MOTHERS

MOTHERS

Chinese Whispers Book II

Mark Whitworth

This book is a work of historical fiction. Names, characters, and incidents are a product of the author's imagination or have been derived from Chinese myths, legends, and ancient history. Any resemblance to any living persons, or anyone having died in the last three millennia is entirely coincidental.

Further information about the Chinese Whispers series may be found on my website at https://www.markwhitworth.rocks/books.

Cover design by Scott Taylor & Mark Whitworth

Map design by Scott Taylor & Mark Whitworth

Cover photography by Mark Whitworth

Cover copyright © 2024 Mark Whitworth

Publicaciones Ili Pika, (Ili Pika Publications)

Patzcuaro, Michoacan, Mexico

Copyright © 2024 Mark Whitworth

All rights reserved.

ISBN 13: 979-8-89379-022-1

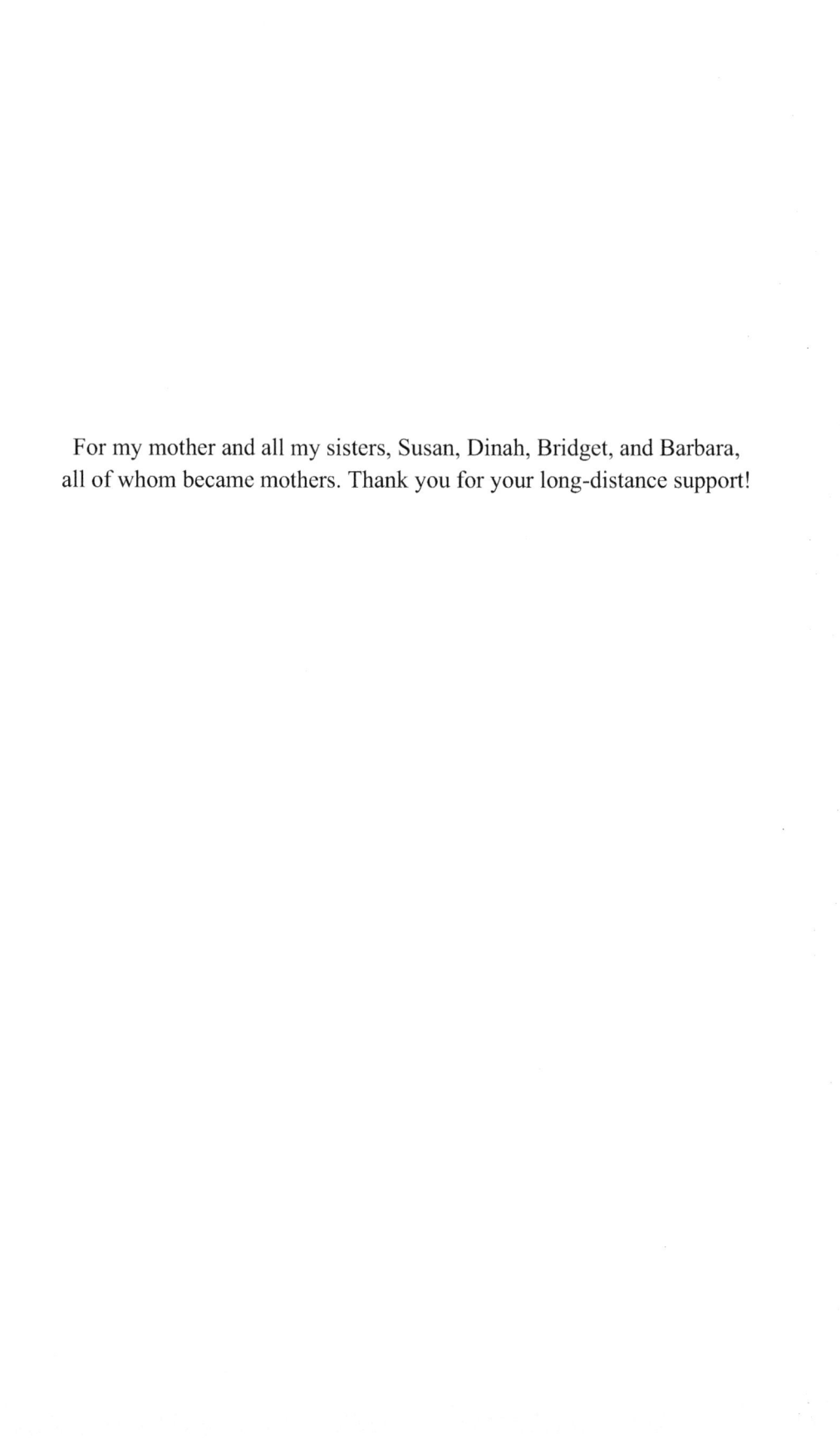

For my mother and all my sisters, Susan, Dinah, Bridget, and Barbara, all of whom became mothers. Thank you for your long-distance support!

Contents

Preface	viii
Chinese Whispers – The Series	ix
Acknowledgements	x
Introduction	xii
Map of China After 1905 BCE	xiv
One: The Appendage	1
Two: The Captive	11
Three: The Wolves	19
Four: The Farmer	27
Five: The Scorekeeper	36
Six: The Barman	45
Seven: The Shepherdess	53
Eight: The Empire	61
Nine: The Fire Starter	68
Ten: The Father	76
Eleven: The Visitor	83
Twelve: The Mothers	91
Thirteen: The Apprentices	99
Fourteen: The Assassins	106
Fifteen: The Brat	115
Sixteen: The Reunions	124
Seventeen: The Machinations	132
Eighteen: The Inveiglement	140
Nineteen: The Blackmail	148

Contents

Twenty: The Femicide	157
Twenty-one: The Boy	164
Twenty-two: The Homicide	173
Twenty-three: The Youth	180
Twenty-four: The Girl	187
Twenty-five: The Mute	194
Twenty-six: The Election	202
Twenty-seven: The Turnabout	210
Twenty-eight: The Bonding	218
Twenty-nine: The Evidence	226
Thirty: The Confession	234
Thirty-one: The Passage	242
Thirty-two: The Arrest	251
Thirty-three: The Imprisonments	258
Thirty-four: The Escape	264
Thirty-five: The Shāng	273
Thirty-six: The Emperor	280
Thirty-seven: The Tigers	290
Thirty-eight: The Spies	298
Thirty-nine: The End	305
Forty: The Beginning	313
Archaeological Evidence, History & Myth	324
Named Characters in the Story	327
Sources	332

Preface

The six years I spent in China were eye-opening. Its extensive history unfolded bit by bit as I visited more provinces. My storyline became fully formed whilst living there, although this book was primarily written in Malawi and Mexico. At times, China's distant past seemed to occupy my working spaces in both these countries, and for long periods, my soul was firmly anchored in the C20th BCE. It was often an effort to return to the C21st CE and cook the dinner!

It was not my intention to produce two books. Halfway through writing **Chinese Whispers - Sisters**, I realised that a single book would have been enormous. I determined then that book one should focus on the fall of the Lóngshān and the second on the rise of the Xià. I hope this makes sense.

There are few guaranteed truths in history. My stories use myths, archaeological evidence, and a degree of speculation; I have attempted to detail the dynamism that must have existed during a period of fundamental change. This tale is a fictional account, but nothing within it could not realistically have occurred.

Chinese Whispers – The Series

Chinese Whispers is a series of sweeping historical novels based in pre-historic and ancient China although it has many other facets.

The first two books cover the gradual demise of individual city-states and the appearance of an embryonic empire. In China, the period spanning the late C20th to the early C19th BCE followed a time of climatic and environmental disaster, the rise of agriculture, the transition from stone to bronze age, and the earliest signs of civilisation as we understand it today.

A key focus is the plight of females, as their traditional roles are eroded, and equality seems but a distant memory from way back. Defying the debased authorities, women fight back, and regaining lost rights is a cause for jubilation. However, what has been earned may also be stolen, a concept that resonates loudly four thousand years later.

The struggle between the elite and the masses is ongoing and rebounds down the ages. Nascent capitalism rubs shoulders with increasing demand as living standards improve. Warlords craving wealth and status ring themselves with elite troops, paid for by the hard work of ordinary men and women. Warfare and individual violence are commonplace. Oddly, weapons of mass destruction exist in this distant era; drought, starvation, and disease are manipulated for good or bad, depending on your standpoint.

Acknowledgements

In writing *Chinese Whispers - Mothers*, there are many people to whom I am indebted. However, any errors and omissions are entirely my responsibility, and I know that some individuals mentioned below may not approve of aspects of my story.

My dear friend, Ian Self, was the first to read this book. To him, my most grateful thanks for providing feedback on the storyline and suggestions regarding grammar and punctuation; he was immensely supportive.

Sue Scott, in New Zealand, has done an excellent job proofreading these novels. She executed this task superbly, for no remuneration, and at great speed; sometimes, I could not keep up with her. Sue also gave me content feedback at various points and reassurance that the story was worth reading.

Petrina McGregor provided a mix of proofreading and content advice on the first of the two books. Her advice was invaluable and given for no reward.

My good friend, Peter Barker, advised me on various medical aspects, such as wounds and scarring. He became so perplexed at the questions I was asking that he requested he read the book himself. Having done so, he gave me further input regarding anachronisms. Cheers, Pete!

My sister, Susan Swanston, conducted the final proofreading of both books accurately and rapidly. Thank you, Sue!

My eternal thanks must also go to my wife, Andrea Kidd. She has been there for me throughout and was the third person to read this novel. Sometimes, you wonder, when writing about violence, sex, drug-taking, and death, how much your partner might go off you. Andrea has not done so yet, although I keep reassuring her that the characters are a product of my imagination, not alter-egos!

It was intended that a section at the end of the book would identify all the sources I used. Unfortunately, this proved a little lengthy. Instead, in the section titled Sources, there is a link to my website, which gives greater detail. These have been listed in categories, such as 'Food and Drink', as I felt a themed approach would be better than a standard bibliography. However, below, I identify those people or organisations that have influenced me the most and, in some cases, those who contributed to telling these stories.

The first is an extensive group of individuals, Chinese archaeologists. Without them, I could not have told these tales. Their work from the middle of the Twentieth Century to this day has been incredible. In the earlier years of the People's Republic of China, they focused on proving the Yellow River as a single origin point for the Chinese people. Their findings demonstrated the opposite that Chinese culture had influences from its furthest flung reaches. There are far too many of them to thank individually, but two stand out, people whose work has enthused me enormously. They are:

Professor He Nu of the Archaeology Institute of the Chinese Academy of Social Science, primarily for his work and many research papers on Taosi.

Professor Li Liu, whose books cover a wider field, examining the transition from the Neolithic to early Chinese civilisations.

I also extend my thanks to Astro Pixels. They provide data concerning the moon's phases right back to 2000 BCE. These phases were critical to people living without modern lighting. This information is given freely through the Moon Phases Table, courtesy of Fred Espenak at www.astropixels.com. It is an excellent resource for writers of history. Thank you, Fred.

Finally, my thanks to the great Scott Taylor. Scott has contributed artistic flair to the cover design and the map; his down-to-earth approach greatly assists in keeping me on the rails.

Introduction

The stories in ***Chinese Whispers - Mothers*** are a continuation of the first book, ***Sisters***. The events in ***Mothers*** occur between 1905 and 1886 BCE. My first book outlines the crushing of the Lóngshān, and this volume focuses on the creation of the Xià empire. It is possible that someone may pick up this book and read it as a standalone novel, although it is probably better to read both in order.

At the commencement of each chapter, a location is given, and I have utilised present-day names. Most appear on the map on page xv, but an atlas or a modern mapping package like Google Earth would also help you find them. Additional information is supplied: the year in the Xià dating system[1], the animal assigned to that year by Chinese culture, the day of the year relating to the solstices and equinoxes and finally, the date in the Gregorian calendar.

Historians assign various dates to the commencement of the Xià Dynasty. I have chosen a somewhat later one than suggested in the "historical myth", which is more aligned with archaeological evidence. It was a time of significant change in China. Before this, there had been many centuries of climatic change and disaster, almost certainly leading to a massive reduction in population size. Humans were already impacting their environments negatively, and some of these changes adversely affected their societies.

This period also represents the commencement of the Bronze Age. Although bronze had been used for at least a millennium, particularly in western China, it was not particularly significant before the Xià Dynasty. Just as in Western history, stone has continued to be the raw material most of the population has used for thousands of years.

---

[1] This is explained late on in this book, but it is basically sequential and ascending with each new year commencing at Chinese New Year, not on 1st January. (The BCE dates are obviously descending.)

I have attempted to ensure descriptions of landscapes, structures, and vegetation of the time align with the findings of specialists in these fields. However, applying a heavy dose of conjecture is necessary after four thousand years. The locations are real and well-evidenced through archaeology; I have visited many settings. The physical events, such as flooding, reflect actual events. Even though there is difficulty accurately dating some of these, I have tried to apply them logically in my story.

Many characters' names are drawn from Chinese mythology and often fulfil roles similar to those in the myths. Others have monikers that describe their personalities, albeit in Pinyin, the official Romanised system for standard Mandarin Chinese. In scrambling around for minor characters' names, I used the name of a cleaner I employed in Suzhou and, for another, that of the Terracotta Warrior who stands in my dining room; clearly, the fictional characters are not representative of either!

On the latter pages is a section on history and mythology, providing links to the tales in the book, and another on the characters' names, roles when they first appear, and meaning.

It is my pleasure to present my version of the birth of Chinese civilisation.

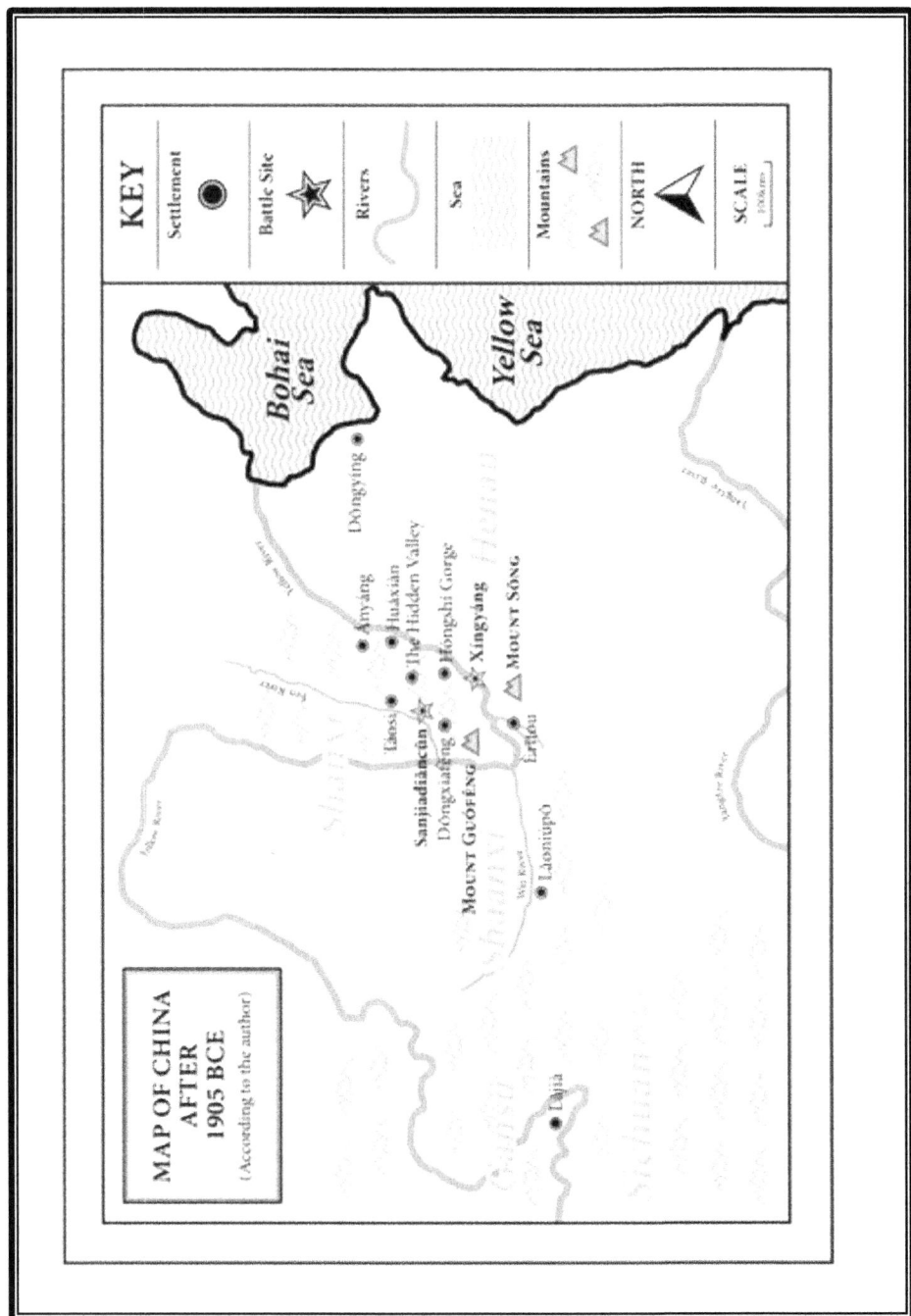

One: The Appendage

Qícūn, Ānyáng, Hénán
Year 90: Year of the Rat
The winter solstice
21st December 1905 BCE

Líng looked to the skies. There had been eight full moons since the Battle of the Yellow River, and she had yet to observe one of them. Tonight, the moon shone brightly in the heavens, and although it was only just past full, stars sparkled and stretched to the horizon in all directions. How many of those full moons anyone had seen was open to doubt; a gem-studded sky was a rarity in the Year of the Rat. Rainfall over the northern plains had been torrential from midsummer right through the autumn; ever since then, barely a day had seen clear skies. However, there would be a frost tonight, and some of the flooded fields would undoubtedly freeze over.

Her vantage point overlooked Ānyáng from the southwest. Over the town hung the Seven Stars constellation[2], which was always considered a symbol of sovereignty. That concept made her laugh this evening, as did the Heavenly Wolf, slightly dimmed by the smoke from cooking fires. The moonlight reflected from waters that still encompassed much of the town. The great river was hardly a day's march to the east, although no one could cover that distance without a boat. Ānyáng's two rivers, which embraced the town, making it a formidable defensive proposition in more normal times, were backed up by the Yellow River flooding. As the excessive run-off from the western mountains continued, it left the urban area as a series of small low islands around which the

---

[2] The seven stars constellation is commonly known in the west as the Plough, the Big Dipper, the Great Bear or Ursa Major. The Heavenly Wolf is Sirius, the Dog Star or Alpha Canis Majoris

Qícūn, Ānyáng, Hénán

redundant city wall poked out of the waters here and there. Pinpricks of light emitted from the cooking fires of the few brave souls still living there, a population subsisting on frogs, turtles, and fish if they were lucky, and the odd rat if they were not.

It had not been a joyful period for those living in what had been Lóngshān lands. If the battle had been perfectly executed, then the same could be said for the re-routing of the great river. The summer's flood would have been disastrous under normal conditions, but with the river exploring a new northern route, it had ravaged the countryside. At one point, the floodwaters had lapped against the foot of the hill on which she now stood. To the south and east, there was devastation. Nine large towns no longer existed; countless numbers had lost their homes, and even more had lost their lives.

However, the urban centres were of minor concern to Líng. After the drought of the previous year and the Lóngshān's gross mismanagement of resources, this year's flood had destroyed four-fifths of the farmland in northern Hénán, western Shāndōng and southern Héběi. There was little food.

Those settlements where her predecessor's advice had been heeded were better off than most. Thousands had undertaken evacuation prompted by the eclipse, but many more remained and were now paying the penalty. Those who had moved early, hoarding what little they could, were now coming under increasing pressure as refugees flocked to centres where there were resources. Líng's news was gleaned from evacuees, although it was seriously deficient as no one had managed to cross the new Yellow River since June; her information only came from the western bank.

Estimated deaths from flooding were compounded a hundred-fold by lives lost to starvation and disease. For some older inhabitants, who had been forced northwards as youngsters, it was the second time they had faced such a crisis. For many, the circumstances were so desperate the tragedy led them to take their own lives.

From her earliest years, Líng had worked to create the catastrophe that had unfolded. She held herself responsible. The Sisterhood's grand plan had been an enormous success. The addition of terrible weather was unnecessary, but it certainly enhanced the strategy's effectiveness. The

One: The Appendage

Sisterhood had destroyed Lóngshān culture. It was now up to the populace to rebuild, with assistance from the Xià. Líng had already turned her attention to the longer term.

She had travelled north directly from the battle, bringing with her Tú, baby Yùtù, Mǎjié, Yěmǎ and Kùàimǎ. It would have been dangerous to leave Tú in Èrlǐtou; she was unpredictable, and the last pieces of the Sisterhood's grand plan needed to slot into place smoothly down south. The three other women had been keen to return to Ānyáng; they had their roots in western Hénán and little interest in what Èrlǐtou had to offer.

When Yěmǎ and Mǎjié had shown her with Hú and Xí's cloaks, gold pieces bursting from the seams, Líng had been decisive. Èrlǐtou did not need gold, but she knew it would be of use where they were heading. She had been correct. While men, women, and children around Ānyáng were dying of starvation, there were always some for whom the insatiable lust for gold did not diminish. The five women did not advertise the fact, but they generally ate well. Líng had stashed the remainder of the precious metal under a long drop latrine pit; it was awkward and unpleasant to access but would surely never be found by accident.

The societal breakdown had made for an exciting journey. What had begun as a leisurely ride had become increasingly urgent as the days passed, and it became clear that severe flooding was becoming a reality. After skirting Xinxiang, they followed the treeline at the foot of the mountains, running northwards, not to avoid the rising waters but to avoid the lines of refugees. At night, Jīnxīng[3] had proved adept as a guard dog, and with Mǎjié, Yěmǎ and Kùàimǎ armed to the teeth and still wearing their body armour, their group was not a target many would wish to take on.

If the women were of the same age, albeit Tú was a couple of years younger, they had undoubtedly had different experiences. Líng questioned the Fire Horse Three about their names, as all were born in the Year of the Ox. It turned out that their mentor, Líng's lamented boss, was indeed born in the year of the fire horse[4]. The previous Grandmother had

---

[3] Venus

[4] There is an east Asian traditional that women born under the fire sign, in the Year of the Horse, would make notoriously difficult wives.

initially seen it as a burden and only later as a blessing; she had felt free of the pressures that might have distracted her from her path. Her charges' names had been light-heartedly applied as Grandmother attempted to trivialise the dire conditions in which they operated. For Mǎjié and Yěmǎ, their treatment at the hands of Hú and Xī resulted in their becoming hardened misandrists. Neither Líng, Tú or Kùaimǎ felt the same way, although Líng had sworn herself to celibacy until her job was concluded.

As Líng saw it, the Sisterhood of the Horse was fading; its function was fulfilled. A new Sisterhood was required, which would work in different ways for different circumstances. It was her task to plant the seeds of that movement, to feed and water it; she would not be around to see the new movement bloom. Although she had masterminded death, destruction, and the overthrow of the Lóngshān by using and attacking men, she desired the next Sisterhood would take a more consensual path. It was a plan that would face repeated challenges, some sooner than she could imagine.

Qícūn was the name they had chosen for their new home, one that had been picked with delicate irony by Líng. Yùtù had just taken his first few steps, enjoying being fussed over by five mothers, four of whom had no idea of his real identity.

"Líng!" The call came from over her shoulder from the direction of the room they had allocated for cooking. "Líng, your dinner's ready!" Kùaimǎ sounded impatient, which was nothing new. Líng took one last sweeping gaze at the moonlit vista before focussing on the Heavenly Wolf. Briefly, an excited tingle went up and down her spine before she turned and strode towards her meal.

"Shut that door!" hollered Tú. It was warm in the room. The chill draught from the open door had caused one or two frowns. Líng slipped into a picture of domestic bliss.

Their solidly built home sat under a heavy beamed roof, and off the main room, there were doors to several others: a pantry, kitchen, store, and two bedrooms. The whitewashed interior walls were unadorned except for five charcoal sketches, one contributed by each woman. Yěmǎ, Mǎjié, and Kùaimǎ had each drawn a horse, the latter quite expertly. Tú had wanted to paint the symbol of the Motherland until Líng pointed out it may attract the wrong sort of interest, so Tú had converted her drawing

One: The Appendage

into a gnarled tree. Tucked away in the kitchen area, Líng herself had contributed a perfect circle with a square formed inside, its corners touching the circle's circumference. She had begun to fill the square with writing; the sole purpose was to keep the others reading; the lines were sometimes common sayings, and others offered complete nonsense.

There had been empty properties on each of the Ānyáng islands. It was not a question of bartering for a home but simply finding one first. In this respect, they were lucky, arriving in Ānyáng before the enormity of the circumstances had struck home with the majority. They had chosen higher land, a well-built structure with ample storage and plenty of land for crops. It seemed they may have stumbled into one of King Léigōng's old hunting lodges; it was certainly comfortable. It was far enough out of town to attract no passing interest, yet close enough for an easy walk into the centre.

The other four women knelt on dried rushes around the copper cook pot taken from the fire using long hardwood poles. It now sat on the earth floor encircled by five empty clay bowls. As Líng entered, Mǎjié picked up the first bowl, dipping it into the broth and waiting for Líng to kneel herself before passing it to her, then repeated the exercise for the others.

"Is there any fresh bread tonight?" Líng asked.

"Sorry…I forgot," Kùaimǎ reached behind her for a platter on which resided five flatbread and a few scraps of *ròugān*[5]. "Tú, do you want me to take him?"

"No, it's fine," Tú had been feeding her son and now carefully detached him from her breast and lay him to the side before taking her bowl. "He's fallen asleep anyway."

By the current standards in Ānyáng, the spread before them was a feast. The five women chewing, slurping, and burping were the only sounds that disturbed the still night until Jīnxīng stood and growled quite suddenly.

"What's that, girl?" Tú asked of her. "What do you hear?" The bitch's hackles were raised, and the hair along her spine stood also. Mǎjié, Yěmǎ and Kùaimǎ rose as one, broth spilling across the rushes as they

---

[5] A dried meat similar to jerky or biltong.

reached for their weapons, while Tú grabbed one of the fire torches. They were ready, but there was indecision about the next move. Open the door or keep it barred?

"Food. Food, please." A man's plaintive voice sounded through the oak door. "Please? Do you have food?"

"Stand back from the door! Stand back five paces! Now! We're coming out! Stand back!" Mǎjié's tone was commanding.

"I will…I will. Wait." The stranger made it obvious he was moving away, shuffling his feet.

"Wait, girls," whispered Líng as she rose and skipped to the wooden batten covering the window. "There's a crack here. Shhh!" The moonlight still flooded the yard outside, where a solitary older man shivered. "It's alright. He's alone. You can open the door."

As Yěmǎ swung the locking bar upwards, the door burst open, throwing her across the room. Three heavily armed men wielding axes crashed through, positioning themselves quickly to prevent resistance. One stunned Jīnxīng with the heft of his axe; the bitch promptly slumped to the ground unconscious. Within seconds, the older man sauntered in to join them.

"Sit! Now! Against the walls! Do it!" Líng nodded at the others, and they backed down, lowering themselves into seated positions against the earth wall, except Yěmǎ, who remained spreadeagled. "Kick those weapons away from you!" There was no movement. "Do it…now!" Again, after a brief nod from Líng, the women kicked their short swords towards the axe bearers.

"Well!" His voice was no longer plaintive, and he certainly did not look like he was starving. "What have we here? One, two, three, four and," he kicked Yěmǎ, who still lay sprawled on the floor, "…and five! Five women and only one child! Where are your men on this beautiful evening? You!" He pointed down at Yěmǎ, "You, girl. Tell! Where are they?"

"Hunting, my lord," Yěmǎ had been in these circumstances before and knew well the importance of appearing submissive. "Please don't hurt me. I can make you very happy—"

One: The Appendage

"And so you could…and so you could. Perhaps. Perhaps when we know what's going on here, you can all make us happy. Isn't that right, boys?" He rested his axe head on Yěmǎ's back. "But perhaps you need to know how serious we are first." He ground the axe into the base of her spine so hard that she screamed. "You see, for me, it's a hard decision…the lure of food or the lure of you 'making me very happy'!" The older man scoured their faces whilst his troops stood over them with axes raised.

Líng was all about planning, and she had plans for many scenarios, including a moment such as this. All the girls had been coached; they were fulfilling her expectations and doing precisely nothing right now. The current balance was not good, and the odds needed to be improved before they could act. As usual, Líng's plan hinged on the men misbehaving and behaving without forethought.

"Zhāng, bring that one here."

"Yes, Captain." Zhāng reached down and, placing a hand under Kùaimǎ's arm, heaved her to her feet. She showed no resistance as he pulled her across the room towards his superior.

"Yes! I like this one! You say the men are hunting. When will they be back? There's a good moon; it's a clear night, and…" he leaned towards the cooking pot, "and there's no food for them! They're not due back tonight, then?" Grasping Kùaimǎ's chin in his ham-like fist, he turned her head this way and that before allowing his hand to come to rest on her breast. "What do you say, girl?"

"No, Captain, they'll not be back tonight." Kùaimǎ's voice shook. Líng, Mǎjié and Tú confirmed her story by shaking their heads, looking down and appearing as despondent as possible. They were all aware the first stage of Líng's planning had gone somewhat awry as it was not supposed to be Kùaimǎ in this position; of the five, only Líng had less experience of men.

"You can have me!" Mǎjié volunteered. "I'll give you a good time and—"

"You! Shut up! Shùn! Kick her!" Mǎjié was grateful her captor delivered a relatively minor blow to the side of her buttock. "I'll have who I want and then the next one! Maybe all of you! Then, when I'm finished, well, Zhāng, Shùn and Péng might just want some of you as well! Don't think for one minute you're going to be left out. Now..." The captain's hand firmly grasped Kùaimǎ's upper arm. "She is coming with me, aren't you, girl!"

The captain led her towards the door, which he guessed provided an entrance to their sleeping quarters. It was an assumption that proved correct. As the door closed behind him, the remaining women could hear Kùaimǎ begin to flatter him. She had remembered the plan; the question was whether she would have the courage to execute it. They exchanged nervous glances with heads bowed while surreptitiously feeling through the dried rushes for their concealed daggers. The odds were improved, although taking one more of the men out of the equation would be a massive advantage.

The moans from behind the door gradually increased in volume. Two of their guards grinned at each other whilst the third looked somewhat embarrassed. The women were waiting for a signal, one which would mean they were back on track. All eased themselves unnoticed into cross-legged positions from which they could rise more quickly. When it came, Kùaimǎ's voice was loud and clear. She had almost shouted.

"Oh! I want to suck on that!"

This time, Zhāng and Péng snickered out loud. Again, Shùn hung his head.

"Shùn?" Líng picked on him for his little shows of kindness. "I need to feed the baby. Would you pass him over, please? Carefully."

As the two other captors continued to exchange excited glances, straining to hear what might come next from the bedroom, Shùn placed his axe on the floor and picked up the now wriggling baby.

"He's beautiful, isn't he?" Shùn was enamoured, "About a year old, I guess. He's—"

The scream from the bedroom would have woken the dead. Mǎjié and Yěmǎ sprang instantly, slicing at the faces of the two guards whose incessant giggling now morphed into a genuine panic. Jīnxīng, still groggy, attached herself to Zhāng's ankle, refusing to let go. Tú stood with Shùn's axe in her hands, its blade hovering in preparation for a blow over his left ear. The child still lay in his arms, utterly undisturbed by the circumstances.

One: The Appendage

"Keep your distance!" Líng hollered, "Mǎjié, Yěmǎ! Kick into their guts! Wind them, then get in there and kill them!" The girls had trained to fight larger opponents, closing only when they had the advantage. "Tú, have you brought him under control? Yes?" Tú nodded. "Don't kill him. Knock him out if you have to, but keep him alive!"

"He's not moving anywhere, Líng. You've got to check Kùàimǎ! Quick!"

Líng glanced around to see Zhāng and Péng had been driven to their knees, blood streaming from their wounds as they came under sustained and punishing attacks from the two girls. Jīnxīng had now switched her attention to Péng's ankle, causing the man to scream louder still. Although her friends had suffered minor injuries, they were not enough to slow them down. They would complete their tasks within seconds, allowing them to reinforce Tú.

Líng grabbed one of the fire torches from the wall, opened the bedroom door and stepped in. What was immediately evident was the amount of blood. There was far more of it than Líng had imagined possible. The captain lay on his back on the bedding, naked from the waist down. A gaping slit across his throat accounted for most of the gore, although the remainder appeared to have pumped from his groin. Kùàimǎ knelt on the floor crying.

Líng closed the door behind her and moved to kneel with her friend. It seemed she was in shock.

"You mustn't tell them, Líng," Kùàimǎ sobbed.

"It looks like you did a good job, Kù. What's the problem? We're all proud of you. Everything's under control. You did just what was needed. It's just…It's just we never thought it would be you." Líng put her arm around the crying girl's shoulders.

"I couldn't do it, Líng, I couldn't! You mustn't tell them!"

"Mustn't tell them what?"

"I couldn't bite it off! It was too tough! I tried, but I was gagging on the blood!"

"So, what's this then?" Líng held up a bloodied and shrivelled appendage between finger and thumb.

"Líng…I cheated. I did that afterwards to make it look like I did. I did that after I slit his neck. Please don't tell Mǎjié and Yěmǎ. They'll laugh at me. Even Tú!"

"No, they will not. You won the war for us! Who cares if you bit his penis off before or after his death? It's all the same to me!" It was slowly sinking in that Kùaimǎ's reaction had little to do with shock.

"You promise you won't tell?"

"I promise."

"And Líng…I'm still a virgin."

"That's even better news! You want to hear my big secret?" Kùaimǎ nodded. "So am I!"

Two: The Captive
Qícūn, Ānyáng, Hénán
Year 90: Year of the Rat
Four days after the winter solstice
25th December 1905 BCE

Líng would have happily kept her promise, but within a day, Kùàimǎ had spilt the beans herself. The other girls had heaped her with such praise that she had opened up when she no longer felt they would laugh at her. Her confession led to further bonding within the group; it was a happy time. However, three significant concerns needed addressing, and Líng spelt them out over dinner a few days later.

"We have to make some decisions," she mumbled through a mouthful of stale bread. "First, we have to decide what we will do about Shùn. We can't keep him tied up and guarded all the time. Jīnxīng is getting tired of watching over him!"

"Is true." Mǎjié was likewise afflicted with a half-full mouth. "We have to kill him."

"I think you forget the other problems, Mǎj. We took a big risk last time and can't hope to be as lucky again. The second problem was that my plan was deficient!"

"It worked, though!" Yěmǎ's eyes shone. "Kù came through for us. She—"

"We've heard a hundred times what she did, and it becomes more exaggerated each time, mainly because you're doing the telling. Leave the poor girl alone!" Líng smiled as she spoke. They were all still in awe of Kùàimǎ's exploits, and Líng was equally as proud of the way Yěmǎ, Mǎjié and Tú had handled the situation. "We can't expect it to work next time. What if there were ten men? What if they'd been more interested in food or just killing? What if—"

"Ow! There are lots of 'what ifs', Líng, but we can't cover all the possibilities." Tú had the child at her breast again; the sudden appearance of some very sharp teeth had made feeding somewhat uncomfortable.

"But we have to cover as many as we can. It may have been luck, but the plan worked. The basic strategy, the divide and separate, the kicking to make distant strikes, closing in to counter their extra reach; all these things worked. Perhaps we need to re-think keeping one alive; a straight stab at killing is the better action, even if we do not find out what they know. We cannot go on like—"

"May I speak?" Jīnxīng growled deeply at the words, and the five women turned as one; it was the first utterance Shùn had made since the morning.

"You may, Shùn, carry on," Líng commanded.

"I don't want you to kill me." He spoke slowly and apparently without fear. "I really don't. It wouldn't be fair. You wouldn't be alive today if I hadn't been nice to the kid. I helped you and—"

"And if you hadn't been running around the countryside looking for victims to rob and rape, you would never have been here at all!" Mǎjié was fired up on anything to do with Shùn, as was Yěmǎ.

"She's right, Líng. He shouldn't have been here at all. It's his fault," said Yěmǎ, waving her eating knife in Shùn's direction.

Both Tú and Kùaimǎ were much more conciliatory in tone. Both argued that he needed to explain himself. Líng wanted information from the man but also had her eye on other possibilities. Three variables needed pinning down, and those were Yěmǎ, Mǎjié and Shùn himself.

"I said he should talk…so he should talk. Yěmǎ, Mǎjié. Shhh! Tú, would you put Jīnxīng outside for a bit? Shùn, explain how you found yourself breaking into our home?"

Shùn commenced his tale by relating his running away from the battle on the Yellow River.

"You were there?" Tú's surprise mirrored in the faces of the other four women.

"Well…I was there, but then the dragon began to eat the sun, and we turned and ran. I was in the infantry, and for the most part, we was just ignored. We'd been told there was nothing to fear, a bunch of women, no

Two: The Captive

disrespect to you all, of course, and some stupid tales about fake wizardry. Then it happened. The dragon began to eat the sun. I couldn't believe it. We was scared. We was petrified!

"So, we didn't see any fighting. Not that any of us were fighters anyway. We was all farmers. They forced us off our farms to go and fight. Then they tell us we'll be fighting women farmers, no disrespect intended, but all we got to do was to run away."

"Where are you from, Shùn?"

"Me and me mates, we were from Huáxiàn…not that it exists now. It's been washed away. It's a crime. It took four days to walk home. We gets there and finds our womenfolk was slain. Not just killed, either. They were all raped and beaten first. They—"

"Who did that, Shùn?" Kùaimǎ's look was of deepest sympathy, which caused Yěmǎ to sneer. She started to object before a long look from Líng silenced her.

"I'm told it was the King of Dōngyíng's men. The king, well, he's called Fēngbō, sounds like a nasty sort. He and his troops had deserted the night before the battle. Seems they was making their way back when they came across Huáxiàn. All our men had been taken for the army. There was only women left there, no disrespect intended. They'd come through three days before we got there and," tears filled Shùn's eyes as he tried to control his wavering voice, "And…and they raped and killed every woman in the town. It—"

"It's alright, Shùn, it's—"

"No. It's not alright. It was terrible. They deliberately left one old woman alive so she could tell the tale. They was animals. She died shortly after telling us what went on. They killed the boys and the babies as well. Just kept the young girls alive, well, those old enough to keep up with them. We was, well, we didn't know what to do. There was little enough food as it was, and they destroyed the granaries. Some men…Some thought their daughters might be alive like, and they decided to go on to Dōngyíng to find them. It's right up north, on the Bóhǎi Sea, I'm told. My wife lay dead. She'd been terribly beaten. We'd never been able to have kids, so there was nothing for me to chase after."

"That is terrible, Shùn. You must have been all messed up," Tú voiced all their concerns. Even Yěmǎ and Mǎjié were beginning to soften slightly. "What did you end up doing?"

"I cried…I think I cried for two days. I hardly ate. Then we started to hear about the flooding and everyone moving. You probably don't know Huáxiàn, but we had a small river, nothing to shout about, really, but it started to get bigger and stronger quite quickly. Our homes were gone. I mean, what am I saying…they're gone! My farm was on the eastern bank, and it flooded first. There's a hill a short distance away to the west, a place called Hóutòngshùncūn. I headed there, but so did many people. It wasn't a hill for long; in a couple of days, it was a very overcrowded island."

"How long were you there, Shùn?" Líng queried.

"Maybe seven moons and a bit, maybe eight. I say moons - we never saw a moon - ever. The skies pissed water, and the river leaked it all over the land. It was wet. We was in some caves for shelter, but even that got wet. People was starving, and people was sick, and people was fighting each other. I even heard that people was eating each other. It was terrible.

"I was fat before the flood. Look at me now. But it was the fat that must've kept me alive. We had to float the bodies off into the flooded fields; there was hundreds. That's when Captain Jiāng turned up. He had a boat, you see. Those two you killed the other night; they was with him: wrong'uns, all three of them. There was nothing for them on the island, nothing obvious anyway, but it turns out they had killed the only one of them that could sail a boat. You need to sail. Punting or rowing wasn't powerful enough with those currents. You had to know what you was doing.

"Anyways…the first thing they ask is if anyone can fix a boat. I'd been a river dweller all my life, so I volunteered like. That's when they made me a captive. They push the boat off from the island with me in it and tells me to sail northwest. Tells me they'll kill me if I don't do what I'm told. Tells me they'd get me food as well. Tells me lots of things, to be honest, but I never trusted them.

"It was like a sea. Now and then, there were islands and always the same story. Dead and dying people. Sickness and starvation. It was

Two: The Captive

obvious Captain Jiāng was headed for Ānyáng, but I don't know what they expected. We gets there, and it's the same thing—dead and dying people.

"What I do know is that Captain Jiāng thought he would be able to take over in Ānyáng. You see, he knew that old King Léigōng had died; he–"

"She killed him!" Yěmǎ's eyes came alive as she pointed at Líng. "She killed him! She cut off his balls and stuck a knife into the top of his head. She did! Líng!"

The man eyed Líng with a level of respect that he had so far reserved only for the Fire Horse Three.

"She did, did she! Well, that's one for the campfire. Sitting here chatting with Léigōng's assassin," he nodded toward Líng, "and Captain Jiāng's executioner!" He smiled at Kùàimǎ, "Wonderful! I suppose I should be even more scared than I am."

"You're scared?" Tú asked.

"I was scared in Huáxiàn, I was scared of the floods, I was scared of those three that might've killed me, and I'm very, very scared of these two!" He nodded towards Yěmǎ and Mǎjié. "Wouldn't you be scared? I guess I'm so used to being scared I've stopped looking like I am, but I am! Very, very scared!"

Líng stood, bringing out her knife. Stepping across the circle of kneeling women and skirting the copper pot as she did so, she stood high over the still prone Shùn. Crouching, she slashed twice, once for the bindings on his feet, the second a little more carefully to the bindings around his wrists.

"Tú has been a captive, Kùàimǎ has been a captive and Yěmǎ, and Mǎjié were as good as captives for many years. I don't want to feel responsible for someone else joining the list. You are a free man."

"I thank you from–"

"Don't thank me. We need someone to help us find a solution to our problems. While you are scared and bound, you are an encumbrance, not a solution. I'm giving you the chance to join us. Of course, if you run away, I might need to send Yěmǎ and Mǎjié after you. Will you go outside now, please? Relieve yourself, stretch your legs and come back in when we call. Go!"

Shùn stumbled awkwardly towards the door as four women looked on with mouths wide open. As the door shut, Yěmǎ spoke.

"What are you doing, Líng? We didn't agree with that! He's not safe! I don't trust him. What if–"

"I trust him. We're still at war, and I'm in charge. This is not like Táosì, where you all get to vote on things. We must iron out a few firm rules to cope with Shùn, but we will. Look at him. Did you see him weep? Did you see the hatred in his eyes when he talked about those other three? When he returns, we'll ask him how he came to be at our door. Meanwhile, he can sleep, unbound, in the shed.

"Trust, Yěmǎ, begets trust. Until one side trusts, the other will not," Líng paused. "We need information, and we need some men here, not just one. If we have no men here, it'll be as if a target is painted on the side of this hill.

"Get him back in. Let's try and sort it out."

Kùàimǎ eased herself out to fetch Shùn while Yěmǎ and Mǎjié knelt, exchanging angry and silent messages between themselves with intense stares.

"I could do with some *baijiu*[6], I really could," Tú's words eased the atmosphere, which had descended like a cloud in the room.

"And we have some. Yěmǎ, would you be a dear and fetch out six cups for us?"

"Six?" Yěmǎ scowled at Líng.

"I count six adults sitting down for a chat, don't you, Tú?" Líng's voice remained light as if unconcerned, "Six if you don't mind, Yěmǎ."

When Kùàimǎ returned with Shùn, there were two available places in the circle; they both sat.

"Right! We're sitting here trying to work out what we should do next. Shùn, this concerns you more than anyone else," Líng smiled at the man. "We have some decisions to make and need to know more about what you were doing here. We've heard your account of the disasters in Huáxiàn and your being taken captive and mistreated. We are very sympathetic. What we haven't heard is what you were doing here with

---

[6] A popular grain spirit in China, made from millet in Hénán at the start of the Xià Dynasty.

Two: The Captive

those three. You weren't tied or constrained. You were armed and seemingly acting of your own free will. What you say and do now is important. Two people are sitting in this circle who would happily kill you. So, please explain."

Shùn rubbed his wrists and ankles as he began to speak and shuffled into a more comfortable position. He was very evidently relieved to be rid of his bindings.

"We was fetched up just off one of the Ānyáng islands. It had taken three days to get there, and we was hungry, but it was clear there was no point in going ashore. Crowds were trying to get to the boat, trying to take it or whatever we might have had that could be food. Not that we had any." Shùn coughed. "They was all dying. It didn't look good. We couldn't stay."

"When was this?" Kùàimǎ asked.

"This was the day before we fetched up at this place. In the afternoon, we was searching for somewhere to tie up, somewhere with no people. The wind was pushing us southwest, and we could see this land rising out of the water. We saw no movement. It was getting dark when we tied up. It was a joy to be off the boat."

"When did you notice us?" Tú wanted to know.

"That evening. When we saw the flicker of your fire, Captain Jiāng made us keep a lookout all that night and again the next day. During the day, we was hidden in some trees, but none of you came close. He only told us he was going to do a raid at nightfall. He thought you had men off on a hunting trip. He said that's why it was just you. He said we'd be quick, in and out, just take the food we needed. He said nothing ab–"

"About what, Shùn?" Líng leaned forward, "What did he say nothing about?"

"He said it was about food…that was all. He said nothing about killing and…and rape. The other two, Péng and Zhāng, kept making some comments, but he ignored them. Or he ignored them when he thought I wasn't in hearing distance. I did overhear them talking about getting rid of me after this raid. They said they didn't need a boatman any longer and that I was useless to them. They all agreed. They was only waiting until after they got the food, then they would only have to split it three ways.

"If the truth be known, I don't think I knew what I was doing…I just wanted a way out. I wanted to run away. If you remember, apart from bursting through the door, I did nothing to harm anyone. Please believe me. Please! I don't want them two to keep looking at me like that. I'm still scared."

The women agreed, and Shùn was not killed. They took him on to farm the land around the home and to act as an additional deterrent. He performed his work diligently, and over time, he and Kùàimǎ became closer and closer. The two, both of whom knew a thing or two about captivity, were at last free. In time, they chose that freedom to bind themselves to each other.

Three: The Wolves
Qícūn and Ānyáng, Hénán
Year 91: Year of the Ox
Ten days to the spring equinox
11th March 1904 BCE

This would be the worst of it: the next two months. Whatever food stores had existed were now depleted; a year of drought followed by a year of the worst flooding ever known had ensured that. It was now the planting season, but grain for sowing was nowhere to be found. The winter deaths had proved a blessing in some respects, for there were now fewer mouths to feed. Nobody tried to put a figure on it, but at least half the population was gone, and that was just the outlook from the areas that had been safer; it was probably much worse further east.

The flooding had receded, leaving behind land that would be barren for a few years yet. Ironically, freshwater supplies were dwindling. It seemed too many sources were contaminated, which led to more deaths. It was a blessing the floods had taken away the bodies in the early months, for many corpses were still piled up in areas where the flood currents had eddied.

Those bodies had attracted rats, and rodents were now becoming a staple food for most people. Eating rats may have assuaged hunger, but their diseases killed many. Lucky were those with any food stockpile, blessed only until they were raided and killed for their fortune.

As well as finding a suitable home, another of Líng's early actions had been to buy up stocks of as much preserved or dried food as they could get their hands on. Even waiting a few days would have meant bloated expectations of exchange, although it would have been unlikely any supplies would remain. By acting early, a few goats, a milking cow, and, quite surprisingly, some chickens and a rooster were acquired. The animals, brought north by an enterprising trader, were all snapped up, along with the man's cart and pulling bullock. Buying in quantity was necessary, not simply because massive food shortages were around the corner but also because their sole wealth was in pieces of gold. It was impossible to buy a few eggs and a handful of rice when all you had to trade was the yellow metal. Their stores of rice, millet and barley filled the cart four times over, and it had been necessary to exercise a degree of subterfuge over their destination. When anyone had asked, Líng had always pointed towards the western mountains with a vague wave of her hand.

The shock of the flooding and the waves of refugees coming a little later had wiped away any memory of the band of strangers and their bulk purchases. Whilst their persons might be forgotten, the land on which they resided would still have seemed attractive. However, the people of Ānyáng feared Qícūn Hill. Its reputation over the years was as a place of slaughter and sacrifice by their king and his lackeys. It was a reputation that Líng ensured was maintained. Mǎjié and Yěmǎ were the primary conductors for the disposal of intruders, Kùàimǎ, Tú and herself spreading news of their bloody actions in whatever way they could. Only strangers to the area, such as Captain Jiāng's gang, were foolish enough to enter the woods of Qícūn, even if they were now accessible by dry land.

It was coming up to the planting season; finding seed was one thing, but finding extra hands to help with the work was also a priority. Líng had a shortlist, so short it need not be written down. Firstly, she wanted another man like Shùn, and secondly, she wanted some girls of perhaps four to six years of age. It may have been a short list, but it could not easily be satisfied. Although she desperately wanted to attend to the task herself, logically, she was the worst prepared for such a venture; her own experiences were primarily theoretical. Mǎjié and Yěmǎ only wanted to be involved because of the potential violence; she could hear them sharpening their daggers. Tú was desperate to get out, but still, Líng had a longstanding mistrust of Tú's inclinations when it came to instructions. It would be Shùn and Kùàimǎ who would venture forth; the fact they had become a deeply bonded couple made their cover even more complete.

"But you said I would be able to go!" Tú shouted when Líng announced her decision.

Three: The Wolves

"No, I did not. I said I was considering all the options."

"It's not fair!" Tú's petulance was reminiscent of her days as a young teenager. "I want–"

"I know what you want. I know you've got your eye on finding a man. I know that Kùàimǎ and Shùn are sorted. I know that Mǎjié and Yěmǎ keep each other warm at night. I know that you want someone too. But this is not the time! We need someone to get down and dirty on the farm. Not in your bed! Do you understand this?"

"No!" Tú was furious. "No, I do not! I do not understand why I cannot find a man for me who also works on the farm. I...do...not...understand!"

"Tú," Líng softened her voice. "Your judgement would be brought into question. What would your priorities be? Now, if it so happens that you like the man that Kùàimǎ and Shùn find, then so be it. If you do not, then you'll have to wait. We need a good farmer. I would also remind you, Tú, you have a baby to feed!"

The scowl that this last remark prompted shocked the whole group. It was unnecessary to physically restrain Tú from following when the pair left, but it was a close thing. Líng had Mǎjié and Yěmǎ observe her for the whole day. Then, they could only wait.

Líng had trusted Kùàimǎ with the information about the children and Shùn with the requirements for the man. Still, they were expected to agree with each other before risking return and the possibility of exposing their home.

Kùàimǎ determined to pretend she had lost her child. In those days, it was a common enough occurrence. They had both donned the poorest and most ragged clothes they could muster. Shùn adopted a limp and used a crutch. Kùàimǎ carried herself bent almost double; her face half-covered as if disguising a disfigurement. They took no signs of wealth, only a little secreted food and a copper drinking cup. They had skirted eastwards, looping around and now approached Ānyáng from the direction of the rising sun, from which most derelicts arrived.

"Have you seen my baby girl, sir?" She asked a man with twenty dead rats drying on the ground where he squatted. He looked up, and momentarily, a look of sympathy slipped across his visage.

"No. Have you seen mine? What's she look like?"

"She's small for her age, about five years old. She has short hair."

"You've just described every young girl around these parts. Any scars, missing parts, anything to go on?"

"No, not really."

"You could try near the ferry crossing…there's a bunch of kids hanging out there. Are you by yourself? I could give you a couple of rats for a quick fuck."

"No, sir. Thank you, but that's my husband there, and he'd not approve."

"Well, don't say I didn't offer. I hope you find her."

Kùàimǎ turned, joining Shùn and pulling him in the direction the man had indicated when he suggested the ferry crossing. After stumbling through thick mud for three hundred paces, they found what they sought. A group of naked kids were on their hands and knees in the thicker sediments on the riverside, searching feverishly.

It was only clear what they were after from the rare occasion there was a success. It seems worms, snails, and slugs were highly prized, but the odd insect was also devoured.

"Poor kids!" Kùàimǎ muttered to Shùn, "I hope I never end up that desperate."

"You should have seen us on the island at Hóutòngshùncūn. It was as bad as that and worse. Sometimes, if you didn't eat the mud worms, you simply didn't eat.

"Look at that one." He pointed to a young girl with a lugworm held in one hand, fending off two bigger boys with her other. "She's feisty!"

"That was some hit!" Kùàimǎ took in the girl just as a left hook exploded under the chin of one of the boys. He fell, poleaxed, as his associate scrambled out of harm's reach. The girl turned her back and began to squeeze sand from the worm.

"If you don't do that," Shùn explained, "All you'll have is a mouth full of sand. "Look, she's done it." The girl lifted the worm into her mouth, chewed hard a few times, and then swallowed. "That'll keep her going for today."

Three: The Wolves

"You had it hard, didn't you?" Kùaimǎ asked. "Last year was the Year of the Rat, and it seems they provided your best meals most of the time."

"Not as hard as most. Remember, I'd lived by water my whole life. I'd not have eaten that lugworm if I could use it for fishing. That's what that lass is missing: a line, a hook, and the skills."

"Time for a lesson?"

"I don't think she'd take too kindly to a lesson right now. What she needs is some decent food, a wash, and some downtime before she can cope with a lesson. Look at her now!"

The little girl had zeroed in on another kid's find and was wrestling a boy one and a half times her size. Unfortunately, he had a solid stick that he brought down on her head with a sharp crack; she collapsed in a pile.

"That's our chance, Kù. Let's get her out of here. Make sure she wakes up with some food and water in front of her, or she'll go wild. I'll carry her. Come on!" As Shùn heaved the girl over his shoulder, Kùaimǎ glanced around.

"If we head out this way, we'll get to clearer water. Come on, Shùn. Quick before she comes round."

When they found a spot where they could sit and bring out the flatbread they carried, the girl was beginning to wake up. Tears filled her eyes, although she made no noise. The blood streaming from her head had dried and matted her hair even more. It took a few moments before panic set in, and the girl looked this way and that for an escape.

"Here, eat this," Kùaimǎ held out a single piece of bread, which was snatched from her hand instantly and rammed into the girl's mouth before you could blink. "There's more. Slow down. We'll give you more, but take it easy."

"Now, drink." Shùn handed the girl the copper cup brimming with relatively clean water. Again, she snatched it away, which caused most of the liquid to spill. The empty cup was thrown to the ground, and when Kùaimǎ leaned forward with more bread, it was once more snatched away and immediately stuffed into her tiny mouth.

"There's still more," Kùaimǎ whispered. "You can take it easy."

"Food!" It was the girl's first utterance. "Food! What want?"

"We don't want anything, little girl. What's your name?"

"Dunno!"

"You must know your name. Everyone does." Shùn smiled at her as he handed over the cup he had refilled from the flowing stream. "I'm called Shùn. This is Kùàimǎ," He pointed at himself and then at his partner. "What are you called?"

"Call Láng[7]."

"You're called Láng? Who calls you Láng?" Kùàimǎ realised they were getting somewhere but had extreme doubts about the girl's ability to use language to anything other than a limited extent.

"Boys call Láng. Food!" Kùàimǎ handed over the last remaining bread, only to find the process repeated. After a few quick chews and a big swallow, it was gone. "Food!"

"There is no more," Kùàimǎ smiled as gently as she could. "There's no more food here, but if you come with us, we'll bring more." As soon as she finished speaking, the girl launched herself and ran.

"Tomorrow! Same time! Be here! More food!" She shouted after the departing girl before turning to Shùn, "How do you think that went?"

"Hard to tell. One thing's for certain, though. We better be here tomorrow, or she might just kill something or someone."

Their return the following day was through largely rural areas, so they felt more comfortable bringing a bag with them. As well as bread, there was a little *ròugān* and a flask of goat's milk. Once they had settled down to wait, Shùn shuffled closer and whispered in her ear.

"Kù."

"Yes."

"Would you like to have babies with me?" He had reddened somewhat, having found it difficult to find the right question.

"What are you asking, Shùn? Are you asking me to have your babies, or are you asking me to marry you?" Kùàimǎ's grin did not ease his worries.

"I'm asking if you want our babies. I don't know if I can get married cos, I've already been married. That makes it complicated."

"You loved your wife, didn't you?

---

[7] Wolf.

Three: The Wolves

"Yes. A lot."

"But you never had babies?

"No, I don't think we could."

"But you think you want to have babies with me. Do you love me, Shùn?"

"Yes, a great deal."

"Well, let's think about it. You want me to have your babies. Yes? You say you love me. Yes? You would like to marry me. Yes?"

"Yes!"

"Well, Shùn. Here's the problem. I want to have your babies. I love you. I want to marry you."

Shùn turned a brighter shade of crimson, "Really?"

"Really! So, Shùn. I think that means we are married. Don't you?"

"Yes. I thin–" Their romancing was rudely interrupted.

"Food!" Neither of them had seen Láng creep up. But, there again, they had also failed to see the miniature copy of Láng that stood behind her. "Food! Sister! Xiǎoláng[8]! Food!"

It proved a little complicated, but the pair were able to make their way home, tailed by Láng and her tiny sister, who looked little more than three years old. Láng insisted that she should be referred to as Dàláng and her sister as Xiǎoláng. It was a decision that would lead to many misunderstandings over the years, as Dàláng grew only a little in later years, whereas Xiǎoláng turned into an enormous adult.

It was the start of an incredible adventure for the five women and Shùn, as not one of them had any experience raising two young girls. It would be several months before the two children stopped running off and longer still before they spent time in any locked area. Láng's language skills returned reasonably swiftly, although her terrible eating habits were to remain with her for years.

As far as Líng was concerned, they were perfect: tough street kids with bundles of energy and keen intellects. These were attributes that had kept them alive in the harshest conditions. They would become the new Sisterhood, and she felt that same tingle return, the one from the stars, the one from the Heavenly Wolf. That was it. The Sisterhood of the Wolf

---

[8] Xiǎoláng meaning little wolf and Dàláng, big wolf.

would rise from the ashes to fulfil their destinies. Everything seemed to be falling into place.

Líng only had one complaint, which she raised over dinner a few nights later.

"Shùn."

"Yes, Líng."

"Shùn, you were supposed to find us a man as well. People will start believing you are keen to surround yourself only with women. You'll get a reputation!"

"Sorry, I–"

"No, sorry, please. Now take this." She passed a cup to Shùn, then a second to Kùàimǎ. Each of the girls brought a similar vessel out from behind their backs. "We all want to say…congratulations!"

Four: The Farmer
Yú's Farm, Èrlĭtou, Hénán
Year 91: Year of the Ox
The spring equinox
21st March 1904 BCE

Yú had found much of the previous year quite tiresome. Although he had time to work on his land, his responsibilities to the town had kept him indoors more than he had hoped. He had also been unlucky; whilst others had managed to work around the regular heavy showers, there was a downpour each time he went out. Èrlĭtou had suffered to a lesser extent than the areas in the north of the province, but his misfortune still meant his eventual harvest would be more limited than other folks.

Most Èrlĭtou farmers had enjoyed their time since the frosts had finished. Not only had they avoided the heaviest rains, but there had also been minimal flooding in the town. Gŭn's incredibly sophisticated irrigation and drainage system had held up well. The farmers had been able to break up the soil and add lashings of manure and compost. The primary planting season was coming to an end, and they were full of optimism.

Yú had attacked the preparation of his land with gusto. Now, his seed was in, and the irrigation sluice opened judiciously to ensure sufficient water for germination. He saw the first seedlings feeling their way into the sunlight. It had been six weeks of hard labour interspersed with bureaucratic duties; he should have been feeling on top of the world, but something niggled him. Now should be the time to admire his work, but as his eyes scanned the fields, he could feel something was not quite right. A call interrupted his thoughts; he looked up to see a somewhat excited Túshānshì rushing towards him.

Yú's Farm, Èrlǐtou, Hénán

"We've news from your mother, Yú. Nüxi finally had a message from Líng. One of the pigeons must have got through."

"It must be important news to find you running across the fields! This might be the first time I've seen you out here!"

"Don't be silly, Yú. Do you want the news or not?"

"Of course…of course, I want the news! As I said, having you running out here means it must be important!"

"She says that there's still a pocket of Lóngshān resistance, and they're preparing to expand from their base in Dōngyíng. The king there is called Fēngbō; he–"

"Wait, wait, wait! How can a pigeon carry all that information? There's way too much detail. I suspect my mother has been storing information from several sources for some time. She really shouldn't do that; it's a control thing. A pigeon only tells you what the pigeon fancier wants you to hear. Do you remember that saying?"

"I do. It was your mother that made you learn it. And don't you think it's a bit unfair to get upset with me about it? There was more to the message; do you want to hear it or not?"

"Yes, I want to hear it, you know that. Come on. Tell me."

"Your mother's coming. She'll be here tomorrow. We'll get to see your father as well, I hope."

"Oh no! Here? Really? Why?"

"Yes, really. She's already set out," Yú's wife had turned and threw the response over her shoulder, "I'll go and prepare a bed for them. They can sleep with Qí; your mother will like that. And it'll give us some time alone. That'll be good for us!"

Yú had become quite used to Túshānshì's manipulations. As time passed, he had learned to systematically ignore some of her machinations. However, he felt unprepared to have his mother and wife together again, working him over in tandem. He would have to be at his most diplomatic yet stubborn. He would yield on matters of lesser importance and dig his heels in on things that mattered. He knew that Túshānshì had been becoming increasingly frustrated by his resistance and would be rubbing her hands with glee at the thought of teaming up with his ageing mother.

Strangely, the two women did not seem to like each other very much, but they managed to gang up on him to achieve whatever objectives

Four: The Farmer

they might have in mind. It could be tiring. At least he could spend time with his father discussing water management; it was not a subject that Túshānshì found interesting.

He looked around once again. The plans to improve his buildings would have to go on hold. That would involve too much time around the house. It was a tough decision and the last thing he wanted to do, but he determined to call a council meeting. It was the one place he could guarantee to be away from the pair of them. He would have to hear his mother's news first. That would provide an excuse for the meeting. Hopefully, his mother would spend her first evening besotted with Qí; after all, she had not seen her grandson since she and Gǔn had left last summer.

Calling the council together was an easy process. A series of flagpoles was dotted across Èrlǐtou, one rising in his backyard. Running up a message would result in all others with flagpoles raising the same flag; it was rare that such a summons would not be known across the whole town before the end of the day. A council meeting in two days' time required a yellow banner; members were always given a couple of days' notice. There should not be a problem as most councillors would have completed their sowing already, but Yú did not have enough information to call a faster emergency meeting. He would have to remember to change the flag the following day. A red one meant one day's notice. When he pulled on the rope to raise the sheet, he did so quite ruefully. It might give him a chance to escape the house, but it would mean he would face all the moans and groans from the community.

Not that there had been many moans and groans. The state reserves had kept the entire population well-fed, kicking in as soon as individual stocks had run low. Gǔn's hard work ensured the granaries were overflowing, and there was plenty to keep everyone going throughout the spring and summer, even after the sowing grain was in the ground. Although there was little variety, there was a complete understanding of the circumstances.

Throughout the sodden year, fishing had overtaken farming in bringing home fresh food. Farmers had brought their animals into their homes through the winter months, sleeping cheek-by-jowl with pigs, sheep, goats, and cattle. Most houses had chickens roosting in their rafters,

Yú's Farm, Èrlǐtou, Hénán

and as spring had crept in, the livestock had already begun to mate or lay eggs. There would be no famine in Èrlǐtou.

For all the successes in the Year of the Rat, Yú had received the credit. For the final migration from Táosì, for the crushing win at the Battle of the Yellow River, for the reliability of the flood control systems, and even for hoarding sufficient grain to see them through the entire period, allowing fields to be sown. Yú was even given credit for diverting the great river, the new stretch from Xíngyáng to the Bóhǎi Sea, often referred to as Yú's River. It mattered not that Yú consistently credited Hòutǔ, Bóyì, Líng and Gǔn. For the town's residents, he was the one and only hero. After all, Hòutǔ was somewhere in Shǎnxī, Líng and Gǔn were also gone, and Bóyì appeared to have taken the lowest profile possible, working an isolated farm in the east of Èrlǐtou, ignoring everyone but Jīngfēi and seemingly blissfully happy.

There were forces at work promoting Yú's hero status further, and the greatest of these was Túshānshì. Her natural ability to convince anyone of anything was worked to the bone. Systematically, she elaborated on her husband's involvement in every success. If she had found it easy to sway public opinion behind Yú, it was because there was so little resistance when the man was already so widely loved and admired. The only resistance she had met came from Yú himself.

The previous year, at the council meeting before last year's summer solstice, the attendees had been jubilant. They had won the war. As far as the townspeople were concerned, one man had won it for them. Every man, woman and child had flooded the streets to welcome the returning hero and his triumphant army. That day, they had not only offered Yú the position of leader for life, but they had also requested that he wear yellow, a colour they planned to ban for anyone else. Much to Túshānshì's irritation, her husband had first refused the role and then laughed at the idea of someone picking his clothes. He accepted he would become leader, although he insisted that annual elections should be held.

Túshānshì had fumed for months. She now desired the prestige associated with her attachment to the great man; perhaps a new home, even a palace, which would undoubtedly have come with helpers, maybe a cook, possibly cleaners and especially a nanny. There were plenty of people out there who would kill for such jobs. Anything to be close to the

Four: The Farmer

seat of power. What did she now have? She worked as a farmhand, mother, cook and cleaner alongside Yú on the farm. As much as Yú felt anxious about his mother's visit, Túshānshì was elated. Although she did not like the woman, if there was one person she could depend on to assist her cause, it was Nüxi; in fact, she was the only one who could provide practical help.

The following day, Nüxi turned up on a sizeable four-wheeled cart, with only the driver for company. The flatbed was heavily loaded, carrying grain to the centre to supplement the stores there. The arterial east-west road had been maintained in the best possible condition to accommodate the larger wagons; on rougher tracks, the two-wheeled version was still more practical. Only in the worst of the rains had the road fallen out of use, and for a short time, the only way to transport anything had been in shoulder bags. Not only was the arrival of such a vehicle evidence that the meteorological crisis was ending, but it was also proof that technological advances were continuing.

Nüxi dropped from her seat beside the driver, the man tossing her small bag after her. Túshānshì was waiting with open arms.

"Well, *Bǎobǎo*[9], how are you doing? It's lovely to see you. Where's Qí?" She kissed and hugged Túshānshì before peering over her shoulders for a glimpse of her grandson.

"He's sleeping, *Māma*[10]. We'll wake him later. You'll have to wait. But where is Gǔn? I was so looking forward to seeing him?"

"Later, later. At my age, waiting is not something you want to do for long! You better make sure I don't die before he wakes!"

"Don't be silly, *Māma*. You can spend some time with Yú and me before Qí wakes. Besides, he can spend the night in your bed. You'll have the whole night with him."

"I'm not sure about that, *Bǎobǎo*, but I'll bounce him around after dinner. Ah! There's my son! Hello, Yú. Now, have you been behaving?"

"Yes, Mother, you know I have," Yú hugged her before holding her hand. "Where's my father?"

---

[9] Affectionate term meaning baby.
[10] Affectionate term meaning mother.

"Let's get settled in before we have many questions, shall we? Come on, take my bag. Put it where you want me to sleep unless it's in the stable! Wait. Give me that cloth bag from the top first - that's the one - I made some treats for Qí."

"What about me, *Māma*? You used to bring me treats? Is there nothing for me?" Yú adopted a whining tone that sounded remarkably similar to one he had used as a toddler. In response, he received a whack round the head from his mother, followed by another hug.

"It's treat enough my being here to see you, Yú. Fancy teasing your loving mother that way!"

The three entered the house and were soon sat around a low table, sharing some of Yú's homemade beer. It seemed the news, in order of importance for Nüxi, was that Líng, Tú and Yùtù were well. That Gǔn was sick. Then she forecast a good summer for the crops, but that famine would continue across northern Hénán and Húběi for a minimum of another five years. Finally, she came out with the information that Fēngbō was re-establishing a large Lóngshān fiefdom spreading out from Dōngyíng. To Yú, her priorities should have been reversed, although he knew better than to argue with his mother.

They spent the remainder of the evening playing with Qí. Nüxi repeatedly tried to persuade the child to chew on the rusks she had made, but the pile only diminished due to Yú's sleight of hand in making them disappear. Nüxi avoided the subject of Gǔn's health. At least whenever Yú asked, his mother changed the subject. Yú determined to grill her about this and other matters before leaving for the morning meeting. It allowed her to focus on spoiling his son.

The following day, after Yú had quizzed his mother and then departed, Túshānshì and Nüxi sat down together for a long chat. The antagonism between the two women was put aside to focus on practical matters. It had proved hard for them to converse seriously the previous summer. Gǔn had left for the west while the celebrations were still in full swing, deliberately provoked into going by Nüxi, who was trying to clear a path for her Yú. Her unexpected ejection from the Sisterhood council still rankled. It also annoyed her that Túshānshì was not considered to replace her; they had both been comprehensively cut out. Líng was taking

Four: The Farmer

the Sisterhood away from Èrlǐtou, just as she had taken so many of Nüxi's pigeons. Both women felt slighted.

Whilst Nüxi, as a member of the senior Sisterhood, had been at one with the Sisterhood's plans, it had been unclear whether Túshānshì was entirely on board. Now, both were ploughing independent furrows, cast adrift from the organisation they had fought for. It was as if they had both become a problem for Líng rather than the solution, and it was not a place either wished to be. They were now struggling to find a common cause; being united in ambition had not brought personal reconciliation.

If Líng was moving the Sisterhood in a different direction, then both Nüxi and Túshānshì were adamant that the previous plans of the Sisterhood should be seen through. However, their motives were not entirely selfless, as both wished for personal and familial aggrandisement as much as anything else. Both women wanted Yú to be the emperor, and both wanted Qí to succeed him. Whilst the selfishness of their desires was evident, it was something they could justify as being compatible with the Sisterhood's plan, at least the Sisterhood they remembered.

What was becoming important was knowing the secrets and understanding whose secrets were true. In Ānyáng, Líng believed that Túshānshì did not know the identity of the child she was raising but that Nüxi did. Líng also thought that only she and Nüxi were aware of who Qí's grandparents were, when in fact, Túshānshì also knew. Túshānshì knew a lot more than anyone thought she knew, including some information of which Líng was unaware.

Yù's refusal to take on the position of anything but council leader, and that only on an annual basis, was something both women wanted to change. No one would consider, let alone propose, an order of succession for someone who was simply an elected council leader.

"When will you finally persuade him to take control?" Nüxi's question was to the point, and her tone somewhat damning.

"I don't know. I thought this would be easy. It isn't as if it isn't something that everyone wants. The only person who doesn't want it is Yù. I've done all I can. I've worked on him from every angle. The only thing I haven't tried—"

"What is it you haven't tried? Maybe it's time to try that?

Yú's Farm, Èrlĭtou, Hénán

"Well, you know...everything I've tried has been, er...nice. I haven't tried to be unpleasant or threatening yet. I've never had to in the past and–"

"What would you rather be, the emperor's mother or the emperor's wife? It's as simple as that. If Yù does not do the right thing, we must manufacture it so that Qí takes over. There's no alternative."

"I know. It's just that–"

"There's no 'It's just that...' about it. Qí will not come of age until he is fourteen. I know he's technically two now, but seriously, he'll be a very young fourteen when he comes of age[11]. That means you must keep Yù in power for twelve more years as a minimum. If there's a vote each year, on and on, this will not happen. It doesn't matter how good they think he is now; he'll have made a mistake in twelve years. There'll have been a plague, a flood, a war. He'll commit a crime–"

"No! Yù would not commit a crime."

"That just depends, doesn't it? Rules change. What was not a crime before can become a crime. Do you see what I'm thinking here?"

"Yes," Túshānshì could see clearly what Nüxi was suggesting, and it alarmed her enormously. "It's only us, isn't it? Nobody else knows?"

"Anyone who did is dead, and the secret died with them. I worried about Líng, but I know she'll not speak of what she knows. There's Gŭn, of course, but no one would believe anything he says with the state he's in, you wouldn't believe it. He–"

"How is he? Really?" Tenderness shone in Túshānshì's watery eyes.

"Gone. Completely mad. Can't remember what day it is. Can't remember if he washed or not. Can't remember who I am half the time. I didn't bring him because it would have saddened you both. He's still trying to fix up the final pieces in the western irrigation scheme, but his men must do anything he does again. They're very sympathetic to him and–"

---

[11] Birthdays were celebrated on Chinese New Year. Thus, Qí who was born just before the new year, was now two, even though he was actually only thirteen months old.

Four: The Farmer

"It sounds awful. Are you coping?"

"No!" Nüxi sighed. "It's one reason I'm here. Not just to get away from him, that would be cruel, but I need to find some fresh upas tree latex; I–"

"You're going to kill him?"

"Yes. What else is there to do? It would be cruel not to. The man's going to hurt himself or someone else."

"You…you better not tell Yù!"

"Don't worry, *Bǎobǎo*. I'll not tell my son I'm planning to kill his father! What do you think I am - a monster? It might be time to take his mind off things, though." Nüxi considered for a while.

"You're going to have to work harder on him. I'll send sister Shíliu over to see you. She's been practising her trade for over twenty years, and you only see smiling men come out of her bedroom. She'll teach you a few more tricks. Listen, Túshānshì; it has to be Qí, not another."

"Yes."

"Do not get pregnant again. Promise?"

"I promise."

Èrlĭtou, Hénán

Five: The Scorekeeper
Èrlĭtou, Hénán
Year 91: Year of the Ox
Three days after the spring equinox
24th March 1904 BCE

The first session of the council meeting was over, and there was a short break before they were due to recommence. Bóyì and Yú sat, attempting to warm themselves in the pale afternoon sun. Yú had been surprised to see Bóyì hanging around, but it did give him an opportunity. The compound and its surroundings had altered little since they arrived in Èrlĭtou a year earlier. The only significant change was that a few rules were now written on each of the four sides of the compound wall, escaping the effects of the weather under protective awnings.

They had found themselves a spot away from flapping ears, sitting on the bank of the *Huángjiā Hé*[12]. Yú had already introduced his protégé to his big idea.

"When was the last time you worked as a farmer?"

"It…" Bóyì stumbled for a moment, "in Táosì - it was the second or third year after the–"

"No. You did not. We were working on a cooperative. You were not a farmer, did not have your own land, and did not run your own farm." Yú was as direct as he could be. "Even now, Jīngfēi is doing all the real work; you're just a second-rate farmhand."

"That's not fair, Yú. I'm learning. I can tell you all about the diseases that affect foxtail millet!"

"And what about Sorghum Millet? Eh, Bóyì? What about rice?"

---

[12] The name the locals had for the irrigation ditch surrounding the central compound; it meant royal river.

Five: The Score Keeper

"Come on, Yú, I told you, I'm learning."

"But what I'm asking you to do is something you do well. Something you already know and something you can teach others. Thousands of people could farm better than you, but no one could do this job better. No one. You're a natural."

"I haven't got your gift, Yú. I can't turn huge crowds onto something. I can't–"

"Rubbish!" Yú laughed. "And who is talking about big crowds? We're talking about an army here, not the whole town. You are the man for the job, and if you were only a little less modest, you'd be prepared to admit it."

"I don't know, I–"

"It's ridiculous! Look, this is a fantastic deal. Not only do you control the standing army, but you also get double the land here in town with workers to do the farming for you. I'm a farmer, and I can tell you that it's hard work; it's even harder when you don't know what you're do–"

"Stop! Enough of these put-downs about my abilities on the farm. You must understand what you're asking me to do. You see, I'd be the only one! People will hate me because I've got more land."

"That's not the case. It's not just you. The same system will operate for the four posts. There's the army, the bronze controller, one for irrigation and roads and one for the granaries. That's four people who all get the same deal. It's not just you! And then there's Háng. I'm not sure about–"

"Ah! Háng, there you go! What sort of mess is that going to make? He's thinking very differently, and some people are getting quite upset by it all. Anyway, you haven't appointed anyone for the other three positions yet, so it would just be me to start with."

"True. The fact is, we can cope as we are for a few months before we appoint the other three, though come the new moon, closest to the longest day of the year, we'll be announcing them. We need you to get working now. This is not a minor issue up in the northeast. It looks serious, and I think we can both agree on one thing. We both want Fēngbō stopped."

Èrlǐtou, Hénán

"On that, we agree, Yú, but you must remember I was not in the council meeting. I don't know the details." Bóyì had been slightly irritated at being overlooked in the previous year's council elections. He had also experienced irritation at the popular conception that Yú alone was responsible for all Èrlǐtou's successes. However, he considered Yú a good friend and carried his frustrations close to his chest. The euphoria surrounding Yú had been such that any contradiction of the widespread misconception would have been shouted down. Besides that, he had no wish to appear disloyal.

"I know you're not on the council, Bóyì, and I doubt you'll be on it after the next vote. We're changing the way we do things. Each group of five hundred farms will appoint two councillors, one woman and one man. At the moment, your farm, right out on the edge, will fall into a group of relative newcomers. They don't know you. Now, it would be different if you had picked a farm closer to the centre or the later Táosì arrivals. The problem is that you didn't! You're not on the council now and will not be in midsummer. Nor will Jīngfēi, and just by the way, we are not allowing couples to stand in the same area, so even if you moved, only one of you could stand."

"*Cào!*[13] You're pushing me into a corner here, Yú. I think you're doing it deliberately. I think–"

"You think I've set up the entire state system to get you to take the army job? Really? I know you have a high opinion of yourself, but–" Yú broke down laughing.

"*Cào!* Alright. There's one thing, though. I need to talk to Jīngfēi. I'll need two days and–"

"So, I can go back in there and tell them you're on board? Yes?"

"No! I said I needed–"

"You think I haven't already spoken to Jīngfēi? She says she'll do anything to get you out of her fields! She says–"

"You went behind my back, like–"

"Yes. Now, you take your two days. I'll do what I can in there, but I will say you are almost certain. Understand?"

"*Cào!*"

---

[13] Meaning "fuck!"

Five: The Score Keeper

Everyone had known a significant reorganisation was necessary. Those who thought most about it knew it would be essential to have people working full-time in the service of the state. One of the major problems was that no one had a name for what they were trying to set up. The information from Nüxi had been the trigger, and Yú had brought forward his presentation to the council. His plan was fully formed, but he would have preferred to have had more time to perfect his address; whether it really was his plan was debatable. Many of the broader ideas had originated with Líng, some more specific to Èrlǐtou from his mother. There were only a few that had not passed the honeyed lips of his wife. The Sisterhood may have withdrawn from Èrlǐtou, but its core ideals would become interwoven in its new constitution.

Yú was not particularly bothered about Bóyì's indecision. He knew he could win him over. He was equally unconcerned about getting approval for the other full-time posts. However, three issues were lying in wait for him in the second part of the council meeting, and they would be more difficult.

If the external aspects of the building were relatively unchanged, even if the inclement weather had pounded the exterior walls, the inside of the *huìyì shì*[14] was now spectacular. With plenty of time and a need to remain indoors much of the year, it had enabled the more artistic councillors to adorn the previously whitewashed walls and ceilings with delicate drawings of local plants and trees. Yú's favourites were the cedars that stretched from floor to ceiling and occupied much of the wall he commonly faced as chairperson. The beautifully executed drawing utilised the cedar uprights that supported the wall and roof as trunks, to which the unknown artist had added the branches and leaves. The colours were vibrant. One other change was that each councillor now provided their own chair, and as a result, there were a variety of styles and sizes; Yú's choice was quite deliberately the smallest he could get away with and the most basic.

When the meeting resumed, the first item on the agenda was the matter of Háng. A councillor raised his hand, and Yú indicated he should speak.

---

[14] Meaning meeting room.

"Yú, I know this is an issue that is splitting the community, but I have to speak on behalf of Háng, who resides in my ward. He asks why he is being discussed in a council meeting, as he has broken none of the written rules?"

"This is true…er…"

"It's Táng, the name's Táng."

"I'm sorry, Táng, I must do better with names. Apologies. I think the problem is that although he has not broken any written rules, he does appear to have broken some unwritten codes. This has upset people. Also, he appears increasingly well off compared to the rest of us. This has also upset people. However, the major complaint seems to be that he refuses to serve anything but inferior beer to those who do not have an 'arrangement' with him. This has upset people most."

"I do not deny any of those points, Yú; I just have to represent his point of view. Unless that is, you would like to invite him to the meeting. He's outside." Táng was desperate for Háng to represent himself; the last thing he wanted was to have his reputation twinned with the barman's own just before an election.

"Alright," Yú sighed, "let him in. Councillors, feel free to ask Barman Háng any questions you wish. Just let me get in the first one. Alright?" There were nods all around as Háng waddled in. So that everyone could see, a few councillors at the far end of the table opened up a gap for the man to stand in.

"Good afternoon, Háng; it seems ages since we met." Yú adopted his most charming smile.

"Good afternoon, Yú. It's good to be here and good to see you ag'in!" It was noticeable that unlike most in Èrlĭtou, Háng had put on considerable weight over the last year.

"Now…Háng, what's this I hear about you serving poor quality beer?" Yú cocked one eyebrow.

"It's untrue, Yú, completely and quality…quanti…fiably untrue."

"But you have a better quality beer; is that not true?" A voice piped in from another councillor.

"It is indeed. If I say so myself, the finest beer this side of Mount Song and possibly all the lands south of the Yellow River."

"So, you have both poor and good quality beer?" Yú asked.

Five: The Score Keeper

"No, Yú, I have an excellent beer, and I have a standard beer. The standard beer is perfectly satisfactory. I think the problem is comin' because people thinks they should all be allowed to drink the excellent beer."

"And why are they not, Háng?" Táng now felt able to switch his perspective.

"For the simple reasonin' that it costs me a lot in time an' materials to make the excellent beer. The agreement I had in Táosì and, it seems here, is that I didn't have to work on the land if I served beer to the people at no cost. This I do; I serve the standard beer."

"So, how does someone get an excellent beer at your place?" Táng enquired.

"They have entered into a financial trans…tran…saction."

"With whom?" Táng again.

"With me!"

"What sort of transaction?" Yú queried.

"It varies. May I call a witness, Yú?"

"This is not a court, Háng, but if you must."

"Would you call in Bóyì, please?" Háng's request finally led Yú to understand why Bóyì had been loitering outside the *huìyì shi*. Upon entering, he looked a little sheepish. Háng continued without allowing Yú to welcome the new arrival. "Bóyì, will you be explainin' what is meant by a medium of exchange?"

From this point on, the council meeting descended into heated arguments. Many concerned the merits of a monetary system and some the benefits of greed. Most councillors had heard of cowrie shells[15] but became completely lost when Bóyì expounded on scarcity, supply and demand, costs and benefits, and incentives. It went exactly as Háng had intended. By the time Yú brought the meeting back under control, the poor quality of the barman's standard beer was long forgotten.

"Háng, I'm going to explain in simple terms what the problem is." Yú was exasperated but knew he had to hold the barman to some account. "It seems that you have spent much of your time establishing a

---

[15] Widely used as a medium of exchange in southern Asia, but mostly for long distance trade.

Èrlĭtou, Hénán

beautiful drinking area, much of which is covered and protected from the rain and sun. According to you, you have also improved the quality of your 'excellent' grade beer. However, you have entered into a series of deals to do so. I cannot fault you regarding the accusation that you supply 'excellent' beer to those who helped you construct your bar; that seems fair enough. But it has come to the council's notice that you have taken to yourself the land of three other farmers, that they now have no land and are working for you. May I ask what standard of beer they receive?"

"They get none."

"None?" Táng was doing his best to distance himself from the barman.

"None. The reason they're workin' for me is to pay off their debt for the beers they did the drinkin' of. Seems fair enough."

"Right. This is the problem," Yú determined to wrap this up. "Èrlĭtou citizens are supposed to have a farm; you have taken their farms away. It means that the council must find a way to give them land. The–"

"But it's only what you're plannin' to do. I hear there's talk of appointin' four state workers. I hear there's talk of givin' them second farms. I hear there's talk of them havin' workers. If the state can do it, then why can't I?" Háng had it all worked out. "And I don't suggest you go givin' those three families new land."

"Why not?" Yú asked.

"Because they'll just be drinkin' it all away again, and I'll be endin' up with more land still! That's not good business for you, although it works out fine for me!"

"Stop!" Yú's irritation bubbled over. "I'm going to call for a vote. We need to think about this. We need some time. I want a show of hands, please. I propose two things: That the council considers this further. Not in the next few meetings, but perhaps in our meeting, erm, just after the autumn equinox; that should ensure the new council is bedded in. I also propose that no one is allowed to take possession of someone else's farm until that discussion has taken place. Hands, please?"

Yú was slightly surprised that the joint motion had only just passed; he had expected a full endorsement.

"Háng, you can go now. I'll clarify that we'll see you in half a year. In that time, you must not take anyone else's farm, and you must

Five: The Score Keeper

keep those workers well-fed and housed. Understood?" The barman nodded before turning and exiting.

The next issue was even more complex, although for entirely different reasons. It seemed a brother and sister had conceived a child on one of the farms in the west. It would probably have gone unnoticed. However, the girl was under fourteen. It was an issue brought to the attention of the local councillor. Further investigation revealed the bigger problem.

The councillors had a month to consider the facts and a few proposals for possible action. It became clear there was little argument amongst the group; all believed that incest should be added to the list of rules. It was simply unacceptable. There were two further issues, however. One was what to do with the young couple, and the other was what to do if it happened again.

Lài was the local councillor, and she had done everyone a favour by going around all the members beforehand, soliciting a consensus.

"We have broad agreement on our course of action, Yú. These two were kids; that much is clear. It's difficult to punish them for their mistake. Everyone thinks their parents should take some blame, but we're unsure what that should mean. If they had been adults, we would have banished them from Èrlǐtou with their baby. However, we do not feel this would be appropriate for this pair."

"That's quite clear. Well done!" Yú slipped a sideways smile. "How about we bring in the parents for a lecture from the whole council and write up the new rule in front of them? How about we leave the girl with her parents to bring up the baby, but was the boy older?"

"Yes, Yú, he was," Lài was undoubtedly in command of her information.

"Then how about we send the boy to the east? That's punishment enough for the parents. I have just the place for him to stay. We can limit his movements for, say, five years, maybe until he has a proper partner. Does that sound reasonable?" There was a murmur of agreement around the room. "Then, case closed. Get that boy to me, Lài. Get the parents for our next meeting, and Lài, you can write, can't you?"

"Yes, Yú."

"Then would you draw up the new rule for the wall? I'd like it displayed as soon as possible. Let's move on."

Notwithstanding the fractiousness of the early part of the meeting, the remaining business went very well. The four state posts were agreed upon as expected. Not only was the remuneration for the posts accepted unanimously, but they also agreed appointments should be made by the council leader, with a simple vote of approval required in the council. He had to complete a double-take when they registered unanimity regarding the changes to the council wards; it would be a decision that would cost many of them their seats on the council, but they had thought it through. Which only left the budget.

"The final issue on the agenda is the provision we make for funding all this."

"Passed!" Zhèng called from the other side of the table to laughter all around.

"What's going on here?" Yú was perplexed. "We've discussed some contentious issues, and the council has voted how I would have liked. Now…Well, now, I haven't even told you what people would have to hand over at harvest time, and you're shouting 'passed'. Has the whole world gone mad?"

"Yú, it's obvious. We don't want you to stand down. We want you to stay. We'd vote to call the day as night if we could only keep you." As Zhèng spoke, there were nods and cheers around the table. "A little bird told us you might be stepping down and–"

"That little bird didn't happen to be a pigeon, did it? My mother is in town!" The laughter reached a crescendo. "Alright, alright, one more year! If you vote me in, that is!" There was plenty of backslapping around the room as Yú's face reddened.

"Taxes…" Yú waited for quiet. "The taxes will remain the same. I know they are currently high, but this is to replenish the granaries and to ensure a good start for the new council. I strongly recommend they come down next year if the season proves to be as good as it looks now! Meeting closed!"

Six: The Barman
Èrlĭtou, Hénán
Year 91: Year of the Ox
Three days after the autumn equinox
25th September 1904 BCE

The council meeting had concluded the night before. It had amounted to little more than a back-slapping session. The harvest was more extensive than anyone could have imagined. The granaries were bulging; the sheer volume of grain had necessitated the construction of new ones. Many farmers had pulled in early harvests and were now racing to see what secondary crops they could produce before the sun fell further. Others had herds of animals grazing and shitting contentedly on their land, improving the soil for the following year. All had worked hard to improve and repair their homes. Not a soul would go cold or hungry in the coming winter; no one feared the idea of a bad harvest in the next couple of years. As a farming community, Èrlĭtou was proving itself to be a success.

If the people were content, then the controller of the granaries was over the moon. Lài had impressed Yú in their meeting in the Spring. She had done all the leg work on the incest case in advance and had greatly simplified the job of the councillors. Only a few meetings with her were necessary for Yú to realise her potential. Her command of numbers was incredible; she used a flat sandpit with pebbles and a clay tablet on which she made imprints to facilitate her accounting.

"On our last count, Yú, we have enough grain to take us through this winter, next summer and the following winter. If needs be, we could probably push that through another summer." Lài was smiling, but her eyes gave away a minor concern.

"What is it, Lài?" Yú asked.

Èrlǐtou, Hénán

"It's the amount of barley and wheat that Háng is requesting. It's not enough to make a serious dent in our reserves, but he keeps coming back for more. I'm not sure–"

"Keep an eye on it, Lài. Keep me informed. We're going to have to look at his bar operation anyway, so we'll do it together. Keep your eyes and ears open."

Yú struggled to understand her counting system, although Bóyì had spent some time explaining it to him. Háng, who had confused Yú by asking him for the job of granary controller, also understood the system but dismissed Lài's decision to use a base of ten, preferring himself to use eight. It had seemed odd that Háng might want the job to start with, but he did not appear overly put out when Yú proposed Lài to the council. The barman seemed to have spent the summer months without breaching the conditions imposed upon him, although he was eager for change.

"Growing into Èrlǐtou!" had become his motto, a phrase that embellished both doorposts to his further improved drinking area with, "There is no such thing as a free beer!" over the archway. His intent was unclear, and the messages remained largely ignored. For many, they were also unread, as the early reading and writing schemes set up in Táosì had ceased to operate for the most part.

Bóyì had recently returned from subduing the Lóngshān. His campaign had also been successful, although, by the standards set by previous Xià battles, he had suffered many casualties. Over thirty troops did not return, and of those who did, ten suffered significant injuries they would carry for the rest of their lives. One of the concessions from the meeting was to set up long-term support for those who needed it, with land allocated to them but worked through the rotating state labour scheme. The heroes would not be allowed to go hungry; the system supported the active troops and those who had returned injured or lost a partner.

Bóyì's campaign had confined itself to the areas south and east of the new course of the Yellow River. Fēngbō was driven back to his hometown, Dōngyíng, where Bóyì had planned to starve the town into surrender until his opposition escaped by boat. It seemed the wily Fēngbō was now beating up settlements across the river, working his way southwards through Húběi towards Ānyáng. What little information came

Six: The Barman

out of the area suggested there was so far no attempt at developing a base; each town taken was pillaged and left in ruins.

Providing some support for Kāifēng was the prime goal. It had not been Bóyì's brief to cross the great river. He had successfully ensured Fēngbō was distanced and separated from their new ally. Some troops from Kāifēng had fought alongside his army, and he had been suitably impressed. He was also determined to return early so the wounded would receive more support. The Lóngshān issue would raise its head again the following year; that was inevitable. The question was whether they would find a home in Ānyáng.

In the meantime, Bóyì had some time on his hands before serious training commenced again. Yú determined he would use him in his investigation into Háng's exploits. Bóyì seemed to understand Háng, although Yú was never quite clear how or why.

Hétóngzǐ had the job of maintaining and improving the irrigation network, drainage, and road systems. He had been a recommendation of Nuxi's, as she had watched him work with Gǔn over many years. All three aspects of his job appeared to be running faultlessly. To what extent this was down to the new controller or due to Gǔn's long-term planning was still open to debate, but the man appeared to know what he was doing. Unlike his ex-boss, Hétóngzǐ got on exceptionally well with his crews, the public, and the council members. The lad involved in the incest scandal earlier in the year was placed in his care and was doing well as an apprentice in the east, learning to control the floodwater escape channels. It always amused Yú that Hétóngzǐ meant water boy; he was unaware that it was a nickname given to him by Gǔn.

It was seemingly a bizarre coincidence that Hétóngzǐ should bring up the subject of Háng's bar. His concern was that the growing numbers using Háng's place were creating a menace with effluent and that it was beginning to taint the irrigation waters to the east of the drinking establishment. It was another item added to Yú's list of things to bring up with the barman.

The choice of a controller for the bronze had been more difficult. Tradition dictated that men dealt with all things bronze. However, Yú wanted to maintain a balance between males and females in the controller jobs. Not simply for appearance's sake but to ensure that children would understand their potential was not limited by gender. Yú had insisted that Bóyì ensure the army was balanced, that Hétóngzǐ's work crews were and that Lài similarly complied. It had been Lài who had argued the most, insisting that females were far more capable and much more precise in their work. Yú understood that she may have had a valid point, although he pointed to various imbalances in both directions and insisted that she comply.

Měnghǔ was chosen to ensure the bronze workshops functioned, that resources were brought into Èrlǐtou promptly, that the foundries' output was of a decent standard and that they had a trading surplus. She was also responsible for the big festival due next spring when the leaders of the states would meet and cement their places within the empire. Although she was a fierce tiger of the highest order, she was loved by all who spent time with her.

Měnghǔ also had a problem with Háng. It seemed he had been opening his bar at lunchtime. In itself, this was not an issue, but the bar's location was right opposite the entrance to the bronze foundries. More than one bronze worker had suffered injury after enjoying a lunchtime beer. With her team generally being specialists, they were hard to replace. The demand for replacement spear and arrow tips peaked after Bóyì's return. The orders for ploughshares reached a record high. Měnghǔ was beginning to feel the pinch. She asked if the bar could be closed at lunchtime.

One of the unresolved issues at the previous night's meeting included Háng and his debt recovery system, which was first raised half a year earlier. Yú was now going to Háng's bar to conduct a less formal meeting with the barman. He was meeting Lài and Bóyì there as well, hoping they may give him some insights into how to cope with Háng's little ways.

"The problem, Yú, is that you're not believin' that anyone should be any wealthier than anyone else. Is that not the case?" Háng smiled as he spoke. He had little wish to be more confrontational than necessary, but he was not a particularly subtle man.

"It's true, Háng, it's true. It makes no sense. Why should I have more than you? Why should Lài here have more than Bóyì? We've just had a bumper harvest; everyone's got enough food, everyone's got a roof

Six: The Barman

over their heads, and everyone has clothes, water, and a fire to keep them warm and cook. Who needs more?"

"But we're not talkin' about 'need', Yú, we're talkin' about wants. They're not the same thing at all. Forgive my askin', but what are you two thinkin' about this?" Háng indicated Lài and Bóyì just as their beers arrived.

"I was thinkin' that we'll be drinkin'!" Bóyì neatly imitated Háng's voice before taking a long draught. "It seems we have the excellent beer!"

"You'd be wrong thinkin' that! That you're drinkin' is the superior beer. There are now three: standard, excellent and superior!"

"Mm!" Lài took a small sip, wrinkling her nose as she did so. "I've never been a beer drinker, Háng. I'm not trying to upset you; it's just that it doesn't do much for me."

"If you're not drinkin' it, darlin', then there's more for us. No worries!" Háng may have voiced a lack of concern, but his expression suggested complete miscomprehension.

"Alright, Háng. You know what we're here to talk about." Yú determined there had been enough small talk. "It seems to me that you identified the problem right at the start. You want to be richer than someone else."

"That's true enough! I'm a wantin' to be richer than anyone!"

"And the problem from our side is that if you want to be richer, someone has to be poorer. Is that not true?"

"In relative terms, yes, it's true."

"And we don't want people becoming poorer."

"But they are not becomin' poorer in real terms, only in relative terms." Háng looked at Bóyì for support.

"What Háng is saying, Yú, is that just because someone gets richer, it doesn't mean someone has to get poorer." Bóyì was not entirely keen on being forced onto Háng's side again.

"So, how does that work then?" Yú was exasperated; his explanation had seemed so simple.

"May I speak?" Lài asked, only continuing when she was sure she had received nods all around. "What Háng's suggesting here is that people

Èrlǐtou, Hénán

only get poorer if there's no growth; if there is growth, which there is, some people can become a lot richer and some people a bit richer."

"Exactly! Yú, it's like if four people is eatin' one sheep, then you'll be gettin' one leg each. Do you see? Then, if the sheep has six legs and there's still four people, you'll be gettin' mo–"

"Hang…sheep don't grow six legs! That's stu–"

"He's picked a bad example, Yú." It was Lài interrupting. "If we have a flatbread, four of us have one quarter each. Got it? But if the flatbread were twice the size, each quarter would be twice as big. This–"

"This means that you don't have to have a quarter each." Bóyì laughed. "Three people could have a sixth of the bigger flatbread…this means they have the same as when they had a quarter of the smaller flatbread…but one person could have–"

"–half of the bigger flatbread, and he'd be havin' much more. See! Everyone is benefittin'!" Háng was smug as he rounded up.

"Aaargh!" Yú had followed much of the argument, but it was edging to the limit of his understanding, "Here's a problem. Why do you want more bread than you can eat? And here's another one. Who chooses which person benefits more than the others? Would you like a third, because there's–"

"Yú, it's all makin' perfect sense because the person workin' hardest is gettin' the most bread. What's more, he might just be givin' that extra bread to someone who's needin' it." Háng desperately wanted to return to the actual situation rather than hypothetical examples. "Look! I'd be makin' beer because I'm good at makin' beer. I'm skilled! I should be benefittin' from that skill. Now, your average farmer; well, he's not so skilled as me and—"

"Stop! That's it!" A light had come on in Yú's eyes. "Hang, I have the solution! If we had more people making and providing beer, then you would be just like that farmer—"

"You don't want to be doin' something like that…they could…well, they could poison someone. They could serve terrible beer. They might–"

"And they might just do it better than you! Eh, Háng?" Lài grinned.

Six: The Barman

Their discussions continued well into the night, by which stage Háng's workers had attached fire torches to the holders around his compound. It was clear that many would be staying a good deal longer. Over and over again, Háng pointed out aspects of his work that cost him personally. As he had pointed out, it was hard to call it a business because it depended on free raw materials and customers who could not pay.

"If they have no means to pay, the only way of coverin' these costs is for them to go into debt! It's as simple as that, Yú. No one's a-thinkin' this is a good idea. I need a payin' system. It's as simple as that. Do you hear what I'm a-sayin'? As simple as that!" Háng finished the last of his eighth mug of beer with a huge gulp and belched. "I could always close the bar!" He shouted his last sentence, and heads turned from their beers to look. "I said...I could always close the bar!"

"It's still early, Háng. What are you talking about?" The words were thrown from a darkened corner where perhaps ten people had been noisily enjoying themselves.

"I didn't mean tonight...I meant forever!" Háng hollered back.

A moan escaped from the gathering, becoming louder, and it was clear there were far more people in the compound than Yú had believed. The calls became angrier, increasing in volume by the moment.

"Now, Yú," Háng whispered, "you're a popular man...a popular leader...but are you a bettin' man? Cos' I'll be bettin' I'm more popular than you in this place. I really am a-thinkin' you'll not be wantin' me to close down my bar to become a farmer?" Háng stood again and raised his voice. "It's alright! I was only jokin'! Just askin' will bring the workers around with a new mug of beer. My superior beer! That's right! My superior beer. The first one is free for the askin'! Drink up!"

"You're right, Háng, of course, you're right. But you didn't ask them if they would like other bars to open. Would you like me to ask that question?" Yú had pinpointed the weakness in the barman's circumstance and would not let it drop.

Digging some long drops was easy enough for Háng to cope with, and it sorted out the pollution issues. He was also surprisingly cooperative in considering not opening at lunchtime. It seemed he didn't feel it was particularly worthwhile anyway. He even appeared content to ease off on insisting on a medium of exchange, which had shocked all present. What he was sure of was that he did not want any competition. Not under any circumstances.

Seven: The Shepherdess
The Hidden Valley, Shǎnxī
Year 91: Year of the Ox
Eight days after the autumn equinox
30th September 1904 BCE

They had travelled light for the journey from Dōngxiàféng. Twenty horses carried four adults, the ten children and their few personal possessions. It had been a relaxed and pleasant journey; the light autumn winds were still southerly and warming, the rains had ceased, and only occasional clouds flecked the sun. The wide-open spaces of the Fèn River valley made for an easy ride, although the devastation wrought by too many people and their demands on their environs was evident. Only on the third day, when they began their climb into the mountains, did they leave the wasteland behind them. It was only proper that those lands they left behind had time to recover.

They had arrived just before the equinox, giving them enough time to settle in and prepare their winter clothing. The mountain pass had brought cooler winds, and some of the patches of deep shade cast by the conifers were more than chilly. Their descent into the mixed woodlands had warmed their hearts again, and they were a happy band as they took on the final leg of their journey into the hidden valley.

The welcome that had greeted them was almost as emotional as the farewells when they had left Dōngxiàféng. Two homesteads had been built, a barn for winter fodder and a comprehensive animal shelter. The land had been cleared in a square of some three hundred paces around the buildings. Fencing surrounded the clearing and divided it into nine smaller and equal squares; the buildings occupied the central plot. It could have taken several years if it had been necessary for them to have undertaken

The Hidden Valley, Shǎnxī

this work themselves; instead, they had homes and a farm ready for occupation.

The care taken in construction was evident. That experts had built the homes and barn was clear. All the buildings sat on perfectly levelled and raised rock platforms. Stout tree trunks formed the uprights, and local stone was used in the infill. A mortar had been used; they discovered later it was a lime-based substance. The roofs were ridged with lighter trunks, a lattice of solid beams holding the thatches in place, built steep enough to ensure the winter snows would slide off.

The interior of the homes was a delight. They had not expected separate rooms, but care had been taken and off the communal area was a small dormitory for the children, a bedroom for the adults and a large, shelved storeroom or pantry. Astonishingly, each room had a stout door, almost as strong as the main entrance doors to the structures. All the furnishings were made of the finest oak or cedar and were functional rather than fancy. The two houses proved to be mirror images of each other, positioned on either side of the barn and animal shelter. The adults had stood in various states of shock for ages. None of them had ever envisaged they would ever live in such luxury. The kids they brought with them looked in awe at the amenities.

The provision of livestock was less of a surprise: a bull and five cows, a ram with a flock of one hundred sheep, a string of goats, and a pair of pigs made up the mammals. Someone had found a Jiangsu rooster and twelve chickens as a particular concession to the new shepherdess.

As the sun began to set and the crescent moon hardened its outline against the aquamarine sky, the shepherd and shepherdess sat on the ridge overlooking their new farm, counting their blessings. There was another clearing here, atop the hill, affording all-around views. It was a place they had ended up at the close of each day since their arrival. Today had been busy, focussing on the human residents rather than their beasts; it had been the first day of school.

They had left Dōngxiàfēng with six children, and now there were ten, the four additions being foundlings picked up on route. The original group had been orphans of the Xīwǎ based in the town; those caring for them had been delighted to have their burdens eased by passing them on. The six were of similar age, around seven years old, whereas the

Seven: The Shepherdess

additional four seemed a little older, a little more aware, although undersized through malnutrition. However, the final additions fulfilled the initial plan; there were now five boys and five girls.

Hòutú rolled and threw her left leg and arm over the prone form of Kànménrén, kissing him firmly on his cheek.

"I seem to remember you telling me that we were both too old to be having children!"

"And I seem to remember you countered that by spending the winter rutting with me, trying to prove me wrong!"

"Are you complaining?"

"I am not! I'm looking forward to the coming winter to see if it works out the same way!"

"It's not going to be quite the same, Kàn. We've got mouths to feed now. We won't be able to stay wrapped up warm in the bearskins until midday."

"True. Although we can share that work with Jiǎn and Lín. They're keen to help with the rearing, just not so keen on the schoolwork."

"That's because they cannot read and write, Kàn. Although, you know, we could teach them as well. It would be fun!"

"I'm not sure, as it would be fun for them to learn with the kids; it would be embarrassing for them."

"Not as embarrassing as when the youngsters have learned, and they're both still illiterate. That wouldn't be so good."

"Jiǎn and Lín will cope. They've both got skills they'll teach the kids, just not reading and writing. If you want to have them learn, you can ask, but I suggest you do it out of earshot of the young ones."

Jiǎn and Lín had offered to come with Hòutú and Kàn. It made little sense for a couple alone to attempt what they were doing; they asked for volunteers. There had been hundreds. Kàn had whittled down the list to a handful of couples before he and Hòutú sat down for a few beers with the prospective pioneers. For whatever reason, the pair had been unable to have children and were positively enamoured with the idea of helping to raise a large group. However, their skills with livestock had been the deciding factor, although it also helped that they were warm, intelligent, and great company.

The Hidden Valley, Shǎnxī

From the ridge, it was possible to scan the entire horizon. It seemed there were low-rolling mountains in all directions. It took a sharp eye to identify the low point to the southeast, where the river snaked out between the interlocking hills. Besides the land cleared for the farm, the area was heavily forested. The evergreens provided dark greens, and as the year turned, along came the oranges, yellows, and reds of the deciduous trees, which were now beginning to shed their leaves. Only on the higher ridges surrounding the hidden valley did the wind stunt the tree growth. However, in the lowest parts closest to the streams, the woodlands thinned out somewhat, indicating annual flooding and abundant game.

That the valley was pleasing to the eye was a given. That it was an ideal location for the two lovers, and their tribe was given away by the solitary plume of smoke. Other than their settlement, the valley was unpopulated.

The welcoming committee responsible for preparing their farm had left, trudging back to Dōngxiàfēng. They had taken their tents and pack animals with them, leaving behind their love and an entire working farm. It had been the Xīwǎ peoples' gift to Kànménrén for his lifetime's work in guiding them. As their leader, he had only one responsibility remaining: attending the spring festival in Èrlǐtou to officially introduce his replacement.

The extraordinary meeting had been arranged for some time, but the organiser, an Èrlǐtou official going by the name of Měnghǔ, had failed to consider how early the new year would fall that winter. If the date remained unchanged, it was likely that Kàn would commence the trek in deep snow. The whole thing had not been ideal. Appeals were made to have the event switched to the full moon before the spring equinox rather than the second new moon after the winter solstice. It was a difference of some forty-five days and would make life so much easier not only for Kàn but also for those travelling from Dōngxiàfēng, Sānménxiá and Lǎoniúpō. It was typical that a resident of Èrlǐtou would overlook the difficulties of those living in more extreme climes.

The departing Xīwǎ had taken some pigeons with them; ones already acclimatised and at home in the hidden valley. As Hòutú had brought more with her from Dōngxiàfēng, communication was certainly not going to be a problem. She had heard the network now included both

Seven: The Shepherdess

Ānyáng and Kāifēng, although the former lay outside what could reasonably be called Xià lands. In the short term, they waited for confirmation of the delay to the spring festival; in the longer term, Hòutú wanted some news from Tú.

Kànménrén had asked Hòutú to go with him to Èrlǐtou. She had declined, insisting she must stay on to avoid Jiǎn and Lín having to take over entirely for a couple of months. She did wrangle a concession from her husband. When he returned and was busy with the lambing and planting millet, she would leave him to visit Ānyáng. The kids could focus on their outdoor education while she was away. Kàn had been resistant to her trip due to the dangers. He was attempting to find a way to ensure her safety.

Hòutú pulled herself upright, then lowered her arms to raise Kàn.

"I'm off to prepare tomorrow's lessons, and you…Kànménrén…you will have to go and kill one of those fat sheep for dinner. Deal?"

"Deal!"

They sauntered down the slope towards their farm.

All ten children sat around the massive oak dinner table the following day. They were disappointed there was no food in sight. Instead, ten small pebbles were in front of each child; their teacher had a morning of arithmetic planned.

At the head of the table sat Hòutú. She had a similar group of ten pebbles, but they were somewhat larger, not only so the kids could see them better, but they fitted more comfortably in her hands. She had also hefted a large piece of rock onto the table. About the length of her arm, half as wide and a handspan deep, it had been heavy to lift from the floor.

She beckoned the children to crawl toward it on the table before asking, "Who thinks they know what these marks are?" On the rock's surface were clear, wriggly lines appearing to originate from holes.

"Writing!" One of the oldest piped up.

"Drawing!" Another chimed in.

"Worms!" said a third.

"You would think I would know, wouldn't you, but I don't," Hòutú smiled. "They are not writing, and I don't think they are a drawing, but they do look awfully like wormholes and casts, don't they? Come outside and see if we can find a real worm cast."

They all trotted out and returned with a hardened soil slab with a clear worm track and cast. Hòutú laid it down next to her rock.

"It's definitely worms!" said one boy.

"Worms can't eat rock!" exclaimed a girl.

"Could if they were dragon worms!"

"Couldn't! They…"

"Sh! I don't think there's such a thing as dragon worms," explained Hòutú.

"Why?"

"Because I don't think dragons really exist, so if that is true, then dragon worms don't exist."

"My aunty says dragons exist; she said they sometimes eat the sun!"

"Well, your aunty might think that, but it's not quite true. Dragons do not eat the sun."

"Could they be baby dragons?"

"If dragons existed, they could be baby dragons, but I think they're worms. Now, what have they done to the rock if they are worms?"

"Eaten it!"

"Jumped on it!"

"They've marked it!"

"Good, well done! I think perhaps these were worms a long time ago. I think they made their marks in the mud, just like the worm we found outside. Then I think that the mud went hard, dried out, and left marks in what is now rock. What do you all think of that idea?"

There were a few slightly confused expressions around the table, although there was a general acceptance their teacher may have a point.

"Now, these worms have left a worm message behind. Is that true?"

"Maybe!"

"Yes!"

"Don't know!"

Seven: The Shepherdess

"Well, when we teach you how to read and write, we use sandpits. When we teach you to add up, we're using stones. If I come in tomorrow, will I see what you have left behind? Yes or no?"

"Nooo!" The answer was collective, but one boy added, "Because you always make us tidy up."

"That's true. But these worms left their mark, didn't they? All the time we're working, I want you to come up with ideas for how you might leave your mark, either for writing or adding up. We–"

"You could do it in the mud!"

"And–"

"If you did it in the mud and let it go hard, it would still be there the next day."

"Excellent! Now, that would be one way. I want all of you to spend this week thinking about other ways to keep a record of what we have done. Will you promise me you'll do that?"

"Yes, Hòutú!"

"Now! Back to your seats!" They all shuffled back off the table onto their stools. "Take two stones. Put them by themselves. Take two more stones. Put them by themselves. That's two stones and two stones. Correct?"

"Correct!"

"Now push them together. How many stones do you have?"

Nearly everyone exclaimed, "Four!" but the youngest had not quite got the hang of it and had pushed the entire set of stones together. She now sat there completely confused as to why everyone was shouting "four" until her neighbour provided help. Hòutú considered just how many stones they would need by the end of the week.

One girl hovered at the door when she let the kids out for a run in the fresh air.

"Hòutú, are you trying to say we should be like old worms?"

"No, it's not that at all."

"So...what are you trying to tell us?"

"I'm not trying to tell you anything, *Bǎobǎo*, just trying to get you to work out how you can leave a lasting impression. Now. If this worm can do it - do you think you might?"

The Hidden Valley, Shǎnxī

After the kids had gone to bed, Hòutú related the story to the other three adults. They were getting into a routine of eating together in Jiǎn and Lín's house, whereas the children's lessons took place in the farmhouse occupied by Kàn and Hòutú. At bedtime, it was just a matter of taking the passageway to the back of the house for the girls. The boys had to walk back to the other home. Regardless of age, they were already programmed to clear up after themselves and did so cheerfully before taking themselves to bed.

"What I'm trying to understand, Hòutú…is your intention for these kids. It's clear you want them educated, but I'm not exactly clear as to why." Lín's soft, melodious voice almost inclined the listener to sleep.

"Well, Lín, it seems the new Xià state is becoming successful. Everyone will spend a lot of time farming, cutting trees, making bronze, and so on. Now, while all that's going on, all the children will end up learning skills. You see?"

"Yes, that's clear. Farmers' kids mostly," Jiǎn was astute and interested in everything. "They'll not need reading and writing, that's for sure!"

"Well, probably. The problem is that they will need people who can read and write to run the empire. The other problem is that those same people will also need to know how a farm should be run and have the skills to milk a cow, kill a sheep, plant crops, and set up an irrigation scheme. There's a lot to know. These people who can read and write will be the people who run the empire." Hòutú smiled, "I know precisely what you're about to say!"

"You mean to say…you really mean to say that this bunch of vagabonds we've just had around the table…they are going to run the Xià state? No! I can't believe it!"

"You will, Lín, you will. This lot and the next lot, and then the lot after that. You see, Kàn and I have a plan!"

Eight: The Empire
Èrlǐtou, Hénán
Year 92: Year of the Tiger
Fourteen days to the spring equinox
7th March 1903 BCE

If the timings had gone to plan, nothing would have been ready; Měnghǔ considered herself lucky the date had been pushed back, even if it had made her look slightly foolish. The event had taken on a life of its own now. She could do little but master the ceremonies, hoping everything would go to plan.

The old *huìyì shì* had been too small; an entirely new structure had been constructed nearby. Yú had asked that they ensure it be circular to give all participants equal access and opportunity; the council rejected his proposal. Měnghǔ had been tasked with telling the council leader, and it was not a happy scene. Her argument that the council sought a building that would stand for hundreds of years infuriated Yú more. Their discussion had not been an easy one.

"I don't like the fact that it's not round. I wouldn't say I like that it has only three doors, all on the south side. I particularly do not like this raised platform. In fact, I will not use the platform. I will not sit raised above all others. You'll have to find something else to do with it. You know, I go away for a month, and everything I asked for has been turned upside down. What I want to know is, who is behind this design?"

"It was a group of the councillors," mumbled Měnghǔ, "not one individual." She was lying through her teeth as the driving force behind the entire thing had been Túshānshì, who had argued that Yú was being modest and deserved better. Yú's wife had been in every councillor's ear; when her husband visited Mount Song, there were opportunities. Not only had she persuaded them to make the changes, but she had also insisted that they remain quiet about the origin of the ideas. To her great delight, Túshānshì realised her powers of persuasion were undimmed.

"What we cannot do now is have an audience ring the five tables; they just won't fit!" Yú seethed. He then paced out the positions he proposed. "So, we'll have the tables on the floor, in a circle around the chests. The seats at each will all face the centre of the circle. The audience will have seats ringing the tables, facing inwards, and on that side, the chairs go on the stage."

"But the audience will be higher than the leaders!" Měnghǔ was horrified. "That's not going to go down well with the other leaders even if you–"

"Leaders are only as important as the people who appoint them," snarled Yú. "I want everyone in this town to understand that idea, and I want all those attending this event to take that back to their states. This is important!

"I'll tell you what. We won't have chairs on the stage. We'll have kids in the audience, and they'll be happy to sit up there without chairs; just put down some rugs for them."

"But I haven't accounted for children in the numbers. It'll–"

"Well…you can start counting them. They're the most important citizens in this town!"

He had terminated their conversation by walking out. It was rare for Yú to lose his temper, and he did not want anyone to see him in this state. Fortunately, one person in town would understand; he found Kànménrén sitting alone at a table in Háng's bar.

"I swear, Kàn, they want this place to return to the bad old days!" Yú accepted a beer placed in front of him by one of Háng's attentive workers.

"Well, Yú, it's good to see you as well. It's only been two and a half years since I saw you last, and you walk in with a face fit to kill! How about a hello?" Yú leapt back up and embraced his friend.

"Sorry. My apologies. I've just come from the new *huì táng*[16], which isn't anything I'd wanted. Nothing at all."

"What was wrong with the old one?"

---

[16] Assembly hall.

Eight: The Empire

"Too small. Well, too small for tomorrow's event. We needed room for your head, Kàn!" Yú was cheered and eased back into his usual self. He was now in the company of one of his best friends.

"And you're calling that thing a *huì táng*, are you?" They could see the roofs of the new building towering over the compound wall. "Well, I've been in town for three hours and heard it referred to several times, but never as a *huì tang*. People are referring to it as *jīn bì huī huáng*[17], one that's fit for a royal palace. You've certainly impressed some around here! It's the best and the biggest building in town by a long, long way. You should ask them to build you a house as well! You should see what my people did for me; I live in a palace!"

"But...I did not do it, Kàn! It's not me! I didn't ask for that. You know me, I–"

"I do. But I also know the people around you, and I think it might be the work of someone closer than you think. Anyway, let's change the subject. Hòutú sends her love."

The discussion took off on different strands, and by the end of the evening, they had caught up on all the missing information. Yú had loved the story about Kàn's unworkable ideas for melting the ice, whilst his friend had nearly wet his pants when Yú described the work of the Fire Horse Three after the battle.

Yú had become more serious over the description of Líng's killing of Léigōng and had exclaimed, "She did that for your family; you should be proud of her. It's strange, isn't it, Kàn? That girl finds it difficult to kill a mosquito."

When they rolled out of the bar, both were the worse for wear. The two men spent the night snoring on the straw in Yú's barn. They were discovered the following morning, already late for the preparations for the big ceremony. Túshānshì had thrown water over them and stripped the pair before encouraging them to clean themselves up properly. Whilst Yú had a new set of clothes laid out, Kànménrén had no idea of the whereabouts of his fresh clothes and ended up attending in one of Yú's less worn smocks, one that dwarfed his frame.

---

[17] A dazzling sight (gold and jade in glorious splendour).

Èrlĭtou, Hénán

When they finally made it to the new hall, it was to find Měnghŭ ushering in the audience. She stared at Yú for a long time before pointing out his seat, placed precisely where he had asked. When she tried to prevent Kànménrén from entering, Yú had to explain who he was and that it wouldn't be a good idea to leave him outside; her expression was withering.

As Yú entered, everyone stood and roared. Banners depicting the symbol of the Motherland adorned every wall, each the brightest yellow on a red background. The slight breeze in the hall caused them to flutter slightly, giving magical life to the place. The kids on the stage were dancing jigs, the outer circle of invited townspeople cheered, and the inner circle of councillors clapped and clapped. Everyone at the delegates' tables beamed and welcomed him, which enabled Kànménrén to slip into his place relatively unnoticed.

Yú's first move was to visit each of the five tables and introduce himself to those he had not yet met. It was a waste of time; they could not hear him, and he could not hear them. Smiles and handshakes had to suffice. The racket went on for an age before it finally began to subdue.

"I was asked to chair this meeting, and–" Yú had to stop as another roar met his first words. He raised his arms for silence, which eventually came, although a few of the more excited children could not stop themselves from gossiping. "I've been asked to chair this meeting. I suggested someone else, but they said no. That means it is up to me to welcome our guests. In fact, I should not call them guests, for this is their home just as much as it is ours.

"Kàn! Please commence with the delegation from Dōngxiàfēng because I know you want to leave the table as soon as possible; it's best if we start with you." Yú's request somewhat irritated Měnghŭ, as she had planned to introduce each table; she now slid against the wall, waiting to see what other random changes he might introduce.

A somewhat shaky Kànménrén stood to address the throng; his speech was concise.

"I have stepped down as Xīwǎ leader. I come to introduce Jiālíng, who has taken over the leadership of our council in Dōngxiàfēng. I want to express my thanks and those of my wife, Hòutú, for the wonderful farm they have given me to live out my retirement. I will now shut up and leave!

Eight: The Empire

To my old friends here - I'll see you for a drink before I leave town. Farewell!"

As Jiālíng introduced her deputy, one of her controllers and another Dōngxiàfēng council member, Kànménrén snuck out. Jiālíng then outlined what she was bringing to the table, which could be summarised by the word meat and the offer of protection of the northwest borders. When she sat down, there was long and sustained applause.

The second leader to speak was Yúntóng from Kāifēng. He attracted the most interest, as everyone in the place knew he had formerly been a Lóngshān warlord. After introducing his team, offering protection in the east and emphasising his town's mass pottery production, he addressed the issue head-on.

"As some of you know, Kāifēng was a Lóngshān town. When I became king, I could see there were problems. Some years ago, I attended a meeting in Ānyáng with almost twenty fellow Lóngshān kings. Their attitude was so awful that they convinced me of the need to turn away from their way of doing things. It has taken time. Just last year, I stepped down as king and asked the people of Kāifēng if they would allow me to stand as their council leader. They agreed, and here I am. Please understand they may vote me out of my office at a time of their choosing. So far, they have chosen not to." A huge smile replaced his previously worried appearance. "And if any of you want to know what it's like to have been a king...I'll talk to you over a beer later!"

As Yúntóng sat, the cheering swept the hall again, his humility appealing to the audience. The two final groups then took a turn.

Héměirén silenced the crowd when she stood. She was as tall as a tall man, and her hair was also wavy. For many in the audience, they had never seen such a thing. She spoke for Sānménxiá, the guardians of the Yellow River gorge and their boatbuilding capabilities. She also addressed the central point of interest immediately.

"I know my hair attracts attention. It always has. Sometimes, I have cut it off, hoping it will grow back straight; it never does! As far as we can understand in my family, the reason is that my great-grandmother came from the far west, where she came from a tribe, all of whom had curly hair. If you do not like it - I can always wear a hat!" Her final comment brought the house down, the laughter increasing out of all proportion when she pulled a hood over her locks.

Last to go was Bórén, from Lǎoniúpō, in the Wei Valley. He explained that they would guard the routes from the south and west but admitted they had struggled to develop a trading speciality. Only when it had become clear that the mulberry trees of the central and eastern areas were devastated during the torrential rainfall and flooding did he realise their strength would be in silk. His offer of abundant warm clothes to trade was a real crowd-pleaser.

When the four had finished, Měnghǔ managed to wriggle through and insert herself into the centre of the desks. It took her a while to command silence, but she did so.

"We have prepared these gifts for our visitors!" Four huge, ornate chests were brought into the hall at her beckoning. Four men carried each, clearly struggling under the weight. Once they had removed the carrying poles, a pair from each group opened the heavy lids before exiting. "I would ask our guests to gather round to view the contents. Please, come!"

The delegations from Lǎoniúpō, Sānménxiá, Kāifēng and Dōngxiàféng left their seats to crowd around the boxes. It was clear from the expressions on their faces that they were stunned at what they saw. Each chest contained hundreds of bronze spear tips and thousands of bronze arrowheads. Lying on top of the weapons were the moulds to manufacture armaments themselves. In addition, there were moulds to make ploughshares and axes. At this point, Túshānshì slipped away unnoticed, merely another crowd member but the only one to be departing. As all the others returned to their seats in obvious awe, Yú rose to speak.

"These, my friends, are simply a token. These are a symbol of our unity. Much of the bronze you see here comes from the stashes of Táosì. We took it from the Lóngshān and are now giving it back to the people they made suffer." He paused to allow the significance to sink in. "Our contributions to unity will be defence, specialist bronze manufacture, and something even more important. Today, in Èrlǐtou, we now have some of the finest craftsmen and women in irrigation, bronze manufacture, granary management and accounting, not forgetting a superbly trained army. What we offer today is to share those skills with our comrades from Lǎoniúpō,

Eight: The Empire

Sānménxiá, Kāifēng and Dōngxiàféng! Only by sharing will we make ourselves one, as equal parts of the Xià Empire!"

It had been scripted but was highly effective. Each leader of the four visiting delegations stood to speak in turn.

"I, Bórén, from Lǎoniúpō, ask that henceforward we be known as the Xià!"

"I, Héměirén, from Sānménxiá, ask that henceforward we be known as the Xià!"

"I, Yúntóng, from Kāifēng, ask that henceforward we be known as the Xià!"

"I, Jiālíng, from Dōngxiàféng, ask that henceforward we should no longer be called the Xīwǎ but should be known as the Xià!"

Finally, Yú stood.

"And I, Yú, from Èrlǐtou, ask all that we should continue to be known as the Xià!"

"And I…" A powerful voice came from outside the door, "And I, Kàn, ask that all you Xià should look after your new Motherland. That will be the greatest gift you can give to your people!"

A multitude surged from the building's doors when the formalities were over. They found an even greater crowd waiting outside. Everyone wanted to see the treasure chests, but equally, everyone wanted to rub shoulders with their new Xià comrades from the sister states. Chants of "Xià! Xià!" continued for the rest of the day and half the night. Háng's bar ran out of beer; he was the only one of two people in town without a smile on his face.

The other sat alone at her kitchen table, fingers hammering a pattern on its oak surface. She was mightily unhappy; in fact, tears streamed down her face. A turning point was reached, and her anger would not easily be assuaged.

Èrlĭtou and Lóngmén Forest, Hénán

Nine: The Fire Starter

Èrlĭtou and Lóngmén Forest, Hénán
Year 92: Year of the Tiger
Twelve days to the spring equinox
9th March 1903 BCE

It was when the copper pan smashed square into Yú's face that she had finally broken. She hardly waited to assess the damage done before leaving. It was clear she had broken his nose, and it appeared a front tooth was missing, but her husband was out cold. She did know that he was still breathing, perhaps not easily; the blood pouring from his nose ensured that, but he would live. Túshānshì briefly wondered whether she may have damaged his brain, but in her present state, she could not decide whether that would have a positive or negative outcome.

He should not have walked in halfway through the night yet again. He should have been sitting on a throne as Emperor of the Motherland. He should have been lauded by all, with her sitting next to him. It was the dream she had been promised would come true since before she could remember. All those years of waiting. All those years of pandering to her him and all those years of putting others first. What was her reward? Nothing! Still a farm girl! Still a skivvy! A mother, a cleaner, a cook! No longer a warrior! She was never going to be an Empress!

Túshānshì was unsure where to run to when she left their farm. Taking Yú's horse had given her more range, and she drove it hard, Qí strapped tightly to her back. Heading westwards and then southwards allowed her to put more distance between her and her husband; any other direction would have quickly brought her to a river's edge. Fanciful ideas skipped through the strands of her insanity, such as riding back to Sìchuān and her childhood home on the slopes of Mount Tú, after which she was named. Ridiculous! Yet nothing seemed to focus her thinking; it was one

Nine: The Fire-starter

mad scheme after another, each rushing through her mind as fast as the wind ran through her hair.

A physical intrusion finally forced her to concentrate. It had been some time since she had been on a horse at full gallop, and indeed, there were the usual moans and groans from unused muscles, but there was something else. Her nipples felt sensitive against the fibres of her underclothes, and her breasts were unusually swollen. It was not a breastfeeding discomfort but a tingling irritation and a heaviness that came and went, but mostly, it came. She slowed her pace, focusing all her attention on her body rather than events. Her condition probably staved off a complete meltdown. The realisation she may be pregnant slowed her headlong rush further. Túshānshì pulled her mount to a halt and took in her surroundings.

It was unlike Túshānshì to lose her temper, and she had never experienced anything quite like the emotions of the last few days. It was time to bring things under control, however big a mountain she would have to climb to achieve that goal. However, it was not necessarily a time to appear as if she had things under control. It was complicated.

She had come a long way, almost past what was now regarded as the edge of town and certainly past the edge of sanity. Behind her, the faint tendrils of dawn lightened the sky, and ahead loomed dark hills cloaked in dense fir. To her left, she could hear the waters gurgling through the rapids of the Yī River, but otherwise, there was silence. In the distance, at the forest's edge, she spied two men dodging in and out of the trees, moving closer but hoping to avoid being spotted. It was perhaps time to turn around; Nüxi and Gǔn's house would mean backtracking fewer than a thousand paces.

The plan became more fully formed as she retraced her steps. As the council leader's wife, Túshānshì was aware of most of the happenings in the area and quickly realised she had stumbled across a pair of bandits. The term bandits was loose; basically, they had been proving a minor nuisance, stealing eggs and the odd grouse, nothing that had yet meant any action would follow. People believed they must be hanging around in the Lóngmén Forest caves, though the pair were relatively low on anyone's list of priorities. She smiled; perhaps they now had a purpose.

Èrlǐtou and Lóngmén Forest, Hénán

When Nüxi opened the door, it was clear that everything was wrong and nothing was right; for both women, Túshānshì's arrival was horrendously mistimed. Qí was thrown onto the straw in the corner of the room before Túshānshì turned and tripped over the prone form of Gǔn lying on the floor.

If Túshānshì was in a desperate state, then Nüxi was hardly much better. She had chosen the timing of the empire meeting to finally put an end to Gǔn, who, towards the end, was being spoon-fed like a dribbling child himself. He had died in the late evening, after which his wife had promptly entered an exhausted sleep, assuming she would attend to his body in the morning without interruption; she had been wrong.

Nüxi supposed that having the old man out of the way was a blessing, as it did enable her to focus more clearly on matters at hand, although having his body out of the house would have helped even more. The chaotic circumstances had not improved Túshānshì's state, and the wailing had re-doubled when she realised her father was dead. Nüxi wanted Gǔn in the ground, but now it was both a matter of finding the opportunity and persuading a distraught Túshānshì to help.

Túshānshì appeared inconsolable. She sat at the kitchen table, kicking at the legs, pulling her hair out in clumps with tears streaming down her mud-splattered face. She refused to feed Qí, who remained on the straw in the corner and completely ignored his crying. Nüxi managed to sort Qí out to an extent, but what to do with Túshānshì was another matter.

It was not hard to figure out what had most upset Túshānshì as she hadn't stopped raging about it since her arrival. It had not been easy to pick out all the threads of her rage, but Yú stood at the top of the pyramid. What was tricky was working out the best course of action. Nüxi determined the time had come to be completely open, but it would not be an easy subject to broach. Before revealing anything, it was essential to have a plan to move forward, one that Túshānshì would accept and one that would not raise any suspicions among the townspeople. Nüxi waited for an interlude in the sobbing.

"Now, Túshānshì, let's look at what you really wanted."

"Wanted! It's ruined!"

Nine: The Fire-starter

"Now, you can't say that. It just looks like a mess right now. We can change the outcomes, you know."

"What? After I hit him?"

As Túshānshì expected, the biggest shock for Nüxi was learning of the suspected pregnancy; it would force her to talk. The cold reality of the circumstance would lead her to reveal who knew the bigger secret.

"*Bǎobǎo*. It is time to tell Yú."

"Tell him what? About being pregnant? What good will that do when you tell me to terminate it."

"No. We can sort that out easily enough. About you and him."

"No!"

"It is. It's the only thing that will now move him the way you want him moved."

"I can't. It's...This is what you were telling me when you came into town. You want me to turn into this monster. I am not a monster!"

"Well, that's not that difficult. You appear to have made a good start by smacking him with that pan. We need him back under control."

"If you're going to try to convince me to continue the sappy and sentimental approach, you'll see I've got a lot of mountains to climb to get his trust back."

"It will bring him to heel if he knows. He dare not say anything."

"So, you want me to go to war? You want me to tell him? You want me to threaten him with that for how long?"

"As long as it takes, *Bǎobǎo*. Until Qí is old enough."

"So, I spend ten years fucking his balls off, and now you're telling me I've got to spend another ten years, but this time shitting on him?"

"Yes, it's time. You've made the problem much bigger, however."

"How's that?"

"You're pregnant, which means we've got a problem. You'll have to get rid of it. The sooner, the better. We're just lucky the switch worked with Qí."

"So, I've got to abort this baby. Then I've got to tell Yú I'm his sister. Can you hear yourself?"

"But–"

"Then I've got to live with that for how long? If he talks, then that's it. Finished! Over! For all of us! If he doesn't talk, then – well - and when do I tell him I found out?"

"You can tell him that Gǔn told you on his deathbed."

"He won't believe that! He'll only believe it if it comes from you! Who actually knows anyway?" It was the big question, the question she needed an answer to; it had slipped out easily.

"Me…you…Gǔn, of course, but he's dead…and Líng."

"Is that it?"

"Yes. I believe that everyone else who might have known is dead. Not one would have passed the information on."

"So, it's me, you and Líng?"

"Yes!"

The dagger slid from Túshānshì's smock unnoticed. As the older woman turned to look down on Qí, it was plunged with some ferocity into her upper back, downwards and close to her spine. The dagger remained in place as Nüxi twisted round to face her daughter-in-law.

"It comes to this—"

"It does come to this," Túshānshì whispered to the dying woman. "But…I'll tell you a secret to take to your grave."

"But—"

"I've got news for you! Surprising news! For me, it's good. For you, who knows? Is anything any good anymore?"

"What…can you tell me…that I don't already know?" The words stuttered out between gasps for air.

"Ha!" Túshānshì now looked directly into Nüxi's eyes. "The switch didn't work! Líng thinks it worked. You think it worked! It did not! Do you hear me? Do you think I'd allow it? In my house! With my midwives! I fooled you all! Qí is my son!"

"But…that dog…what's its name? Jīnxīng? Jīnxīng called the switch," Nüxi was turning a horrific shade of white whilst blood began to pour around the dagger in the wound on her back. She was shaking violently, "Líng told me."

"Well, it's good that Líng doesn't know much about dogs then, isn't it? Qí is my son! My son is going to be emperor! This will happen whether your son and my brother knows or not!"

Nine: The Fire-starter

The air in the room could not have been more still once the shouting ceased. Nüxi slumped sideways before crumpling onto the floor. For a few moments, Túshānshì was a statue, her arms and fingers splayed across the table, an expression of triumph radiating across the killings.

It was a dreadful satisfaction. Túshānshì had told Yú's mother a truth she would not have wanted to know in her moment of death. Qí was the son of Yú and Túshānshì. Líng was wrong; she had taken Tu's baby to Ānyáng. Now, only she knew this truth. That Líng knew the more dreadful truth, that she and Yú were sister and brother mattered not, for she would not act when unaware of the first truth.

As she sat, she began to make other connections, some of which would compel her to take even more extreme actions. Her mind was still operating at full speed, although her emotions forced her thoughts to veer wildly across all the possible outcomes; it was logic of a sort, but not logic that a sane individual would have recognised. Èrlǐtou would not react well to its leader smashed into unconsciousness. Simultaneously discovering their leader's mother and father were dead would provoke outrage. Both Èrlǐtou and Yú would need satisfactory explanations, and when there was only one person who might have been present at both the assault on Yú and the death of his parents, it did not look good.

She considered Nüxi's body coldly. Where would she have put the remains of that upas tree latex? It was unlikely it was all gone. Standing, she pulled the bow and quiver from its place on the wall. Taking careful aim, she shot her dead father in the chest and then repeated the action, hitting his guts. The corpse stubbornly refused to bleed. In desperation, she changed her aim, taking her mother through the neck. Deep crimson welled from the puncture. Túshānshì scooped it up in her cupped palms, liberally spreading it around her father's new wounds.

The day had rolled by, time flying unnoticed. It was time to leave, but something had to have gone missing; there must be an apparent cause; a botched burglary would suffice. A shoulder bag with two flagons of her father's homemade spirits would do. She also scraped the ròugān into it and a pile of flatbread that sat ready for heating. It wasn't much, but it would suffice for her purpose. Her very recognisable dagger still protruded from her mother's back; it was quickly pulled and cleaned.

Túshānshì made a double-take of the man she had never been allowed to call father and then one last look at the woman she had never been allowed to call mother. They had never fully understood the consequences of their decisions so many years ago. Although they had accepted the possibility of creating a monster, they had not believed that was the outcome; their grandson looked normal. However, the beast they had raised disguised herself well; it was an evil that only now Túshānshì realised herself.

She knew it would be wise to end her pregnancy. There was little point in taking such a risk again. She knew that if what she planned came off, Yú would take her back in. She would be cared for, and she would be able to try to work him around again, perhaps with more luck. What she assumed was that she could use the bandits as cover. It was a risk that she would never have taken if she had been thinking as clearly as she imagined and was probably indicative of her growing insanity.

One last subterfuge was required. Spilling the remains of a half-empty flagon across the floor and dragging a few hot coals from the fire should start a burn. Slow, perhaps, but it would eventually suffice as a signal, drawing people first to the house and most likely the following morning to track down the culprits.

Strapping Qí across her back once more, the bulging shoulder bag hanging over her stomach and partially resting on the horse's back, she left her parent's home for the last time. It was a short and easy journey, although she went out of her way to scrape against every bush and to have the horse step in every bit of wet mud as she tore pieces of her clothing to drop along the path. No tracker on earth could fail to follow the signs she left.

When she came across the bandits, once again ducking behind a shrub, she temporarily brought her mount to a halt before kicking it back into a gentle trot. Within a few steps, they reappeared on either side of the path ahead. They were dishevelled and unkempt; it was clear they were sleeping rough.

"Hey, sister!" one man called.

"Hold up there!" shouted the other.

Túshānshì brought her mount to a halt and gazed down on two of the most abject specimens she had seen in years.

Nine: The Fire-starter

"And what do you two want?" A whole drama played out in her mind as she spoke the words. Sharpened ideas incorporated what had previously been hazy thoughts. The entire concept had now come to her as one, suddenly and seemingly fully formed. It was time for the charm.

They took her to the cave they were using; it was more of a mess than they were. They talked excitedly about her joining them, and she had persistently upped the ante. They were not particularly aggressive individuals; it seemed they wanted company more than anything else. Quite what kind of company they expected was a different matter.

Bolstered by a few slugs of Gǔn's homebrew, she soon had them going, offering encouragement with her behaviour, continually readjusting her clothing, exposing legs and breasts in alternating and tantalising glimpses. It had not been difficult to persuade them to mount her, but convincing them to hurt her proved more problematic. When she finally faked a colossal orgasm to show them what pain would do to her, they became more enthusiastic, indiscriminately beating and biting as she howled in apparent ecstasy. She waited until they were utterly exhausted and sleeping before stabbing each neatly through the heart.

If there had been dangers in her actions with the men, it was nothing compared to the risk she now took. Using a bamboo shard, she cut into her vulva and vagina before inflicting similar damage to her cervix and womb. With a few short, sharp stabs, the unborn inside her would be as dead as the two men lying beside her.

It was a brutally cold dawn when she finally heard the scrabbling outside the cave and the call of her name. As they entered, torchlight must have lit her form, for Túshānshì could hear their gasps. She lay semi-conscious and wholly exhausted. Blood pooled between her legs; scratches, cuts, bite marks, and bruises covered her body.

It took a week for anyone to have the courage to transport her damaged frame back to the centre. After burying the charred remains of his mother and father, Yú sat with her throughout her convalescence, holding her hand. When it became apparent that he had no memory of what or who had struck him, Túshānshì also claimed complete ignorance of the events of that day. It led to much speculation, although no one ever resolved what had occurred, nor were any fingers pointed.

Ānyáng, Hénán

Ten: The Father
Ānyáng, Hénán
Year 92: Year of the Tiger
Seven days after the spring equinox
29th March 1903 BCE

Kànménrén, having taken advantage of the spring river conditions, had crossed out of Xià lands some seven days before. Since hitching a ride with an expectant fisherwoman, he had travelled alone, unknown and on foot. He was unaware that he was retracing the route used by Líng two years before, although it was his objective to meet up with his daughter. His aims were two-fold: firstly, to check on his child, but secondly, to scope out Ānyáng to assess whether it was safe for Hòutú to visit her daughter. When he tossed the idea around, he found it odd that their offspring had ended up together, although it was particularly convenient.

The atmosphere north of the river starkly contrasted with what he had left behind on the south bank. Èrlǐtou had a contented air, driven forward by Yú, a feeling growing spatially but one that had not yet stretched its tendrils into these lands he now crossed. It was not as if there was poor Lóngshān governance, for there was no governance. A state of anarchy prevailed, which had little time for the weak and allowed local bullies to create a reign of terror. Undoubtedly, this was the counterweight to the successes of Èrlǐtou; starvation and disease walked hand in hand with mistrust and violence.

Nothing about his appearance suggested who Kàn might be, where he might be from or what his previous status may have been. However, it was clear that most folk on the tracks avoided him, ducking for any available cover and hiding, just as he avoided the settlements where groups of young men strutted, blocking any from entering their fiefdom. It was the big black flies that appeared to have benefitted most.

Ten: The Father

In each village, surly youths stood guard beneath the dead and dying, strung from gibbets, advertising the welcome strangers would receive. The black flies paid little regard to who was dead, dying, or alive and swarmed the men on guard duty to the same extent as their victims.

It all resulted in his journey proving to be a series of zigzags. Gradually, he took to higher and higher land with more woodland cover to travel in something approaching a straight line. What was abundantly clear was that by destroying the Lóngshān leadership, the Sisterhood had not benefitted the ordinary people of this area one iota. Instead of top-down, organised violence, they faced disorganised, chaotic violence that impacted their day-to-day lives to an even greater extent. Everyone was scared, even the bullies, knowing there were bigger bullies in the next village, over the hill or around the next corner.

The houses showed the most significant damage from the storms of the year before last. There was little sign of repair. Most fields were weed-filled, and only a few had been prepared for spring planting, which should have already occurred. It seemed likely that people had eaten any remaining seed stock. Some farmers may have prepared land out of habit or had hoped to receive supplies. Kàn reminded himself of the devastation of the Fèn Valley, but this was on another scale. It seemed a vastly reduced population was hiding in shelters that afforded a little cover, watching the land and doing little else but praying for a miracle. From what he could see, there was little sign of any miracle on its way.

Even the woodland on the higher slopes was ravaged. It was evident that little care was taken. The objective of those who were able was to hack firewood and kill any game to keep themselves going until tomorrow. Then, it would start all over again. It was hand-to-mouth living. There was seemingly no concern about the day after tomorrow and certainly not for the following year.

Kàn had spoken to almost no one since the fisherwoman; either they were too frightened of him, or he was too scared of them. He had judged every likely meeting carefully, but when he had determined the consequences were safe, it seemed the other parties had not. His loneliness came to an abrupt halt when he threw himself into a ditch to avoid being seen by a roving band of young males.

"Watch out! You almost crushed me!"

Ānyáng, Hénán

Kàn had dived into an innocuous stand of bent reeds, but it seemed they were already occupied by an individual displaying the same caution as himself.

"Sorry. Shush! They're not a hundred paces away."

"Well, stop moving. Look at the reeds. They'll give us away. Stay still!" The whispers were hushed but commanding.

The pair lay there in silence for some while. Several pairs of feet passed perilously close at one point, but eventually, the sounds faded into the distance, and the two men could readjust themselves and sit up.

"I'm Kàn. What are you called?"

"Chéng. Where are you from, Kàn? Why are you hiding from them vagabonds?"

"Same as you, Chéng; I'm scared shitless of them. I'm going on to Ānyáng, looking for my daughter. You?"

"More or less the same, 'cept I'm looking for my missus."

"In Ānyáng? Is that where you're from?"

"No, mate. It's a long story. I'm from Huáxiàn originally. It's not two day's walk from here." He pointed in a southeasterly direction. "But I've been travelling a long time now. I'm still searching."

"Searching a long time, then? Surprised you haven't given up by now."

"I almost did. But then I was passing back through Huáxiàn, and I was crossing the river, and it turns out I knew the boatman. He'd been looking for his kid, been up to Dōngyíng just before the worst of the floods hit. Says he saw my missus being taken in a cart by the Fēngbō's troops. She stands out, my missus, a beautiful woman, but she has white hair and very pale skin."

"She's an albino?"

"Yes. I'm surprised you know the term. She must avoid the sun, and they had her out there on the back of an open cart. I'm praying she's alright. What I'm thinking is that, because of her condition, they might just keep her alive. Some people see it as good luck to have an albino around, although it has to be said many more do not. She was almost killed at birth; her parents threw her out. Some good, caring people rescued and protected her, then took her back to Huáxiàn, where we met.

Ten: The Father

"So now, I've heard that Fēngbō has fetched up in Ānyáng. If he's in Ānyáng, then Cāngbái might be there too. I'm going to rescue her."

Kàn eyed Chéng up and down. He was an honest-looking guy but not one to take on the Dōngyíng army alone. Chéng mirrored Kàn's assessment, concluding the stranger was just an older version of himself. It was an easy decision for them both to share the burden of the rest of the trip; agreement came without words, although the details needed thrashing out. Both preferred to travel alone; however, they agreed the overnight stops were the most nerve-wracking. If they could spend the days apart and meet up each evening, it would maximise their safety. It would still be a few days to Ānyáng, as the roving bands would considerably slow their progress, and once there, it would be necessary to spend time scoping out the town.

Before settling down for the night, they shared the little food they had before taking turns to sleep.

Kàn knew Ānyáng and the passes that crossed through the mountains from there into Shǎnxī, although his memories were not entirely happy ones. His last visit had been to rustle beasts for the first trekking train from Táosì; on that occasion, he had taken away more than he had brought with him. However, on his previous visit, his first, he had lost considerably. His wife and two sons had been taken by Léigōng and tortured to death in front of him. Whereas the memories sharpened his remembrance of the geography, his eyesight became afflicted by the welling of tears. He had never forgiven the Lóngshān and never would.

Approaching Ānyáng from the west, they used small trees and shrubs that dotted the ridges as cover. It was a complete accident that they should come up behind the small hill that comprised Qícun. There, they found an ideal scrape for a night's sleep. Tomorrow, they would begin to edge closer to the town. Both men were nervous, being this close to a larger settlement. The outcome could have been entirely different if it had not been Kàn, who had taken the first watch.

When an arrow thudded into his left arm, just south of the shoulder, Kàn controlled himself enough to restrict his reaction to a low yelp. It brought a surprising result, for out of a thicket bounded an excited dog, jumping up at his chest and attempting to lick his face. He just found it in him to call out before a second arrow targeted him.

"Don't shoot! It's me, Kàn!"

Líng was devastated she had shot her father. She was an awful archer, and in living memory, she had never struck a moving target. It had been a challenging shot in the half-light of dusk. No one was quite sure how to react. Whilst Kàn was welcomed into the home and guided to a seat to have his wound tended, the women were more circumspect regarding Chéng. Whilst they let him in, Mǎjié stood over him with a bent bow.

The string was beginning to cut into her fingers when Shùn joined them. As his eyes adjusted to the light, he realised two men were in the room and that he knew one of them very well indeed.

"Chéng! Chéng! How long, my friend?" Shùn went down on his knees to greet his old friend face to face. "It's alright, ladies, it's Chéng! I knows him! I'll vouch for him! Chéng, my old mate! What are you doing here?" He turned momentarily. "Was it you that's brought in this bandit here? Shot him, did you? Well done!"

"Shùn, that's not a bandit," Kùàimǎ took him by the arm, "that's Líng's father."

"Who shot him?"

"I did." Líng, who turned from dressing her father's arm, looked somewhat paler than usual. "I shot him…and before you say anything…anything, Shùn…think about it first!"

"You needs to aim for the chest, a bit lower and–" His remark was halted in its tracks by a fearsome stare from Kùàimǎ, who had prepared herself for just such a comment; it was a look matched by Mǎjié, Yěmǎ and Tú.

It was late by the time Líng finished with Kàn's arm. Everyone was tired and wanted their beds; the catching up stories would have to wait for the morning.

After breakfast, all gathered under the magnificent oak that dominated the top of the hillock. From here, there was a line of sight for most of the immediate environs, but with Jīnxīng's nose twitching and seemingly in good working order, they would likely receive early warning of any approaches.

They had agreed to a joint meeting because of so many shared strands of interest. Tú wanted to hear about her mother but also Yú. Líng

Ten: The Father

was interested in any news from Èrlǐtou, although, unlike Tú, she shied away from asking about the council leader; she also wanted information from the east of the new river. The Fire Horse Three wanted to know if anyone had escaped the battle and, if so, whether they might find they had arrived in town with Fēngbō.

Shùn wanted to catch up with Chéng so they could compare notes on what had happened since they had both left Huáxiàn, Shùn westwards and Chéng to Dōngyíng. It was a private conversation they had intended to have, but it seemed something that also fascinated everyone else. This tale then linked to Fēngbō and his arrival in Ānyáng. They had heard little of what was happening in the town; it seemed surprisingly quiet. Chéng's only interest was whether his wife was in Ānyáng and the prospects of rescuing her.

Kàn had remained surprisingly quiet. He sat in the fork between two massive, raised roots, with Líng hanging off him like a baby. Only Tú had previously observed this behaviour from their leader, and the almost childish adoration for her father shocked the remainder of her group. Líng even asked Kàn to preside over the proceedings rather than take on the job she usually did herself.

While Kàn was ready to take on anything he could, he was more interested in the two young girls darting around the outside of the circle. He had heard the term Wolf Sisters, although he was unsure of its meaning. It seemed to him that there might be a potential conflict between Hòutú's aims in the hidden valley and what Líng might be attempting to do here. He ensured it was not raised in the morning's conversation.

As the sun reached its highest point and the shade from the old oak became a blessing, Kàn summarised their discussions.

"This is what I've gleaned from this morning's chat. I'll add a summary of my observations on Èrlǐtou as well.

"It seems that east of the new river, which I believe some are calling Yú's River, conditions are considerably better than here. Farming has resumed, and although there is little food, no one is starving anymore. Bóyì's army has spread the news about the new Xià Empire, and many are hoping for a helping hand from Èrlǐtou. Things look like they may be heading for eventual inclusion in the empire. Is that right, Chéng?"

"I'd say so."

Ānyáng, Hénán

"Èrlĭtou is stable and thriving. Yú has things under control, although Túshānshì's mental health should be monitored. I've thrown that one in myself because it was my biggest concern before I left. The four satellite states have reached a high level of cooperation with the centre. Trade is beginning to boom.

"Here, west of the new river, it would appear we have a state of anarchy all through western Hénán and possibly Húběi. Famine and disease are widespread. Ānyáng may or may not be under the control of Fēngbō and his army from Dōngyíng; this is something we need to establish. Do we all agree?"

"Chéng's wife may or may not be in Ānyáng. She may or may not be with Fēngbō's retinue. Let's focus on Ānyáng before anywhere else; it makes sense. It is something we need to find out urgently."

"Immediately, as far as I'm concerned!" Chéng sounded desperate.

"Agreed, Chéng. Agreed! I'm interested in the mountain passes to the west. There are two reasons for this. Firstly, I want to establish whether any of the people from Hénán and Húběi are spilling through the mountains. Hòutú and I have our home there, and I'm keen to ensure our security."

"Yes, you must do that, *Bàba*, as a matter of urgency," Líng looked up into his face. "Urgently."

"Secondly, I want to know if the passes are safe for Hòutú to visit Ānyáng. She wants to see Tú, but I think it would be useful for you to talk to her, Líng. I'll talk about that with you later." He smiled down at his daughter.

"So, first things first. How do we get information from Ānyáng?"

The meeting broke into informal discussions between couples, but most focused on Kàn's final question. It was challenging to be a spy when every stranger was treated with the utmost suspicion, and newcomers were likely murdered before they even posed a question.

One thing they had on their side was Chéng's wife, who, in his own words, stuck out like a sore thumb.

Eleven: The Visitor
Ānyáng, Hénán
Year 92: Year of the Tiger
Ten days after the spring equinox
1st April 1903 BCE

The decision had been made. This time, Yĕmă was to take on the part of a mother searching for her child. There were arguments that Kùàimă was a far better choice, but with her having performed the same role previously, there was a possibility she may be recognised. How many children might she have mislaid?

Yĕmă displayed little in the way of motherly intent and seemed averse to the prospect of having to well up with tears. All agreed she was the most likely to escape if things went awry, but it was proving almost impossible to take her seriously as a desperate parent searching for her son. Only when Líng suggested she should try a bit of insanity did Yĕmă's character come to life; it seemed she could play mad far better than a mother.

By the time Yĕmă left Qícun, she had convinced everyone she was the maddest witch this side of anywhere. It was a perfect disguise but a little too perfect for the people of Ānyáng, where everyone she met held the same opinion. Witches were to be avoided, particularly strangely mad, vagrant witches. No one would speak to her; everyone she encountered ran away. Only through extraordinary good fortune did Yĕmă glimpse the white hair through a broken wall, but in an extraordinary piece of bad luck, Fēngbō, on hearing there was a witch in town, determined to have her followed.

On Yĕmă's return, Chéng was overjoyed. The only other piece of news Yĕmă was able to relate was that it did seem as if someone had set themselves up in residence in Léigōng's old palace, although she had no idea who it might be. Even the guards around the walls had vanished as she approached.

A plan was needed. Kàn restrained Chéng from running into town and attempting to storm the palace single-handedly. Level heads were required. Even if they succeeded in freeing Cāngbái, the very nature of her condition would make her easily identifiable by anyone. The others felt an escape needed to be thought through in detail before they even considered breaking into the palace. They had re-grouped in their meeting place under the oak.

"I suggest Chéng and Cāngbái come with me." Today, Kàn was the quickest thinker and realised the couple needed to be clear of Hénán. "If we have horses, a full moon and an early start, say just after it gets dark, I'll be able to get them safe on the road up the–"

"Safe from whom?" A smartly dressed man approached. "I don't suggest you pull your weapons; I really don't. My troops have your three children gagged and tied, and they've already killed your dog. They like killing - my troops do. They like it a lot." He sat down on one of the tree roots. "On the other hand, I'm not opposed to keeping people alive…if they're useful."

There was silence. No one moved. Although the group sat on a near armoury of weapons, none had the confidence to bring one to hand.

"You killed Jīnxīng?" Tú asked.

"What?" The man looked confused. "We killed a dog."

"She was a bitch, and she was called Jīnxīng. You killed her?"

"Yes."

"Are the children safe?" Líng asked.

"For the moment. However, two things might make my men twitchier. The first is any movement from you. The second is if those kids don't stop biting them."

"Could one of us go and calm them down?" Líng's voice was shaky, but her mind was utterly focused. As to whether Tú was up for the task ahead was causing her emotional acrobatics. Tú had been primed but was often random.

"One of you may. Unarmed, of course…and you'll have to prove it."

Eleven: The Visitor

"Tú, you go; they've got Yùtù and the girls. If they let you bring them all back."

Tú rose carefully, winking surreptitiously at Líng before slipping off her smock and walking the thirty paces to where the children were being held. The Wolf Sisters calmed immediately, and Yùtù's crying stopped immediately when she put his mouth to her breast.

"It seems I've found what I'm looking for!" The stranger announced. As Tú returned to the group with her child, he examined her body. "I learned there was a witch in town, and it seems there is.

"Let me introduce myself. I am Fēngbō, once King of Dōngyíng and now King of Ānyáng. So, I have told you who I am. I think it might be time for you to offer me the same courtesy.

"Men! Bring those two youngsters over here. Let's take it easy on them but keep knives at their throats. Only hurt them if they struggle. If they try to run, err...Kill that small one first." Fēngbō turned back to the anxious group. "Have you got that? Make sure they're under control, and I'll make sure they live. Understand?"

"Yes," Kàn answered for them all. A wrinkle roved across his forehead; for Lóngshān, these seemed highly unusual tactics.

"You! What's your name?" Fēngbō indicated the breastfeeding mother.

"Tú."

"So...you are one of the Sisterhood...it seems your pretty *wén shēn* gives you away. Are you?" From behind his back, Líng was making frantic nodding motions towards Tú. "And I don't need anyone helping you with the answers here!" He turned sharply, glaring at Líng before turning back to Tú.

"You don't need help. Do you know why?" Tú shook her head. "Because the members of the Sisterhood are always clever, that's why!

"So, you must be in charge up here. Yes?"

"Yes," Tú nodded.

"Not him?" Fēngbō poked a boot in Kàn's direction.

"No. He just looks after our chickens. He's deaf." Tú was struggling to allocate advantageous positions that group members could use later.

Ānyáng, Hénán

"And not one of these two?" The king pointed at Chéng and Shùn, who were sitting together.

"No. We took them in because they're a bit simple. They're farmers; they just turn the soil and dig the long drops."

"And not big mouth over there? The one that keeps sending you signals."

"No. She's just mouthy and older. I give the orders."

"And these three? Who are they? One of my men swears he recognises one of them; he just can't place her."

"They're my night guards. Of course, they used to have a dog as well."

"And now they have no dog. I apologise." Fēngbō even managed to look sincere. "So, Tú. You and I are going to have a little chat. Give that baby to the older, mouthy one. Put on your smock and come with me."

"Yes, sir." Tú was enjoying being the focus of attention immensely; if she had any nerves, she did not exhibit them. The man seemed nothing like the descriptions she had heard of Lóngshān warlords. As she reached for her smock, she managed to ignore all the hand signals and facial expressions directed at her by the group. After all, even if she were again sacrificed for the Sisterhood's goals, she was going for a walk with a king, and they were not; she may as well enjoy herself.

"Men!" Fēngbō called up two more of his troops. "These two are minding those children. Your job is to mind these adults, although I'm led to believe they're not right in the head. If they move, shoot them. Arrows loaded! Got it?" The additional troops arranged themselves to cover the group. "And do not…and I mean, do not…engage in any discussion with them. If they speak, shoot them! If they nod or wink at each other, shoot them! However, you may allow them to breathe!" He laughed at his joke before turning and heading for the rocks overlooking the town of Ānyáng, calling over his shoulder, "Tú! With me! Now!"

It was a critical moment in Líng's plan. Her worst nightmare was that Tú should get this wrong. It was not that she was incapable; it was the fact she had become so unpredictable. Líng would have done anything she could to avoid it being Tú that could influence events further;

Eleven: The Visitor

however, she was the only option. That marking on her body had handed unknown power to the girl; the question was whether she could control it.

Tú was fascinated rather than scared. She had no doubts about her abilities. Having spent considerable time with Túshānshì, she believed that she was able to manipulate just as well as Yú's wife. She needed more information, for without knowing just what Fēngbō was after, it would be impossible to lead him down a route better suited to herself. She was not entirely selfish. Although she blamed the Sisterhood for not having ensured it was she ruling Èrlǐtou with Yú rather than Túshānshì, she wished no harm to come to Líng. Neither did she want any harm to come to the others, presently under the eagle eye of their guards. What she wanted most was for everyone to come out of this mess safely, with herself as the heroine who made that possible. She eyed Fēngbō's profile as they walked; she might have to spend some time with him.

"Here. We'll sit here." Fēngbō slid his bottom onto one of two smooth-faced rocks. Tú followed suit and found they were facing each other squarely.

"I thought you lot always made people sit below you?"

"Mm! Not if we want to see if they're telling the truth. So, you want to know why you're here?"

"I would. I assume you've moved away from your men and my people to ensure no one else can hear. That means you have a secret, or you'll tell me to have sex with you."

"Let's deal with the secret, shall we?"

"Oh! Alright." Tú managed to look crestfallen.

"And don't pull silly faces at me! It never ceases to amaze me that your sort looks at my sort and thinks we must be stupid. Do I look stupid?"

"No."

"Did I not say a few moments ago that you were Sisterhood, and you were, therefore, likely to be intelligent?"

"You did."

"Well, we're going to talk serious, grown-up talk, and you never know…we might just come to a mutually beneficial arrangement. Let's give it more time before you try to tempt me with sex. Got it?"

"I have."

Ānyáng, Hénán

"Let me tell you how I see things from where I'm sitting. I've taken control of Ānyáng. Ānyáng is a mess."

"I agree."

"You don't need to agree until the end. I'm in a train of thought and must get this out in order." He looked at her expectantly. For once in her life, Tú obediently kept her mouth shut.

"I was chased out of Dōngyíng by an army of the Xià. You know of them?" Tú nodded. "I believe they control everything to the south and east of the new river. It means I cannot go back. If I am going to rule, then Ānyáng will have to be my base, which means I need to sort out Ānyáng. Correct?"

"Yes."

"I believe that the Xià will eventually control Ānyáng, which does not appear very good for me at first glance." Fēngbō finally smiled. "Although…although if…in time…I was to ally with the Xià, then…well, I would have power and wealth and a set of new friends. How does that sound?"

Tú was stunned. Nothing he could have said was less likely than what he had said. She had nothing prepared as a response. It was her opportunity to think on her feet, and she was failing badly. The only course of action was to bring it back to herself.

"And…where…exactly…do I fit into all of this?"

"Do I look like a farmer?" Tú shook her head. "That's because I'm not. I know nothing about farming. I know a bit about fishing theoretically, but that's not quite the same. Ānyáng, I am led to believe, is surrounded by good farming land. Yes?" Tú nodded. "And you, if you are Sisterhood, have certain skills to keep these farmers on track. Is that right?" She nodded again. "You know about the stars and the sun and the moon and such and about the weather and how the seasons work. Yes?"

"This is true."

"Well, Tú. Let me explain. You need me so my troops don't kill you or your companions. Correct?"

"It's true."

"Well, I could kill them and take you to town, but you might not cooperate. Correct?"

Eleven: The Visitor

"That's highly likely." Tú was beginning to see signs that her strategy was on course; it was a different matter as to whether it was time to go for his balls.

"Well, Tú. I need your help with these fucking farmers. Without the farmers farming and farming well, there'll be no point sitting on a throne in Ānyáng. Correct?"

"Correct." Tú's smile was wide as an ocean. "I think we might have a deal." It was time. "There's one thing, though…"

"What's that?"

"Well, King Fēngbō, I always fancied sitting my arse on something much more comfortable than some hillside rock. I always fancied sitting my arse on something that resembled something quite different."

"And that would be?"

"Now, who's being slow?"

"Wait, I've—"

"I've always fancied sitting my arse on a throne. Is there any room on the one in Ānyáng?"

"What you mean…you mean…you mean you want me to step down?"

"Slow, slow, slow!" Tú reached her forefinger under the king's chin. "No, I don't want your throne. I want to sit with you on the throne. Have you got it yet?"

"I believe so."

"And is there room on the throne? No jealous wife back at the palace?"

"No."

"Right!" Tú had turned the tables completely. "I will agree to sort out your farmers. I will help you make Ānyáng rich once more. Yes?"

"I would appreciate that."

"You, in turn, will ensure the safety of my friends here in Qícun. When there is evidence that things are moving in the right direction, well, then you will marry me and put me on the throne next to you. Is that a deal?"

It was not quite the deal that Fēngbō had expected when he came up the hill not long before. He had imagined dragging an old crone down

Ānyáng, Hénán

the slope, imprisoning her, and torturing her for information. Instead, he seemed to have cooperation of a sort, albeit one that came with a particular yet unimagined cost. He remembered for a moment what she had looked like without her smock. She would have to keep the *wén shēn* a secret; he could not have that getting out. She seemed eminently desirable, but there was plenty of other meat around if she proved not to be. He looked directly into her eyes.

"I believe we have a deal."

Fēngbō called his troops off without returning to the group. He strode directly down the hill while they scurried after him.

Tú sauntered over, plonking herself on the ground and taking Yùtù from Líng.

"Guess what?"

"Come on, Tú, what happened?" Líng was almost desperate.

"Go on…guess?"

"You offered to have him?" Yěmǎ howled.

"No! I'm getting married!"

Twelve: The Mothers
Ānyáng, Hénán
Year 92: Year of the Tiger
Eight days after the autumn equinox
30th September 1903 BCE

Fēngbō was finding the demands of living with Tú somewhat different to what he was used to, although he was beginning, albeit grudgingly, to enjoy it. His experience of women, whilst numerically extensive, was most definitely one-track. Previously, his routine had been to pick a woman, force her into bed, have sex to his satisfaction and then discard her when bored. He willingly confessed to Tú that finding the process particularly pleasurable had become more challenging. His new wife ensured he had neither the time nor energy to return to his old ways.

Tú had breezed into his life just as he was considering whether the albino servant might make his sex life more enjoyable. Fortunately for Cāngbái and Chéng, he had failed to act on his initial impulse. It was probably fortunate for Fēngbō as well, as Chéng had sworn to terminate the life of anyone who dared touch his wife. He was not a man known to fail to make good his promises.

Tú was the happiest she could remember. Fēngbō might only be a job for her, but he was proving quite pleasurable. She had a man who would do practically anything for her in bed, and she also had a man who was the boss. In a complete reversal of her experience in Táosì, she could shout it from the rooftops if she wished. Her dissatisfaction with her previous circumstances, with no man and no apparent purpose, had been eating away at her. Now, she was involved in everything she wanted and had even found that she did not have to apply her manipulative wiles often. Occasionally, she thought she might not mind it going on forever until she focussed on the bigger picture again, and her residual allegiance to the Sisterhood kicked back in.

Of even more satisfaction for Tú was to have moved from a position where she considered herself bottom of the pile to one where she could lord it over the women with whom she had lived. She had stopped short of having herself called Queen Tú. Although Fēngbō was a king, he seemed tired of the title. It did not sit particularly well with the new world order, and that new world order appeared to be emanating from Èrlǐtou.

Yùtù was also thriving in his new environment. He was spoiled, not only by Tú but also by the palace guards and servants. Even more surprisingly, Fēngbō seemed to have quickly become attached to him. Tú had given up feeding him from her breasts when it was clear that wet nurses were available. Although she insisted on breast milk in the morning and early evening, she no longer had to put herself out as the task was done for her.

In the new set-up, both Shùn and Chéng worked under Tú's guidance and were now supervising the somewhat late harvest in the fields around Ānyáng; in effect, they were working for the new king. It had been a difficult season due to the lack of preparation. Tú, having learned from her experiences in the first year under Yú's command in Táosì, had outlined the requirements. Shùn and Chéng had put together the workforce and issued the orders. On odd occasions, Fēngbō's troop sometimes had to provide the necessary coercion. Not that most people needed it. When faced with the prospect of long-term famine, it was unsurprising that the majority worked as hard as their frail frames would permit. It was a whole community effort, albeit a directed one.

Fēngbō's army's primary function was to prevent too many outsiders from taking advantage of the improved situation. In this role, they were also the first to spot game or domestic animals that had gone feral. They were becoming adept at stopping strangers at the border yet ushering home pigs, deer, sheep, and the odd cow. It proved to be a lifeline for the citizens.

The harvest may have been late, but it was also huge, thanks to ideal growing conditions. The problem was storage. Líng had kept herself clear of the town for the most part, but like everyone else, when she could see a need, she stepped in. Granary design was not her speciality, nor was

Twelve: The Mothers

carpentry, but she had absorbed enough to apply the skills required over the years. Six tall structures were going up on one of Ānyáng's low hills. Rats were the most significant problem. Líng had always been obsessive; that aspect of her character suited the challenge of the rodents.

All the granaries were raised above the ground. A shield surrounded the legs of the structures to prevent the rats from climbing in. All trees had been removed from the area, ensuring the rats could not gain access from above. All the vegetation had been scraped clear in a large circle around the buildings, which were checked daily for access holes. Líng insisted that all the grain was stored in sacks, which were tightly bound, and all spillages were cleared up immediately. However, to her enormous frustration, not a night passed without one of the granaries being entered by one or more intruder. Until that is, she introduced the leopard cats.

In the early part of the year, the Wolf Sisters had hurled a rock at a local cat, killing it stone dead. The next day, they began to hear mewling, and Shùn uncovered four kittens still in their nest with unopened eyes. It had been a massive effort to save them; goats, cows, and even Tú's milk were used to keep them going. All four survived, three females and a male. As autumn drew in and the leopard cats attained adult size, they were re-housed in the granary area. The rat problem disappeared overnight.

They were beautiful animals, but they had failed to learn to clean themselves somewhere along the way. It was a regular sight to see them being petted and groomed by the guards at the site, for whom it became a matter of pride that their cats were in the best possible condition. At their best, the animals were majestic, their tawny fur splattered with brown and black rosettes covering their bodies and tails. So admired were they that people argued that the current year should be the Year of the Cat rather than the Tiger, as no one had ever seen the bigger of the two beasts.

It was with all this going on that Hòutú arrived. Somewhat fortuitously, she had made her way to Qícun Hill under instructions she had received from Kàn. Even more fortuitously, it turned out that Líng was present when she arrived. There had been communication between Ānyáng and the hidden valley, but it was limited in scope. Líng saw it as her job to bring Tú's mother up to speed before Hòutú made discoveries

Ānyáng, Hénán

about her daughter that may make her unhappy. For now, Líng did not want anything to upset the apple cart.

"Yes, she's married him. Well, they're living together as man and wife; to my mind, that means they're married."

"When did she move in with him?"

"It was pretty quick, actually. I think Tú thought he might change his mind until she had him by the balls. I was terrified, I'll tell you. It all looked wrong. Tú is impulsive; this time, there were no constraints because of whom she was with. However—"

"What's he like, this Fēngbō?"

"That was a shock. He's not as bad as his reputation suggests. He does listen. He takes advice. It doesn't seem to matter if it comes from men or women. He certainly listens to Tú, which is more than useful, and he adores Yùtù. Since he–"

"How's he treating the people, though, Líng? Is he shitting on everybody as all those Lóngshān bastards do?"

"No, he's not. It's almost as if he's realised the dead-end nature of that policy. When we first met him, he wasn't too bad; quite polite, in fact. However, it worries me how he will influence Yùtù. I hate to say this, but he sometimes reminds me of Yú, which is remarkable, but it does mean he needs someone holding his hand and dragging him through life. He's a safe haven for Tú and her son right now, and that's what we need until the time comes. Remember, Hòutú, that my family was tortured and killed in front of my father and me while King Léigōng gave the orders. I am not one to defend a Lóngshān king, and I will not hesitate regarding his removal."

"I'm trying to get my head around this. What do you think has changed him?"

"If you're asking my opinion, I'll give it. Although I must say, I've no proof."

"Go on!"

"I think he was marginal in the Lóngshān. Look where he was from, Dōngyíng. Right up in the northeast. Did you hear what happened at the battle?" Hòutú shook her head. "Well, he took his troops away the day before…he never fought the Xià."

"He ran away?"

Twelve: The Mothers

"No. It doesn't look like that. From my interpretation, he had to play the part in front of King Léigōng. You know, be a hard man, be a nasty bastard. But, if he wasn't terrible, and there's only one thing I've heard about that's awful, then perhaps he became fed up with all that."

"What's the awful bit?"

"Huáxiàn. We've two guys here from Huáxiàn. They say his army killed and raped indiscriminately in that town before heading off to Dōngyíng with all the young girls. That's the only bad thing I've heard specifically; the rest is just rumours."

"And since he got here?"

"Good as gold, really. Improving since Tú moved in with him. He's not always walking all that well; I think your daughter is slowly screwing him to death."

"That would be Tú!"

"I'll take you down the hill when you're ready. Today or tomorrow?"

"Let's go tomorrow. I could do with resting my bones before walking again. You could spend the evening telling me about the Battle of the Yellow River. Yes, perfect! Have you got food in?"

As the evening passed, they became progressively more drunk. Both women slept it off, falling asleep in the straw around the eating table. They had never been particularly close, although that night, it seemed things might change. The following day, they shook off their hangovers and went in search of Tú.

"Look at you now, *Bǎobǎo*!" Hòutú's gaze swept around the palace hall. "Look, you've even got a big fancy cabinet in the hall and a huge table. Even bigger than the one Chīyóu had in Táosì. It's quite impressive!"

"Yes, *Māma*. I thought you might be proud of me."

"Líng says he's behaving, your Fēngbō. Is that true?"

"Early days, *Māma*, but I think I have him where—"

"Have me where?" The king sauntered over to the pair. "You must be Hòutú. I've heard a lot about you."

"Including the fact that I'd arrived in town? You don't seem surprised, my Lord."

Ānyáng, Hénán

"You can drop that 'Lord' rubbish. It's Fēngbō to you and anyone else. I heard of your coming not a few moments before from Tú's maid. I know who you'll want to see! Yùtù! Am I right?"

"My grandson. Do you know I've not seen him before?"

"Too sad, too sad! Come, let me take you to him." Fēngbō, to both Tú and her mother's surprise, led Hòutú away by the hand. It was not usual Lóngshān practice; more often than not, a mother-in-law was despatched with a knife in the back.

Tú stood alone in the hall, scratching her head.

During the day, Hòutú inspected all of Tú's projects, Líng's granaries and the final work of the season in the fields. She was impressed. For once, she was full of praise, not only for her daughter but also for Líng and quite eloquent regarding Fēngbō. It was to Líng she turned at the end of the day, leaving her daughter and the king frolicking on a grass bank under the setting sun.

"We need to talk."

Líng and Hòutú returned to Qícun. Their meeting lasted through the night, and they were still going as the sun reached high overhead the following day. Only two issues were discussed. The first concerned the prospect of Ānyáng becoming a part of the Xià Empire and the role Tú might play in that. They were not in complete agreement, but neither were they far apart. They concurred that it was a good idea in principle. However, both were concerned that Fēngbō might not behave as they hoped. They concluded that Tú was doing the best job possible at present.

The second item concerned Hòutú's school for vagrants.

"What do you mean, you just pick them up where you find them?"

"What it sounds like!" Hòutú was irritated by Líng's supercilious attitude.

"What, no check on their parents…nothing like that?"

"No! We take anyone! How do you find the Wolf Sisters? The same way, I bet!"

"They were not random; we chose them for certain strengths!" Líng was back on the defensive.

"What, like the ability to kill cats' mothers? Come on. You picked them because they were hard, tough street kids."

Twelve: The Mothers

"And you're picking them on the sole grounds that they're unwanted! Which is the better method?"

"Ah! But you see, we have different objectives. I don't want all the kids I teach to come out the same. Some will be farmers. Some will be - I don't know – shepherds – and some will work for states. Not everyone can learn to read, write, and handle accounts, you know!"

"So, what you're saying is that you'll take ten…ten, is it?" Hòutú nodded her affirmation. "Ten each year or two…and how many do you expect to end up as qualified to help run states? Six?"

"There's no set number, Líng; it could be ten or none. As we get older, we'll need farming help in the valley. Those that don't make it academically will be sure to make it good as something. Everyone can become an expert at something; it's just a matter of scaling the expectations to the needs or even the needs to the expectations."

"Agreed, but–"

"There are no buts. There are presently five states. Let's say each of those states needs two people to work on their records, accounts, rules, or whatever. That's ten trained people needed as soon as possible. Now, by the looks of things, in the next ten years, there will be as many as ten interlinked states. That's twenty needed, and that's not allowing for the expansion of trade between them. This is not a matter for the Sisterhood; this is necessary for the councils that rule the states. I cannot see that it conflicts with whatever re-direction you establish for the Sisterhood. Which, just by the way, you have not spoken about at all. It's time to talk!"

"You're right, Hòutú. It won't be long before I give all this up. I want to join you where you are now and help with your work if you'll have my partner and me. I want to spend some time closer to my father. You don't mind, do you? I am setting up something I can leave to run by itself. I want a life, and I want my freedom. I want to spend more time with my father before you finish him off! You know, you need to go a bit easier on him; he's not as young as he used to be!"

"What's he been telling you then?"

"Oh…this and that. He's happy, at least. Happier than I've ever seen him, so you're doing something right." Líng beamed, her face breaking up into a picture of delight. "Thank you. It's been hard for him since my mother and brothers died. Keep up the good work."

"You know, Líng, much of it was his idea. He–"

"I know. Much of everything has been his idea. There's a lot I receive credit for, or Yú receives credit for that initially came from my father. You know he was also helping Gǔn early on? That he also helped the late Grandmother with her network?"

"No, but it doesn't surprise me. He never talks about what he has done, just what others have done when he's been around. We're going off the point. Líng, you still haven't told me about the next steps for the Sisterhood."

"Well…it's a bit different," Líng's brow furrowed. "This is not something to go further than you and my father. Promise?"

"I do."

"The network for messaging will remain. We'll use some existing contacts and establish some new ones. There'll be less emphasis on the pigeons, as the land networks will open up more for all; there'll be proper tracks between all the centres. We'll limit the numbers in each centre to three, and they'll have to develop their replacements, but not expand. Then we have the team."

"The team?"

"That's what we're doing right now. Again, they'll have to replace themselves. Again, it'll be a team of three. The whole network will be spying. The team has a special purpose, and they are highly trained."

"Come on!"

"You have to realise how guilty I feel about what has occurred. Sure, there were others involved in the decision-making, but it was I who saw it through. Thousands – no – hundreds of thousands of people have died. Most of those people were not guilty of any crime. They should not have been held responsible for the actions of their masters, but they were. This was a mistake that should not be repeated. Ever!"

"And you have another way?"

"I do. Targeted attacks. Focusing on the individuals creating the problems, cutting out the infections before they spread. I'm training an exceptional group. Very special. They're trained as assassins, Hòutú. Now, you tell me. Is it possible for your trainees to work with mine?"

Thirteen: The Apprentices
The Hidden Valley, Shǎnxī
Year 99: Year of the Rooster
The spring equinox
22nd March 1896 BCE

The progress over their eight years of training had been phenomenal. As expected, not all of the first cohort had shown they would be suited for service to a state. Some had more modest ambitions. Three individuals preferred to remain in the hidden valley. They would eventually take over from the ageing quartet who had brought them up. As if by magic, three high-flyers in the second cohort were ready, at least as seconds, which meant they had ten students ready and willing to go. Hòutú could confidently send out a pair of her students to each of the towns of Èrlǐtou, Kāifēng, Sānménxiá, Dōngxiàfēng, and Lǎoniúpō. The arrangements were all in place; each council leader eagerly awaited their arrival.

Hòutú's apprentices were trained in accounting and detailed record-keeping. They were more than capable of devising farming calendars. After learning more about their different locales, they would be able to apply astronomical principles. They were excellent communicators and had a solid, if not detailed, understanding of the critical principles of farming, irrigation, road maintenance, bronze manufacture, and trade. They had also learned how to train others who would eventually take on their roles. The ability to communicate with both little children and council leaders was a prerequisite. Of equal importance was that each worked to a standard methodology, meaning their skills were transferable to other centres, and they could communicate efficiently. It is what Hòutú had desired: a civil service in waiting.

Many years previously, Hòutú had laid down a challenge for them to develop ideas for writing mediums. It was expected that most seven-year-olds would come up with ideas they had already seen; writing in wet

The Hidden Valley, Shǎnxī

clay, on beaten copper, painting on pots, and carving stone were some such offerings. She had been surprised when one of the students suggested the shoulder bones of sheep; it took her back to the time in Shímǎo when she and Kàn had stumbled across the piles of scapulae. Had they come up with the same idea?

However, the children put forward two completely new ideas. One suggested writing on bamboo strips. It was a brilliant concept, although it might have to wait until they could link the strips efficiently. The other was as simple as it was mind-blowing. One of the younger students was doodling on her smock; an activity discouraged due to difficulties in the laundry. If the youngest had seen it as fun, an older girl took it very seriously. She proposed that they use material on rolls as a record not only of the accounts but also as a diary of important events, thus creating a historical document.

Hòutú had never considered the idea of using cloth before. It certainly worked in terms of application if the paint had the right consistency. However, it would need to last well over ten or possibly fifteen years to make year-on-year comparisons possible. Her more significant doubts were regarding the longevity of using cloth, having had several of her garments damaged by moths. Finding the material and storage method most resistant to those insects was important.

In Hòutú's experience, wool was the worst affected, but it was useless as a writing medium anyway. Linen attracted fewer moths, but it proved more challenging to handle, and the paint tended to spread. Silk was preferred for the ease of writing and storage, but it was more prone to insect attack. Her solution had been to get Kàn to bang together some cedar box containers for the cloth and to have posies of lavender and bay leaves in each corner of the trunk. It was a system soon to become a standard for the empire, all because little Dòngxī could not help drawing on her smock!

The girl stood before her now; although she was no longer a little girl, she was a rather beautiful woman who would shortly be gracing the town of Lǎoniúpō. "Hòutú, what would you prefer to eat tonight? Chūxi said you would want something other than the mutton, and I should ask if you wanted a special dish for yourself."

Thirteen: The Apprentices

"Dòngxī, how many times? How many times must I tell you? We are all equal here. If Chūxi is eating mutton and you are eating mutton, then what do you think I want to eat? Mutton!"

"Yes, Hòutú." The girl's smile widened across her face. "I know; that's why I made up the bit about Chūxi asking, so you wouldn't get mad with me!" She giggled. "But we had to ask, didn't we?"

"What's that all down your apron?" The girl looked down only to find her nose caught between Hòutú's finger and thumb. "Got you!" Hòutú grinned back and hugged the girl, "Without you making a mess on your clothes, where would we be? Now. Go!"

They would have a grand meal tonight. There was no doubt this would be a gargantuan feast. There were now more than fifty students in the hidden valley, of whom ten were leaving—the first graduating class. Hòutú had called a halt to recruiting more students, although she was running out of available orphans in the area. This job would now become the responsibility of the graduates, who would train their replacements in whatever location they found themselves.

It was essential to Hòutú that her charges avoided the idea that they were becoming an elite. She wanted them rooted and understanding of their good fortune. An integral part of their jobs, whilst looking for ideal candidates, was charity. They should support poorer communities and families where able. To emphasise this point, the graduates prepared, cooked, and served the meal the day before their departure. They also had to take responsibility for clearing up. It was a grand opportunity for the younger students to make as much mess as possible.

The barn had been enlarged several times. It now accommodated the extended stock of animals, their feed, and the new school space. Five large wooden trestles stretched the width of the barn, each consisting of four halved tree trunks, their surfaces having been smoothed to perfection, although the undersides still maintained a rough and ready appearance. Each trestle could accommodate twelve with room to spare, and the four adults were to spread themselves out; only the oldest group, whose table remained empty whilst they finished cooking, were left to themselves.

Before the graduates were allowed to serve, Kàn ushered the cooks into the hall, and Hòutú rose to speak. There was immediate and spontaneous cheering that filled the barn to its rafters.

"Students! Students! Shush!" The noise went unabated. Hòutú raised her arms, but even that failed to provoke the usual, respectful attention. Only as tears began to roll down her face did the racket begin to diminish. It was the first time in her life that she was reduced to a blubbering wreck. Unable to compose herself, she motioned for Kàn to come over and whispered in his ear before turning and leaving the barn through a rear door.

"What Hòutú wanted to say can wait. She says she will speak to you when we have all eaten. There are flagons of beer for these tables," Kàn indicated those already full of expectant students, "and for the graduates, your chefs for tonight, there's a choice of beer or *fénjiŭ*! Just don't start on it until you've finished cooking!" There was an immediate round of applause from the thirteen chefs; this was a rare treat. "Now, we'll let the cooks return to work, and I'll find out where Hòutú has gone. Carry on!"

Kàn followed his wife's footsteps, concerned that she might have fallen into a desperate state. Therefore, it was with surprise that he found her around the back of the barn, doubled over and laughing her head off.

"Er…you're going to have to explain this…you left weeping, and now you're wetting yourself laughing. I've–"

"We've done it, Kàn, we've done it. We've done what the Sisterhood could not manage in all those years. We're sending out these young people to make the world a better place. I'm crying because I am both happy and sad to see them go. I'm laughing because of the ease of our achievement."

"It is you, my *lăo pó*[18], who has done all this! I am just the farmer and herdsman."

"No. You know that is not the case. You have guided me all along. You have supported me. You have supported them. You have made this possible. It is you who should give the farewell address. It is you they should all be thanking."

"I think you underestimate yourself. It has been–"

"No. Do you think I don't know? Do you think I do not know how it was you who kept those women feeding me when incarcerated in that

---

[18] Colloquial and endearing term for wife.

Thirteen: The Apprentices

cave? Do you think I do not know that, at the same time, you were helping your daughter plot against the Lóngshān? Do you think I did not appreciate your support in those first years in Táosì when Tú and Túshānshì seemed to be screwing things up? Do you think I did not understand how it was you who inspired the people of the Èěrduōsī Loop into action with the ice dams? You are the guiding hand in this brave new world; I am simply one of the tools you have had come into your hands."

"If you–"

"You are much, much more than that. I'm starting to realise just how significant you are. Not to me, that's obvious, but to the world. You were bigger than the Lóngshān. You are bigger than the Sisterhood. You are bigger than the Motherland. Kàn, who are you?"

"I'm your husband, *lǎo pó*, that is all. I would be nothing without you." He held her briefly before turning her back toward the barn door.

It proved to be the most elaborate meal ever prepared in the hidden valley. There was fresh bread with a soup of fish and onions to start them off. The main course consisted of rice, cabbage and root vegetables accompanied by several whole spit-roasted sheep. There was a delicious, honeyed cake to finish the meal, something entirely new for most diners.

By the time the cooks' table had cleared their plates of the cake, there was a gently bubbling atmosphere in the room. When Hòutú rose to speak, the simmering conversations evaporated; this time, there would be silence for a while.

"I would like to say this is the best day of my life, but it is not; it is the second-best day. For the best day was the day I married the man sitting there on the middle table, sitting in the middle of you, casually consuming his third, or is it his fourth, piece of honey cake!" Laughter rippled around the barn as everyone looked at Kàn, whose mouth was stuffed to overflowing.

"I think you'll agree that Kàn has been like a father to us all. He has guided you through these years here; for the oldest of you, that is a full eight years. Without him, your education would not have been anything like it has; he has inspired us all. Some of you even call him *Qīn'ài de bàba* [19], but–"

"But only when I'm out of earshot; otherwise, there would be trouble!" Kàn had emptied his mouth and stood glaring around the room as the students took up the chant.

"*Qīn'ài de bàba! Qīn'ài de bàba! Qīn'ài de bàba!*" Smiling, he moved across to Hòutú and gave her a quick kiss and a hug. The chanting redoubled in noise, and Hòutú had to raise both arms to quiet them.

"We also have to say an enormous thank you to Jiǎn and Lín, who, more than anyone else, have kept you in food, put clothes on your backs, and even tended to you when you've been sick. Never have I met a couple with as much patience, as much time and as much love…for such a horrible group of dirty, unkempt, and ill-disciplined children!" The room fell silent as she paused momentarily, "I'm joking!" The silence ended with an immediate roar, and once again, she had to raise both arms to settle them.

"This is not the time for a lesson. For the graduating class, the formal lessons are over." The oldest students punched the air in excitement. "They know what they know and hold dear the skills learned. However…However, much as school may be over, your learning is not. You will be learning all your life. Look at Kàn; he's just learned how to swallow his food! It's a new skill! At his age, as well! The formal lessons may be over for you, but there are still lessons to be learned and lessons to be given. Do not forget you are not only students, but you are also all teachers.

"As a people, we are on the threshold of something new. It is time to look at the future and imagine it as a history. Imagine you are all my age and looking back on what you have done with your life. What would you want people to say about you?

"Tomorrow, ten of you will be leaving for Èrlǐtou, Sānménxiá, Dōngxiàfēng, Kāifēng and Lǎoniúpō. Three of you will be staying here to take over the running of this place and hopefully give Kàn, Jiǎn and Lín an easier time as they age. Every one of your roles is as important as the other. Every single one of you has a contribution to make to this new age

---

[19] Dearest father.

Thirteen: The Apprentices

that we are entering. Running the teaching farm here in the hidden valley, keeping accounts of copper shipments through Lǎoniúpō, or writing histories in Èrlǐtou: these are all careers. These are of such importance that it is hard for you to imagine it now. But you will!

"When you look back on your personal history, I want you to be able to say that you are proud of what you have done with your lives! I want you to be proud of what you have done for the societies in which you live! I want you to be proud of what you have done for others!

"I am proud! I have stood naked and proud in front of the tribespeople of the Xīwǎ! I have stood naked and triumphant before the evil twins, Hú and Hum! I stood naked and proud in front of King Léigōng of the Lóngshān shortly before his execution! As an aged and wrinkled woman, I will stand naked proud before you!" She let her robe slip to an audible gasp. Only a few had glimpsed the scarring on her body when washing in the river. It had not been in this context, not in front of the entire student body.

"This is the statement of my life! This is my pride, here in these scars! These wounds represent my personal history! My achievements! This is what we fight for! This is for the Motherland! We are the Xià!" There was silence for a few moments, and then the chanting gradually began.

"Xià! Xià! Xià! Xià! Xià!" No one knew when it ended, but it continued for much of the night. Hòutú slipped her robe back on, took Kàn by the hand, and the pair left for their bed.

Fourteen: The Assassins

Qícūn, Ānyáng, Hénán
Year 99: Year of the Rooster
Two days to the autumn equinox
19th September 1896 BCE

"It's a trial run. No one gets killed."

"What's the point in that?" Dàláng asked.

"Come on! You can't be serious in asking me a question like that."

"I can, and I am. Why not pick a target we can take out now?"

"Because there is no one that we actually want to be rid of at the moment. We can't just pick somebody and kill them for no reason. Besides, if you randomly chose a target, how do you know the individual concerned is not about to play a momentous part in some welcome development? You don't! It's going to be a dry run." Líng felt she had exhausted herself; over three days, it had been the same question, repeated over and over again, albeit phrased slightly differently.

The three younger women sat around the table, each beseeching their mentor in turn. For Líng, her ten years had come and gone; it was time she stepped down from active service. She was tired of their home; the old hunting lodge had seen little improvement since they had taken occupation. Now, she was the only one who slept there; all the others had built more suitable houses around the site. Even the three facing her now had constructed a dwelling for themselves, although admittedly, it was pretty basic.

The three wolves, Dàláng, Xiǎoláng and Kuàiláng, had been champing at the bit for some months now; it was time they saw some action. However, they were not as ready as they thought, and it was true

Fourteen: The Assassins

there was no realistic target for them; this had to be an exercise, however bloodthirsty they might be.

It had reached the point where Líng was becoming irate; it was not an emotion she wished to display. Half of her wanted the job to end and looked forward to her freedom; the other half was simply confused. She stood, arms splayed, fingers arched on the wooden surface, her knuckles whitening. If the irritation were not immediately apparent on her face, one glance at the sinews in the back of her hands would have been enough; she was beginning to lose it and had to regain control.

"Right. Enough. Dà, go and get the three horses, please. It's time you wolves learned a little common sense!"

Dàláng rose from her stool, slipped her wiry frame under the table, and somersaulted before springing upright to open the door. It was not ideal timing; she caught the handle as the door swung open, knocking her back onto the floor. Yěmǎ's mouth opened in horror as she watched Dàláng begin to nurse both her forehead and wrist.

"Sorry, Dà. Are you alright?" Yěmǎ went down on one knee to assist the struggling girl. As she did, Dàláng reached out her hand, grabbed Yěmǎ's sleeve and pitched her forward into a roll, then turned, straddling her victim, fingers poised above a pressure point in Yěmǎ's neck.

"And that is what I'm talking about." Líng's exasperation became very evident.

"But...but...I just floored her!" Dàláng shouted, "I could have killed her...look!" Her fingers closed on the pressure point before she leaned forward and kissed the forehead of the prone woman. "Sorry, Yěmǎ. Will you forgive me?"

"It'll be the thousandth time this month! Why should I forgive you again?" Yěmǎ smiled; she was delighted with the successes of her protégé. "I swear, next time, you'll kill me! It's true, isn't it, Líng?"

"She might just do that, Yěmǎ. This is what I'm frightened about. Dà does not seem particularly careful about who she might kill. That is a problem! As for you two! If Dà does not display enough care, you, Xiǎo, still must learn to disguise yourself better. It's all well and good being so tall, but you stand out like a one-legged centipede; you have to master a disguise. Lying down might help!" Líng grinned at Dà's lofty younger sister. Humour might turn the mood.

"As for you, Kuài! What can I say? If you're supposed to be the brains of this outfit, then it's up to you to help solve both Dà's impetuousness and come up with ideas for cover for Xiăo. I've seen no evidence of either," Líng sighed. "Dà, do you remember what you were supposed to be doing? No?" Seeing Dàláng shake her head, she shook her own, "Fetch Măjié and Kuàimă here, please."

"Not Yěmă?"

"No, you idiot, she's already here. You're still sitting on her."

Finally, when all seven were seated, Líng outlined the possible targets.

"There's Yú. Obviously, that's the big one, but too easy. I believe he takes absolutely no care for his safety. He's coming up to Ānyáng soon, and I'll bet he comes alone, with no bodyguards, nothing.

"Then there's Fēngbō. The problem with him is Tú. He won't remember you, but she will. Only if she goes away, perhaps to her mother's, does that make Fēngbō a suitable candidate." Líng was bursting to tell them that the Ānyáng king would indeed be in their sights at some point but held back for a moment.

"Líng, we are just talking about a trial run here?" Kuàimă was extremely anxious about her adopted daughter's involvement in the Wolf Pack, although she had been unable to prevent the strong-willed orphan from joining. That she now had two children with Shùn was little compensation; she loved Kuàiláng as much as her own pair.

"It is a dry run," Líng smiled. "I know you're worried, Kuàimă, but there's no need. You've done more dangerous things yourself, and you know it!"

"Fēngbō wouldn't be fair! We only get to go to Ānyáng. I want a proper trip!" Xiăoláng's whine was something of a surprise, but her sentiments were understood.

"The other problem with Fēngbō is that he might eventually become a real target. If we use him as a practice, he might learn something." Dàláng had a wicked grin on her face. Líng quickly changed the subject.

Fourteen: The Assassins

"Well, the third option is Yúntóng in Kāifēng. That seems a very realistic option, as none of you has ever met him. It's in a strange town, and he has a rather interesting relationship with the council. Another would be in Lǎoniúpō. An interesting choice for you is this one. There's a girl called Dòngxī. Now, you may never have heard of her, but she's one of Hòutú's graduates, and she's in charge of the copper supplies coming through there from Sìchuān."

"You said a girl?" Xiǎoláng asked.

"Why would we be assassinating a female?" Kuàiláng followed up.

"And how old is she?" Dàláng queried.

"Yes, she's female. I guess she's fifteen or sixteen years of age, although I'm not sure. It does make her an adult. In answer to Kuàiláng's question, you never know who you might need to kill. At the top of my list right now would be Túshānshì, Yú's wife, although that's personal to some extent, so it doesn't count. It could just as easily be a female as a male standing in the way of progress. Your trainers have learned that over the years; isn't that right, Yěmǎ?"

"Well, she's correct, but that doesn't mean killing men isn't much more fun. Mǎjié and me agree on this one; we've talked about it lots. The trouble is, as you get older, some of the fun goes out of all killing - women or men. You've got to take advantage while you're young before you get soft like us; we'll be no more than farmers once you three are up and running," Yěmǎ smiled throughout her little speech, but it was clear she envied the Wolf Pack.

Kùaimǎ did not. "Your targets are selected for you; this is just a dummy run. When this becomes the real thing, you need to remember that you'll select your targets and follow through. You'll be killing real people. Taking their lives away. It's worth thinking about." Since the slaying of Captain Jiāng, Kùaimǎ had been unwilling even to involve herself in the slaughter of animals. When they recruited Kuàiláng, she had first been furious and then dead-set on leaving, taking her daughter as far away as possible. Only Shùn's intervention had persuaded her to remain.

"But…you've killed people, Māma." Kuàiláng objected.

"And that's why I speak as I do. I speak from experience. You three do not. They can tell you," she indicated Yěmǎ and Mǎjié, "but they still have the blood lust; they are still not over their treatment at the hands of Hú and Xí! I have had the blood fury; I will tell you that much. After the Battle of the Yellow River, I was like an animal; I cannot even count the number of men I slew and disfigured. I–"

"We can; we kept a tally!" Mǎjié sniggered, "And I believe you lost the bet! And the loser had to–"

"Shush, Mǎjié," Líng attempted to intervene; she knew that what was coming next would derail the discussion.

"I know what the loser had to do, but we had to rush away too quickly. I made up for it with that horrible man, Captain Jiāng instead! That should be enough!"

"But you said you–"

"Ladies! Enough!" Líng's frustrations were beginning to get the better of her. "You're setting a bad example for these three." She indicated the Wolf Pack. "We'll stop now. I'll talk to you wolves in the morning. Mǎjié, Yěmǎ, Kùaimǎ, come with me to the tree now. Come!"

The discussion underneath the old oak was much calmer. The four did not need to impress each other; they knew each other's faults and accepted them. They were good friends despite all their differences. Although Kùaimǎ was deeply concerned about her daughter's involvement, she had never argued against the principle. They all knew that Líng had been desperate to prevent another genocide similar to the one brought on by diverting the river. They all agreed removing individuals who abused their power was a better route. It did not mean they all approved of murder, simply that they could not develop alternative options.

The three students had been finely honed. Whilst they were all generalists, on the whole, it was accepted that Dà was the weapons expert, Xiǎo the poisoner and Kuài the strategist. Kùaimǎ believed that with this division of responsibilities, her daughter was least likely to become the actual assassin. However, she would have to take as much responsibility as the other two. The older women were trying to determine not only who should be their target on the trial run but also how the girls would prove they were successful. After all, there would not be a body.

Fēngbō and Yú were quickly dismissed; the discussion focussed on Yúntóng in Kāifēng and Dòngxī in Lǎoniúpō. They had still not

Fourteen: The Assassins

decided when Chéng and Cāngbái drifted past on their way to dinner. Cāngbái's hair and skin illuminated the dusk; she stood out like a beacon. It reminded them how dark it had become. Líng called her over.

"Cāngbái, would you assist us, please?"

"Sure." She pecked her husband on the cheek and sauntered over, calling over her shoulder, "Chéng, you start the cooking, will you?" He nodded before turning toward the big house as Cāngbái asked, "What do you want?"

The explanation went on for a while. Part of the need for a new pair of ears was that they were still trying to consolidate their thoughts on the requirements. Gradually, they formed a list, which became longer and longer. In the end, it was clear that they would need more than one dry run. It was Cāngbái who called it.

"Let them visit Kāifēng and Lǎoniúpō. They can do two dry runs, one on Yúntóng and the other on…what's her name, Dòngxī?"

"If they do that, they can visit Èrlǐtou on the way. That would be a good experience for them; to see the centre of things is important." Líng was taken with the idea. "In fact, we could make it a grand tour. They could do Kāifēng, Eriltou, Sānménxiá and Lǎoniúpō, returning through Dōngxiàféng, dropping in on Hòutú in the hidden valley on the way back. That'll keep them busy!"

"Do you mind if I go and help Chéng now? If I don't, you might end up with burned food?"

"Yes, Cāngbái, thank you." Líng was delighted with the input and even more with the idea of the Wolf Pack learning about locations they might have to operate in sometime in the future. "You go and cook! Make sure there's plenty and that it's not burned! We're all hungry from talking too much!" As the albino retreated towards the farmhouse, Líng turned back to the others.

"We now have a longer list, ladies. Much longer!" Líng was more cheerful than she had been all day.

"You'll have to write this on that huge scroll you keep adding things to. The one that Hòutú gave you. What are you writing anyway?" Kùàimǎ raised an eyebrow, "When are you going to let us in on that little secret?"

"It's no secret; it's just not complete. I need someone else to help me with that. However, you're right; I could add a separate section. How about a 'List for Assassins'?"

"How about we go and get some dinner?" Mǎjié grumbled. "I'm a fighter, not a writer; that job's down to you, Líng!"

The group broke up, leaving Líng alone. Mosquitoes occasionally hummed in her ear, breaking her concentration, but the list was gradually coming together. As she gazed across the valley towards Ānyáng, the pinpricks of cooking sites reminded her of fireflies. There were many more now than when they first occupied Qícūn.

Líng felt prepared to present her plans to the Wolf Pack the following morning. She had worked all night to make a written copy on rough linen; she knew it was a draft. Not one of the girls would be permitted to take a copy; they would have to memorise it, but she would make and retain the final version on silk as a more permanent record.

"So, girls, this is how it starts.

"Firstly, you need to establish what your own identities will be; it is unlikely you will use your own. These may vary from town to town, but," She nodded at Xiǎo, "you must also be careful as others move around. A tall girl in Kāifēng is a tall girl in Èrlǐtou; you do not want people making connections.

"Secondly, you should understand your location; have identified a safe house and routes in and out, both overt and covert. Thirdly, you must ensure you have properly identified your target; it is all too easy to kill the wrong person! Fourth, you need to be aware of whether you should make a covert killing or one that is very public. Fifth…"

The list consisted of some fifty instructions; as a manual, it was comprehensive. Líng left the three girls to go through it and formulate questions. It was time to speak to Mǎjié and Yěmǎ again.

Whilst Kùàimǎ had reached a level of peace with herself and her new life, it was clear the Yěmǎ and Mǎjié retained some of their more youthful and psychopathic tendencies. However much they claimed to be over it, Líng knew the scars would never completely heal. She now had a job for them, although it was perhaps not what they might have expected. Once again, they gathered under the oak. The leaves were turning; golds,

Fourteen: The Assassins

yellows and browns adorned the branches and the ground around the tree. Qícūn was at its most beautiful in autumn.

"I want you two to go with them."

"What, the whole trip?" Yěmǎ's eyes lit up.

"I think there's more, Yěmǎ. Wait." Mǎjié was always the slightly more cautious of the two.

"To Kāifēng and Èrlǐtou. Then, they need their own space. However, as long as you don't interfere with their later schedule, I don't see why you can't take the opportunity to visit some new places. We've plenty of gold left buried; there's no problem with funding extensive trips."

"There has to be a catch!" Yěmǎ knew Líng always wanted something in return.

"There's two."

"We knew there would be! Come on, what are they?" Exasperation tinged Mǎjié's question.

"Well...one is that you must report anything you see when you return here."

"Like we were spies?"

"Yes, but general detail. You know, how are things running, are people happy, are there any problems? Things like that. Simple, really."

"And the second."

"Ah! The second is that you will have to maintain your distance from the Wolf Pack in Kāifēng and Èrlǐtou. Your faces are known; theirs are not. You cannot afford to have them linked to you. You must have contact with them, but it must be covert. In addition–"

"You said two catches, and you're about to come up with a third...I know it, isn't she, Yěmǎ?"

"She is!"

"Alright, the third," Líng agreed. "It will be down to you two to set them up for the future. You will need to persuade them to choose a leader. It must be Kuàiláng, by the way - no arguments. It's just best if they come up with it themselves. Understand?" The two women nodded. "You will return to Qícūn before they do and give me a thorough assessment of their performance. They will–"

"I'm starting to count five or six catches, aren't you, Mǎjié?"

"I most definitely am. I thought this was going to be a holiday!"

"Alright, ladies, I hadn't thought it all through. I have been up all night."

"Sorry, Líng."

"When they return here, I will go; they'll be independent. I will leave almost immediately; when I say leave, I mean to leave for good. Leave this house, this town, and this job. There will be one task that I want them to perform. An assassination."

"Oh! Who? Please tell! Perhaps we could get him for you!" Yěmǎ grinned.

"No. I'm not telling you; I don't want them to see it as an order. The best way is if they come to me and ask if I want a leaving present. Then I can ask them to perform this job, rather than telling them. You two will have to set this up. Have you followed my logic?" Líng queried.

"Yes!" Yěmǎ nodded.

"Yes, but this explains why you sat up all night. You were plotting!" Mǎjié poked her finger at her boss, who bit it lightly. "Ow!"

"You know what they say?" Líng laughed, "Once bitten!"

Fifteen: The Brat
Huáxiàn, Hénán
Year 99: Year of the Rooster
Ten days after the autumn equinox
1st October 1896 BCE

It had been Fēngbō who had wanted their meeting to be in Huáxiàn. Yú had complied, although only after insisting his son, Yùtù, should be in attendance. It seemed that Fēngbō was not as keen for Tú to attend their meeting. There was a suspicion that he did not want Yú to see what was happening in Ānyáng. In truth, Yú had inside information about the conditions in the town, provided mainly by Líng but also by traders who were now visiting the northernmost outpost of Hénán regularly.

Yú was keen to meet up with Yùtù. The child had been a suckling babe when he last saw him; he had little idea what to expect. Contact with the boy's mother had amounted to nothing, and once again, Yú had been in debt to Líng for keeping him aware of the boy's health, if nothing else.

He had a whole day and night to wait. A messenger had approached him on arrival, indicating that Fēngbō's journey was delayed by a day. Yú wished now he had gone on to Ānyáng; it would have made more sense.

A trader had recommended rooms to him. The small farmhouse he stayed in had seen better days, but the welcome was warm enough. He was fed and watered as soon as he dismounted; his horse was treated with the same care.

Yú travelled light: a water bladder, a saddlebag, a small backpack, an axe, a dagger, and a bow and arrows. They sufficed. When he travelled this way, he had to wait for no one and rarely went hungry. On the other hand, he imagined Fēngbō's caravan would consist of foot soldiers and cavalry, a wagon loaded with clothes and possibly a chariot for the king and his adopted son.

Huáxiàn, Hénán

Yú was aware that he and Fēngbō had a share in Yùtù and that he had not participated in the child's development. He was both jealous of Fēngbō and ashamed of his own negligible contribution. It was just one of the many things that would keep him from sleeping tonight.

The other was the Ānyáng king's request. It had come out of the blue, although there had been some speculation that such a question may arise following Fēngbō's demise; it had not been expected in his lifetime. He had asked to join the Xià Empire as a satellite state. If there was one reason Yú should have visited Ānyáng, this was it. He would have liked to see what progress had been made as regards throwing off the shackles of the Lóngshān, and a trip to Ānyáng would have been ideal.

Yú lay on the straw, wrapping himself tighter in his cloak as the sky finally darkened. It was overcast, and a southerly wind threatened rain. His meal was not sitting easily in his stomach, and he struggled to get comfortable. As expected, different scenarios competed for his focus, although a repeating vision of Èrlǐtou dislodged the whole raft of thoughts. It was strange. The last thing he was worried about was the situation at home. Still, his subconscious kept promoting this specific thought ahead of concerns about his upcoming meeting with Fēngbō and all the variations it might present. It was as if someone was whispering in his ear.

Eventually, he rolled off the straw and sat on a stool positioned so he could gaze out of the window. There was little to see. He ran his finger down his crooked nose; it was still an experience that came as something of a surprise. The sky had cleared a little, but with the moon having set, there was little illumination. The obscurity changed instantly when a massive bolt of lightning crashed into the ground directly in front of the house. Within a millisecond, the wall of sound hit; the shockwave knocked him off his stool.

Yú blinked and blinked again. It seemed the brilliance of the shaft of light had left an image on the insides of his eyelids. After seeing visions of Èrlǐtou all evening, the new scene was a delight. Rolling hills and a log cabin. Beside the house was a woman, and although it was unclear who, she appeared to be trying to speak to him. He blinked once again, and the vision departed.

Fifteen: The Brat

Yú was not a man who believed in fairy tales. He had no time for soothsayers and their predictions for the future. He did not believe in fate, ghosts, gods, or any guiding hand in life's path. Yet what he had seen seemed to be an image of his future; it was simply unclear where it was, and indeed, he had no idea who the female was.

As he came to his senses, the lightning forked again but further away. The thunder, which rolled in waves, was beginning to diminish. The period between the bolts and grumbles grew longer quite quickly. He lifted himself back onto the platform, adjusted the straw and immediately fell fast asleep.

In the morning, Yú could not rid himself of the feeling that something significant had happened. Although his memories of the previous night's events were undiminished, it still nagged him that there was some message he could not interpret. It would prove to be the commencement of a full day of breakdowns in communication.

With time on his hands, he meandered around the small village, chatting with anyone who also had a few spare moments. It was a dry and dusty place, freshened up only slightly by last night's rain, which had been insubstantial compared to the sky's other activities. With the harvest in, people were preparing for the winter months, which in these parts seemed to consist mainly of moving animals between fields of stubble to fatten them up before slaughter. All and sundry were ready to chat, and most were focused on the past rather than the future.

They all agreed that Huáxiàn had been a significant town. Close enough to feel the influence of old Léigōng in Ānyáng but strong enough to have an independent leader and not to feel threatened by their larger neighbour. At least, not very often. Yú winced when he heard the descriptions of the damage inflicted by the great flood. Today's numbers added up to fewer than a twentieth of the original population. Estimates varied, but it was thought that four or five thousand had died and a similar number had fled, although it was a commonly held view that those who had fled would have met their end somehow. If not, why had they not returned?

To Yú, it was not entirely clear why they should bother returning, although he was told that the soil was finally improving. It seemed they had been assisted in preventing further floods by selecting defensible lands. Finally, an older man spelt it out for him.

"We feels safe here. We always feels safe here. The old king wasn't too bad; he looked after us, and now there's Fēngbō."

"What does he do for you?" Yú was sceptical.

"He protects us. He's been the one who sent the advisors on flood defence and irrigation. He sends his cavalry if bandits threaten us; they'll be here within a day. He's a good man."

"But isn't it true that he came through here years ago and pillaged, killed, raped, and kidnapped? I was told he caused as much damage as the flood." Yú was curious how the stories related to him in previous years seemed so much at odds with the ones he was hearing now.

"That wasn't Fēngbō; he'd long gone when that started, headed for Dōngyíng. It was some of his troops alright, and few of us escaped them. They was nasty sorts. But he got them!"

"What do you mean?"

"When Fēngbō found out…well…he had all the ones rounded up that came up to Dōngyíng late. He questioned them. Actually, I believe he tortured them, but there's not many who would say that out loud, and then he had them killed. On the spot!"

"And the women they were supposed to have kidnapped?"

"There was hundreds to start with, I believe. But many died on the way, most at the hands of those men—only four or five survived by the time they fetched up in Dōngyíng. I'm told that Fēngbō took them on as servants, and they was treated very well. I'm also told that one of them had white hair. Not grey hair like, but white hair; she was a youngster."

"You mean an albino?" Yú queried.

"A what?"

"It doesn't matter. So, you like this Fēngbō then?"

"I do!"

"What do you give him for what he does for you?"

"We gives him a quarter of our harvest and livestock. He's coming to Huáxiàn soon to collect. You could well meet him!"

"I will be, old man; I have a meeting planned with your king."

Fifteen: The Brat

"Oh dear, I hope I haven't said nothing amiss. If that's the case, though, and just out of curiosity's sake, may I ask who you might be and where you be from?"

"I am from Èrlǐtou; my name is Yú."

The older man nodded. "That's the same name as the man who rules in Èrlǐtou. You wouldn't be trying to fool us, would you?"

"No, old man, I am Yú, the council leader in Èrlǐtou."

The man spat on the ground between his feet and smiled. "I bet you're not as good as Fēngbō!"

Yú said his farewell and waved to a gaggle of children as he reversed his steps to his accommodation. When he reached the courtyard of his rooms, it was soon apparent there were new arrivals in town. There was a cart with a still sweating bullock under rein. There was a group of six odd horses drinking from a trough. A groom urgently shovelled out shit from the yard. As Yú entered the open area, a man strode toward him, raising his hand in greeting.

"Yú! I was told we would find you here. My name's Fēngbō!" The stranger reached out his hand, which Yú grasped firmly. "Shall we walk and talk? My arse is still sore from the horse. I could do with a stroll."

"Greetings!" Yú was taken aback; he had expected a considerable degree of pomp and was disarmed by the casual nature of the man. "You're earlier than expected. I was planning to change."

"No need for ceremony here, no need at all. It's one reason I suggested Huáxiàn. Back in Ānyáng, someone might expect me to dress up, and I can't abide that. How long did it take you to get here?"

"The whole journey took about a week. The river's down now, so the crossing was good as well. I got in last night."

"Did you see the storm? That lightning nearly blew the roof off the palace in Ānyáng! It scared me anyway!"

"I did, I did. It almost took me out and threw me backwards off a stool. I can still see the flash."

The two men wandered down the town's main track. As Fēngbō was recognised, they were not interrupted, although many waved and smiled in their direction. Their monarch waved back when he spied them. It all seemed very cheerful. After small talk about the weather, the last farming season, and an exceptionally pretty girl they passed, Fēngbō halted.

"So, Yú! We'll talk about the reasons for our meeting a little later. I wanted you away from the others to start with, firstly to get a feel for you and secondly to tell you about my companions."

Yú turned to face him, "Right, go ahead then."

"Let's start with Yùtù. I've brought him along. It's only proper for him to meet his birth father. I must caution you, though; he may not be that friendly. That's not entirely my fault; Tú has been a major influence on him, but do not be offended if he does not take to you."

"I understand completely; I haven't seen him since before he could walk. He cannot know me and can only base what he does know on what he hears. I understand if that has not always been good. That's life."

"There's another thing about Yùtù. He's going through a bit of a phase right now. He's taking on airs and graces, some entirely inappropriate, but I will not admonish him over it at this time; it would not be appropriate."

"Also understood. We have some issues with Qí, although I'm not sure it's just a phase with him. It sometimes seems like he's not all there. Do you know what I mean?"

"I do. Let's change the subject. I've brought someone with me who you do know! Kùàimǎ. It's–"

"Kùàimǎ! Fēngbō, you are fortunate you did not meet Kùàimǎ at the Battle of the Yellow River!"

"Really? Why?"

"Well, you would have lost your manhood at the very minimum; she had the blood fury!"

"Well, it was really her husband I wanted to bring down, but they're inseparable, and anyway, she has a message from Líng for you. She seems sweet as apple pie to me! I can't imagine her with a weapon in her hand.

"Back to the others. I brought Shùn, Kùàimǎ's husband, because he's originally from Huáxiàn, as are Chéng and Cāngbái, who are also with me. I hope you get time to talk to them about what we've been doing here in this town. So, now you know, why don't we go back to the house

Fifteen: The Brat

and give you some time with Yùtù and Kùàimǎ before we sit down for further, more serious discussions? Is that alright?"

Yú agreed, and they turned to retrace their steps. Once again, everyone smiled and waved as they passed.

Yú's get-to-know-you session with Yùtù was entirely unsatisfactory for both parties. The whole thing got off on the wrong foot when his son insisted on being called 'sire'. It went from bad to worse, with the boy refusing to answer any of Yú's questions, instead asking a few of his own, most of which were barbed insults. In the end, Yú gave up, leaving the boy alone in front of an enormous plate of fruit. Not once had Yú been asked if he would like a piece; Yùtù hogged it to himself. Yú could not stop comparing him to Qí, a lovely boy but one who seemed to lack any character or fire.

His next meeting with Kùàimǎ was much better. They did not know each other well, but they had fought together and had plenty of common ground and friendly discussions. Yú quizzed her about Yùtù's attitude, and it became clear the boy's issues were not confined to his approach to his biological father. Kùàimǎ used the word 'brat' on several occasions. She steered clear of discussing Líng but did bring a message written on a piece of silk. Much to Yú's embarrassment, he found he could not understand it and asked if Kùàimǎ would read it to him. It was short and cryptic.

"Add two years to the ten I foretold. Meet me in the hidden valley in the Year of the Pig. Remember, every picture tells a story, but not all are true. Come in secret. When the storm hits, I will be your shelter." Kùàimǎ glanced at Yú as she finished the final sentence. "Do you know what it means?"

"Some, but not all. It was a long time ago. She said something, although it sounds so vague."

"The hidden valley is in Shǎnxī; it is where Kànménrén and Hòutú have a hideout. The Year of the Pig starts in a year and a half. So, you have a time, and you have a place. It sounds like she wants to look after you. That's nice!"

"Why does she want to look after me? What do I need shelter from? I like the woman, but–"

"It's not a forecast, Yú. It is not a prophecy. I think it's an offer. She says, " If you have a problem, she will be there."

"No, Kùàimǎ, she says, when I have a problem, not if! I just cannot see what this supposed problem might be! And this stuff about pictures, well, that's completely beyond me."

As they were about to rejoin the others, Kùàimǎ grabbed Yú's wrist. With the other hand, she placed two fingers on his palm, then repeated the gesture and finally put four fingers on his palm, all the while shaking her head. Yú opened his mouth to speak but was hushed with a single finger across his lips. If it was a message, it seemed to say two and two do not equal four and be quiet about it. It was certainly confusing, and it seemed like a strange way to conclude a conversation that appeared quite open.

When he had finished with Kùàimǎ, it was time to sit down with Fēngbō and the others. Fortunately, Yùtù had fallen asleep, and no one showed much inclination to wake him. Yú was introduced to Shùn, Chéng and Cāngbái, all previous inhabitants of Huáxiàn, although they now resided mainly in Ānyáng. Cāngbái was startling: long white hair with skin colour and texture that looked like wax. Yú immediately made the connection.

Fēngbō put his proposal on the table. He wanted to join the empire as a client state. He appeared happy to step down from the monarch's role, even to the point that he suggested he stand for election to an Ānyáng council, something that did not yet exist. He seemed eager to allow his citizens to do the talking, and when Yùtù awoke, he picked him up and took him outside to play.

His parting words were, "Why don't you four tell Yú what it's like in Ānyáng and what we're doing here in Huáxiàn? Go on, give him the details without me influencing him, warts and all. Good and bad! I want Yú to go away with a comprehensive idea of what it's like around here."

They did this for ages and ages. There was the odd negative, but all in all, their remarks painted a glowing picture of the situation. Cāngbái was full of praise for Fēngbō's care for her in the early years. Chéng and Shùn went into enormous detail about the work they had been doing in Huáxiàn, fully resourced by Fēngbō. Only Kùàimǎ was less glowing,

Fifteen: The Brat

although she mainly limited herself to the beneficial and protective role that Fēngbō's troop had offered the farm at Qícūn. Yú did note that although they talked a great deal about happiness, not one of the four wore an expression that could have been said to reflect that emotion.

When Fēngbō and Yùtù returned, they had almost finished their discussion; the smell of hot food was wafting in from the outdoor grill.

"We had better eat," Fēngbō looked around. "Everyone happy?"

"It seems we might be on to something," Yú grinned. "It looks like we'll be able to make a deal."

"About time!" Yùtù actually stamped his foot. "We've been three days here so far, and I want my proper bed!"

For a moment, there was silence. A cat had slipped out of a bag, but no one was sure what that cat was, who else had noticed, and whether it was relevant. Indeed, no one was in the mood to bring it up.

The following morning, the six from Ānyáng waved off Yú, watching him as he and his horse disappeared into the distance. By the time he did, they had commenced their journey in the opposite direction. If they had followed the Èrlǐtou leader, they would have found he stopped and tied his mount fewer than a thousand paces from the village. Yú wanted to spend more time with the old man now that he might feel under a little less pressure.

Sixteen: The Reunions

Qícūn, Ānyáng, Hénán
Year 100. Year of the Dog
Thirty-one days after the spring equinox
22nd April 1895 BCE

It was an inconvenience she could have done without. How could it be that the Wolf Pack should return the night before her send-off celebration? She burned with indignation over their tardiness, but it would not be made apparent to the giggling trio. Mǎjié and Yěmǎ had reported favourably from the group's outings in Kāifēng, and whilst the pair of them had been in Èrlǐtou at the same time as the pack and kept their eyes open wide for a sighting, it had proved fruitless.

The Wolf Pack had now had a night's rest and were lounging on the straw floor of the kitchen of the Qícūn farmhouse. It was an informal and friendly meeting, but several issues needed mutual attention. Líng's first questions had to do with their early stops; she wanted to know if they considered Kāifēng a success and how they had gone underground in Èrlǐtou.

"Here, you'll like this!" Dàláng handed Líng a bow wrapping a few strands of black hair.

"What's this?"

"That Líng, is Yúntóng's hair! I took that on the first night we got into his bed-chamber!" Dàláng was whispering, although her enunciation made it remarkably akin to shouting.

"Now, look at this!" Kuàiláng grinned from ear to ear and handed Líng a similar bow.

"Is that what I think it is? It's not? It's pubic hair!" Líng flung the gift away. "Ugh!"

"We acquired that the second time we went in, a week later," Kuàiláng laughed as she retrieved the bow.

Sixteen: The Reunions

"I hate to think what you'll give me, Xiǎo. Come on, let's get it over with."

Xiǎoláng presented Líng with a slipper. "I'm afraid I was too big to climb through the same hole. These two sent me up with a hooked stick; it's the best I could do, I'm afraid. It's one of Yúntóng's slippers."

"Well, I prefer it to what Kuài gave me!" Líng smiled, "Now, tell me how you did it?"

"Basically, we scouted out the area for a week. I'll not go into all those details. I'd think that Mǎjié and Yěmǎ have filled you in." Kuàiláng was taking the lead, much to Líng's delight. "What we did was get Yúntóng blind drunk on three occasions. We did that to show you we could have poisoned him. Easily! Then we had to enter the bedroom. That took a bit of planning, but we found a route and–"

"And we had to disable a guard." Dà was getting frustrated the story was taking as long as it was. "So, when I was the first to go, Kuài and Xiǎo kept him busy while I went to the outside wall and through this hole. From the state of it, I'd say it was the place they swept the shit through; it stunk!"

"And how did you keep the guard busy, Xiǎo?"

"Erm…I let him play with my breasts while Kuài sucked his dick." It was clear she was a little embarrassed.

"And when Kuài was up there the next week, Xiǎo sucked him off, and I took her role. He seemed ever so happy and was more than willing to do it the following week. We were scared Xiǎo might get stuck, you see!" Dàláng was clearly excited to be relaying the tale and had no qualms, unlike her younger sister. "After the last time, we promised we'd be back the next week, but we left town that night. There was little reason to stay. Job done!"

"Well, it sounds like a good job, anyway! Well done! So, what about Èrlǐtou? How did you evade Mǎjié and Yěmǎ?"

"We didn't. We were around them all the time. We even spoke to them. They saw us all right; they just didn't recognise us! It was wonderful," Kuàiláng couldn't stop laughing, "Xiǎo, you tell her!"

"In Èrlǐtou, Kuài and me dressed as two old men. Dà was dressed as our granddaughter; we treated her so, so badly! We spent just over a week in Èrlǐtou, familiarised ourselves with the place and saw some leading players. We saw, Háng, Yú, and Bóyì, we saw–"

"Why did you put Háng first?"

"Easy. He seemed like the most powerful man in the town. We also spent a lot of time in his bar; it proved a good place to learn stuff." Kuài had recovered her composure.

"But Líng, do you know what they did?" Dà was pouting, the other two girls snorting, whilst Líng herself knew that if what Dà was about to say was even slightly funny, she would be unable to contain herself. "Do you know what they did?" Líng shook her head. Behind their comrade, the other two wolves were now silently crying with laughter. "They said…they said I couldn't have a drink…they said I was too young!" By this time, Kuài and Xiǎo were rolling on the floor whilst Líng struggled not to wet herself. "One whole week! One whole week without a drink. They should be punished!" Looking around, she finally noticed her friends' antics and leapt on them, rubbing their heads with her knuckles. The laughter only increased.

Still on the floor but turning back to Líng, she said plaintively, "And then they tried to marry me off! To some old bumpkin! Really, it was too much!"

Líng rushed out, making the latrine pit just in time. When they resumed, it was clear there were no hard feelings. They outlined their time in Sānménxiá and Dōngxiàféng, spending a little more time on Lǎoniúpō, where they had their second trial run.

"It was too easy, Líng. Too easy. This girl, because that's all she was, could have been murdered anywhere, anytime, and it would have been even easier to get away with it. I don't understand why you set this one up as a trial, Líng; it should have been harder." Kuàiláng was deadly serious.

"You must realise that Dòngxī may have been easy, but so might other targets you could end up with. Was she important?" Líng asked.

"Well, from what we heard, she had only been there for a year. She and this boy who was helping her were effectively running the town. Of course, they've got a council leader called Bórén, but he's stepping down this year. Some have suggested that Dòngxī should become their leader, but Líng, she's younger than me!" Kuàiláng sounded indignant.

Sixteen: The Reunions

"Youth isn't necessarily the important factor here, but I suspect inexperience might be. If she's as good as you say she is, she'll say no! She'll get on with sorting out their taxes and administration for a few years."

"I think she did say no. They have someone else lined up now. Someone related to Bórén, she's–"

Líng cut her off. "Related, that doesn't sound so good. We don't want dynasties forming here! Related in–"

"No, not like that; she's his third cousin or something. You must know what it's like in Shaanxi; everyone's related to everyone else!" Kuàiláng was laughing again. "Oh! Guess what? Dà found a boyfriend in Sānménxiá!"

"No, I didn't! He wasn't a boyfriend! I was cold! Anyway, after you tried to sell me to that old man, I needed to restore my confidence."

"You were noisy enough!" Xiǎo joined in with the teasing. "But Líng, we're still trying to find out why he started screaming. Such a noise! He wouldn't stop. We think she showed him the–"

"Enough!" Líng was delighted with their camaraderie. It was clear that Dàláng was enjoying their mucking about; it was equally clear that they were competent practitioners. The big question was whether they could handle the choices. "So, who's in charge?"

The sisters both pointed at Kuàiláng. "She's the boss; we're the workers. How do you always say it? 'We're the hammers that drive the pegs in!' That's us! She's the brains behind the outfit. Isn't she, Dà?"

"Yes! Less thinking time means more drinking time - that's what I say. We'll let Kuài burn out her brains before we have to use ours!"

"Good. I'm pleased you worked it out. Now–"

"Líng, we think we're ready." Kuàiláng sounded assured. "We think we have a plan for replacing ourselves. We have set up good contacts around the empire. We are grateful to you for all you've done. We have a question for you before you retire: is there anything we can do for you?"

There had been a nagging doubt, one that had grown and grown over the previous ten years. Líng had observed Tú and Yùtù closely; it was remarkable how his looks resembled his mother's. "Did you see Túshānshì and Qí when you were in Èrlǐtou?"

"We did. You interrupted us earlier," Kuàiláng scolded, "We saw quite a lot of them. You told us that Qí was Tú's son. Well - I think that's rubbish. He looks a lot like Túshānshì–"

"Just like Yùtù looks like Tú and–"

"And there's no way they got mixed up; that's what she's trying to say. I think she didn't want to tell you that you were wrong about–"

"Enough!" Líng 's mood had undoubtedly changed. The three girls were embarrassed, "I'll need to talk to Tú…this is bigger than you might think."

Although Líng did need to think about it and needed discussion with Tú, she had already worked out a strategy for such an eventuality. The Wolf Pack sat, their ears twitching, as she went into considerable detail with a twin-forked plan. By the time she had finished, all three were surprised but understood the need and the signal they would be given. As expected, it was more than the single favour they had offered; Líng outlined several alternatives.

*

The last news she had received had not put her in the best of moods, but she forced herself to appear happy. If the meeting with the Wolf Pack was supposed to mark Líng's last piece of work for the Sisterhood, the second get-together was to celebrate her next step: retirement. Kùaimǎ, Mǎjié and Yěmǎ had organised the event without any other consultation. Líng was somewhat shocked by what they had put together. It was ten years, near enough, since eight women had ridden across the plain and faced up to the Lóngshān in the parlay. Like that day, there was a new moon; like that day, eight women were gathered.

Sadly, Mài had died a couple of years earlier, but the three horses had even considered that little problem. Hòutú was invited to step in, and everyone agreed it was what she deserved because of her significant role.

For the occasion, Kùaimǎ, Shùn & Chéng constructed a peculiar building. The structure was set away from the main house, and they had been quite secretive about its purpose. It was intended for long-term use, but today, it functioned as the perfect venue for eight people to sit in a circle with an uninterrupted view of each other. The four main supports

Sixteen: The Reunions

for the roof also supported the seating, dividing it into four pairs. The table formed a circular band, and servers could access the central section, where a small fire burned. Smoke vented through a hole in the roof, although the ingenious addition of a second smaller roof prevented precipitation from entering. Although the sides were open, rush fences were manoeuvred to shield the diners from the wind, and the lower roof overlapped sufficiently to protect them from the sun.

Líng believed many of the Lóngshān kings would never have eaten in as luxurious a setting. As for the company! She scanned the seven ladies, who were so engrossed in their conversations that none had noticed her entrance. She then came to a very sudden realisation; all seven had once been members of the Sisterhood. The Fire Horse Three and herself, until moments ago, Tú and Túshānshì until the Battle of the Yellow River. Jīngfēi had been an early leaver, having felt the organisation insufficiently protected women and Hòutú! Well! Hòutú. Was she still a member? If so, she was part of a vastly different Sisterhood than Líng had been running. She moved to the vacant place and threw back her hood as she seated herself. The group's reaction was as immediate as it was embracing. In twos and threes, they all left their seats to hug and kiss her; for the time being, any personal differences remained outside.

When all had resumed their seats, everyone started talking at once. Kùàimǎ had to raise both her hands to persuade them to fall silent. She had taken it upon herself to be in charge and asked Cāngbái if she would mind serving the food, which kept Shùn & Chéng in the kitchen with the cooking duties. It was to be an all-female affair in the new roundhouse. She was halfway through explaining the situation when she was interrupted for the first time.

"I don't see anything to drink!" Hòutú volunteered, "If we want to have a toast, we'll need some drink!"

They started a chant, "Drink! Drink! Drink!" If Kùàimǎ had believed for one moment that they would have a polite dinner party, she was quickly disillusioned.

"I thought we could start with a few words from Líng; after all, it is a party in her honour." Kùàimǎ looked flustered. "I'll ask Cāngbái to bring some beer and some *fēnjiǔ*."

Qícūn, Ānyáng, Hénán

There were cheers around the table. "Drink first, Líng second," Yěmǎ had just realised her boss was no longer her boss.

"Why not drink first, food second and Líng third?" Mǎjié asked.

"I think it will take a while to understand what's happening here. Are you just realising that you're all equals now? It happened to me years ago!" Jīngfēi smiled.

"And me!" Tú had been one of the quieter participants. She was now beginning to get into the swing of things. Only Túshānshì seemed somewhat remote.

"I'm going to speak first!" Líng shouted.

"No, you're not. Here's Cāngbái with the drinks!" Mǎjié grabbed two flagons from the tray and passed one to Yěmǎ. "Here you go, Yě!" Everyone soon had a drink before them, and Líng began to talk.

"I had not realised quite what you organised. It is a wonderful surprise to see you all. I guess Kuàimǎ sorted out some of this, but–"

"Mǎjié and Yěmǎ were a great help," volunteered Kuàimǎ.

"Well, thank you, all three of you, and thank you to all of you for coming. First, I would like to have a silent thought for Mài, who cannot be here for obvious reasons today," Líng raised her drink, looking wistful.

"Secondly, we've all been on a long journey these last few years. Some of us have known each other for as long as twenty years. At a minimum, it's been ten." She looked around the group. "I've just realised that some of you hardly know each other; perhaps you will by the end of the day!"

"Finally, the last thing I want to say concerns the future as much as the past. As you know, I've now had this leadership position for ten years. In those ten years, I have made some major changes, including getting rid of the title of 'Grandmother', mainly because it made me feel so old!" Laughter rippled around the room.

"It was important to look back at our successes and failures…and believe me, there have been both. We sat on our horses at that parlay ten years ago and were not scared; that was a triumph! We battled the Lóngshān and won a great victory, helped to a huge extent by Hòutú in the Èěrduōsī Loop." Líng raised her drink to Hòutú, and all followed her example.

Sixteen: The Reunions

"Our major failure remains evident to us all. It is something that has weighed heavily on my shoulders these ten years. Too many died, swept away, bogged down, starving, or contracting fatal diseases - hundreds of thousands of lives. It can never happen again, whether the cause is a man or a woman. It was wrong!

"Some of you may have felt you were edged out of the Sisterhood, that I abandoned you. Yes, this was the case. We had to change. Only a few, sworn to secrecy, know what has replaced our old ways. The Sisterhood will continue to exist. The Sisterhood will do more to protect women," Líng nodded directly at Jīngfēi, "but the Sisterhood will have a more targeted…a more focused existence. It will act effectively but not cause widespread distress as we did ten years ago. I cannot tell you more, but I hope you approve." A round of applause went around the room.

"So, I am no longer Grandmother! I am no longer leading the Sisterhood! That being the case, things might already have changed without me knowing! You do not know how relieved I am to have let this go. I'm thirty-three years old this year. It's time for me to lead a normal life and have fun! If you allow me, I will continue to call you all - Sisters!"

The eight women continued their party into the early hours, fed to overflowing, drunk to the point of collapse and deliriously happy. Even Túshānshi fell under the spell of the occasion. Only two of those present had any idea how these eight women would be torn asunder over the forthcoming decade.

The following morning, Líng took Tú aside for a lengthy discussion. It seemed Líng's definition of retirement did not match that of her peers.

Seventeen: The Machinations

The Royal Palace, Ānyáng, Hénán
Year 100: Year of the Dog
Thirty-two days after the spring equinox
23rd April 1895 BCE

It had not been possible for Túshānshì to come to Ānyáng for Líng's party without making an official visit to the palace. At least, she could have done but would have had the discomfort of travelling in secret. As she had always yearned for attention and status, she had spent little time before dismissing all but the official option. It would mean a formal meal with Fēngbō and Tú, where she would, in theory, be speaking as Yú's representative.

She was filled with self-importance, having only acted in such a role once before. Finding she was to be treated as royalty only inflated her ego further. She was given a vast room with a hearth and a real bed covered in fine silks; these were luxuries that Yú would not countenance on their farm. Two teenage girls also attended to her. They would run at her command, bringing any other amenities she requested; hot water had been first on her list.

In addition to the two units of troops, despatched more for protocol's sake rather than to provide protection, accompanying her on the trip was Háng. He had pleaded with Yú to be part of the delegation, claiming his eyes were on a commercial deal trading alcohol with their northern neighbour. Over the years, Háng's status in Èrlǐtou had risen dramatically, although it was unclear to many why this was the case. The number of bars he ran had increased, as had his manufacturing processes, but how his business operated successfully was not entirely transparent.

Háng knew much about Yú 's wife and had used the information very carefully to exert a growing control over her. Túshānshì, well-used to manipulating others, was not entirely at ease with being influenced

Seventeen: The Machinations

herself. Information was not the only thing Háng supplied her with; their relationship was becoming particularly complex. In Èrlǐtou, Háng had attempted to use Túshānshì as a lever against Yú. Every pressure was to encourage acts by the council to benefit his business. Now, her string of failures was mounting up, reaching the point where she, as with many others, was seriously indebted to him. The payments had become physical as her political interventions failed and her use of hallucinogens increased. Háng had her where he wanted and had her as often as he wished but had not yet benefitted to the extent he felt justified the costs.

Túshānshì was almost blissfully unaware of her actual status as the barman's whore. She took comfort in sharing some of her thoughts with him, although they were increasingly confused. Perversely, she had become isolated in Èrlǐtou, not wishing to lower herself by socialising with the other farmers. Without the Sisterhood, she now had no alternative social circle.

Háng was aware of this; he had initially become a confidant, supporting her desire to become the Empress of the Xià. He knew he could push her to extreme lengths to force Yú to act. He also knew she had information with which she could blackmail her husband. She had not yet revealed entirely what that information was. All he knew was that it had something to do with her desperate search for a woman in Sìchuān called Āyí Zhū; he had assisted her with the investigation.

Háng's reluctance to fully commit to Túshānshì's ambitions had two causes. Firstly, it was clear she was unstable, something that could be used, although it could also have unexpected effects. The second was even more complex. In the event of non-compliance by Yú, Túshānshì intended to put her son on the throne and become the emperor's mother. As this would involve not only the removal of Yú but also the accession of her son, Qǐ, the proposal appeared to be something of a long shot.

Háng had spent valuable time cultivating Qǐ, acting as a benign uncle to the boy. The lad was eleven, although it was clear to any who knew him that he had the mental age of a toddler. The boy tired quickly, had difficulty concentrating, was always short of breath, and seemed as pale as a ghost. He also had trouble sleeping, to the extent that Túshānshì would spend several nights each month comforting him.

The Royal Palace, Ānyáng, Hénán

It was mid-afternoon when they all met in Fēngbō's feasting hall. There were four key players, but each had expectations that did not necessarily align with those of the others. Agreements would only be reached if the participants kept their true intentions to themselves. For all the food on display, it was clear their individual discussions were of far greater importance than eating.

The room was decorated with strung banners; the Xià standard of the Motherland was as surprisingly prominent as Fēngbō's flags. Troops lined the walls, unarmed, each bearing only a tray on which titbits were offered. Although the main table was already groaning under the weight of too much food, the main meal would wait until dusk.

"I'd like to introduce my son, my Lord." Túshānshì's voice was soft, her expression demur.

"It's Fēngbō, please, no formalities."

"This is Qí, my son. Qí, this is Fēngbō." The pair rather formally clasped hands.

"And this is Yùtù, and of course, you know Tú well." Fēngbō pushed his adopted son towards Qí, "Why don't you both go off and chat for a while. Go!" he gestured for them to move away.

"I'm not sure what Yùtù will make of Qí. He's…a little…how should we say…slow on the uptake." Túshānshì's comment was at once protective and dismissive, almost as if she were confused about her son's role in life.

"Mmm! He could make an ideal leader if he had someone strong standing behind him! It's not a crime to be slow and not always a disadvantage." Fēngbō smiled, "Now, you pair were enjoying yourselves yesterday. I believe Líng had quite a party. Are you recovered, Túshānshì?"

"Fully, my… Fēngbō, fully. I think Tú and I are more than capable of holding our own when the drinks are flowing. Is that right, Tú?"

"It's true, alright. I'm going to see how Yùtù and Qí are making out. Do you mind if I slip off? I think Háng is anxious for an introduction. Háng! Come over here, meet Fēngbō." Tú's timing was perfect: a public demonstration of a motherly concern she certainly did not feel.

Seventeen: The Machinations

The barman waddled over, taking Tú's place in the triangle. He was soon deeply involved in discussions about potential trade and how it might benefit the Ānyáng leader personally. Háng also introduced his favourite topic, that alcohol was a religion, keeping the people happy regardless of their actual quality of life. Fēngbō was undoubtedly interested in the potential savings, grasping the economics fully, yet stumbling with the apparent ideology. Quickly, the discussion became focussed on the accession of Ānyáng to the Xià empire. When the conversation became more sensitive, Túshānshì edged the group away from any flapping ears.

"It is my belief, Fēngbō, that Yú will either accept popular opinion and grant Ānyáng the status it deserves, or he will stand down. Either way, you will end up with what you want. Although, I have a question for you." She lowered her eyes. "What is it you really want?"

It was clear that Túshānshì was now flirting with the king. Háng made a pretence of looking more than a little uncomfortable. She was so good at focussing her attention on one person, even in a small group, that the barman felt ignored even with his intimate knowledge of her.

"What is it that any of us want?" Fēngbō was curious about the direction of the conversation and had never knowingly closed down any option until he was sure of its potential. "I think, like most people, I want a bright future. I want to be happy, yet at the same time, I want excitement and challenges."

"Am I a challenge?" Túshānshì had edged herself closer, so close their clothes were touching, and the king could feel the rise of her breast through the fabric.

"Er… Háng. Would you fetch the lady and me another drink, please?" He gave his goblet to the barman before taking Túshānshì's and passing it over.

The moment they had planned had arrived. Háng glanced momentarily at Túshānshì before moving away. It was easy to see how she readily played with men's feelings. Whilst no longer the beauty she had been when he first knew her, she had an irresistible draw when she chose to use it. Fēngbō was being sucked into a whirlpool from which he would find it difficult to extract himself, while Háng span into an eddy.

The Royal Palace, Ānyáng, Hénán

Satisfied that one of his plans was coming to fruition, Háng determined to launch into his backup. He told the guards that his companions needed more drinks before going off to find Tú.

In the courtyard, the two boys practised fighting with wooden staffs. It was immediately evident that the smaller of the two had a considerable edge in both technique and athletic ability; Qí was suffering a beating.

"Come on, boy!" Tú hollered at her son, "Left down! Right up! Swing! Now again! Go!"

"It all seems a bit one-sided." Háng's concern was genuine.

"It is…it is, Háng," Tú whispered behind her hand. "He'll kill him if I let it continue." She raised her voice, "Boys! Enough! Now, go in and get washed while I talk to an old friend. Go!" The two boys dropped their weapons, ran into the washroom and left the two adults alone.

"That's an unusual term to use. I don't recall us ever being what you might call friends. Is there a–"

"A reason? Yes." Tú looked him straight in the eye. "There is a reason, a good reason. I'm guessing that at this moment, Túshānshì is trying to seduce my husband. True?" Her direct approach disconcerted Háng. "I take it from that screwed-up expression on your face that I'm right." Háng nodded. "Don't worry, I expected it from her. However, I think you're behind it as well. You are here with me now to sniff something out. Correct?"

"Well…err…it's not–"

"I can see through lies, so please don't lie."

"We had a plan of sorts, it–"

"You probably forgot that I know Yú intimately and was his lover for years."

"I was not forgettin'."

"You may have also forgotten that I know Túshānshì, perhaps better than anyone else does…even you. Are you sleeping with her? Don't answer that; of course you are!" Tú smiled.

"So, I'm going to tell you what your plan is. Túshānshì is going to try to persuade or force Yú into becoming the emperor of the Xià state. She is unsure whether she can do so. She will force him to step down as council leader if she cannot. I'm unsure how she will do this, but some

Seventeen: The Machinations

rumours exist. Knowing Yú as well as I do, he will never become an emperor. That leads me on to your role in all this."

"My role?"

"Or your roles, for it will depend on which route you go down. I know more about you than you may think. I know you're the richest man in the empire, an empire in which no one is supposed to be rich. I also know you have no real inclination to become a leader; you're not the type. You want to pull the puppet strings, not be a puppet. You want to be richer than you are, and you want people to know you are rich. You want them to know that you are a big man. You cannot do this at present."

"But I–"

"I haven't finished! You think that you and Túshānshì can leverage Qí into succeeding Yú. However, you need my husband on board to provide a bit of military might. Seeing what I've just seen, it could be possible to persuade that idiot boy to do what you wish. The problem is that the people will not vote for him when they realise that although he might be Yú's son, he is vacant, as empty as an empty flask. You might bribe them, blackmail council leaders, or whatever, but Qí will not become emperor!"

"You have a proposal?"

"Yùtù is also Yú's son."

"This is true, but he's completely unknown in Èrlǐtou. You're not goin' to bring in a child, say he's Yú's son and have people a votin' for him. Remember, keepin' power might be different, but to gain power, you must be elected in Èrlǐtou."

"So, you propose to put a known idiot into power in Èrlǐtou while you pull the strings. Yes?"

"If you put it–"

"Yes, I put it like that. It's a useless idea. Look at that boy Qí. He's sickly, as well as thick. Chances are he would be dead in a year or two. Now, if we were to get Yùtù into power, you could run things as you want."

"Why would that be the case?"

"Because, dear man, I control him. I am making a deal with you, not my son. Do you understand?"

"I'll go back to my earlier point. Why would anyone vote for a child they know nothin' of?"

"They will not. They will vote for Qí."

"You're mad! What you're sayin' doesn't make sense. How does Yùtù get into power when they's a votin' for Qí?"

"We switch them."

"Switch them?"

"Switch them. Yùtù becomes Qí, and the real Qí disappears."

"There's three big flaws in your plan, three huge holes that are impossible to reconcile. Firstly, the two of them are a lookin' very different; in fact, Yùtù is smaller. Secondly, how are you explainin' away Yùtù's disappearance, particularly to Fēngbō? And, thirdly, Yú and Túshānshì would see through it all. It just won't work!"

"Let's deal with those in reverse order. Firstly, I forecast that Yú will have left and Túshānshì will be dead. Secondly, I can handle Yùtù's disappearance as long as I also dispose of Fēngbō. Thirdly, there are things we can do to make their appearances more similar. It would help if you remember, they are both growing quickly at this age, and their voices will begin to break soon; they–"

"But their faces…their faces is different."

"I believe Yú's face was changed some years ago; it–"

"You believe right, smashed up with a big broken nose! But you couldn't–"

"Couldn't break my son's nose? I'll do more if necessary. Ridding us of Fēngbō is high on my to-do list, but that isn't very easy and needs perfect timing. Now, at the moment, this is all me, all my effort. I will need you to commit; otherwise, this conversation is purely hypothetical.

"Just by the way, if you ever attempt to mention any of this…I have the means to kill you, but I also have Fēngbō, who is awfully keen on torturing people if they so much as look at me the wrong way. This evening, there are four people here, all of whom will believe they have at least one ongoing and one new agreement. Two of them are probably screwing each other right now. We two do not need to be screwing each other; we need to be screwing them. Got it!"

"I'm understandin'."

Seventeen: The Machinations

"What you need to understand is that I am not Túshānshì. You cannot and will not control me. If we have a deal, it is from positions of strength for us both; don't forget this. We each have information that could burn the other.

"So, if the richest man in the empire wants to continue to be the richest man and, in fact, wants to become even richer, that's fine by me. If the richest man in the empire wants to expand his business up here in Ānyáng, that's fine by me. That rich man would also have more power, and more government decisions would favour him. But! That man has to deliver two things."

"They are?"

"Identifying Yùtù as Qí, that's first."

"It won't be easy!"

"You'll make it easy. The second is to deliver a council vote to make him leader as soon as he turns fourteen."

"What if Yú disappears before then?"

"He will, so it would be in your interests to keep the council seat warm with someone who can readily be removed. Do we have a deal?"

"We have a deal." Háng grinned widely, "What sort of deal do you think Fēngbō and Túshānshì are makin'?"

"Well, he's a right bastard, and she's a rutting whore! Who cares?"

Èrlĭtou, Hénán

Eighteen: The Inveiglement
Èrlĭtou, Hénán
Year 101. Chinese New Year. Year of the Pig
Thirty-seven days to the spring equinox
12th February 1894 BCE

It was the first day of the new year, that of the pig. The significance of the council meeting, due for later in the day, was lost on no one, least of all the council leader and his wife. That Yú would attend was a given; that Túshānshì would not was also to be expected, although it still rankled.

Túshānshì had reached the point of despair many years ago. Since then, she had teetered on the brink of breakdown rather than succumbing. The kratom[20] powder was the only thing that kept her going. Monthly supplies had cost her dear in terms of her self-respect. She knew not where Háng sourced the stuff, but the payment meant accommodating him in various perversions.

The balancing act had brought out some of her finest and worst moments. She now stood on the brink again, and as to which way this would play was the great unknown. Her skills had been failing her of late, and everything depended on those abilities. Now, it was time to apply additional enhancement. It caused her genuine physical pain to use some of her little helper on Yú, but it was the last chance. If she could not change his mind, then she could perhaps alter his mind. If this failed, there would be no more attempts; Fēngbō now provided a last-gasp alternative if she had to remove Yú. There was balance; should she fail in her finest moment, she would succeed in her worst.

Yú had woken less troubled than his wife and gladly took the steaming mug offered him as she climbed back into bed. Some matters would make the day difficult, but nothing was insurmountable. Accepting

---

[20] A tropical tree native to Southeast Asia, with leaves that have mind-altering effects.

Eighteen: The Inveiglement

a majority view different from his own was becoming somewhat easier for him. The primary issue hanging over the meeting would be Ānyáng. Yú had determined they should not allow the northern city-state into the empire, whereas the majority, led by Háng, believed they should be admitted. Their leader had a trick up his sleeve, for he had estimates of the cost of such a venture. The requirement for increased taxes may well dissuade them from voting against him.

Túshānshì's objective was to hijack the meeting, not in person, but through her influence on Yú. Ideologically, she cared not one jot whether Ānyáng was in or out; she had little interest in taxation rates, and her only fundamental opinion regarding Háng was that he should continue to supply her. Túshānshì's goal remained unaltered; she wanted the status she deserved. It had become an obsession. Three routes remained; two required Yú to maintain his leadership; in one, he became emperor, and in the other, he nominated his son. The third route saw Yú dead and Fēngbō coming in as a protector; it was a scenario that only Túshānshì, in her madest condition, could envisage.

It was freezing outside; the ground was rock hard from over a week of continual frost and a persistent northerly wind that made it feel ten times worse. Inside the farmhouse Yú shared with Túshānshì, it was at least somewhat warmer. It was not comfortable enough to encourage Yú to leave their bed, and Túshānshì had to spend some time warming herself against his body before she was again snug. For much of the time, theirs was a functional arrangement when it came to sleeping; long gone were the nightly sexual trysts that bound them so tightly. Warmth was now the overriding factor. For the last ten years, any sexual advances made by Túshānshì invariably meant that she wanted something; any made by Yú were borne solely out of frustration.

When Túshānshì's now warm hand slipped around his genitals, Yú's immediate thought was of the likely demands she would make. Not sexual, but political. He was still unclear how she rooted ideas in his mind but had come to recognise some of those that did not belong. It left him with a controlling hand; sometimes, he played along, and sometimes, he did not. He knew his body would react; he knew she would spend time bringing him to an incredibly aroused state and knew he would not resist. He would actively engage, and their lovemaking would be as passionate as it had been when they were teenagers, perhaps more so. As she slid down the bed and took him into her mouth, he groaned, but in his mind's eye, all he could see were the faces of the councillors. He wondered momentarily which of them was sucking his cock right now?

Túshānshì had stood over an abyss eight years before. Now, as her tongue tripped around the underside of Yú's penis, her thoughts were elsewhere. Her body performed the motions while her mind observed from a distance. They were motions she had trained herself to excel at; they needed no thinking. Her attack on Yú and even Nüxi's murder were not things she was ashamed of in principle. However, she had let herself down regarding both the timing and the removal of a possible witness. In those eight years, Túshānshì had been busy. Yú was still a work in progress and would always be so; she had almost given up on his becoming emperor of his own accord. If she could make him, that would be an achievement; if she could not, the fallback was her son. She had brought under control the violent madness of her breakdown, but the fury still bubbled under the surface, and no observer would have considered her thinking rational. At no time since her mistake had she regarded Yú as anything but the enemy; he was simply an enemy to be directed through mind games. Whatever the outcome, when she was finished with him, she would also take great delight in killing him when his powers were no longer helpful.

She lifted her head from his groin, levering herself up his body, sliding her breasts and stomach over his erection as she did. In a series of deliberate pulsing movements, her pubic hair rubbed against him as she used her legs entwined with his own to roll him over her.

She would make one last attempt to persuade him to accept before forcing the issue; this was the final throw of the dice. It had been difficult to retrieve the situation with Nüxi dead; she blamed herself repeatedly for her reckless behaviour. Tracing contacts in faraway Sìchuān, identifying who would know and more, who would speak out, had been complex but achieved. Āyí Zhū was walking, talking proof, and never had she found a woman so eager to speak. For the time being, keeping her quiet wasn't proving easy. What had been harder was persuading her to walk. Getting her off the slopes of Mount Shān alone took over five years and the offer of considerable reward.

Eighteen: The Inveiglement

Yú rolled with the pressure, finding himself lying chest to chest with his wife as she gradually opened herself, bringing her legs around his thighs. He pondered what wishes she would express afterwards. It was usually something relatively minor, starkly contrasting her actual wants. Her attempted mind control on significant issues was always disguised by the more mundane. Instinct took over as he slid inside her. Túshānshì's feet were now crossed behind his back and forced him deeper. He believed it would be Háng; the barman was always in his wife's ear, and his son's, for that matter. There was something about the man Yú admired, but it came with an equal measure of irritation. What would he want?

He felt her muscles start to flex around him. In his experience, which was admittedly limited, only Túshānshì could manipulate herself in such a dedicated manner, pulsing and tightening against his penis. It was not something she had done when they were younger. He thought for a while, concluding that this particular trick had arrived in their bed shortly after he had broken his nose. Strange. It was not something he wanted her to stop. His consciousness was sliding into the realm of ecstasy, and his thought patterns were becoming less focused. Just as he felt he was about to come, she squeezed so hard he could not. It was a pattern that repeated itself over and over. When he finally did, it was in an orgy of delirium. There was no up, no down, no yesterday or today. The intensity and power of his repeated ejaculation was almost painful, the pleasure absolute. Yú blacked out.

Túshānshì had not taken herself to the same extremes she had taken her husband. She could have found similar, if not more fantastic, satisfaction if she had desired. Now was not the time. It was control she wanted and control she had. This was not a one-act play; she would drain him until he could no longer move. Rolling him once more required more significant effort; temporarily, he was a dead weight, but she was a strong woman. As she felt him soften inside her, she loosened the grip from her legs and began to slide from underneath. By the time she was astride him and had rolled him onto his back, he was ready. Again, her hand slipped downwards, this time directed solely to his sodden penis; she began to bring it back to life, taking her time and with a gentleness she did not feel.

Yú came around to find their roles reversed, his wife touching him with her fingers and gently licking at his right nipple. The meeting and councillors fleeted briefly in his thoughts but would not adhere; his focus was gone. Retaken into Túshānshì's trap, it was a delightful place to be imprisoned. His entire self had slipped from his head to his groin, where her fingers were reawakening him. She was preparing to bring herself down onto him. There was almost a thud once his shaft had slipped deep through the mess of fluids their glands had produced, and then she began. Up, down, rotate, up, down, rotate. Slow and easy, not tightening as before. Her down strokes swallowed him whole; her upstrokes left the tip of his penis tantalisingly close to exiting her vulva. Yú's mind had gone wandering once more as he began to thrust upwards as she came down. Without intent, his hands felt for her breasts, which swung heavily from the crashing motion of their engagement.

Túshānshì knew she had done enough. His pupils were pinpricks. She was now able to let herself go. Disengaging herself from Yú's needs, she brought the seesaw action to an end. Now, instead, she was grinding down, her clitoris exposed to his hair, a scratchy tingling, at the same time irritating yet turning her on more and more. She could feel his fingers on her nipples, but her intense focus was much lower. Plunging her fingers inside, sliding them against the rock-hard shaft, which repeatedly thundered inside her, with the fingers of her other hand, she massaged herself, heightening her arousal. Closer and closer and closer. The warmth spreading outwards from her pubis became a more juddering and intensely pleasurable sensation. She was coming; her frame contracted and stretched uncontrollably. She no longer had any power over her body; its master was itself. As she felt wave after wave of her orgasm crash through her entirety, deep inside her, Yú exploded. How many times she could not count, for she collapsed forwards as the entire universe swam around her mind.

She remained slumped over her husband for a long time as he began to snore gently. Bringing herself round with a vast shudder, she remained astride him but brought her lips to his ear, throwing her long hair over his face and chest. It was then she began to whisper.

It was midday before Yú awoke. His erection felt enormous. Túshānshì was still draped around him, and Yú found it easy to twist around and penetrate her once more. It was a mechanical action, one

Eighteen: The Inveiglement

intended to rid himself of an inconvenience rather than to achieve a level of pleasure. She woke.

"I want–"

"What do you want, Túsh?"

"I want you to follow your instincts, that's all."

"That's all?"

"Do what's best for you."

"I will!"

Yú charged into her, reinvigorated. He soon came. This time, he immediately rolled off her and out of their bed. It would be for the last time.

Yú had not enjoyed breaking the ice that covered the water's surface in the washing bucket. He had enjoyed it even less when he had to apply the wet cloth to himself. He wondered momentarily whether his manhood might drop off or vanish entirely; it was that cold. At least it woke him up more fully; now, he could try and interpret messages left within him during the night.

Follow your instinct. That had been the waking command that Túshānshì had given him. That was not the important message, for he usually followed his instinct. What was she trying to persuade him to do? What was the subliminal message she had left him with? Certainly, she had spent enormous time and effort; it must be important. Whatever it was, Yú could not place it. During the short stroll to the *huìyì shì*, his mind churned. Bumping into Bóyì did not awaken anything either.

"How are you doing, Bóyì? I told you living so far out would not always be for the best. You must be freezing after that walk!"

"Good day, Yú! It's bracing, that I'll admit, but it keeps me fit. Look at you," he poked Yú's tummy. "What's this? It looks like you're being fattened up for slaughter!"

"Maybe I am! You know what, Bóyì, I will ask them to make me emperor today. Emperor for life, I think!"

"You've decided what?" The look on Bóyì's face was one of utter shock. "But you've always said–"

"I've got a feeling it's time, it's..." Yú paused. The expression on his face changed from one of genial bonhomie to horror. "Did I say what I thought I just said?"

"Yes. The council will accept immediately, but–"

"Bóyì. Something is very wrong with me. 'Follow my instinct,' she said. That's what she said. Yet my instinct is not my instinct. You know, I will ask them to make me emperor today. For life! It makes sense. Follow your instinct. What instinct? Whose instinct? Bóyì. Something is wrong! You know, I will ask them to make me emperor today. For life! Follow your instinct…life…emperor…Bóyì…something is wrong with me. Really wrong!"

Bóyì took Yú's hand, leading him into one of the antechambers of the *huìyì shì*. Seating him carefully on the table's edge, he wrapped his arm around the back of Yú's neck, his right hand on his arm. With his left, he beckoned to a passing councillor and whispered a single sentence. The councillor scurried off into the main hall with a message that the meeting was delayed by a day. Bóyì knew it would not be popular, but there was little else to do. He also asked that Jīngfēi be summoned; he had left her trying to warm up at Háng's bar.

Yú continued to mutter to himself. There was some coherence, although little seemed in character. When Bóyì's wife arrived, she took one look at the ailing council leader before uttering one word.

"Poison."

"What sort of poison?" Bóyì's concern was genuine.

"I don't know. Look, he's sweating and shaking. Look at his eyes; the pupils are almost gone. Yú! Yú, are you feeling sick?" As if ordered, Yú retched over his friend's wife.

"Get him on his side. Not his back, his side." Bóyì adjusted his position and lay Yú down. "Bóyì, careful. If he vomits again, we don't want him choking. Hold his head, make sure!"

"What do you think he's had? We should ask Túshānshì; she would know."

"Bóyì, if this is poison, where do you think he's got it?"

"At home."

"Yes. And if he got it at home, who do you think gave it to him?"

Bóyì closed his eyes for a moment, trying to square his idealised vision of Túshānshì, a woman he both openly admired and secretly lusted over, with the picture of a murderer. "No!"

Eighteen: The Inveiglement

"You don't think so! Are you aware of how she's treated him for years now? Everyone thinks it was her that broke his nose; everyone knows she gives him a hard time, or at least every woman knows. You should open your eyes!"

"What are we going to do?" Bóyì felt impotent.

"First, we'll help him recover…away from her. Then we, and by we, I mean all three of us, will confront that woman. Now, let's get him to his father's old house. There's some bedding there, and we can get a fire going. Get a messenger to go round to Túshānshì and tell her Yú has headed off to, to–"

"To inspect the army!" Bóyì finally found something he could offer.

"Yes! Now you sort that, I'll sort Yú, but come back with more bedding, firewood and water and find someone to give you some hot broth for him. Go!"

Jīngfēi spent the remainder of the day and the entire night nursing Yú back to health. Bóyì popped in sporadically, but only when he felt he was not being watched. They had no desire to attract attention to the situation.

The following morning, Yú had recovered. He awoke to find himself wrapped in the arms of Jīngfēi, which was something of a shock. When Bóyì entered the room, Yú hastily disentangled himself, although his friend seemed unbothered. Bóyì, seeing him better, experienced a rush of delight and bounced over to hug them both. It was an action that confused Yú further.

"Could someone tell me what's going on?"

Èrlĭtou, Hénán

Nineteen: The Blackmail
Èrlĭtou, Hénán
Year 101. Year of the Pig
Thirty-five days to the spring equinox
14th February 1894 BCE

To the further annoyance of the councillors, their meeting was not only put off for another week, but they also received a somewhat cryptic message from Yú. It seemed he wanted the news spread around the town that he would never accept their annual offer of lifetime leadership status. As he had said the same thing every year, it seemed odd to repeat it now and even more bizarre that he should want the statement widely disseminated.

Their irritation at the delay varied considerably with the distance each representative had to cover to come to the centre. Yú's popularity dipped further amongst those newest to the town who were the furthest flung for the most part. In the centre, Yú remained a hero, but for many, he was a distant figurehead, someone they had never met and who appeared to have an inflated opinion of himself.

Of course, the image had little to do with reality. Yú was embarrassed by the accolades showered on him by those who attributed every piece of good fortune to him. He was embarrassed others were not given the recognition they deserved. He yearned to address the whole town and get to know the newcomers; however, it was impractical. He had tried several local meetings, particularly in the more distant parts of the town, but these were unsupported by local councillors and poorly attended. There were now too many people living in Èrlĭtou for him to walk the streets to get to know them.

He had proved to be an inspired and level-headed council leader, something that surprised Yú himself, and indeed, there was nothing he

Nineteen: The Blackmail

had done wrong. Each year, his popularity diminished due to complacency rather than rejection. Certain corners always fought and tried to stir things up, but they were generally the lone voices of people with their own agendas. In the election due this summer, Yú would undoubtedly win, although perhaps as much as a third of the vote would go against him.

Notwithstanding his general popularity, it was a somewhat rattled Yú that accompanied Bóyì and Jīngfēi on a visit to a home he had always considered his own. He knew what he wanted to say. He knew what he wanted to ask. Unusually for Yú, he did not know the answers or where this particular meeting might take him.

Túshānshì had seen the three of them coming and met them at the door. Someone else was inside, but no clues were offered about who it might be. In an act of what could only be described as defiance, she kept the three of them standing in the cold.

"You've been telling people you'll not take a lifelong leadership role. An odd thing to do considering you've had no meeting and you've not been offered it since last summer."

"Don't you think we should start on something else?" Jīngfēi was more than prepared to be confrontational, even if the two men seemed more deferential.

"Such as?"

"Such as how this one ended up in such a state," she glared. "Poisoned! Now, we need to know first what it was, so we'll be able to find out if there are any more steps we should take to get him back to health."

"It was kratom; he'll get over it. He'll be fine." Túshānshì was dismissive and seemed surprisingly controlled.

"What's going on? What's kratom?" At last, Yú found it in him to speak. "Why did you do this to me? Have you no remorse, no apology?"

"No."

"No? So, this is finished, then? Are we over? I don't understand."

"I want you to come inside. I'm going to introduce you to someone. Yú, you might remember her; she is a stranger to you two. Come in."

Èrlĭtou, Hénán

Túshānshì turned and led them into the kitchen, where an older woman tended a well-banked fire.

"This is Āyí Zhū. Yú, does she stir a spark in your poor old memory? You would have met her at least twice?" Yú shook his head. "Not surprising, really. She was my nanny, although she knows an awful lot about you."

"I'm pleased–" The old nanny was cut off.

"Not now, Āyí Zhū. Later. Later, there will be time for you to talk." Túshānshì held a single finger up to her old nanny. "Not now. Would you leave us for a while? If you're going to Háng's bar, I'll send a message to you there."

"Alright, but I can't see why I can't stay. I'll be missing all the fun! It's cruel!" The older woman left, and Túshānshì indicated the visitors should all sit. She was treating the home as her own; it was clear that Yú was not a co-host.

"So, let me understand this; you have come here to ask me questions? Correct? The first question has been answered. The second was a string of blather from Yú that was hard to follow. So, let's start again. In fact, I'll make things a lot easier for you.

"Yes, I poisoned Yú. I used kratom powder in his morning drink. No, I did not intend to kill him. What's the next question?"

"I have a question," Bóyì opened his mouth at last. "Why did you poison him?"

"Well, that's a long story, Bóyì, but let's just say I was trying to get him to do something, which Yú knows only too well."

"It was a final attempt to get him to become emperor, wasn't it?" Bóyì sneered. "So much for that, then. It didn't work, did it?"

"You're a soldier, Bóyì; you command the army. That is true, is it not?"

"It's true enough."

"And in that role, you often make plans, yes?"

"Yes, but where is this going?"

"And you have backup plans in case something goes wrong?"

"True."

"Well, so do I. I had hoped that Yú and I could have reached a satisfactory conclusion ourselves. I hoped we could handle this as a family

Nineteen: The Blackmail

matter, but clearly, you two are now also involved. I planned that it would be clean, simple, and precise, and no one would get hurt."

"But you poisoned him! How is that not hurting someone?" Jīngfēi was still fuming and having difficulty coming to terms with this scenario unwinding in this hearth of domesticity.

"He survived. The only trouble is that he didn't do what he was supposed to."

"Which was for me to become emperor? Why? I don't want to!" Yú's face wore a twisted grimace.

"No, you don't, but I want to be an empress, and I want Qí to take over the throne."

"So, you've failed! This has been going on for so long; how often have you failed?" Bóyì was becoming more and more irritated by the pointlessness of it all.

"But I have not! I told you there was a backup plan. The problem is, instead of just one person getting hurt, the consequences of this is that several people could get hurt and much worse than a tiny bit of kratom poisoning."

"How can you stand there and pretend you have any control left in this situation? I'm not coming back to you. This is the final straw! I will fight you and win for the supervision of Qí. After what you have done, I know the council would recommend banishment. It hurts me to say it, but you will not be calling Èrlǐtou home for many more days." Yú had finally fully understood what she was saying and ended in a more pitiful tone. "It is so sad that–"

"Wrong! Wrong! Wrong! If you could only see yourselves, all sitting there with a more righteous-than-thou attitude! Bóyì, Jīngfēi, you are not in the wrong. You are here only by association, but it might just bring you down as the head of the army, Bóyì!"

"Túshānshì, you're crazy!" Jīngfēi had no sympathy, "How could you bring down the head of the army? Madness!"

"So, madness, is it? I'll admit, I was mad when I smashed the pan into his face! Perhaps not mad enough, though, for I intended to kill him!" The two men's jaws dropped. "Yes, it was me! Now, I'll confess to more! Do you want to hear? I think you probably do not, but you're going to anyway!

"I killed Nüxi!" For a moment, there was stunned silence.

"I killed those two vagrants!" She laughed triumphantly.

"And I killed the baby that was inside me!" It was as if a maelstrom of insanity had filled the kitchen.

"And you want to know something more? You…" she pointed at the three of them, "…you will tell no one!"

"I will!" Screamed Jīngfēi. "I'll stand up at the council and repeat everything you've said, and so will Bóyì. I cannot speak for Yú, but you may just have crossed a line admitting to murdering his mother!"

"And my father?" Yú was crying. His emotions were not ready to explode, but he could not stop the tears.

"No! He was dead already. Nüxi killed him! I just put two arrows in him to make it look as if there was another killer. It's been eight years or more, and no one has ever realised." She looked down and calmed herself, "There's no one outside this room who ever will."

"You cannot be allowed to get away with this, Túshānshì. With luck, they'll take the view that you're insane, but they'll not let you see the streets of Èrlǐtou again." Bóyì sounded calm, but he was as outraged as Jīngfēi and as upset as Yú.

"You think? Well, I do not. For you see, Bóyì, I have a secret, a dreadful secret, it—"

"Another one?" Jīngfēi was scornful.

"Oh no! Not your average pathetic secret! I said a dreadful secret, and I meant dreadful. Ultimately dreadful!"

"But you've just admitted to killing your mother-in-law, two vagrants, aborting your baby, defiling your father-in-law's corpse, and assaulting Yú. How much worse can it get?"

"Much worse! You see, Gǔn was my father, and Nüxi was my mother!"

"Not mine?" Yú was frozen, as still as a statue, as if he had seen a ghost. Only his lips moved. "Not mine?"

"It's obvious that they were your parents! The simple fact is, they were mine as well! I am your older sister!"

The words hurled across the room; no more followed them for a while. The only sounds came from logs cracking in the fireplace. The

Nineteen: The Blackmail

three visitors sat with their heads down, trying to absorb the information. Finally, Yú shook his head.

"It's not true. It cannot be true. You are making a grievous accusation and—"

"Yes, I am! Think a moment, Yú, just think. You say it's untrue. I say it is true, and I have a witness. Āyí Zhū holds the proof. I told you there was a backup plan. I told you that you would not like it. Now! Well, now you must live with it. No one else will know if you behave; you have my word. This truth will only be believed if both Āyí Zhū and I swear to it, which leaves things in your hands, Yú. There are only two choices."

"How? How are you saying this happened?" Yú looked up at his wife's face.

"You were born when I was coming up to two years of age. Shortly afterwards, I was taken away. Āyí Zhū and her husband brought me up. I did not know our parents until I was older. I was brought back into the area when I was fourteen. I was told I would marry you. I had been coached into it for years. Can you imagine the terribleness of serving a cause that wants you to bed your brother, not just once, but for your whole life? What's more, they would not allow me to fall pregnant. I was to remain childless, but not you! No, you were to have a child by Tú. It is the Sisterhood to blame for this sick mess, not I. You think I'm mad, well, maybe I am completely insane, but this is the truth, and you had better understand it!"

The room was silent once more. Yú continued to shake his head from side to side. Bóyì sat in frozen silence. Only Jīngfēi was animated. She stood and poked a finger into Túshānshì's chest. "There is another option…"

"And that is?"

"We could kill you!"

Túshānshì brushed her hand aside. "Which is why one other person knows. You dare not kill me! You dare not kill Āyí Zhū. If you were to, the truth would come out, and he…" she directed both arms in Yú's direction, "would be on charges of murder! In addition to incest, that is! And think about it; where would that leave Qí?" Túshānshì smiled. "You know, Jīngfēi, I've always had him by the balls…always…but now…now I have it all! Yú, you might want to reverse your decision about leading the empire. Do you not?"

"Bóyì, pick him up." Jīngfēi motioned to Yú to take him outside and get him to the horses. Now! Go!"

Bóyì struggled to lift Yú, who was reluctant to leave, but the younger man had a firm grip. As they exited, Jīngfēi turned once more on Túshānshì. She stepped into her personal space, pushing herself chest to chest with the taller woman, their noses almost touching. If Túshānshì was scared, she showed no sign.

"I am going to explain something about friendship. Yú is our best friend; we love him. You have never been our friend, simply the partner of a friend! I stand by my friends, whatever the circumstance. You are accusing Yú of incest, but I would point out it would appear to be unwitting incest, and that is only if the story is true! I am going to make a promise tonight. I promise that I am going to kill you. Sooner or later, it matters not! When I kill you, it will be a horrible and painful death. I will not spare you any agonies. I will tear your guts out. I will gouge your eyes from their sockets and put a spear up your arse. I hope, Túshānshì, that you remember what I have just said, for I do not break a promise. Ever!"

With that, Jīngfēi turned and stormed through the door.

Outside, Bóyì, having managed to persuade Yú to mount his horse, signalled his wife to double up with him on her mount. Yú raised his eyes to the heavens in despair. The sky twinkled with stars, although now it seemed there was a new addition. A line, a streak, an arrow? It was unclear, but it pointed towards the spot where the sun had set some hour before.

"You are coming with us, Yú. To our house." Bóyì pulled on the reins his friend had allowed to hang loose. "We'll talk or drink or sleep; the decision is yours. There'll be no arguments."

"I'm not arguing." His voice was the sound of a broken man. "Look," Yú pointed to the heavens, "it's a message."

"I don't know what it is, Yú, but it's not a message. You don't believe in messages," Jīngfēi whispered.

"Maybe I do now. I don't know what to believe."

"Come, let's get home; it's too cold out here. When we're home, we'll talk." Bóyì dug his heels into his steed's flanks, wheeling it through

Nineteen: The Blackmail

half a circle to head east. Yú's horse followed without any response from its rider.

They had spoken no further during the ride and were now settled with three mugs of beer in Bóyì's kitchen. It had become a standing joke that Jīngfēi referred to it as such, for she was the one who spent most of her time here. She had promised Bóyì that once his job with the army was over, he would cook all the meals. It was something that kept her husband determinedly in his position.

Yú had spent some time repeatedly banging his forehead on the kitchen table to the extent that his nose was now bleeding. Only realising that he was making a mess of his friends' furniture caused him to desist. Jīngfēi had gone off to find some rags.

"My sister! I won't admit there's any truth in this, Bóyì."

"I know. What's your thinking, though?"

"My sister! I believe her. It makes me sick to say it, but if it were true, too many strange loose ends would be tied off. How would you feel, though? My sister!"

"But why? Why would anyone think this was a good idea? Your mother?"

"She said it! It's something to do with my mother, Tú, Túshānshì and the Sisterhoo–"

"The Sisterhood! That was the one thing she said that makes some sense!" Jīngfēi re-entered the room in a combative mood. "I left the sisterhood because they were doing no good. It seems they've been messing around diabolically this time!"

"My sister! I'm finding it hard to believe they would countenance incest," Yú was becoming angry. "Incest! If it's true, I'm guilty, but I'm the innocent one in all this. She's right. She does have me by the balls. If I don't become emperor, they will find me guilty, and I'll not only be banished but also lose my good name, which is far worse. Qí might be allowed to stay; he's underage, but Túshānshì will not–"

"And there, Yú is the problem with her plan. If this does come out, she is affected as much as you are. She might be mad, but she would not want that consequence, would she?" Jīngfēi appeared to have come up with something, although all three tried to make it fit with a desirable outcome for Yú.

Èrlĭtou, Hénán

"What would happen if you simply went away?" Bóyì asked.

"More than that, Yú, what if you disappeared?" Jīngfēi smiled for the first time all day.

"If I disappeared? Well! I could not be council leader anymore—"

"And?"

"That means I could not be emperor."

"And?" The couple spoke in unison now.

"That means she would tell her story, but—"

"But?"

"She wouldn't because it would only damage her and Qí. Not me!"

Yú walked to the door, allowing an icy blast to enter the kitchen. "Come, come here!" He beckoned the two of them outside and turned to the west. "Look! It's an omen[21]. It's a sign. It's telling me where to go! Whatever it is, I will follow. Through the Qínlĭng Mountains to Sìchuān. It's taking me home!"

"Tomorrow, we will secretly get you out of here, Yú." Jīngfēi linked her arm through his.

"Before you do…I need to meet with the controllers. I need Lài, Měnghŭ and Hétóngzĭ, as well as Bóyì. I want to make a statement they can take to the council. Suppose I make the statement in front of the four of them. No one will be able to contradict them. I'm worried about Túshānshì and Háng in this regard; neither would dare challenge the word of the controllers."

"I'll round them up at first light and bring them here. It won't delay your departure by much. There's only one proviso, Yú!" Bóyì mirrored his wife's position; the three stood, arms linked, with Yú in the middle. "You have to find a way to tell us where you've gone. I'll not want to be drinking alone in my old age! Nor spending my time doing all the cooking!"

---

[21] Halley's Comet, but only named as such thousands of years later.

Twenty: The Femicide
Èrlĭtou, Hénán
Year 101. Year of the Pig
Thirty-two days after the spring equinox
2nd May 1894 BCE

In the end, Kuàiláng's question of two years before as to why they would be considering assassinating a female had come back to haunt her twice over. Líng's request sounded reasonable now, if only because the leader of the Wolf Pack had greater access to information. The circumstances had changed little. Removing Túshānshì and Āyí Zhū from the present equation made sense. The idea of eliminating Fēngbō had cheered them enormously. What did not make as much sense was taking down Túshānshì's son. Kuàiláng pondered whether she really was in charge.

Kuàiláng had begun to doubt whether Líng had stood down from active duty or whether she was still pulling the strings. All the information they received appeared to have Líng's character and ideals laced within its design. It was not raw information, which had to be analysed and then a plan of action constructed. It was information passed in such a way that the desired pathway also seemed implicit. As the Wolf Pack leader, she would have to take responsibility for these actions, but it was doubtful whether they were the actions she would have taken, given unbiased information.

No matter, a job was a job. Xiǎoláng and Dàláng had agreed on the overarching plan. It was now a matter of filling in the details, ensuring they had ample opportunity for the murder of the two women and could escape from Èrlĭtou with a boy, who was to be observed as alive by as many as possible. It was the third stage that was driving them to distraction.

"He's got to be seen. By as many people as possible. Us too, but without revealing our identities. This is not going to be easy, Kuài!"

"I know, Dà, it's not going to be easy at all. Xiǎo, have you got anything to suggest?"

"I do, but we have a minor problem with your and Dà's sizes. I was going to suggest that we dress as soldiers and—"

"Not this again," Dàláng rolled her eyes. "What's wrong with my size? I can dress like a soldier. They plenty of female soldiers in Èrlǐtou, there's—"

"There is a problem, Dà. I was not thinking about Xià troops but those of Ānyáng. Fēngbō does not have female troops. You two are too small to get away with it.

"Wouldn't someone question how three of Fēngbō's army were marauding around the centre of Èrlǐtou?" Dàláng was scathing, "Don't you think it would have been picked up on at the gate?"

"I haven't got a better idea. It's as simple as that, Dà," Xiǎoláng sighed, "do you?"

"Wait a minute, you two. Xiǎo. Dà. Let's not become despondent about this. In killing Túshānshì and Āyí Zhū, we do not need to be observed. In abducting Qí, we do not have to be seen. As we escape, we must have the boy seen. We do have to be identified. It's just that they need to think we're someone else. That would get rid of the size problem. We—"

"Across the river!" A huge smile crossed Xiǎoláng's face.

"What are you talking about, Xiǎo?" Dàláng's expression did not mirror the joy of her comrades.

"Ah! I see it, Xiǎo. Good thinking! Looking at Dà's face, you might have to give a little more of an explanation before it sinks in. Look, she's going to sulk! Explain!" Kuàiláng smiled.

"This is how it works, Dà. We take out the two women. We kidnap the boy. We do this in whatever disguise we see fit, whatever works. We leave by one of the gates and ensure Qí is not observed. Then—"

"But we know he has to be seen. That's the point, isn't it? He must be seen being abducted. Simple as that."

"No, Dà, he does not have to be seen being abducted. He can be identified after his abduction. What I am suggesting is that we let people see him after we have got him out of the gates and…across the river!"

Twenty: The Femicide

"It's brilliant!" Kuàiláng laughed. "We just need to pick a part of the river where there's plenty of people on the town side, no one on the other and where the river is quite narrow and not easily crossed."

"I've got it!" Dàláng's face had furrowed in concentration as she came to terms with Xiǎoláng's idea. Now she leapt onto her younger sister, her legs wrapping around her waist, her arms around her neck. Quite solemnly, she planted a kiss firmly on her forehead.

"Well, if you've got it, I must have explained it exceptionally well!" Xiǎoláng grinned and pretended to sag under the weight of her sibling.

"So, girls, which of the two rivers and where? We've not much time. Scouting out a spot starts now," Kuàiláng directed. "We'll split up, take the horses, and meet back here in two days. Each of us comes up with two suggestions as a minimum, more if possible.

*

Túshānshì was having immense difficulties trying to keep Āyí Zhū's mouth firmly shut. No amount of logic could dissuade her that letting the cat out of the bag now would only harm themselves. As a result, they had become reclusive; Túshānshì out of choice, Āyí Zhū through coercion.

Túshānshì existed in a world of her own. She felt divorced from the Sisterhood and at odds with everyone in Èrlǐtou. Even the barman had stopped coming over to see her. Not only was she alone, but she was also suffering withdrawal symptoms, having lost her supplier. If the days had become stressful, her nights were now awful. There was constant nausea; she shook and sweated prolifically, and the muscle spasms caused her guts to crease with the agony. She realised she both missed and wanted Yú, something she would not have considered possible.

She had become increasingly paranoid. Discussing her fears with her ex-nanny at least kept the older woman from wandering out too often. Túshānshì believed that Jīngfēi would have convinced Bóyì to send the Èrlǐtou guard to take her out. She feared the Sisterhood to a lesser extent, although it was not a threat to be dismissed.

Èrlǐtou, Hénán

Túshānshì had moved out of the home she had shared with Yú; it was just one more thing to irritate her. She had moved of her own free will, knowing the house would soon be reallocated to the new council leader. She suspected it would be Bóyì, and the thought of him and Jīngfēi rolling around in her bed irritated her enormously. At least her new home was away from the centre, although it took little time to walk there if she could be inclined to wander out.

The move meant they were now living in a smaller home than before. It meant sharing her bed with her son. Qí was particularly grating. He missed his father and took it out on his mother. Túshānshì no longer considered him her passport to a life of greatness, now only finding him irritating. Trapped on their farm all day, in the close company of the garrulous Āyí Zhū and her whinging son, she was on a downward spiral from which she saw no escape.

Túshānshì's lack of information was one of three strands causing her downfall. The second strand was the need for fresh food, and the third, which proved her complete undoing, was choosing to leave her son at home when she went out. Unwilling to allow Āyí Zhū out alone, she had instigated a weekly trip for them both down to the riverside to buy fresh fish. Without a thought, they never varied the time or the route, always used the same fishmonger, and hung around the riverbank for far too long. Túshānshì had no idea they were being spied on continuously and would have been surprised to have discovered the extent of the Sisterhood's network. She enjoyed the fresh air and the added time away from Qí. It was an easy pattern for the Wolf Pack to pick up on.

*

There was a point where the Yi River turned, meandering north up to its confluence with the Luohe. On the eastern bank were thick bushes; on the western, the farmlands of the fishermen gave way to their wooden piers. The piers protruded into the fast current, providing platforms for the best catches.

The rapid flow was caused when the Yi narrowed to less than twenty-five paces. For no known cause, it was here that the silver carp enjoyed jumping out of the water, often reaching twice the height of a

Twenty: The Femicide

man. Those fishing played a waiting game, holding nets ready to cast under the leaping fish. It was a skill not many mastered. The carp were not only difficult to catch, but they were also difficult to eat due to their spines. However, they were hugely popular as they were tender and flavourful, mainly cooked in *baijiu* with fresh herbs.

On one bank, Túshānshì bartered over the cost of three fish. The seller wanted two bowls of millet, but Túshānshì had only one. She still had some persuasive powers, even in her present mental state, retaining an aura she had used throughout her life to bring deals to a close. She bent provocatively, pretending to inspect the fish again, moving her head from side to side and allowing the vendor to glimpse her breasts as they swung slightly under her smock.

"You can have all three for one bowl if you let me see those properly," the fisherman grinned.

"And what would you be talking about? You want to see the fish better?" Túshānshì lifted her head but kept crouching, ensuring the man could see enough but not quite everything. As far as she was concerned he could look at her body for as long as he wanted if she walked away with three fish. "Is that better?"

"It's better, but it's not enough. Why don't you just take your smock off?"

"You mean...like this," Túshānshì raised the smock over her head. Completely naked beneath, she heard the man take a sharp intake of breath and felt him reach a hand onto her flesh. "Touching as well! I think you'll be giving me the fish after that."

"No! You'll only get the fish for free if you let me do a deal more than touch you. I heard you were the one who wanted to be an empress. I've always fancied having an empress, even if you're not one. What do you say?"

As she pulled the smock back over her face, considering whether the offer was worthwhile, an arrow flew sliced straight through the man's hand and into her heart. She died instantly, a half-smile on her lips; she had intended to agree to his deal.

The fishmonger's squealing caused Āyí Zhū to come running; it also proved her undoing. A second arrow screamed out of the bushes on the far bank, taking Túshānshì's old nanny in the neck. It was intended as

Èrlǐtou, Hénán

a second chest shot. Dàláng was disappointed in her aim, although the woman had ducked at the last minute to inspect her mistress's breast to which a man's hand was now firmly pinned.

"It's no matter, Dà. She'll be dead in minutes. You got her neck. That stuff spreads fast. That fisherman will succumb fast enough. The upas tree latex will have him before evening." Xiǎoláng forced a smile. "Kuài managed to smuggle the boy out. She's waiting by the horses."

"I don't know, Xiǎo, I'm not sure about—"

"Later, Dà, later. I can see you're upset, but this is not the time. We've got a show to put on. Come on!"

There was a slight clearing in the bushes. Kuàiláng was waiting, crouched down, pinning a struggling youth to the ground. Dàláng joined her, kneeling on the boy and using her dagger to make a light incision across his scalp.

"That'll bleed and bleed a lot. It's time to raise some noise and get noticed! They'll be close enough to see his face and to see he's bleeding. Ready, Dà? Ready, Xiǎo? Remember, deep noises, nothing shrill. Dà, stand here, make yourself look tall." At Kuàiláng's signal, they rose as one, shouting and hauling the boy up with them. The three made a big show of displaying him and ensuring their makeshift Lóngshān uniforms were seen by the growing crowd on the opposite bank. At least thirty pairs of eyes now swivelled from gazing at the semi-naked and clearly deceased form of Túshānshì to view the performance on the far side of the river. Seeing the young boy being prodded, pushed, and shoved around brought an instant reaction. Fists were raised, threats made, and curses sworn. However, no one was prepared to risk the swift current of the Yi River.

Finally, when a few fishermen had collected their wits together and headed off for weaponry, the Wolf Pack determined it was time to leave. Ducking back into the bushes, Xiǎoláng and Dàláng carried the struggling boy between them. It took mere moments for them to truss him up across the packhorse before swinging onto their mounts.

As Kuàiláng moved away at a trot, Xiǎoláng put her hand onto her sister's arm, "Dà, I'm not sure about all this. Killing women and boys is not what I signed up for."

Twenty: The Femicide

"True, sister, it's true. I almost changed my aim when I saw that man fondling Túshānshì's breasts. No matter what she's done, she doesn't deserve a groping. Now we've got the two of them dead, and we're supposed to kill this kid. I'm not sure it makes sense."

"We'll talk later, Dà, and talk to Kuài. I think she might feel the same way." Each looked up as a voice floated in from ahead.

"It's going to be a long ride, girls! Two days! South, then west, then north, then back east. Hùtóu Cave, here we come." Kuàiláng dug her heels into her mount's flanks. "We overnight at Xīshān Sēnlín. Let's go!"

Hùtóu Mountain Cave, above Èrlĭtou, Hénán

Twenty-one: The Boy

Hùtóu Mountain Cave, above Èrlĭtou, Hénán
Year 101. Year of the Pig
Thirty-four days after the spring equinox
4th May 1894 BCE

It was a beautiful spot, one unlikely to be disturbed. Their cave opened to the east, which shielded their fire from the valley, although another wide ledge provided a view to the southwest. In that direction, the wooded slopes below gave way to the flood plain of the Luòhé River, the main fording point, a clean scar from cartwheels extended north and south from the water. On the far bank, the palisades of Èrlĭtou centre stood tall with an extensive patchwork of farmland stretching from east to west. The arable land halted abruptly along a wavy line that must have been the more distant Yī River, although its flow was invisible anywhere but at Èrlĭtou's southern entry point. In the far distance, the crags of Wan'an Mountain stood tall, rising high above the plain. Within weeks, the view would become more obscure when the rains swept in from the south as they did each year.

It was in a beautiful spot, and the cave was clean and functional. Temporarily abandoned by the shepherd who raised meat for the valley's inhabitants, it served the three members of the Wolf Pack well. The fourth occupant was a great deal less content with his circumstances. Bound and gagged, he cried almost continuously, to such an extent that Kuàiláng was increasingly concerned that he might dehydrate.

"You've got to make him drink!" Xiǎoláng exclaimed, "If he keeps on like that, well…he'll flood the cave!"

"You try…go on…you try! It's not as easy as you might think. If I pull his gag off, he screams. You try pouring water down the throat of someone who is screaming. They start to drown." Dàláng was trying,

Twenty-one: The Boy

although she was increasingly irritated by the puny male specimen lying at her feet. "If we must kill him, let's do it now."

As the words left her lips, the crying ceased immediately. The boy struggled against his bindings and appeared to indicate they should remove the gag. Dàláng took another look and had second thoughts.

"Here, we'll take it off. Just you be quiet for a bit. And drink the water, won't you." She bent down, unknotting the gag behind his neck. The boy gulped for air.

"I'll drink the water. I won't scream. Just don't kill me!" The words came out in short, sharp bursts. Dàláng raised the leather water bottle to his lips. This time, he drank and kept on drinking; it was clear he was thirsty.

Kuàiláng had been watching the scene unfold; she had been trying to give herself thinking space, although the boy's antics had prevented it. Líng had been quite clear about the boy's fate, although executing a plan hatched six days' ride away and out of sight of their victims was proving a little more complicated than it had sounded on Qícūn Hill.

"You've killed my mother, haven't you?" The boy trembled slightly, "Is that because she was going mad?"

"Yes." Kuàiláng grasped at the most straightforward response.

"She was being very odd. She climbed into my bed and stroked me." The innocence of his facial expression did not match the words tumbling from his mouth. "She kept me from my *Bǎobà*[22] so much. It was nasty. She used to be a nice lady. Not now." He picked at the scab that had formed over the scratch on his scalp.

"Look, Qí, the girls and me are going to go outside for a bit." Kuàiláng shimmied over and cut the bindings on his arms. "Here…take this flatbread. Would you wait for us? Without screaming." The boy nodded. "We'll be a few minutes. Sit here." She indicated the bench she had occupied earlier. "Now…eat!

"Xiǎo. Dà. Come with me." She led her comrades out of the cave and onto the southwest-facing ledge. They ducked low to avoid distant eyes; the air was clear today, and spotting them from the valley would be easy.

---

[22] Father.

Hùtóu Mountain Cave, above Èrlǐtou, Hénán

"Come, sit. You know, I don't think I can kill this kid." Kuàiláng put it straight to them. "He's a mess. It sounds like Túshānshì ended up treating him like a plaything. When you listen to him, it's like listening to a five-year-old, and he's more than twice that. It's so awful that–"

"You know what Líng asked for, Kuài. We're just fulfilling her request. Dà and I have already agreed we don't like this. We might be getting fed up with the crying, but it must be done."

"No…it does not have to be done. I am in charge here, not Líng. She may have asked, but that does not mean she gets. I'm trying to devise a solution that does not involve killing him but satisfies the circumstances. Why does she want him dead?"

"She wants him dead so that Yùtù can take his place, Kuài, even Dà knows that much!" The tall woman smiled at her comrades in arms.

"But…but that does not mean he has to be dead, does it? Look at Yú. He's gone missing. If Yú can go missing, then why can't Qí? And if Yùtù replaces him–"

"Then no one will come looking for Qí!" Dàláng rarely concluded their round table discussions, but on this occasion, she was proud to have come up with a solution, "And if you think about it…there's no need to disfigure him either. I never liked that bit of the plan. I understand we need to rearrange Yùtù's face, but if we're not going to kill Qí, why can't we keep him in one piece?"

"It's not quite as easy as that, Dà. There is another reason Líng wants him dead. A big reason. She doesn't want him breeding. He's the son of a brother and sister. You know that's bad enough. I mean, look at the boy; he looks sickly from every angle. Xiǎo, you know more about this sort of thing than me, but don't tell me that having a father and mother from the same family didn't cause that!"

"I have an idea!" The look on Dàláng's face was one of near wonderment.

"Two in one day! Kuài, she'll be wanting your job next. She must have gone off the idea of stabbing people!"

"I didn't stab the last two; I shot them and…and you, Xiǎo, poisoned the arrows…and I was only doing what Kuài told me to. You're trying to make out like I'm some mad killer when I'm really–"

Twenty-one: The Boy

"Verbose! Cut out the squabbling and tell me your idea! Xiǎo, don't start her off again! The idea, Dà, what is it?"

"Well, it would mean we don't have to kill him, and I'm not very keen on that, nor is Xiǎo. I don't know what you would call it, but shepherds always do it. They do it to the male sheep they want for late slaughter. They cut the bottom of the ball sac and chop out the balls." Dàláng broke into an ever-widening grin, "If it stops rams from having lambs, it should certainly stop Qí from having babies!"

"It's called castration, and I'm not sure, Dà, that Qí will be as enthusiastic. From what I've seen, the shepherds bite open the bottom of the ball sac and remove the balls with their teeth. I suppose you could do it with a knife. Whatever, Qí is going to struggle and–"

"Dà's idea is good, Xiǎo, it's great. Your job will be to knock him out. If you can get him to sleep for a few hours, then Dà can do the knife work." Kuàiláng smiled at her partners, "Leave the boy here with me. Dà, go and find that shepherd. You know the one. We saw him on the hills to the west yesterday. Talk to him. Nicely! Find out how to do it. Do not tell him we're doing it on a boy.

"Xiǎo, go and find the herbs you need. Remember, you need something to keep him out cold and something to prevent infection. Oh! You might also find something for pain. I'm not sure how much this will hurt him afterwards, but you've seen what it's like when a man gets a kick in the balls, their faces go all funny and screw up, and they bend over double. I suspect it might hurt him. If we get started now, we'll have more time for him to recover before Yùtù gets here with Tú. Go!"

Kuàiláng returned to the cave to determine what she should or should not tell the boy. She had managed to justify the assassinations of Túshānshì and Āyí Zhū to herself. Yú's wife had deliberately become an actual and active danger to the Motherland. Unfortunately, Āyí Zhū had become entrapped in the business, but it was not simply through association; she had gone out of her way to stir things up further. Shutting them up had to be a final act; any form of distance gagging would not have been enough. The boy was a different matter; he was wholly innocent.

Kuàiláng wondered whether she was overcomplicating things; it would be simple enough to do away with the boy. It was only then she

Hùtóu Mountain Cave, above Èrlǐtou, Hénán

considered Yú. What would he want? She did not believe that Líng could have asked him; she likely decided by herself. What would Yú prefer? A castrated son, a dead son, or a breeding son? Kuàiláng tried to put herself in his shoes and concluded that the first option was the most likely, knowing that Yú understood the boy's physical heritage. Castration it would be. As she slid into the cave, she hoped her partners in crime would not leave her alone for too long with the boy.

Xiǎoláng considered her role the easiest, although finding the devil's trumpets before the rainy season was challenging. The plant was ideal for knocking the boy out and far more subtle than the alternative, which would have meant a sharp blow to the jaw. As it was the dry season, she had to find a flowing spring, which meant dropping down the hill somewhat and possibly exposing her location to anyone passing. She came across the spring soon enough; unsurprisingly, two other people were there. She skirted through the thicker parts of the woodland to afford herself a better view, digging herself into the wet undergrowth.

Dàláng was not the best actor in the world, but she was perfectly capable of extracting information from a lonely shepherd. Her technique had been applied equally to guards, carpenters, and hunters in the past; she had never failed. The shepherd had been taking his flock down the hill for water, which meant she had to take a wide arc to avoid startling the sheep. When he arrived at the pool nestled in the woods at the foot of the hill, it was to find Dàláng with her smock pulled up, nursing her knee.

"What have we here?" The man was surprised to find anyone, let alone a young woman, at the watering hole.

"I think I've twisted my knee. It hurts."

"Twisted knees are a bane to me, striding these hills. Hills are no place for a twisted knee. I sometimes wonder why knees are designed quite like they are!"

"Will you take a look, please?"

The shepherd cast an eye over his flock; the sheep seemed delighted to have been brought to the water. "Yes, I'll come over." He dropped his staff and bounded to where Dàláng had propped herself against a boulder.

"It's here." She pointed to the inside of her right knee. "Feel."

Twenty-one: The Boy

The man lowered himself in front of her and, placing both hands around her calf, carefully dragged them upwards, his thumbs brushing her kneecap.

"Seems sound to me. You may have twisted it, but it's not sprained. That's good news, by the way. Sprains is the worst news, worse than a break. Sprains do not go away easily."

"Your hands felt good. Would you do that again, please?"

The shepherd looked at her sideways, "You have no idea what my missus would say if she knew I'd been stroking a girl's leg for no reason. She'd have a fit! They might be nice legs, but I think I'll be leaving them for you to feel. Pardon me, Ma'am, but I'm happily married–"

The snort from the nearby bushes caught them both off-guard. The sight of Xiǎoláng rolling out into the clearing with tears streaming down her face propelled them both to their feet, the shepherd in horror and Dàláng in total embarrassment.

"It didn't work! You didn't seduce him! Always telling me you had perfect technique!" Xiǎoláng's laughter almost prevented her from speaking. She snorted once more. "I think I've wet myself!"

"This is an odd thing." The shepherd had rid himself of his immediate fear and was beginning to see the funny side of his situation. It was possibly a mistake.

"You idiot, Xiǎo! Now we have a problem, and the problem is him!" she pointed at the man. "He'll go and tell all and sundry that he met two women up here…he'll tell everyone. If you had let me do it my way instead of bursting out of that bush, well, if you had, there would have been no problem. Idiot! We'll have to kill him now." Dàláng pulled out a small bronze dagger.

"Hold on a minute," the fear returned to the shepherd's eyes. "What's all this talk of killing? Who would want to kill me, I ask you?"

"Dà, leave him be. Let's sit down. We can talk this through. We don't need to kill him." Xiǎoláng smiled at the man who maintained his nervous expression.

"That would be nice. If–"

"If we can come to an arrangement." Xiǎoláng had focussed him further. "You see, Dà here needs some information. Information that you have. She would have done anything to get that information, but you

Hùtóu Mountain Cave, above Èrlǐtou, Hénán

weren't interested," she sniggered, "and so what she now wants to ensure is that you will not tell anyone you've seen us. Do you see that weapon? That dagger has killed many men; one more is nothing to her."

"That's a bit unfair, Xiǎo, I always say–"

"You always say you have a perfect pulling technique, and that's proved wrong, hasn't it? Now, what I was saying is that we can make a trade. You tell Dà here what she wants to know, and we will not tell your wife that you raped us both. Easy!"

"But I didn't rape her or y…" it was sinking in quickly, "or you. It's not fair to…What? Can you repeat it, please?"

"If you tell Dà what she wants to know, we will not tell your wife that you raped us both. Got it!"

"You won't tell anyone?"

"No, just don't you tell anyone you even saw us!"

"What does she want to know?"

When the shepherd learned Dàláng wanted information about castrating male sheep, he was immediately interested. He may be interested, but he was also concerned. Why would a young woman, with no apparent interest in the animals he cared for, want to know how to take their balls off?

"Now, you won't be doing anything silly with my sheep. They've just lambed. There's nothing to do right now!"

"No, you misunderstand; it's not your sheep, it's–"

"Dà, shut up!" Xiǎoláng wanted to exclude the shepherd from the conversation. "Come over here."

The two women moved away and whispered behind their hands. The question was whether or not they had compromised the shepherd enough to keep him silent, whatever the circumstance. They concluded they had.

As the sun was setting, Xiǎoláng, Dàláng, and the shepherd topped the terrace immediately below the cave. Kuàiláng found accepting the shepherd's presence tricky, to say the least. Many words passed between the three that, in normal circumstances, would have been unacceptable. However, there was no going back.

"So…I'm not going to ask your name…you are responsible for this flock now grazing around this cave? Yes?"

Twenty-one: The Boy

"Yes."

"And you have been threatened by Xiǎo and Dà?"

"Yes."

"You are so scared of what your wife might do to you that you will not speak about us?"

"Yes."

"For how long?"

"Sorry?"

"For how long might this pact hold?"

"Forever."

"I don't believe you."

"If you knew my wife, you might believe me. If there's anything as much as a rumour…Well, she'd have my balls! She's a lovely woman, but she wouldn't stand for any…err…nocturnal expeditions."

"Nocturnal expeditions?"

"She would kill me if I went with another woman. These two are telling me they'll let out the news I've raped them. It's simply untrue. But she might believe it. That's my concern. Do you understand?"

"I do. Xiǎo! Dà! Go away! Leave me with this man. Go!"

The two sloped away, worried they had broken the rules but hopeful they may have brought Kuàiláng a solution.

"Shepherd…what is your name…it's pissing me off to call you shepherd?"

"Jǐ."

"Jǐ. Is that right? Jǐ. Well, this isn't easy. They gave you choices, yes?" The man nodded. "Death, blackmail, or cooperation. Yes?"

"More or less."

"I'm going to give you the same choice. Don't worry; I'm the boss; you'll not have two opportunities to die!" Kuàiláng adopted a sweet smile to disarm him; it did not work.

"Yes?"

"Yes. We have a problem, and you have a problem. We can solve your problem. The question is, can you solve ours?"

"I don't have to have sex with the three of you; please don't make me do that!"

Hùtóu Mountain Cave, above Èrlǐtou, Hénán

"No!" Kuàiláng laughed out loud, "There's no chance of that! We have to perform a castration."

"On me!"

"Stop being stupid."

"On whom?"

"Well…it's not a sheep."

"And it is…?"

"A boy. The only questions are whether you can do it and–"

"And if I can keep my mouth shut? Correct?"

"Correct."

"That's not going to work if you want me to bite his knackers off, is it?" The shepherd smiled for the first time.

Twenty-two: The Homicide

Hóngshí Gorge, below Yúntāi Mountain, Hénán
Year 101. Year of the Pig
Thirty-seven days after the spring equinox
7th May 1894 BCE

It had been a convoluted process. Duping Fēngbō had been easy enough, but arranging to accompany him was quite another. Tú breathed in deeply as she led her pony down the pebbly riverbed, which opened onto the plains of Hénán. Following a few steps behind was her enthusiastic, although somewhat nervous, son. They were both dressed to travel. Behind her loomed Yúntāi Mountain, towering over the Hóngshí Gorge, where she had left her husband. Everything was down to the Wolf Pack now; if they failed, she and Yùtù would be exposed and would have to go to ground. That was an undesirable option to any of those involved in the plot. She put the thought behind her. In one smooth movement, she mounted her horse, kicking it into a trot on a southbound course. Yùtù copied her. It would be two days before they reached the mountains around Èrlǐtou, the town destined to become their home for a few years.

Tú had seen Dàláng and Xiǎoláng briefly as she descended and they climbed. A few words sufficed because the set-up was flawless as far as she was concerned. Fēngbō was in position and alone; it should be enough.

Higher up, Fēngbō perched, dangling his legs over the ledge, whittling bark from a stick. The pieces fell the height of ten men before fetching up on the rocks below. It was a relief to be out of Ānyáng. It was a relief to be alone for a while. Below him, the waters of the Hóngshí River gurgled across and splattered the smooth rocks lining its course. He felt the last three days had gone well. During the daylight hours, Yùtù had done some growing up, and at night, Tú had been more than usually

Hóngshí Gorge, below Yúntāi Mountain, Hénán

attentive. As far as he was concerned, they were now safely on their way back to Ānyáng. His armed guard would pick them up as they turned northbound.

If the Ānyáng monarch had anything troubling him, it was in trying to understand why Túshānshì would wish to meet him here. He understood it could not be Èrlǐtou and understood why his hometown was impractical, with Tú likely to disrupt the intended tryst. He looked around. It was a beautiful, secluded spot.

Fēngbō had become particularly fond of his stepson. He wondered idly if Tú had produced a son by him, would he be as keen on Yùtù? Discarding the thought, he focussed again on how he had brought Tú's son to manhood. It had taken years of coaching, culminating in the killing spree in the last few days. Teaching the boy to hurt people was something that had occurred in Ānyáng. He had been more subtle about torture and had taken regular trips with the boy into isolated areas, where screams would go unheard and the dead would go unnoticed. It was here, though, that Yùtù had first killed.

They had started with smaller animals. It could have been called hunting, but Fēngbō and Yùtù were so comprehensive that it became a slaughter of the wildlife. Nor were they interested in swiftly dispatching their game. The longer the prey suffered, the better. The king wanted his stepson to observe their pain, feel their fear and enjoy their deaths. On the second day, they had progressed to the more dangerous species, taking down a brown bear and a wild boar. It proved less satisfying for Fēngbō, for their violent behaviour when wounded was such that it was necessary to end their lives before Yùtù had time to play with them in their agonies.

It was on the third day that Yùtù killed his first human. They had brought the other boy with them; a street kid picked from the dozens in Ānyáng by Tú. Ostensibly, he provided the prince with a sparring partner, a role he had performed well. Fēngbō never learned his name. With the promise of a rich reward, the lad had easily slipped into the part where he had to put up good fights without seriously damaging the heir apparent. It might have been somewhat different if he had known his own demise was likely.

The two boys were of equal height and weight. Yùtù had the advantage of classical training with the right arms, whereas the street kid

Twenty-two: The Homicide

had skills honed to perfection in his desperate life, where dangers lurked around every corner. The stranger was an intelligent lad, though, and now ensured he held back when he could go for a kill. The rewards on offer were far more important to him than besting Yùtù.

On that third day, their usual training took place. As the boys sat gasping under an old tree, Fēngbō pulled out a rope, grabbed his stepson and began to bind him. The urchin watched in astonishment as Yùtù was firmly tied and secured to the trunk.

"Now, boy, I want you to pick up that knife and jab it into the tree, as close to my boy's flesh as you can. Have you got that? Don't touch him, though. This is to practice not flinching. Yùtù. Do not move. If you move, he'll cut you. Go!"

"You really want me to do this?" the boy asked, somewhat plaintively.

"I do! Go!"

Hesitantly at first but gaining confidence, the boy pricked the bark around a terrified Yùtù. Thump, thump, thump!

"Harder. Harder and faster! Now!" The order barked out. The prince screamed as the blade grazed his flesh. "Enough!" Fēngbō put an arm out to hold the boy back before untying his stepson. "Now. Now we change it around. Yùtù, now your hands are free, take the remainder of those bindings off. When you've done that, tie this boy up as I tied you. I'm off for some water."

Left alone, the two boys comfortably changed positions, with Yùtù tightening the ropes around the street kid's feet and drawing his arms tightly to the tree. When Fēngbō returned, the boy was immobile; even so, the king checked the bindings.

"Right! Now, we'll repeat the exercise. Yùtù, attack!" The prince responded by placing a few well-aimed thrusts around the static form. "Stop! Now. Now the rules change." Fēngbō smiled. "So far, you've stabbed a thumb's width outside him. Now let's go for a thumb's width inside."

Neither boy understood immediately. Within seconds, however, the street kid began to squirm. Within a few more, Yùtù's face wore a look of shock. It was only after a few deep breaths a cruel smile began to

Hóngshí Gorge, below Yúntāi Mountain, Hénán

form. "You mean I can stab him? Like we did with the rabbit after we broke its back. Really?"

The king nodded. "You may."

"You hurt me." Yùtù moved closer so that his eyes met those of the bound boy. "You hurt me, and you must know I'm going to hurt you!" The thrusts were more violent now, much harder, and more accurate. Each tore into the boy's flesh, but they were only flesh wounds.

"Stand back, Yùtù. Come here; let's talk about this." Fēngbō took his stepson by the hand and led him twenty paces away. "Are you enjoying yourself?"

"Yes."

"Do you want to hurt him more?"

"Yes."

"Then, think about it. You want to hurt him more, but you can only hurt him more if he's alive, can't you?"

"Yes."

"So, think about the rabbit, the pigeon, and that small deer. How did we keep them alive while you cut them up?"

"We made sure the wounds did not compromise their lives."

"Well done! So, here's the test. How long can you keep that boy suffering? Till noon, until it's time for dinner, until tomorrow. How long?"

It turned out that Yùtù's first murder took longer than it would to skin, gut, and butcher a bullock. It was a long and painful death. When the end was near, the king encouraged his stepson to try to extract an apology from the street kid; none was forthcoming. Yùtù took the opportunity to place the point of his dagger under the boy's ribcage, holding it for a moment before exploding his blade upwards into his heart.

Fēngbō cut himself. His concentration on the whittled stick had not been what it should be. The murder, execution, call it what you will, was done and dusted. The boy's body lay nearby; the king had no intention of burying it. Yùtù and Tú had left. The lad had a good soaking in the river to wash the blood off.

There was a rustling on the path. It was too early for it to be Túshānshì; if it were her, she would have bumped into Tú on her ascent, which would not have been helpful at all. He concluded it must be another bear and began to rise.

Twenty-two: The Homicide

His assumption may as well have been correct in effect, although he had the wrong species. Due to a minor navigational error, Xiǎoláng blundered into the grove. Meeting Fēngbō, there and then, was as unexpected for her as it was for him. The first thought that crossed her mind was to ensure that Dàláng did not break cover; that was essential, and she had to warn her.

"Ah! King Fēngbō. How nice to meet you!" She was as loud as it was possible to be without appearing out of the normal.

"Who the fuck are you? Wait. I've seen you before, in Ānyáng, with Tú. Has she sent you?"

"No!" Xiǎoláng looked around and spotted the boy's broken body. "You know, if you leave that there much longer, you're going to be joined by all sorts of wildlife, some of which might just eat you." She smiled.

"What? You'll be joining that boy if you don't start explaining what you're doing here." Fēngbō had become more accustomed to speaking to females, but he did expect a degree of deference. He felt for his weapons, but they were lying several paces away; there was only the short dagger handy with which he had been carving the wood.

"And you would be using what to dispose of me?" Xiǎoláng smiled again, this time tossing her *bàng*[23] from hand to hand, distracting the king somewhat as she watched Dàláng creep through the undergrowth to his left. Xiǎoláng took two steps closer, for more was needed as a distraction. "That little toy you have in your right hand. Look at me. I could use that as a toothpick!"

Fēngbō was very aware that his position was far from secure. He had some confidence that his fighting abilities would be more than a match for the woman, but he could be in trouble if she knew how to use that bang. As the woman closed, he could fully understand that she had other advantages over him: her height was impressive. It was time to talk.

"I think you'll find that we can come to some agreement. I have food and drink over there if you need it. You look thirsty. It's a thirsty climb up that gorge in the sun."

"No. I'm not thirsty." Xiǎoláng kept her eyes glued on his, but at the same time, noticed that Dàláng was almost directly behind him. She

---

[23] A Chinese quarterstaff.

Hóngshí Gorge, below Yúntāi Mountain, Hénán

considered what move she could make to force him to step back. Her *bang* was a heavy stick fashioned from red oak. It was a weapon anyone would wish to avoid having contact with in a fast hit. She needed to make it work with a single blow. He would think of moving back and then forward as the staff's arc passed by him. "But I am hungry!" She shouted. With Dàláng now in position and slightly to the left, she slid both hands towards one end of the *bang*, then raised it over her right shoulder, making it evident to him from which direction the blow was coming.

Fēngbō crouched slightly, ready to defend before launching an immediate attack; he had read the situation perfectly. She could only swing one way from her position, and he primed himself to counterattack the move.

"Any last words?" Xiǎoláng asked before bringing the *bang* down at full force in a wide-sweeping right-to-left arc aimed at his chest.

The king's timing was perfect; however, his judgement was faulty. He stepped back with only a hand's breadth separating the oak from his body. As he moved, his right leg encountered Dàláng, who made matters worse by rolling away.

Both women enjoyed the sight of Fēngbō teetering on the cliff edge. Nothing would stop his fall, but every muscle, every one of the tendons in his body, was trying to prevent the drop. There was a sudden whirling of arms as gravity finally took command, and the king attempted to support his weight in thin air. The women were not fast enough to see him land, but from the mangled position of the body, it was clear he had broken his neck.

"Thank you, Dà. Perfect. I would probably have had him, though."

"Not with that shot, Xiǎo. He would have been back at you."

"I changed the shot when I saw where you were, silly!"

"You know, all that planning, all Kuài's work, and we end up getting him almost by accident."

"It's true, Dà, we make a good team." They embraced. "You know, it seems to make up for knocking off the two women; I feel good about this one."

"That's right, it does. Have you seen that boy, though? We'll have a hard time making it look like he died in a fall. He looks like a pincushion.

Twenty-two: The Homicide

We can smash his face up as planned; that'll make him look like he was Yùtù, but how will they explain the wounds?"

"I don't think it matters, Dà. These guys are always fighting. They fight strangers, they fight friends, and they fight family. It'll probably be explained away as a family tiff. Our job remains the same. Smash the boy's face, tip him over the edge, and throw both bodies into the river. Fish, birds or animals will likely gnaw at their corpses anyway."

"I guess what they find and how they find it doesn't matter then. If Fēngbō's recognisable, they'll assume that it's Yùtù. What I'm left wondering is how Tú can explain her disappearance. We better get done here quickly and catch up with her."

The two women set to work quickly and efficiently. They were done as the sun dropped below the mountains to the west. Apart from the facial rearrangement, they treated the boy's body with as much respect as possible. For Fēngbō's corpse, there was none.

They would rest the night before making a speedy journey southbound.

Hùtóu Mountain Cave, above Èrlĭtou, Hénán

Twenty-three: The Youth

Hùtóu Mountain Cave, above Èrlĭtou, Hénán
Year 101. Year of the Pig
Forty days after the spring equinox
10th May 1894 BCE

"When this is all done, you'll see a new moon emerging. Let these few days slip by, and forget the pain. This is your chance to rule. There will only be one. Are you listening?"

Yùtù was spending his time examining Kuàiláng's breasts as she bent over him and had little interest in focusing on his mother's advice. The stirrings in his groin were intense as this strange and slightly bizarre woman scored charcoal down his face. His fascination grew as he lifted his head slightly to glance inside her smock at her nipples. The reward was a hard, cold slap across his face.

"Ow! That hurt! I killed the last person who hurt me!"

"Just try it! I'll hurt you more if you keep trying to look down my top. This is not being done for fun. This is your future. This is not the time to try and get off on a pair of tits." Kuàiláng was becoming exasperated with the youth. He was unfocused and self-obsessed. They were not traits she found endearing, and the boy himself left so much to be desired her list was endless. Why should this miserable specimen be thought of as suitable for leadership?

"Tú, get your boy to behave, will you?"

"He's a teenage boy; what do you expect? Cover yourself up, and he'll be more acquiescent. It's just the way they are!"

"The last one I dealt with didn't have this sort of problem."

"Maybe not, but this boy will get a hard-on with just a glimpse of female flesh. There's nothing I can do about that!

Twenty-three: The Youth

"Right! I'm going." Tú rose to leave, "He's in your hands now. Just bring him through alive, and - just in case you're thinking of any additional form of unusual punishment - we need him alive and fertile! Certainly not dead like my dear husband. I'll be back in two days to take a look."

Tú left without looking at her son, who seemed more compliant once his mother had left.

"I'm looking forward to the next bit," Kuàiláng whispered to herself and smirked at the thought. "It'll maybe get his dick to lie down as well." She completed her work with the charcoal. She had drawn a precise target across the lower half of the boy's nose. It would be Dàláng who must hit him.

"Now, go outside, have a piss or whatever you must do, and come back shortly." The boy heeded Kuàiláng's instruction, this time without objection. He must have been primed and calmed for this event, even if he did not appear well-prepared for behaving in a socially acceptable manner in life.

If Kuàiláng had doubts about dealing with Qí, she had none regarding Yùtù's transformation. The boy was obnoxious, and his mother did little to control his unpleasantness. She had shared her thoughts with Xiǎoláng and Dàláng, and they had all concluded that they would accidentally forget both the relaxants of the devil's trumpet and any painkillers they had.

It had been so different with the childlike Qí. Ultimately, the shepherd had baulked at performing the procedure himself, although he had remained present. The three women had drawn lots as to who would castrate the child and then did so as delicately and carefully as possible. The wound was left to drain, a fine cloth keeping flies at bay and Xiǎoláng administering regular small doses from her devil's trumpet flowers to ease the boy through his pain. Almost a week later, Qí spent time with the shepherd while his wounds healed fully. He was pain-free, appeared in better health than ever, and did not seem to notice his missing glands.

Not one of them had any thoughts about easing Yùtù's pain. Keeping him alive was a priority; making him comfortable was the least of their concerns. If he were unconscious, it would not be through their desire to relieve his agonies but simply to stop him from struggling.

Hùtóu Mountain Cave, above Èrlǐtou, Hénán

Saving Qí was something they had invested in personally; re-arranging Yùtù's face was regarded as a chore, albeit one from which they might derive some pleasure.

Tú appeared to be on a different plane. Fully accepting of the agonies about to be inflicted on her child, it seemed that her knowledge of Túshānshì's death had propelled her into an orbit somewhat different from the one that mere mortals occupied. She had spent nine years occupying Fēngbō's bed and had adopted all the airs and graces one might expect of a queen. Her son seemed little more than a tool for her to propel herself even higher. It was an attitude that every one of the Wolf Pack found more than sickening. If Tú had excused herself for the day of the transformation, it was not to avoid her son's pain, merely to avoid the possibility of dirtying her clothes.

Yùtù returned to the cave. It was hardly moments later that Dàláng's wrapped fist smashed into his nose. The blow floored the boy, although Xiǎoláng caught him before he hit the rough rock below; it was not time for accidental injuries. She laid him on the bed he had risen from a little earlier. The three women positioned themselves to weigh him down and prevent movement. Dàláng straddled him, clamping his head firmly between her thighs before bringing her dagger to his blood-splattered skin.

Dàláng had flattened the boy's nose; he would undoubtedly snore for the remainder of his life. She admired her handiwork before cutting into his flesh. Her knife swept from the top of his right ear to the side of his mouth. It was a deep surface wound that would scar but not do undue harm. With difficulty, she repositioned her knife and dragged a second line, bisecting the first, from his nostril to his earlobe. The boy groaned.

Turning her attention to the other side of his face, Dàláng took one more cut from the outside line of his eyebrow to his earlobe before pausing. "One more, Wolves, where should it be? The charcoal's smudged off." As she spoke, a pair of eyes blinked open, one on either side of the mashed pulp in the centre of his face. They all leaned down harder as the boy began to buck and scream. "Come on! Where?"

"Put a hole in his cheek!"

"And cut his earlobe off!"

Dàláng acted immediately, and Yùtù passed out.

"Dàláng, you did both!" Kuàiláng admonished.

Twenty-three: The Youth

"I slipped! He shouldn't have moved, should he."

"It looks perfect to me," Xiǎoláng grinned, "just perfect!"

When their victim came around, he started to blub. They found it was necessary to drug him so that they could get a little peace. There were no salves on offer, nothing to make the boy feel good, just the knockout drop to prevent him from disturbing their sleep. If he were going to act like a pig, then they would treat him like one. Dàláng offered several times to kill him and put them all out of their misery, but Kuàiláng held firm.

"He lives! There's nothing to be gained from killing him and much to be lost. I will confess, the operation we performed on young Qí was necessary and tough, but if we had to do the same to this boy, I'd not be bothered at all."

"Why not?" All three women turned as Tú entered the cave. "To be honest with you, I've harboured thoughts of murdering him for years. I never went through with it. I cannot kill him, and you cannot because the Sisterhood wants his seed. My only personal concern is as regards my position. If he reproduces earlier, it doesn't matter if he dies. I'll be the emperor's great aunt instead of the emperor's aunt; it's not something I'm worried about. If he lives long enough to reproduce legitimately, then I'll be set to live the good life. That's all! I came back because I had a moment of enlightenment that made me think I needed to protect his balls! I was right!

"You've made some pretty patterns on his face! It's a good job he'll attract a mate due to his position because he won't do so with his looks. Well done! I suppose my job is confined to making him look a little taller!"

"You're not bothered about what we've done…only bothered if we castrate him? Look at him. He's your son!" Dàláng was struggling with Tú's coldness.

"What do you want for your son? A happy home, a loving father, and security. My son has known none of these and probably never will. Anyway, he's an objectionable shit. As to whether I care, well, I'm unsure. Perhaps not. I've learned to care about myself."

"It's not just his height you need to worry about; it's his voice. And there's the timing. To cover your tracks, the news of his return to

Hùtóu Mountain Cave, above Èrlǐtou, Hénán

Èrlǐtou will need to reach Ānyáng, and then you need to add a week for the journey. You'll have to spend your time here in this cave."

"I was born and brought up in a cave…I'll cope. When you allow him to return to consciousness or pass him as fit enough, get him into Èrlǐtou. It is only then that I'll continue his training. Remember, he's not going to become emperor until he's fourteen. That's the plan."

"I do not understand the plan," Kuàiláng surprised her two colleagues. "I do not understand why we want an emperor. I do not understand why it should be him, and I certainly do not understand you."

"Then there's a lot you don't understand. Just as I do not understand very much, I only know that this is what the Sisterhood wanted. All I know is what I had to go through. All I know is that I've followed my instructions as best as I possibly could. That meant allowing myself to be impregnated by Yú and then bedded by Fēngbō for all these years. And each of those acts was to ensure that he…" she pointed directly at her son "…that he was born and raised in safety!" Each of the Wolf Pack looked surprised. "Yes…you thought that was my idea…it was not. Never! Just like my mother followed instructions, so did I, and it was all to do with getting that little shit," she pointed at her son again, "into the position he's going to be in a few years!

"So do not think you are the only ones who follow orders. Do not think the hand of the Sisterhood will not take you in directions you would prefer not to go. What you should remember is that the reason we all got into this mess is that it was Túshānshì who failed to follow instructions when she fell pregnant with Qí. By her own brother, no less!

"So…our jobs are to clean up the mess she made. Our jobs have been to get our hands dirty, simply because she could not bear the thought of my having a baby and her not. That's what it comes down to. You may not like me, and you may not like my son. In fact, I do not like my son. But it is what it is: we followed our instructions at the end of the day.

"I believe, Kuài, that you are now the Sisterhood. This mess was not of your creation. However, I think you will now have to keep things in check. Until that is, you pass the job on. Now, ask yourself a question. Have the actions of the Sisterhood in our lifetimes, or even my mother's, been consistent with their stated objective? They were supposed to assist the plight of women whom men were subjugating! Have they? It seems to

Twenty-three: The Youth

me that there may have been a temporary improvement but in Èrlĭtou alone. Their aims are supposed to be long-term and widespread. With an emperor in Èrlĭtou running the Xià Empire, well, I see this lasting no more than a couple of generations before we see the return of the Lóngshān social systems.

"For me...for me, it's almost over. Three more years to do what I am told to do. When that is over, I'll tell you, when those three years are over, I will sit back and enjoy whatever benefits I can. There'll be no more orders followed then.

"So...for the time being...don't touch this boy's balls, and don't let him die. You satisfied your blood craving on Fēngbō. Now, you must follow your instructions, as I have for my whole life!" With a flourish, Tú rose and stormed out.

"It seems we may just have acquired ourselves another assassination target. Three years will pass quickly." Kuàiláng smiled at her comrades, whose jaws were only now coming off the floor. "Meanwhile, you two have a little job to do up in Ānyáng. It's time to go!"

*

A week later, Yùtù turned up at the ford across the Luòhé River. The boy had been given an additional roughing up by Dàláng that morning. He had been without food and water for a full day and night. He was on his hands and knees when found and rushed into the guardhouse. No one made any connection between Qí's disappearance and the discovery of a beaten youth at the riverside.

It was more than convenient that Háng was supervising building work on his new bar, which was nearby. With inordinate haste, he took it upon himself to visit the stranger lying in the guardhouse bed. It seemed only moments before he had satisfied himself with the youth's identity, pointing to a tiny bluish scar behind the ear. The news that Qí was alive spread like wildfire, and the tales of his injuries compounded daily.

Háng insisted on keeping the recovering Qí isolated for days. It was becoming something of a struggle; Bóyì and Jīngfēi were asking to see the boy. It was fortuitous, therefore, that another piece of news hit

Hùtóu Mountain Cave, above Èrlǐtou, Hénán

town. It seemed that in the mountains to the west of Ānyáng, Fēngbō and his son, Yùtù, had been killed. A flash flood had done for them. It was a crisis of state that kept Bóyì, the council leader, from having the time to see the boy. By the time he did, Háng had ensured the whole town had visited the lad and had brought the boy's mourning aunt down from Ānyáng to care for him.

With the punishment the boy had received, it was no wonder there were changes in him. There was virtually no suspicion. As a youngster, Túshānshì had always kept him at home. He was hidden from the eyes of those who might realise he was a boy with problems. As Háng pointed out, male development was always a lottery, coming in fits and starts. There were only four people in Èrlǐtou who knew the truth: the boy himself, Tú, Háng and one other.

Tú was taken aback when the barman used their shared confidence with immediate effect. Háng seemed to spend as much time with her and Qí as he did on his business and certainly more than he spent with his secretive wife. In one respect, it was reassuring. He gave regular sound advice and suggestions to Qí on modulating his voice. He had been the one to suggest her son should shout a lot; it seemed to shout blurred accents, making them sound the same. Háng had come up with the idea that talking to people through a screen or a wall would help. This simple step both shielded his features and muffled his voice. Háng pointed out that if he looked right, dressed right, walked right, and said the right things, everyone would think that the changes in his voice and looks were down to his accident.

In truth, Tú realised that the barman had a lever on her. It was a question of how he would choose to use that power. The man had already clarified that Túshānshì had bestowed him with sexual favours. She believed it was only a matter of time before he asked her for the same. It was not something to which she looked forward.

Twenty-four: The Girl
Lājià, Gānsù
Year 101. Year of the Pig
Twenty-six days to the summer solstice
26th May 1894 BCE

"Above anything else, I want to know what that thing in the sky was meant to mean. It was unnatural. It was like a frozen shooting star. It did not make me comfortable at all, and now, where's it gone?" Yú pulled at the strands in his bowl. "The other question I have is a bit more mundane. What are these?"

"They're *miàn tiáo*[24]. What did you think they were?"

"I didn't know; I've not seen them before. What are they made of?"

"Millet, silly! These are a mixture of foxtail and broomtail millet. Have you never eaten noodles?" The woman eyed Yú suspiciously as he stirred the eating bowl with his finger, withdrawing it when it became too hot. "Use a stick, silly; that's what they're for, to stop you burning your fingers. When you finish, you can drink the broth from the bowl."

Yú followed her advice, enjoying the dish much more once he had the hang of winding the noodles around the stick. Having mastered one art, he promptly managed to burn his throat, trying to gulp down too much of the hot liquid.

He planned to end his journey in Lājià. The comet was no longer visible. It seemed pointless trudging further and further west, although it had exposed him to some of the traditions and foodstuffs of the Qijia, the ancestral parents of Kan's Xīwǎ tribes. It seemed to him that the further he moved west, the more primitive it became. Only the *miàn tiáo* indicated

---

[24] Noodles

Lājià, Gānsù

an advance not yet achieved in the Motherland. Most of the homes were hovels, most of the cooking communal, and the destruction wrought on the farming lands was something to behold. Clearly, there had once been organisation and order; now, it reminded him of the state of the Fèn Valley. If Lājià was regarded as the capital of the Qijia culture, Yú had little interest in investigating the lesser settlements.

The town had a mixture of *yaodongs*[25] and post-built houses. The people were still practising human sacrifice, a tradition Yú abhorred. More often than not, they buried their dead, both the sacrifice victims and the natural deaths, underneath their own living spaces. Yú looked at their culture as primitive and found it hard to believe that his friend Kan was descended from such brutish people.

The locals seemed obsessed with fish. All their stories featured river life. The town had a moat fed by waters from the gullies leading down from Dàhóng Mountain. This ditch was regularly stocked with river fish, most of which promptly died due to the extent of the human effluent that went into it. The town stunk. When it did not smell of human shit, it smelled of dead or drying fish.

Yú had avoided the local chieftain. There seemed little point in drawing attention to himself. As far as the locals were concerned, he was just a drifter, happy to do some work in exchange for food and a place to rest up for the night. Yú did not disabuse them.

It had been raining for days, which kept the town a little cleaner and perhaps sweeter smelling than when he arrived. He was taken on to assist in moving materials to prepare to build another dwelling, although the timing was hardly ideal. When the earthquake hit, Yú, unlike most townspeople, was outside, soaked to the skin, attempting to cover a pile of straw used in constructing the walls. He was lucky. The force of the ground's shaking was immense, throwing Yú aerially and sideways; he was fortunate the straw broke his fall. As he scrambled up, he was knocked off his feet again.

While the ground moved in seemingly random waves, there was rumbling, cracking, and the thump of heavy walls falling, which went on

---

[25] Improved cave dwellings.

Twenty-four: The Girl

and on. Yú was a brave man, but he was frightened to the core. As the nearest building collapsed in on itself, the juddering and swaying halted.

Then the screaming commenced, or at least, it could now be heard. Yú regained his feet and darted for the closest standing building. Two wailing children huddled inside the door. As he pulled them out, he cast his eye into the dust-filled room only to realise that it no longer existed. The children's family would have been crushed if they had been there. Ushering the pair to the safety of a clearing, Yú entered a second building from which screams emitted. A young woman lay, seemingly unharmed, until he saw the heavy beam that had fallen across her thighs. More people were flooding in to help now, so he called over a teenage boy to help lift the roof beam, but she could not crawl out; Yú suspected her back might be broken. The two called for assistance, and soon, they were joined by a third man who grabbed the woman's hand and heaved her free from under the log. She made no sound or movement as he dragged her; they concluded she had died within moments.

What a terrible place to be living. A new sound broke Yú's train of thought. The rescuers and the rescued turned to look northwards; it seemed their woes were not yet over. From the direction of Dàhóng Mountain, a wall of mud was approaching the town. It was the height of a man, bearing with it trees, bushes, parts of walls and the bodies of those unfortunate enough to have already been in its path. The wall of death flowed faster than a man could run.

Yú's instincts took over as self-preservation became paramount. Around him, people scurried into doorways, making futile attempts to shelter from the mudslide that would be on them in moments. To be caught in the open would be foolhardy, but to be trapped where that sludge might pond would mean death by drowning. Yú sprinted downhill, away from the houses and towards the river, as the flow gained on him.

The cave he had occupied for the last few nights had a beautiful south-facing view, taking in the Yellow River and the foothills of the mountains. The spectacular vista could not have been further from his mind as he dived into its entrance. The roar of the mudflow and the crashing of the objects it carried enveloped his senses, although sight would have been useless; inside the cave, it was pitch black.

Yú edged towards the cave's rear, thankful there was only one entrance. He felt for and then chewed on an old piece of *ròugān*, although it may well have been leather. His water flagon proved to have spilt most of its contents, probably during the earthquake, although he may have knocked it over as he entered. There was only enough for a few short sips. He lay back for a few moments as the cacophony began to diminish. By the time he sat back up, there was silence, not quiet, but a silence. No screams, no calls, no shouting. Nothing. The mudslide had passed. What of the people he had been eating with so recently?

The entrance to the cave was blocked. If no sound penetrated, then neither did any light. Would air find its way in? The only real question was how much time he might have; he knew the cave was only a little bigger than he. How long would the air last?

Yú reached around for his staff. It had been fashioned from ash to assist the more precarious parts of his journey once his horse had given up on him. A metre and a half long with a diameter to fit his large grip, the stick would serve as a quarterstaff if required, although for now, he probably needed a battering ram.

Turning in the cramped space proved difficult. It was almost impossible to position the staff to give himself a chance to ram it into whatever mass had blocked the cave entrance. His first attempts only proved he could cause a cave-in, resulting in less space. In the end, he resorted to prodding gently at section after section. It took upwards of thirty thrusts before the staff sailed through a gap, and a pinprick of sunlight slipped in through the peephole. Now was the time for more care.

Even with a newfound light source, visibility inside the cave was minimal, particularly his view of the newly formed wall. It was clear that some of the mass was mud, but it seemed from touch there were also two large boulders. In yet another area, there was the undeniable softness of human flesh. Yú presumed it must be that of someone deceased. Puncturing the seal had not brought in any sounds; it was eerily quiet.

As carefully as possible, Yú worked the hole wider with his fingers. Once the looser mud came out, there was still only room for him to push his arm through, and the remaining material appeared much more resistant. Having determined he would now be able to breathe for as long as it took, he did what he so often did in times of indecision and lay down

Twenty-four: The Girl

again. He was trying to picture the composition of the blockage. Two boulders, for sure, a body and with his arm fully stretched through the hole, he thought he had felt a tree trunk. This last item was strange, for there were few trees within several thousand paces of the town; the hillsides behind it had been stripped over the centuries. Did this mean the mud had travelled a long way?

Yú ultimately concluded that he should use his staff as a lever on the smaller boulder. He took the risk of a collapse, which could trap him for good, but no other option was seemingly available. It was then he heard a faint and distant voice.

"Help me!" hollered Yú.

Closer now, a young girl's frightened scream pierced the air from outside.

"I'm trapped underground!"

"Are you a devil?" Came a small voice.

"No! No devil! Just a man trapped in this cave!"

"My mother said the devils had come," the voice spoke back to him.

"Where is your mother?"

"After she told me she fell asleep."

"Can you see this stick?" asked Yú, pushing his staff back and forth through this newly forged breathing hole.

"Yes."

"Can you tell me what's around it?"

"A hole."

"No. What's around the hole?"

"There's a big tree trunk. It looks like two boulders on top of it and some legs and lots and lots of mud."

"Some legs?"

"Some legs, but I think he must be asleep as well. Funny place to fall asleep."

"If I move one of the boulders, which would go downhill best?"

"The smaller one."

"Why?"

"Because there's a good slope in front of it."

"I can feel two boulders, but I don't know which one is the smaller. Can you tell me?"

"The left one."

"Which one is that?" Yú thought quickly, "Is it the one in the direction of the sunrise or the sunset?"

"Err, the sunset."

"Are you sure?"

"Yes."

"I'm going to move it. Can you move away? Twenty paces away, please."

"Alright."

Yú dug his staff as far under the right-hand boulder as he could and, whispering words of encouragement to himself, began to press his body weight down on the wood. The ash gave only a little, an unexpected outcome, but the boulder did rise. Yú used his feet to kick material under the rock before it could settle back. He repeated the process five times before it was clear the boulder was ready to move under its own weight. Retreating to the back of the cave and now using the staff as a ram, he was about to shove when a nearby voice asked, "Have you done it?"

"Please, please, please. Go back twenty paces. Not downhill! To the side. You'll get killed if you stay this close. Quick!"

"Alright! I'm gone!"

A sustained shove and the boulder ripped away. Yú saw it bounce twice before he was covered by falling debris. As he brushed himself off, he watched the second boulder and tree trunk descend the slope, followed by a shower of smaller rocks and dried mud. In the slide, a body tumbled, seemingly waving to him as it rolled out of view.

"You're not a devil, but you're very dirty!" A small figure watched as Yú dragged himself up; it was only five paces from where he had been lying in the cave. "I'm Lùduān, and I know who you are."

"When we've found your mother, and only then, I will explain to you what twenty paces is." The girl could hardly have been more than ten years old. She was elven-faced, appeared to have pointed ears, and seemed ridiculously precocious. Yú put it down to shock, although he later found she was being her usual self. "And then you can tell me how you know who I am."

Twenty-four: The Girl

"I know exactly what twenty paces is, both yours and mine. The fact is, I chose to ignore you."

"Right. Which direction is your mother in?"

"I don't really believe she's asleep. I think she's dead."

"Well...shall I go and look and come back and tell you?"

"No, it's alright. I've seen dead people before. Every year, at the new year, they sacrifice someone, usually someone my age. It might be me next year. If I'm lucky, that is."

"If you're lucky?"

"Yes. You should try living here. It's horrible."

"You lived somewhere else before?" Yú was trying to put the girl at ease as they struggled through the debris that had engulfed the town. There were clear no-go areas where the liquid mud appeared treacherous, and several homes seemed to have filled with the flow.

"Yes, in Sānménxiá. That's where I've seen you before. You were different then. They said you were the Xià leader and you wore nice clothes. What happened? I mean, look at you now. You're a mess."

"Well, I could say the same about you. Why did you move here from Sānménxiá?"

"Look! There. There she is!" The girl pointed at a spot thirty paces off, where a woman's head rose from the mud. It was immediately obvious she was dead. There was no need to check, which was fortunate in that getting to her would have been nearly impossible.

"I think we're going to have to leave your mother. I can't get to her, and there's no way she's still alive. You'll have to–"

"It's a shame. She was the best mother I've had. She looked after me really well. I liked her a lot."

"You've had several mothers?"

"Yes. Not everyone has had several mothers. I've been lucky."

"I only ever had one."

"Poor you!" The girl smiled up at him sympathetically.

Lājià, Gānsù

Twenty-five: The Mute
Lājià, Gānsù
Year 101. Year of the Pig
Twenty-six days to the summer solstice
26th May 1894 BCE

"Look!" Yú spotted movement in the mud swept up against one of the homes. "Lùduān, we've got to be careful now, but we'll try and save that person. Look around for a stick or a rope, please."

"Here." She found the end of a twine rope poking from the mud, almost where she stood. Trying to pull it out proved beyond her; Yú took over. She smiled up at him once more, "You're strong. I like you!" The rope snaked out as he pulled arm over arm until he had enough to throw one end towards the movement. It was impossible to say if it was a man or a woman. Lùduān's attention shifted to the object of their rescue attempt.

"Why aren't you speaking?" The figure waved back, but there was still no sound. "It's Xīwángmǔ! She cannot speak. They cut out her tongue. And she's having a baby! She's ever so nice!"

"If you talk to her, that would be best," Yú whispered to his young companion. "Tell her to grab the rope and twist it around her shoulders."

Lùduān complied, and the silent woman followed her instructions. Yú took the strain and began to edge backwards. Initially, there was little result other than her face contorting with pain. Eventually, Yú's exertions began to overcome the suction of the mud, and gradually, she rotated so that her back was towards them. The girl joined him, tugging on the rope, and suddenly, the greasy shape came free, sliding towards them. Both rescuers fell backwards as the force was released. However, the battle was not over; the object of their rescue attempt began sinking again, although this time a little closer to them. It required continual effort to keep her head above the surface. When they had her onto the ankle-deep mud, Yú straddled her waist, cleared dirt from her mouth and eyes, and tested for a breath. Within moments, it was clear her

Twenty-five: The Mute

diaphragm was jerking. He eased his weight off her just in time to avoid the mix of vomit, blood and mud that gushed from her mouth.

"I thought you said she was pregnant." Yú spoke quietly to Lùduān, "She doesn't look pregnant to me."

"Oh, she is. Just not very pregnant. Two weeks, maybe."

"How do you know that? It's not–"

"Shush! I said she could not speak - I did not say she was deaf. That's so rude! Look, she's coming around. Hold her head and tip her on her side."

"I'm doing that. How do you know so much? It's..." Yú was lost for words and needed time to attend to the stricken woman rather than continue conversing with a child. "Look, be careful, but go and see if you can find anyone else who needs help. Go! Be careful!"

Lùduān raced off, sticking to areas with a solid footing while Yú turned his attention to his patient. The woman appeared to be unhurt, or at least as unhurt as someone could be who had been stuck in neck-deep mud. He carefully slid his hands over her arms, legs, and shoulders, but when he reached for her waist, the woman's eyes opened wide instantly, and he received a cuff around the side of the head. He smiled ruefully; the female was in better shape than he had thought. He offered her his arm to assist her in sitting up, which she accepted, although not perhaps as graciously as he had expected.

"Lùduān told me you were called Xīwángmǔ; is that right?" The woman nodded in assent. "She said you could not speak, is that right?" She nodded again. "I was touching you to check if you had broken bones. I had checked your legs, arms, and shoulders; I was trying to check your ribs. Do you want me to check?"

This time, Xīwángmǔ nodded more carefully and held a single finger up at Yú, waving it from side to side. He was not clear what she expected of him. "I'll check your head first." Yú ran his hands around her skull, "Good! Now, the ribs on your back." He dragged his fingers quite forcefully down either side of her back, "Now–"

The woman's finger was up again, and she motioned for Yú to stand and haul her upright. Once he had done so, she covered both her breasts and lifted them before nodding.

"I see. You want me to…" Yú quickly ran his hands down the ribs below her raised breasts. "You're fine. Do you need food?" She shook her head. "Water?" This time, her response was more pronounced; she was thirsty. "We need to get you some clothes as well." She shook her head and indicated with a drinking motion that water was her only priority.

Just then, Lùduān reappeared. She had cleaned herself up a bit, and her smock was wet through.

"Where did you find water, Lù?"

"Don't call me Lù. I don't like it."

"Lùduān, please take Xī and me to the water."

"Xīwángmǔ probably doesn't like being called Xī either!"

"Please, Lùduān, she needs water; she probably doesn't care if she's called *xī, dōng, nán* or *běi*;[26] we need water. Where is it?"

"Well…you should follow me!"

Yú offered Xīwángmǔ his arm, which was gratefully accepted, as they followed the youngster across the town.

The devastation was absolute. There were now a few individuals staggering around. Some were digging with their hands in pools of wet mud. Desperation seemed to have silenced all. Only one spoke to them as they passed, and his only offering was the word, "Why?"

Lùduān led them to a spot where seemingly fresh water was bubbling from the ground. Yú was doubtful, but Xīwángmǔ threw herself into the pool it had formed and almost inhaled the liquid. A little more cautiously, Yú followed her example. It tasted clean, although he had his doubts; however, any longer without rehydrating, he would begin to flag.

"There are some women stuck in this house here," exclaimed Lùduān, "Can we help them as well?"

Yú lifted himself from the ground, feeling refreshed but uncertain about commencing another tug-of-war with the glutinous mud. "Let's see."

She led him over to an open doorway. At least the top half was open; mud blocked the lower, which appeared to have pooled within the

---

[26] West, east, south, or north.

Twenty-five: The Mute

home. An older female arms outspread, cut through the surface of the sludge, which extended up to her armpits. She was weak but conscious.

"We'll try and get you out," Yú reassured her. "Lùduān, would you fetch the rope we used, please?" The girl skipped off as Yú approached the woman as closely as he considered safe.

"I don't think…you'll get me…out," the woman spoke with short, sharp breaths, "My legs…trapped. I'm stuck hard, but my family are inside. Can you see them? There's twelve of them. Some might be alive. Can you save them?"

"We'll see if we can get you out when the rope comes. I'll check if I can. Is there a window?"

"Other side…south side…high on the wall…window."

"Wait." Yú raised himself again and skirted the mud pool to circle the home. There was a window. It was blocked; two pairs of arms and one head were visible. It seemed two of the family had tried to escape. He had to conclude that the remainder were buried inside, their only exit blocked by the bodies. When he returned, Lùduān had readied the rope, but the woman was having even more difficulty breathing.

Yú determined it was not the time to announce her family had been wiped out, "We'll try for the others when we've got you out. Try to catch this." He tied a loop in the rope and tossed it toward her. It fell neatly around her. "Get your arms through the rope. That's it. Now, hands on the line and hold tight!" Yú carefully took the strain and began to pull. As he did so, the woman's mouth widened in horror before she screamed, and with an awful finality, her head lolled onto her left cheek and began to submerge. If she were not dead, she would be very soon. There was no give on the rope; she had become wedged. A single bubble appeared as her mouth and nose disappeared into the mire. Yú hoped she had died before she drowned.

"It's sad," Lùduān whispered.

"What's sadder is that everyone in this house must be dead. Did you see any others with people calling out?"

Xīwángmǔ had come over and was urgently tapping Yú's shoulder with her right hand whilst signalling to Lùduān with her left. "What is it?" Yú asked. It was apparent that the two females had a communication system, although it was one he failed to grasp.

Lājià, Gānsù

She says we should go to the house around the corner; some are alive, and it might be possible to save them."

"Tell her to take me. You find something to cut that rope. Don't get into the deep mud. We don't need to be saving you as well. Join us when you have it."

"You can be so rude sometimes! Do this, don't do that! I'm not stupid, and I'm not deaf! And, you should say please!"

As Yú departed with Xīwángmǔ, he threw the word over his shoulder, "Please!" before hurrying on.

The scene awaiting them had a forbidding similarity. This time, two were trapped, and both were very much alive. Yú wondered momentarily where all the men were, and then he realised they had all been at a drinking party under the awnings in the gully. He tried to put the vision from his mind; there was little doubt of their fate, and he had only missed it by a whisker. One of the tribe's warriors had been trying to draw him into a fight, something he had desperately wished to avoid, which was why he had continued to work in the rain. It had not been a happy town.

The pair were far more vocal than his previous encounter, and whilst distraught, they were alive, if not kicking. Both had become wedged in the doorway and from behind them came the sound of another, clearly conscious, although little light had penetrated the last remaining gap. Yú could not ascertain whether the voice was male or female. When Lùduān eventually arrived with the rope, Yú quickly fixed another lasso before casting it to the closest of the two women. She struggled momentarily but set it around her and under her armpits. There was a satisfying 'glug' as her form rose, followed by a screech as she scraped across unknown debris as he hauled her in. Behind her, the second woman panicked; removing one body had caused her to sink further. The task became more difficult.

"Lùduān, take this lady to the water…please! Then come back as soon as you can. "Xī, I'll need your help; be ready to pull. Is that alright?" Having received a nodded response, he opened the lasso wide once more and cast it perfectly over the second woman. Only one of her arms was free, and the process of bringing the rope tight around her was forcing her head further into the slime.

Twenty-five: The Mute

"Go on, pull it on!" Yú's encouragement was kind enough, but the woman was in grave danger of drowning in her efforts. Finally, she forced her left arm out of the mud and through the loop. "Ready?"

"Yes! Pull!" Yú took the strain as Xīwángmǔ joined him in hauling, "Keep going! Please, pull!" The woman was desperate, desperate enough to live. There was a moment when her head dug into the muck, but it rose again as she gulped for air, and by the time her heaving chest was entirely out, Yú rammed his fingers into her throat to force her to gag.

"This lady says there's a girl in the house and that she's alive." Lùduān had returned with the first woman. "She says you might be able to get through the roof."

Yú hauled his exhausted frame upright once more. "Here, Lùduān, take this lady to the water...please!" He cracked a small smile in the girl's direction before turning to his latest recruit, "Now, you, what's your name, and where's the best place to get through the roof?"

"Dǒng, sir. The best place would be to go to the south side of the building. There's a boulder there, and it gives a step up onto the thatch."

"Come with me, Dǒng. Take me."

She led him around the muddy moat surrounding the house. It was clear that the dip in which the house was sited, added to the sunken floor, had contributed to this disaster. Two sawn trunks had wedged themselves against a boulder, forming a ramp for Yú to ascend. From the height he had gained, it was easy to start ripping off the thatch.

"Careful, sir, we'll need that roof come the wet season."

Yú turned to her in disbelief; no one would be occupying this house again. "I'll try," he reassured her.

The straw and reeds came away readily. Beneath was a fine lattice through which he could punch a hole. With light coming through the top half of the doorway, Yú could make out the absolute devastation. The home had been filled with mud, to the depth of a tall man, but all that remained of the adults were three pairs of hands reaching upwards from the sludge. How they had wedged themselves in such a position was beyond belief, but perched on a short plank, which seemed to hover on the mud's surface, sat a terrified five or six-year-old. She had been precious enough to be saved; all three adults must have agreed to die

Lājià, Gānsù

together in a communal pact to allow her to live. A pair of big dark eyes stared out in desperation at Yú.

"What's your name, *Bǎobǎo*[27]?" The girl just shook her head before tears welled in her eyes. "We're going to get you–"

"Want, *Mama*[28]!" She howled.

Yú pulled his head and shoulders from the hole, turning to Dǒng to ask her to fetch the rope. She returned immediately, asking, "Are others alive in there?"

"There's a girl, maybe five or six years of age. That's it." The woman began to weep herself. "Time to cry later, Dǒng, not now. We've got a girl to save. Give me the rope."

This time, Yú drew a much smaller loop. He had to be accurate and could not afford the girl to overbalance. "Keep still, *Bǎobǎo*; don't move at all. Let the rope fall over you. Do you understand? We don't want you falling into the mud, do we? Will you promise you'll keep still?" The girl looked at him uncertainly, although she dipped her head, indicating she had grasped the idea it might not be ideal to topple.

"Here it comes!" With a restricted throwing angle, it was a miracle that Yú's cast at least encircled one of her arms. "Now, carefully, very carefully, pull it over your head." The girl followed his instructions, but the movement caused her perch to tilt to one side, unbalancing her. "Put your second arm through! Now! Quick!" Whatever else, she knew how to follow instructions. As the plank tilted further, she thrust her arm through the loop just as Yú began to haul it in. The tightening around her chest made her squeal. He had enough height. The girl's feet were in the mud, but nothing more. Wrapping the rope over a rafter, Yú brought her up, hand over hand, until her fingers contacted the roof spar.

"Dǒng, come up here, grab her hands, take her weight and haul her out." Almost instantly, he was joined on his platform, the woman pushing past him to assist the child.

"Here, *Bǎobǎo*, come to Aunty." Her voice was surprisingly low and melodious, "Come - aunty will look after you - come now." She wrapped the youngster in her arms and struggled back to the ground.

---

[27] An endearment for a child.
[28] Mother.

Twenty-five: The Mute

Yú turned southwards and momentarily wondered what had happened to the river; it was missing. Then he fainted.

When he came around, it was pitch black. A small fire smoked the atmosphere; other than that, the darkness was intense. He remembered the girl he had lifted, although a dreamlike quality masked her face. He heard low voices, indistinct but close. He felt the wet cloth on his forehead and warm breath on his face. For a moment, he thought he might be back home in Èrlǐtou with Túshānshì tending him. As the horror of that thought sunk into his consciousness, he came awake with a start.

"Where am I?"

A hand pressed to his chest gently, with little real pressure, just enough to be comforting. Someone moved away, and another took her place.

"Xīwángmǔ tells me you're going to be fine. She says you must sleep. We are all safe. In the morning you will have food. Xīwángmǔ tells me you are going to take us away from this place. It makes me happy. You might be very, very rude, but you're a good man. Thank you for saving the others. We could find no one else to save."

"What about your mother?" Yú whispered.

"It's alright. I have another one now. Go to sleep."

Èrlĭtou, Hénán

Twenty-six: The Election
Èrlĭtou, Hénán
Year 101. Year of the Pig
Eleven days before the summer solstice
10th June 1894 BCE

It was somewhat unexpected that the vote came down so heavily in his favour. Bóyì was delighted that he had all the council members, bar one, backing him for office. However, it was not a position he had ever aspired to, nor one with which he felt comfortable. He had understood and entirely accepted Yú's desire for him to step in as a substitute when he had left. Still, he was flummoxed as to why the council had now voted for him, although they were presumably following the wishes of the people they represented.

He had almost laughed at the swearing-in ceremony when they had undergone the same rituals as in previous years. They offered him the role of lifetime leader and the opportunity to wear yellow, just as they had asked Yú. He wondered what would have transpired if he had accepted, although they had obviously expected him to decline.

Jīngfēi had encouraged him to stand down before the vote. What she disliked most were the hangers-on, the people always after something. She often commented on how difficult Yú must have found it. She knew that Bóyì had been happy with the army leadership; his happiness had declined since his promotion.

One of the sycophants was Háng. It was fortunate that both Bóyì and Jīngfēi had a soft spot for the barman because he was one of the most persistent and nagging citizens of the town. It had been twelve years since they first sat together in Háng's bar in Táosì, and for all the irritation he provided, they still regarded him as a totem of their relationship. In return, Háng had always been kindly to them both. He had gone out of his way

Twenty-six: The Election

to express his support for Bóyì during the election. They would have been thoroughly alarmed if they had seen how many strings he had pulled.

Háng, for his part, knew he could not control Bóyì, neither directly nor through Jīngfēi. However, he believed he could predict the new council leader's actions and knew the opportunity to discuss his favourite topics would always be there. In effect, Bóyì won the election because Háng wanted him to, and Háng wanted him to be appointed because he regarded him as the best choice as a temporary leader. It would also be easy to get Bóyì to stand down when the time came. The barman had been taken somewhat by surprise at how quickly the events of the winter had unfolded; the last thing he had expected was for Yú to go so soon. He knew he had two years, but in the next election, he would need to shore up Bóyì again and yet crush him the following year. Life was not going to be easy.

Bóyì had been required to deal with the fallout from Fēngbō's death while he was still only acting council leader. One of his mantras was always to consider what Yú would have done and do precisely the same. Keeping Ānyáng out of the empire was not Háng's choice would have preferred, but Bóyì held out. The barman would have to wait.

When visiting Ānyáng, Bóyì had hoped for advice from Líng, but she had gone, leaving no information as to her whereabouts. If it still existed, it seemed the Sisterhood had gone underground; there was no obvious way of contacting them.

In this, Bóyì was mistaken. The new Sisterhood had eyes everywhere, but there was no noticeable presence. No one had any idea that the Wolf Pack had responsibility for Fēngbō's death, nor that Yùtù had been nowhere near the scene. Two mangled bodies with ripped and filthy clothes had all convinced the king had died with his adopted son.

Bóyì's visit to Ānyáng had been an attempt to stop the town from falling into an anarchical state. To appear acceptable to the Xià, Fēngbō had put in place a council, albeit one with no power and councillors who were incapable of coping with it anyway. Turning up at the head of an army had quietened the expectations of Fēngbō's more senior generals. They could not compete with the force that paraded before them; thus, negotiations commenced. The lack of consensus amongst the generals meant that Bóyì had to shuffle between individual meetings, each with someone who thought he should be in charge. The new Èrlĭtou council leader did not wish to impose an outsider on the town, yet he could find no one suitable from within. It had been an accidental meeting that led to the solution.

Chéng and Cāngbái had been attending to the cats protecting grain stores. Each had produced a litter annually, and from being a protective force, they were beginning to become a nuisance. Cāngbái had perfected a sterilisation technique for the male cats, but the problem would not disappear, as just one male could impregnate as many females as were available. They had been discussing the issue when Bóyì passed by.

"That's a beautiful cat! Lovely spots! Does it bite?" Bóyì had been more than ready for a conversation about almost anything other than the governance of Ānyáng.

"Yes, but not humans! Just rats and mice and sometimes each other." Cāngbái was sitting in the shade whilst Chéng enjoyed the sun.

"Ah! You must be, err, Cāng…Cāngbái! I've heard about you." Bóyì struggled with the name but eventually got it right.

"There's not many who haven't! The white hair and skin are a bit of a giveaway, aren't they!"

"She's a bit of a novelty for strangers," Chéng chimed in, "but everyone in the town loves her, especially me."

"So, you're not just popular with the cats?" Bóyì joked.

"No, people think she's gifted or something, which of course she is, but–"

"Don't you go saying silly things, Chéng; this man doesn't want to know about what you think!"

Bóyì sat down, "Do you know who I am?"

"Sorry, dear, I'm guessing you're with that Èrlĭtou lot," Cāngbái smiled, "Having to deal with our generals, I'm not surprised you need a sit-down!"

"I'm the leader of the Èrlĭtou council, and you're right; after listening to them puffing up their self-importance, I need a sit-down. I'm Bóyì." He held out his hand, first to Chéng and then to Cāngbái.

"Oo! Sorry, my Lord! We did not realise you were important." As Cāngbái spoke, they both struggled to their feet. "This is my husband, Chéng."

Twenty-six: The Election

"Sit down! And please call me Bóyì. My wife would have a laughing fit if she heard you say, 'my Lord'!" The two sat back down but with straighter backs than before.

"Chéng, you said that people think Cāngbái is gifted. What do you mean?"

"Well, some thinks she's a witch, but an extraordinary witch. She never gets ill, she never gets cross, and she's exceptionally intelligent. She's not a witch, but it doesn't stop people from thinking she is. No one dares say a word against her; it's quite funny! She could say black is white, and people would agree! We have a laugh about it sometimes, mainly because she's so white; it would be funny to think of her as black!" Chéng laughed out loud.

"You say no one would speak against her. Does that include the generals?"

"Let's just say she's like their good luck totem. They'd not have anyone touch her, except me, of course, and they'd protect her with their lives."

The discussion had dribbled on, but the upshot had been that when Bóyì and his army left Ānyáng a week later, the town had a new council leader with a two-year tenure. The new leader's prime objective was to get Ānyáng into a condition whereby it could join the Xià empire. That aim coincided with the wishes of the farmers and the generals; everything since indicated that Cāngbái's appointment had been an enormous success.

A success in Ānyáng did not amount to success in Èrlǐtou, where the delay in opening up the north more quickly went down badly. There were also murmurings that taxes in the capital seemed higher than those in the four satellite states. Citizens in Sānménxiá, Dōngxiàféng, Kāifēng and Lǎoniúpō paid for their community systems, whereas those in Èrlǐtou seemed alone in paying for the superstructure of the empire in addition. It amounted to much more of their harvest being taken from them each year. Even if the town were running well, the four appointed commissioners now being firmly established and Hòutú's people doing an excellent job of monitoring everything, there appeared to be more and more underlying dissatisfaction. There was enough food, water, shelter, wood to burn, and warm clothes aplenty, yet there was a distinct feeling that all was not right.

Èrlǐtou, Hénán

Bóyì and Jīngfēi both missed Yú enormously, not just as a leader but as their one true friend, someone they could rely on totally. They fell back on their lunchtime discussions as a solace to events in the town.

"What I do not understand is Háng's role here. It always seems he's in demand by people, yet not so many actually like him." Bóyì knew he was missing something but could not put his finger on it.

"Well, from what I heard today, he's opening yet another bar, this one on the river to the south. Pretty soon, he'll have bars at all the locations with guardhouses. Perhaps he's begun to target the army for new customers." Jīngfēi smiled and passed her husband a jug of beer.

"He had better not be. They've got work to do. They shouldn't be quaffing alcohol on their working days."

"It's not only alcohol, I'm told. It seems he's come to an agreement of some sort with the whores."

"What's that got to do with Háng? They run their own show. They only have a whore's council so they can be represented at the town meetings. They work as loners generally."

"Mmm! They did! It seems Háng is providing them with space to operate, always attached to his bars. The one in the centre now abuts the central meeting place walls."

"There's been no complaints at council…nothing."

"And you wouldn't expect any, would you? Háng's got the council stitched up. If he says jump, they jump."

"I'll have to go down and see for my–"

"You'll not be visiting any whores, Bóyì, council leader or not! That's if you want to come home and find me here! Sometimes, you might have to listen, but you don't have to sample what's on offer! Unless, of course, you want to!" Jīngfēi grinned at her husband. He had been faithful for twelve years, and she had no doubt he would be loyal to her until the day one of them died. After that, she was a little less sure.

"You know I'll not be doing that. Really! But this thing with Háng! No one ever comes to the council with a complaint about him or his activities. Not ever. I mean, the army gets more complaints than he does, and they're always doing good things. Everyone's always complaining about all sorts of things, and not one complaint about Háng."

Twenty-six: The Election

"He's buried himself so deep with Qí; you'd think he was his father. He's there every day, the way some tell it; he's also there most nights. I wonder what his wife thinks about all of it?"

"What?" Bóyì had lost track of the conversation. "We were talking about there being no complaints about Háng, and you think…you think that it's because he's not around?"

"No, he is around, but he's around Yú's son all day, and I'm beginning to wonder if he's sniffing around Tú every night. I'm still trying to work out what happened to that boy. It's as though he had a new brain put in. And he's so rude! He wasn't like that when he was younger."

"Come on, Jīng, the boy lost his father, his mother was going completely mad, she's killed, the boy's kidnapped, he's cut up and beaten up, and he's left for dead…something like that is going to change a boy."

"There's change, and there's change! There's a change for the good and a change for the bad. He may always have been a slow, difficult boy, but at least he was polite. You should see him now. If there are any more complaints in this town during this year, I'll bet that several are about him."

"And what's Tú doing about it?" It wasn't a subject Bóyì wanted to pursue. He knew the state supported Tú, employing her to supervise Qí. It seemed she did a lot of lying around and not providing much care. "She's supposed to parent him now. This new Qí must be almost as bad as her son. I guess she must still be upset. We can give her some time and space to recover."

"She looks fully recovered to me!" It was a subject about which Jīngfēi felt strongly. "She looks like she's very content. No one would think she's just lost a husband and a son!"

"Going back on things…I've got to visit Háng. Those carts trundling into town, fully laden - what's he bringing in?"

"Why not ask him? Let's go now and surprise him. I'll be betting he's either with Tú, in which case he's screwing her, or with Qí, in which case he's leading him up some path he shouldn't be. Let's see!"

It took only moments for the pair to ready themselves, bouncing out of their house with renewed purpose. It was a major disappointment to find that Háng was not with Tú or Qí. He appeared to be meeting the couple sent by Hòutú to help with the state's accounting. Far from

Èrlǐtou, Hénán

objecting to Jīngfēi and Bóyì's presence, he motioned them in enthusiastically.

"It's my favourite council leader and his esteemed partner! Come in! Sit! We're a-thinkin' we've just got our heads around the problem!"

"What problem?" Bóyì was perplexed.

"The problem I've been bringin' up year after year, of course! We think we've solved it."

"You mean your suggestion that we should have units of currency?" Bóyì smiled, "It was dead and buried. We don't need it!"

"You might not need it, and the council might not need it. These two say they don't need it, although they say it would be helpful, but…you see…I need it!"

"Háng, what are you doing?" Jīngfēi knew of the barman's long-term obsession and understood the difficulties as well as Bóyì, "Are–"

"I'm a-goin' to make my own currency!" Háng was triumphant, "It doesn't need to be a state thing. These two have explained to me how it could work!" He smiled benignly at the two youngsters. "They say there are only two problems, one a bein' the creation of a token that is hard to copy and the other a bein' the fact I have to guarantee its value. What we're workin' on now is the value of the token. I want to guarantee it's worth one mug of my superior beer. They say it should equate to a quantity of millet or rice. Which did we decide? Oh! That's right. Rice! So, we're at the point of decidin' how much rice a mug of superior beer is worth; it's–"

"It's worth nothing if you don't want one!" This argument had entertained Bóyì over the years, but now it was wearing a little thin.

"Well, you can say that, but you wouldn't say that about the rice if you were hungry, would you? You may not want beer, you may not want rice, but you might be a wantin' something else. How do you get it? What if you want a haircut?"

"Jīngfēi cuts my hair, and I cut hers; there's no need to–"

"I was talkin' about someone who cares about his looks." Háng grinned at Jīngfēi, "I'm talkin' about him, not you! If you want a haircut, how will you pay for it? Well, the haircutter is probably sick and tired of people a-givin' him bags of rice. What he wants is somethin' he can use to pay for somethin' else, perhaps a whore?"

Twenty-six: The Election

"Ah, Háng, that's something else I need to speak to you about," Bóyì remembered how his discussion with Jīngfēi had started.

"They're a sufferin', Bóyì, they're a sufferin' because there's no means of exchange. You know I'm havin' to house some of them to keep them from death's door. Whereas, if the whores are paid in exchangeable tokens, well, then they could use them for whatever they wanted!"

"And you, Háng the barman, will guarantee their token is…what?" Bóyì knew this was the weakest link in the barman's plan.

"That's what we've just figured out, Bóyì! A token is goin' to be worth a fixed quantity of superior beer or a fixed quantity of rice, probably the same amount of rice as would fit into the same mug. So, I guarantee that if someone is a-comin' to me with a token, I'll be a givin' them one of those two things in exchange!"

"Which one, the rice or the beer?" Jīngfēi was sure she knew which way this was headed.

"No matter. I'll have enough beer and enough rice to do either!"

"And what is the token going to be?" Bóyì knew that this had always been the deal-breaker.

"They'll be patches of silk!" Again, a triumphant expression.

"But…Háng…anyone can get some piece of silk." Jīngfēi was beginning to think the man had lost his mind.

"It's true, Jīngfēi, they can, but you see those carts over there? See? They're laden down with a special silk I've had woven, with my symbol threaded through it. Only me and the manufacturer have the design; it would be impossible to copy, and the dye is unusual too!"

"And what will you call these tokens, eh Háng?" Bóyì was beginning to realise that the barman was serious.

"We thought we would be a-callin' it *qián*[29]. These two came up with that name. I've got a feeling it might just catch on!"

---

[29] Money.

Twenty-seven: The Turnabout
Mount Guófēng & Dōngxiàfēng
Year 101. Year of the Pig
Twenty-four days to the autumn equinox
30th August 1894 BCE

Yú's journey to Lājià had been cathartic. Following something, anything, even something as mindless as a streak in the sky, had given him an alternative focus. Time by himself, time to ponder, time to allow the realities of the awful start to the Year of the Pig to sink in. With it came the dawning of understanding and his predicament since basing himself in Èrlǐtou. It was not the kind of life he had any desire to re-live.

The accusation, or more, the fact that he had been in an incestuous and controlling relationship for so long, was not something he had been able to put to the back of his mind. However, he had attempted to justify his actions. Running away may have appeared to be the cowardly solution, but the intractability of the circumstance had left him with little choice; he had blunted Túshānshì's attack and perhaps even foiled it. He had left a capable leader in charge, a functioning town, and a growing group of states to call an empire. He had even thwarted Fēngbō's attempts to join the Xià when he had realised the King of Ānyáng was playing a duplicitous game and bullying his citizens to comply.

It was not only the fact that the comet had disappeared from the skies that terminated his westward journey; it was also the realisation that there was somewhere he could go, an offer he could accept, and that he was wanted. If saving the three women and two girls had given him back his ability to live with the man he was, it also gave him a bigger problem. Yú was accompanied on his turnabout. All five females wanted him to take them away from Lājià and away from the Qijia. His journey back east

Twenty-seven: The Turnabout

was as part of a team, four of whom were indebted to him and one to whom he was indebted.

It had taken several days to gather the requirements for their journey, but those days also provided essential recovery time. Although there were a few other survivors, none were close to those in Yú's group, and none had wished to trek east with them. Yú had laughed and laughed when he worked out how prescient he had been on rescuing Xīwángmǔ, for other than Lùduān, the truthteller, the four were named Běidǒu, Nányīng, Dǒng, and Xīwángmǔ; they were very much his north, south, east, and west! He joked that they could use each other as direction markers and that he would hold up Lùduān as a pointer; the young lady was unimpressed and even less so with Yú's inclination to abbreviate everyone's name.

When they found an old horse that had lost its owner to the mudslide, Yú suggested they call it Bùlùduān[30] to differentiate it from Lùduān and to tell them apart, as they were both so stubborn. The joke fell entirely flat with the ten-year-old.

They received interesting news from the few stragglers left around Lājià about the disappearance of the Yellow River. The earthquake had caused an even more enormous landslide upstream, which had blocked the waterway in the Jīshí Gorge. Previous experiences meant the older hands knew what would happen sooner or later; the future floods would be catastrophic; they may even wipe out what little remained of their hometown. By the time Yú's group had set out, most had already gone, the majority headed south or north, away from the impending and murderous floods that were sure to come.

Yú intended to head eastwards and to keep going for a hundred days. There had been potential issues. The route would be dangerous unless they kept to the mountains and clear of the coming maelstrom. Following the comet on his outbound journey kept him on a shade more northerly path than the setting sun. He had proposed to lead his small team directly towards the rising sun, a line he estimated would bring him into the vicinity of his old home in Táosì.

---

[30] This effectively means not Lùduān.

Yú had only admitted their actual destination when they were halfway through the trek. His confession that they were headed for a secret hidden valley he had not visited before brought some derision. When he had further informed them that he was trying to find a woman he hardly knew, who was in her mid-thirties, it was hard to tell if scepticism or ridicule won the duel.

"What are you talking about? She said she would shelter you. From what?" asked Dǒng.

"The storm."

"What storm? There's not going to be another storm for a few days. Even then, we'll see it coming and make the shelter. Not…what's she called, this girl, this old woman…Líng." Běidǒu was incensed. Even Xīwángmǔ shook her head in disbelief, although it was always somewhat tempered by her shy, lustful glances in Yú's direction.

"It makes no sense; you've got three of us here to look after you. It's not like you're going to get cold at night. Come on! Or would you rather sleep with the horse?"

If the three women were giving him a hard time, Lùduān was even worse, "You're a pig! Yes! A pig, in the Year of the Pig! Soooo rude you are! It's like you're throwing up opportunity after opportunity. No one would believe you if you said you were heading east to meet up with an old lady when you've got Xīwángmǔ, Dǒng or Běidǒu to bed each night. You only make sense when you're planning a route or saving someone. You make no sense when it comes to women."

Lùduān had made it clear to the women in the group that she knew who Yú was, albeit she had sworn them to secrecy. Her manipulations were so pragmatic that, in the end, they worked out to everyone's satisfaction, other than her own. To keep warm on the cold nights in the mountains, the three women rotated sleeping with Yú. On their off nights, they slept with one of the two children. It had taken them ten days to have the routine working to their satisfaction; Yú accepted whatever they threw at him. By the time they had hauled up to Mount Guófēng, some eighty days later, Dǒng and Běidǒu had joined Xīwángmǔ in carrying a child. When the pair revealed their news, Lùduān was indignant, furious that Yú would not grant her the same privilege. Yú was unknowing and oblivious to the cause of the girl's temper. That is how the day had started.

Twenty-seven: The Turnabout

That evening, she broached the matter again, perfectly prepared to spill secrets in her attempt to manipulate Yú, even to the extent of dropping her preference for full names. She had managed to sideline him with the excuse of a turned ankle. They were some five hundred paces behind the rest of the group.

"You know that Dǒng is expecting a baby, don't you?"

"No. That's a bit of a surprise. It's even more surprising she didn't tell me."

"And you know that Xī is pregnant?"

"Yes, but she was before this trip; you told me that!"

"Alright, but just perhaps…just perhaps I said…I lied. She's pregnant now, though."

"Well, I'm sure she'll know who the father is."

"What about Běi?"

"What about Běi?"

"She's having a baby too!" Lùduān poked her finger into Yú's ribs, "You made her pregnant!"

"It's possible. It's not a crime, you know. Really, it's–"

"The crime, as you well know it, you rude man, is that you have not had the decency to make me with a child as well. You've not–"

"Hold on! How old are you? Ten? You have to wait, young lady; your time will come, and there'll be this nice boy who–"

"But he won't be you, will he?" Tears began to course down Lùduān's face.

"No, it will not be me! There's nothing wrong with your ankle. Shoo! Go catch up with the others." Still weeping and forgetting her supposed injury, Lùduān ran like the wind to join the women.

Mount Guófēng stood above the flatlands like a tortured wart. Only its lesser sister peak, a day's walk to the east, interrupted its dominance of the plains west of Dōngxiàfēng. There, the six were finally halted by people with the power to do so.

As the riders hove into view, Yú dropped the cowl of his gown over the upper part of his face. They were now a team; everyone knew their role.

"Ah! Such nice horses!" Lùduān had abandoned all her histrionics, "What are they called?"

"They're called horses, girl, nothing more, nothing less." The sergeant was arrogant and had little time to communicate with a child. "Who's in charge here?"

Five sets of fingers pointed directly at Yú.

"Well, sir, tell us your business." She was direct and challenging but not entirely unfriendly.

"We are making a pilgrimage, miss," Yú hissed asthmatically. "We are to climb Mount Guófēng before taking our journey further east into the mountains."

"And you think you'll get up there…in your state?" The sergeant laughed. "There's bears occupy that hill. If you get as far as halfway up in the condition you're in, they'll enjoy a tasty treat, especially with these young 'uns!"

"It is to our ancestors we will pray for deliverance from harm and our weaknesses." Yú knew he was on solid ground; in Shǎnxī, any reference to predecessors was tantamount to holiness.

"And you're…what…one man…three women and…two girls?"

"'Tis true. We have been a weakened force since the death of my brothers. We soldier on, carrying our beliefs and our goal." Yú was uncertain how long he could carry on with the charade.

"And Yú's the best leader ever! It's true!" Little Nányīng's mouth opened into a semi-toothless smile. "He helped me lose one of my baby teeth. Look!" A quiver of panic went through the group at the mention of his name.

"Captain!" one of the troop's youngest spoke hurriedly, "They'll be doing no harm in Dōngxiàfēng. We could be here for a week if we carry on this chitter-chatter. If we ride hard, we'll be in our beds tonight. We all want some good beer and a night of good sleep; can't we leave them be?"

The sergeant managed a brief withering look before her face cracked into a smile. "We'll go!" she turned back to face Yú. "You know, there's devils up there…as well as bears. If you're going to climb it, do not walk in straight lines, do not let them follow you, and do not sleep without a guard." She paused and hardened her stare. "I do not wish to see you again, but I do not wish you harm. Climb Mount Guófēng, beware

Twenty-seven: The Turnabout

the bears, defeat the devils and access your ancestors," she smiled once more at her wit, "and then get out of this valley! Got it!"

"Yes, ma'am." Yú bowed deeply. "Our thanks for your understanding."

"Troop! Turn! Five hours of hard riding, and we'll be in the tavern tonight. Let's go!"

The six horsemen wheeled and galloped into the distance, dust flying from hooves and the sun glinting off the metal studs embedded in the armour on their backs.

"Who were they?" Dǒng asked.

"They, dear Dǒng, are the Xià. Well-trained, well-mannered, and well-dressed. Did you see their discipline? A unit of six, three men and three women. It's another life, but I was proud to be one of them once."

"And that young one spent an awful lot of time looking at your face, and when she heard your name, she even went so far as to interrupt the sergeant." As usual, Lùduān had seen what others had missed and was intent on ensuring everyone knew. "Perhaps you should change your name."

"That might be a good idea now we are back in the Motherland. I don't think anyone would recognise me with this beard and the hood, though!"

"It's your nose! That's why I know who you are and why that soldier recognised you. We can't do much about your nose, but we can certainly stop using your name. Can't we, Nányīng? If it isn't too much to ask!"

"Now, go easy on her, Lùduān; she's only six. It's not her fault."

"So, let's give ourselves a name that we can use. We can't say we're Yú's band or Yú's disciples; we must have a different name." Lùduān paused for a moment, "What about something to remind us to talk to each other before making a decision?" she stared pointedly at Nányīng. "Perhaps *shāng*[31]! If we are always supposed to discuss and agree before taking rash steps, it's perfect. Then Yú, you can refer to Xīshāng, Dǒngshāng, Běishāng, and Nánshāng. You could even carry on shortening their names because they really don't matter. They–"

---

[31] Consult.

"Who are you saying doesn't matter? Bighead! And what about you? Should we not call you Lùshāng?" Běidǒu was making fun, egged on by nudges from Xīwángmǔ and whispers from Dǒng, "And what do we call Yú? It's all getting dreadfully complicated!"

"You must call me Lùduān and nothing else." The girl's stare could have melted the rock on which Dǒng had perched. "And you can call Yú by his name if you wish, but if others are around, you should call him Shāng. I'm not saying all this to be petty like you think I am. I'm not even suggesting it. I'm telling you this is what we must do, and the reason is that it is easy to remember, even for Nányīng, and that's what's important because she needs to have an easy time remembering. And if you want to know why I'm not changing my name, it's because it doesn't matter to anyone what I am called, but it's the only thing I've got that is me!" The tirade only paused long enough for Lùduān to catch her breath, "I've lost mother after mother and home after home. I am not going to lose my name!"

"Well!" Yú managed to catch the eyes of each of the women, "We are the mystical Shāng…all six of us! After that little consultation, we must agree. Lùduān, do you mind being Lùduān Shāng?"

"What? You all agree?" Lùduān was almost open-mouthed in astonishment.

There were smiles all around as airs of amusement and resignation slid together.

"We all agree!" Dǒng smiled, "I've been called a lot worse in my time… Shāng it is then! But Yú? Do we really have to climb up this mountain? Could we have a little consultation about that as well?"

Yú smiled and shook his head before leading the group on the lower path, one sweeping to the north of the peak before resuming its eastward track. He lifted Nányīng onto the old horse, and for once, even Lùduān marched on with a contented smile. Yú wondered how much of the histrionics had been about avoiding the mountain climb. He had wished to ascend the peak due to the views afforded. He had wanted to look down on the beautiful scenery and scenes of his past triumphs. He secretly wished they might pass by the site of the Battle of Sanjiadiǎncūn; it was somewhere he had never re-visited.

Twenty-seven: The Turnabout

Recalling the battle, his mind focused on its architect, Líng. What had she meant about sheltering him? What did he need shelter from? Turning over different ideas led him to focus on their recent meeting with the Xià troop. Their plan had worked to a point, but even Yú shared Lùduān's concern. It seemed only one of the soldiers had registered who he might be; it would depend on whom she shared the information.

*

The troop fetched up at the Dōngxiàféng barracks well after night had fallen. The sergeant went to report an uneventful day while the other five crowded into a full bar for some food and a beer. While waiting for their drinks, their youngest member slipped out to use the long drop. She was gone a little longer than expected.

Twenty-eight: The Bonding

Shāngyuǎncūn & Sanjiadiǎncūn
Year 101. Year of the Pig
Nineteen days before the autumn equinox
3rd September 1894 BCE

The Wolf Pack was in Sānménxiá when they received the information. It was a little vague. One of their agents had spotted a man she believed filled a description that had been circulated. It seemed the man's hair had been longer, an unkempt beard added, and it appeared he was wearing a magician's robe. For company, he had five females of varying ages and an old horse. Xiǎoláng had commented at the time that their own group was even weirder; three young women and a neutered male youth made strange bedfellows.

The information came from the slopes of Mount Guófēng, where a patrolling troop had spotted them heading eastwards. The only additional information was that this group's presence had not found its way into the troop's official report. It seemed they had been considered a somewhat eccentric religious group of no harm to anyone but themselves.

The Wolves' biggest concern had been coping with Qí as they travelled, although it had gone as well as they could have hoped. Dressing him as a female had worked perfectly, and the boy had been quite happy with the arrangement. Renaming him, *Qíqí*[32] had been Dàláng's idea after she caught him studying millipedes. He seemed obsessed with anything that crept or crawled. The three women had grown used to his company and treated him as they would a younger sibling. For his part, the three had become surrogate mothers. Although his mental skills sometimes

---

[32] Creepy-crawly.

Twenty-eight: The Bonding

seemed to hover well behind him, he had proved a fine horseman once his wound had healed, and he certainly had a way with animals.

The Wolf Pack's objectives were hardly simple. First, they must deliver a castrated son to his father. Then, they had to guide that father toward the woman who had ordered his son's death. Finally, they must return to Èrlǐtou bearing proof that Yú had died without actually killing him. It made the killing of Fēngbō seem like collecting chicken eggs.

By allowing Yú to turn up in the hidden valley with his son, it meant Kuàiláng would not have to own up to Líng personally. That was something all three of them desperately wanted to avoid. If that were to occur while they were fulfilling Líng's final request, the staging of Yú's death, she couldn't possibly do anything but come to adore the boy before they met her again. Kuàiláng was confident she could give Yú's group directions without accompanying him.

Kuàiláng had suggested they head for the gap through the hills at Shāngyuǎncūn. It had been hard riding, although the Wolf Pack were used to that, and two days had given them an intercept for a walking group going eastwards. In many regards, the gap was a bottleneck; both north-south and east-west trade routes tended to use the pass there. It had previously been a point for regular bandit attacks, but now, with the Xià peace holding firm, traders congregated there in numbers. There was never any doubt that traders could be persuaded to talk; all too often, the problem was shutting them up. Once they had a lead, Xiǎoláng had the task of eliciting information. If there were further information to be derived, Shāngyuǎncūn was the place.

*

"So, we were climbing this beaten-up old track when we came across this giant panda. I'm not keen on those things; they're unpredictable; sometimes they run, and sometimes they want to wrestle you. One wouldn't have been too bad, but she had a cub with her. Mother pandas can get very nasty when they're looking after cubs; they're–"

"What's this got to do with those religious types?" Xiǎoláng could not help displaying some irritation.

"I'm coming to that bit, don't rush me; I'll forget where I was." The trader had the whole evening, and female company suited him better than being alone.

"You had walked up a path and came across a panda. Then what?"

"She was big, that mother panda, the biggest I've seen. Anyway, I'm just thinking I should move away, carefully like, so she doesn't chase me, and this girl comes down the path. I guess she was eleven years old or so. She was whistling. It was an interesting tune I thought I'd heard before, although I wasn't sure. It's funny how some tunes stick in your head and–"

"The little girl, was she with the others?"

"You're getting a little hasty on me, and there's no rush; there's more to the story for sure, but–"

Xiǎoláng knew she had to speed him along. A white lie might help, "You see, she's my daughter. She's been lost for months, and I need to rescue her. That's why I'm in a hurry. I'm scared of what might happen to her."

The trader looked at her doubtfully, "You're a little young to have such a child; you must have been her age yourself when you had her!"

"I was young, it's true, but it doesn't mean I don't miss her."

"Alright. Well, I'll cut a long story short then, just for you, mind." The man smiled winningly. "She comes down this path and says to the mother panda, 'You're not going to hurt me, move aside!' and blow me down; the panda does just that. The girl even stroked the cub's fur as she passed. Untouched - she was untouched, I say. That's the girl, by the way, not the panda, cos obviously the girl touched the panda cub, but the girl herself was untouched. I thought I should explain that bit."

"But what about the others?"

"Ah, yes. After the panda had scooted into the undergrowth, they came down the track after her. They can do that, you know. Sometimes, they're loud, crashing around, and sometimes they're like ghosts. This mother panda and her cub were like ghosts. I'm not keen on them myself, pandas or ghosts. They're particularly dangerous when they're with a cub. Did I tell you that?"

"Yes, but you haven't told me who was with the girl or where they were going?"

Twenty-eight: The Bonding

"Like as not, but I thought I mentioned them."

"How many were there, men, women and children, and where do you think they were going?"

"They were going down the track. There was one man; he had a bit of a squashed face. It looked like a while back, he'd been in a bit of a fight, I'd say. You know, it's always best to avoid fighting. We see a lot of it moving from town to town; it's–"

"Who else?"

"Well, there was three women and another girl, about half the age of the first, I'd say. What's a group like that doing walking in bear country? Cos there's bears and wolves as well as pandas, you know. Those wolves can be a–"

"Did you speak to them? Do you know where they were going?"

"Well, he was affable enough; they all were, actually. Nice to bump into someone who likes a bit of a chat. Unlike some!" The trader stared harshly at her.

"Are you going to tell me where they were going?" Xiǎoláng was about to lose her temper, a rarity the trader would not wish to experience.

"They was heading to camp by the big bend in the Fèn River. It's not but a short ride from here, due west. That's not their overall direction, though; they were travelling to the east. I guess it's just a stopping point they were…Where are you going? Come on, girl; we haven't finished. We…" The trader was still talking well after Xiǎoláng's departure.

Rounding up the Wolf Pack proved a doddle, waking Qíqí a little more difficult.

"I think whether we go now or in the morning is the question. In the morning, we might miss them. If we go now, it means riding in the dark with this poor, sleepy lad. What are your thoughts?" Kuàiláng often ran things past them, especially when she had already decided, but it was a moment until her companions spoke.

"There'll be no moon this evening and only a sliver in the early morning. It's not ideal." Dàláng was unusually reticent; both her colleagues suspected she had lined up a man for the night.

"It's supposed to be a flat ride on fairly open land. There's starlight to see by!" Xiǎoláng was more anxious, having been the one to have solicited the information.

Shāngyuǎncūn & Sanjiadiǎncūn

"Two beats one! Bad luck, Dà, you'll have to put him on hold!" A scowl met Kuàiláng's sweet smile. "Dà, you get the horses, and we'll sort out Qíqí. With a little luck, he'll be re-introduced to his father by tomorrow."

*

The journey did prove relatively easy; when they arrived at the river, a campfire was burning brightly in Sanjiadiǎncūn. Dismounting, Kuàiláng sent the other two wolves and Qíqí back with the horses towards some caves they had passed, telling them to be ready for her at sunrise. She was off to deal with Yú.

She took the route down the river terrace that many of Chīyóu's troops had taken that fateful night. The campfire sat squarely where the palisade had been—where Líng had sheltered underneath the wagon all those years ago. Although Yú may have known the site intimately, Kuàiláng did not realise its significance.

Her arrival at the campfire caused all six diners to turn in shock. It was not every day a single woman walked in on their supper in the middle of nowhere.

"I'm here to talk to Yú."

"There's no one here of that name," said a young girl. Kuàiláng wondered if it was the one from the trader's tale. "We're all called Shāng, after him." She indicated towards the man, who had pulled his hood closer to his face.

"It's funny that," Kuàiláng smiled, "for I recognise that man's face, and he's definitely called Yú. I'll go further...he's not only called Yú, he's also the previous leader of the Èrlǐtou council. This is Yú, who was the leader of the Xià. Hullo, Yú."

"Hullo." Whilst the five females whispered under their breaths, Yú pulled back his hood. "I am Yú. Your problem, young lady, is that these five have sworn to kill you. Don't take it personally. They are sworn to kill anyone who reveals my identity."

"In that case, I need to tell you some news...some news that may well dissuade your colleagues from taking my life. The first thing is that your wife, Túshānshì, and her nanny, Āyí Zhū, are dead."

Twenty-eight: The Bonding

"Good. That is, indeed, excellent news! I wondered how I would feel when imagining that news. Now I know. I'm happy."

"The second is that I am here to guide you towards your shelter. I suspect you now understand the message my mother gave you two years ago in Huáxiàn."

"You are Kùàimǎ's daughter?"

"I am. She adopted me. So, let me check; you now know what she meant by needing shelter from the storm?"

"I do."

"The third I need to tell you alone. Would you come with me, please?" Kuàiláng offered her hand to help Yú raise himself and turned to the others, "I've no intention of harming him, but you'll have to believe me on that. I cannot speak my next point out loud. I'm sorry."

"If any harm comes to him, you'll not see the sunrise!" Lùduān was the only one to speak. "He's our leader, and we love him!"

"I'm sure you do," Kuàiláng crouched, holding the girl's chin. "There's lots of people who love him just as much. I'll look after him." With that, she turned away, leading Yú by the hand and heading towards the riverbank, where the gurgling flow would drown out their conversation.

As she left, she could hear a louder whisper from behind her, "And if she keeps holding his hand…I'll kill her anyway…Nobody loves him as much as me!" Lùduān made sure Kuàiláng heard her. Once they were alone, Kuàiláng began.

"We were also instructed to kill your son…we have not done so."

"I…" Yú was struck dumb; he had no idea whether Qí's death would have been a good idea. However, his emotions were churning, and he felt slightly sick.

"We did not kill him; I have him with us."

"Where is he?"

"That you will learn tonight, although not yet. I need to tell you something else."

"He's alive, and he's here! Where?"

"Later. Calm down. You will see him. I need to explain something." Kuàiláng took a deep breath. "I know that Túshānshì was not only your wife but also your sister."

"Yes." Yú's face furrowed in intense concentration. "I hope you haven't been telling anyone that?"

"No, I have not, and that is why we killed Túshānshì and Āyí Zhū: to stop any news spreading."

"Good, I don't need to take responsibility for that crime…I never knew."

"We know. We had a problem when we were supposed to kill your son. We couldn't do it. He's so sweet and innocent. He's–"

"He is even freer of guilt than I. Where–"

"Later. There was a problem, though. With his parents being brother and sister, we could not let him have children."

"It'll be hard keeping him away from women all his life."

"It would…that's why we castrated him."

"You did what?"

"We've castrated him."

"How?"

"You don't need to know how. You just need to know that he's very well, he's recovered just fine, he's very much looking forward to seeing his father, and–"

"You cut his balls off? What, like a bullock? You–"

"More like a sheep actually, he–"

"You bit his balls out?"

"Well, not me, but someone I know. He's recovered, he's well, he's fine, and that was four months ago. He's not unhappy. I'm not sure he understands what he's missing." Kuàiláng paused, realising she needed to disseminate two more pieces of information. "I need to admit this, Yú, but to keep his identity secret, we have been travelling with him dressed as a woman. We've also altered his name."

"To what?"

"Qíqí."

"It's a good job you didn't tell me you were bringing good news!" Yú had slumped to the ground before raising his face towards Kuàiláng. "I understand what you're saying. I understand why you did this. I understand, but that doesn't mean I have to like it. Give me a little time, will you? Go and sit with them around the campfire. Ask them for a drink. Tell them I'll be with them shortly."

Twenty-eight: The Bonding

Kuàiláng left him and went to sit in the circle around the fire. She was welcomed cautiously by all but Lùduān, who pulled faces behind her hands. It seemed an eternity until Yú returned, but when he did, the man had a great big grin on his face.

"Tomorrow, ladies, you will meet my son! Kuàiláng has rescued him from Èrlĭtou. I am forever in her debt. Please treat her well. I'll meet him tomorrow morning, and then we will stay at this site for a second night. Then we will have a feast, and I will tell you and my son about our battle here."

*

The following morning, just as the sun rose, Yú and Kuàiláng reached the top of the river cliff. They were blinking in the sudden light streaming directly into their eyes, but it was just possible to see three figures some fifty paces ahead. As Kuàiláng peeled away from Yú, Xiǎoláng and Dàláng dropped their hands, allowing Qí to sprint towards his father. He was still three steps away when he launched into Yú's arms.

"*Bǎbá*! I love you!"

Yú kissed his son, "And I love you, Qí."

After a huge hug, his face buried in his father's chest, the boy raised his head, "Would you make me two promises?" The son looked earnestly into his father's eyes.

"I will. What are they?" Yú smiled.

"The first one is...please don't go away again."

"I promise."

"And the second one is...could you call me Qíqí and not Qí? I like it much more!"

"I promise... Qíqí."

"Thank you, *Bǎbá*!"

Twenty-nine: The Evidence
Èrlĭtou, Hénán
Year 101. Last day of the Year of the Pig
Forty-one days after the winter solstice
31st January 1893 BCE

It was a trader who brought the news. A tall stranger from Lǎoniúpō had wandered into Èrlĭtou with a seemingly far-fetched story of the destruction of a village in Gānsù. It sounded as if the wrath of their forefathers had descended on the inhabitants: earthquakes, mudslides, diseases, then flooding and more diseases. He freely admitted his information was second-hand and doubted some of its integrity himself. It was, however, a tale that lent itself to re-telling, and he found himself showered with offers of a drink, food, a roof over his head and companionship for weeks.

It was the first day in weeks with a bit of sun and wind. The trader took the opportunity to clean some of his clothing and kit, which were left out to dry, hopefully before the evening frost set in. As the wind whipped through, a passing sharp-eyed Èrlĭtou archer noticed something unusual about the trader's quiver, something he recognised. Without any doubt, it was Yú's quiver. Not wishing to challenge the man, he reported the affair to his councilwoman, who passed the information to Bóyì. It had led to the trader sitting down with the reluctant council leader in Háng's eastern bar later that day.

"I'm told you're named Shuĭkè. Welcome to Èrlĭtou!" Bóyì was probably one of the few inhabitants who had not yet met the trader. "I'm Bóyì, and I'm supposed to be in charge around here."

"Greetings. I am Shuĭkè. And may I say that all in all, this has been a hugely welcoming town. Quite unexpected! I suppose much of it has to do with the tale I came in with rather than my charm and good looks! I've never really been treated as well anywhere, except when I go home to the wife in Lǎoniúpō."

Twenty-nine: The Evidence

"You know, one reason they like to hear about disasters is that we don't have them around here." Bóyì kicked out at a rat scuttling past. "Although, if we get many more of those fellas, the new year will be appropriately named. Stinking rats!"

"Ah! Have some sympathy for the poor creatures. This one's just trying to keep warm, probably. They're harmless enough." the trader chucked a scrap of bread toward the departing rodent.

"You obviously aren't responsible for a town's grain store as I am. You wouldn't think them harmless then. We've even brought leopard cats in from Ānyáng to solve the problem. The trouble is, it's not working. The damn cats keep running away. Are you still here tomorrow? It's the new year celebrations starting, and, of course, it will be the Year of the Rat."

"I'll be around. I suspect my welcome is starting to run out, so I won't be staying for all the celebrations. Anyway, with the ground hard and the moon starting to grow in a day or two, it'll make for easier travelling. I'm headed for Ānyáng as it happens."

"I was up there earlier this year. They've got a new council leader, who goes by the name of Cāngbái. Nice lady. She's got white hair."

"She's old?"

"No, just white hair."

"Mmm! Interesting. I'm going up there with some fine silks. I want to establish a regular trade."

"Well, the good news is that the area has recovered from the great floods, and it seems to be getting over the reign of terror that Fēngbō had not so subtly applied. However, I'll come to the point–"

"Aargh! You don't want to hear the Lājià story, do you? I must be on my millionth telling."

"Not really, but perhaps my question might take us there. Where did you get your quiver?"

"My quiver? I bought it from another trader. It was the same one that told me the story about Lājià."

"Is that where he got the quiver from?"

"Her, it was a woman. I met her in Shāngyuáncūn in Shǎnxī. I thought things were going pretty well with her, let me tell you. She was a big girl but kind of foxy and kept pressing against me. Then, all of a

Èrlǐtou, Hénán

sudden, just when I'm thinking I'd got someone to keep me warm for the night, she leaves, just like that. It was a bit strange. That first night, she told me no stories, and we did no trading, although I thought she was up for it, and my luck was in! Then! Gone!"

"So, when did you hear the Lājià story if she left?"

"Two nights later, she reappears. It was a warm night back in early autumn. She settles in on a stool beside me as if she'd not been away. Deep brown eyes, and when she leans forward, oo! You should have seen her breasts. Gorgeous. Erm, you won't tell my wife any of this, will you? I can't have tales getting back to Lǎoniúpō."

"I promise, if I revisit Lǎoniúpō, I will not tell your wife a thing. I suspect we will never meet anyway."

"Well, just you be careful who you tell. Understand?"

"Yes! Please focus on the quiver, not the girl."

"Well, she told me all about Lājià at the bar. After that, we spent the night together, and in the morning, she asks me if I wanted to trade for some kit. She knew I was doing silk and wanted some. I'll tell you; she was big but had such a nice, tight, hard body. It looked great in the fancy red silk I had. She kept putting it on, taking it off and teasing me. She–"

"The quiver, please!"

"Well, it wasn't just the quiver; it was a bow, arrows, a water bladder, a saddlebag, a small backpack, an axe, and a dagger. They were good quality, they–"

"May I see them?"

"Well…" the trader suddenly grew suspicious, "I bought them in an honest exchange; they're not stolen or anything."

"I believe you. I think they once belonged to a good friend of mine. He would never have let them go. If they're his…If they're his…I believe he must be dead."

"That's what this girl told me." The trader was oblivious to Bóyì's emotional state. "She said they'd belonged to someone who had died in the mudslide in Lājià. She said he was a traveller from the east, said he'd been living in a cave, but when the mud came, well, he was out at a bar. It seems the bar was full of the town's menfolk, something about a big fight, but then it got drowned in mud and took all those men and boys away for good. It seems that hundreds died. Anyway, this guy had left his

Twenty-nine: The Evidence

stuff in this cave, and when she realised he must be dead, she goes and collects it. I don't think you can thieve from a dead man, can you? I have to suspect she'd been...Well! She was a horny woman, put it that way."

"And she said this man was dead?" Tears trickled down Bóyì's cheeks before the trader realised something was amiss.

"Whoa. Hold on, young fella, let's not be a-weeping. Was he a friend of yours?"

"Did she describe him?"

"Yes, in some detail. Said his nose was caved in, tall, well-built; in fact, the detail she went into makes me sure she was keeping him warm at night. Do you want to see this stuff?"

Bóyì nodded affirmingly, and the trader lifted a large shoulder bag onto the table.

"Here you go, this is all of it except the backpack and that bow standing in the corner. You can have a root around, but give me that bundle first; that's my silk samples."

Bóyì stood and eyed the bow before passing the bundle of cloth to the trader and delving into the bag. First out was a quiver containing six arrows. "Quiver, yes; arrows, no."

"True, I used the original arrows; these were a replacement from Sānménxiá."

Bóyì next pulled out the water bladder, then an axe, followed by a dagger. With each, he whispered, "Yes," before walking over to the bow. After inspecting the bow tips, he returned to his seat and sighed, "They're my friend's possessions, alright. You may have heard of him; his name is...was, Yú."

"You're not referring to the great Yú, the man who should have been our emperor?"

"You know of him?"

"Everyone's heard of him. Everyone knows he disappeared. I had no idea I was being traded his belongings. I'll hand them back to his widow."

"She's dead."

"I'll hand them back to you. You said you were his friend."

"There's no need."

Èrlǐtou, Hénán

"I can't believe what I've done. I promise…You'll have to find that woman. You should start in Shāngyuǎncūn, in Shǎnxī. That's where it was I saw her."

"Did she say anything that might be important?"

"No, not that I can think of, just this story about the earthquakes and mudslides and the fl–"

"Did she pass on any other information?"

"Not that I can think of…Wait! Yes. It was odd. When she left that last morning, she grabbed my wrist, and with the other hand, she placed two fingers on my palm, then did it again and then put all four fingers on my palm. She was doing this and all the while shaking her head. It was weird. I've got no idea what she meant by it. I wondered whether she was rating me, but I deserved more than a two, maybe a four out of five, but not a two."

"Would you show this to my wife, please?"

"Sure, but don't tell her too much about the girl. You know how women can–"

"I tell her everything. She's here somewhere." Bóyì swivelled on his stool and, spotting Jīngfēi, called her over.

"Now, now, I'm busy here. You can't expect privileges in the bar; look at all the others I've got to serve. And who's this?" Jīngfēi laughed at her husband's exasperated expression. "Come on, what is it?"

"This, my dear, is Shuǐkè. He has brought unfortunate news. Sit down." Bóyì moved so that only one of his buttocks remained on the stool, leaving room for Jīngfēi to join him. Putting his arm around her, he whispered, "Yú is dead." He nodded vigorously as tears welled in his wife's eyes. "It's true."

Bóyì retold the trader's story while pulling some items from the bag. He appeared to have recovered his composure somewhat, although his wife was distraught.

"There's something else. Shuǐkè had a strange parting from this girl. Show her, Shuǐkè." The trader repeated the finger pattern. "Do you understand it, Jīng?"

"I certainly don't, and I need a piss. Where's the long drop?" The trader spoke as he stood and was on his way before one of them could answer.

Twenty-nine: The Evidence

"I certainly know what it means, Bóyì. It's a common Sisterhood signal. We learned it when I was but a girl. It means two and two do not equal four, although you should be quiet about it. You know what that means, don't you?"

"I do. As soon as he showed me, I thought I knew. It means Yú is still alive, doesn't it? And it means he wants everyone to think he is dead. That's why it's not supposed to be spoken of. Is that right?"

Jīngfēi's eyes shone through the pools of water that had collected, "It does. It really does. It's good news indeed. Clever! There's just one thing, Bóyì. What I cannot believe is that this trader is completely honest. What did you call him? Shuǐkè. He accidentally turns up in Èrlǐtou and passes the message on to Yú's best friends as if by accident again. There are too many coincidences. We have to ask him."

"Ask me what?" Shuǐkè dropped his bottom onto the stool.

"Well…what we want to know is how many people you have told…about that finger thing?" Jīngfēi smiled disarmingly.

"Just you."

"And how many people know it is Yú that is dead?"

"Just you. Bóyì just made the connection."

"And why did you tell us about the finger thing and no one else."

"It didn't seem rele–"

"No lies, please." Jīngfēi smiled again, "It seems there's something you're not telling us. What was the girl called?"

"She called herself Xiǎo. She was big and well-muscled. She–"

"I don't know that name, Jīngfēi." Bóyì shook his head as if trying to recall the name.

"Nor do I." Jīngfēi turned from her husband to the trader, "Shuǐkè, she gave you more than one message when she left you, didn't she?"

The trader was looking more and more miserable, "She did."

"She blackmailed you, didn't she?"

The trader nodded.

"She said she would tell your wife if–"

"If I did not come to Èrlǐtou and tell this story, and she told me to only give the hand signals to him." He pointed at Bóyì. "It's taken ages for me to get to this point and fulfil her wishes. I hope it's not all going to go wrong now. What are you two planning to do?"

"Well, Shuǐkè, I plan to blackmail you, too."

"How's that?"

"Bóyì and me are quite likely to visit Lǎoniúpō as part of our civic duties; this could happen quite soon, in fact. Now, we wouldn't want to tell your wife all about your dalliance with this girl, Xiǎo, would we? We especially wouldn't want to tell her that you described this girl as big and well-muscled, perhaps young as well, I suspect. You know, wives don't really want to hear about big, young, well-muscled and perhaps pretty girls that their husbands have been screwing. Well, not in normal circumstances. It's a question, Shuǐkè, whether your behaviour will prevent us from talking to your wife? Will it?"

"You're not going to make me choose…are you? Not between what Xiǎo wanted and what you want because that would not only be unfair but also couldn't possibly work."

"No. It's easy. We want you to continue to tell your story of the disasters in Lājià, and believe me, I've heard all about them, not only from Bóyì just now. The news is all around town. That's what Dà wanted as well, isn't it? For you to tell the tale. Well, keep telling it."

"But–"

"Shush, man, this is important." The smile crept back onto Jīngfēi's face. "We want you to go to the army chief, and we want you to tell him we think you have Yú's gear. We'll back you up and say it's not stolen. Is that running counter to Xiǎo's wishes?"

"No, but–"

"So, there's only one thing extra…and I'm sure Xiǎo would approve…we do not want you to tell the finger story again. Do you understand?"

"That's what she said. Once I'd passed the message on to you, I should forget it."

"And you will, because if you do not, then this girl, Xiǎo, and me are going to be joining forces in a visit to your beloved in Lǎoniúpō. That should be fun!"

"So, Shuǐkè, can you keep this one secret?"

"I can, I promise, really I do!"

Twenty-nine: The Evidence

"I think you do!" Jīngfēi grinned widely, "I must get back to work."

"May I ask a question?" Jīngfēi nodded at the trader's request. "Why is the wife of the council leader working in a bar?"

It's simple, Shuǐkè, I get to meet people I like, as does Bóyì from time to time. We got to know each other in a bar." She blew a kiss in her husband's direction.

"It's true, Shuǐkè, Jīng, you and I probably hang around bars quite a lot. There's a big difference, however. I manage to keep my dick in my pants, and she hasn't got one, although some say she has balls!" Bóyì creased over with laughter at his joke, just ducking beneath Jīngfēi's left arm swipe.

Èrlǐtou, Hénán

Thirty: The Confession
The Hidden Valley, Shǎnxī
Year 102. Year of the Rat
Thirty-nine days to the summer solstice
14th May 1893 BCE

The inhabitants of the valley numbered fewer than one hundred and fifty. All were pioneers, either of the land or the spirit. It mattered not; they were all escapees or refugees of a sort. Slightly more than half of them made the trek up to Shāng Hill.

    The site chosen by Líng for the construction of her home was a short walk to the north of Kànménrén and Hòutú's farm. It would have been a somewhat different proposition in the wet season as, at times, crossing the river could be tricky. Instead of a wicked and risky current, today it was possible to wade through the slow-moving, chilly waters and make an easy fording; the worst floods would not commence for a week or so. Everyone was thankful they did not have to take the boat, pulled across hooked to a fixed wire; it could be a daunting journey.

    Líng's construction lay on the southern slope of a small hill, almost surrounded by the river's meander. It created a barrier across which strangers would at least be delayed but most likely halted. The possibility of those strangers approaching so near seemed extremely unlikely, as to the south, Hòutú's expanding settlement barred the tracks. To the north, grazers loyal to Kànménrén occupied the mountain passes. Woodland straddled the narrow neck, which accessed the defended land. It was tightly planted with wineberries[33] under dragon spruce trees, both a rarity in the area. Together, they provided a thorny shock to anyone attempting to enter from that direction. The defensive attributes of the site

---

[33] Rubus phoenicolasius, a relation of the raspberry.

Thirty-one: The Passage

also kept the stock from wandering off. All in all, it was a shelter, one designed to keep its contents secret and one that Yú had come to appreciate greatly.

Líng had spent much of her time since Yú's arrival trying to become a mother, so far, without success. If she had been shocked when Yú arrived trailing three pregnant women and two children, she did not show it, although she must have been jealous.

Líng had required extensive assistance constructing a home large enough for two adults and perhaps their children. In autumn, when Yú's band had rolled in, the structure simply could not accommodate eight people; adding in the babies, eleven living there would have been a total impossibility.

The barn, recently stocked with hay to feed those animals being kept alive through the winter, saved the day. The structure ended up providing one enormous warm bed. From the autumn equinox until the winter solstice, the rapidly growing Xīwángmǔ, Dǒng and Běidǒu made do with the hay for bedding, sharing it with little Nányīng and an increasingly uncooperative Lùduān. It was fortunate that the snow came late that year. It meant the group could expand the home in time for the three successful births that brought the headcount to eleven while it was still relatively warm.

As a result of the hasty construction, they accidentally created an arena near the house. It was to this bowl the valley dwellers headed. Today, only the women were to gather there. The males and toddlers were left behind to guard the routes up the valley and tend livestock.

The meeting commenced as a light-hearted and joyous event. One of the visitors, a surprise recent arrival, was delighted to observe the uplifted spirits in the valley, so different from her experiences of recent happenings in Èrlǐtou. It seemed genuine happiness existed in the valley, not the idle semi-discontentment that seemed to hang over her home town. She listened through the introductions in a fulfilled daze, pondering how her husband's election preparations were going.

"If anything comes in, we vet it. If anything goes out, it is what we choose to allow. It's as simple as that. This is too important to allow unintentional external contact. We will defend our territory with what some may call witchcraft. In my eyes, it is little more than common sense;

there will be little mystical about it. The stories that outsiders will choose to believe will be those we have chosen that they should believe. If there is one thing above all else that we should all understand…it's that it takes a common belief to achieve the common good. That belief is simple. That belief is in our future. That belief must be held in common; if it is not, we shall fail."

So began the detailed section of Líng's speech to the womenfolk of the Hidden Valley. In truth, none disagreed with her sentiment, although a few rolled their eyes at her arrogance. After all, who was she? The question was soon answered.

"You wonder who I am, why I should speak this way? Well, I shall tell you. I was the leader of the Sisterhood for ten years and a senior member for a few years before that. I am here to tell you that the Sisterhood played a leading role in the obliteration of the Lóngshān. You do not have to believe me; there are others you may ask. Ask Yú or Kànménrén, ask Jīngfēi or Hòutú. If you want to hear of heroic self-sacrifice, ask Kùàimǎ, Mǎjié or Yěmǎ about their personal stories. I am serious. Ask them!" Líng paused long enough for the gathered women to register what she was saying.

"It is time these secrets were revealed. It is time you knew everything about what was going on behind the scenes. For some of you, this will be completely new. For others, perhaps previous members of the Sisterhood, you know bits and pieces. Listening to me now, or asking those individuals, will enable you to fit the pieces together. However, I am not here to talk about our successes. I am here to talk of our failures," there was something of a gasp from the audience, "and how we intend to correct them. My opening words about information leaving this valley are essential, for this information is not for all. This information is for you alone.

"You may wonder why I have asked to speak only to the females in our community. You may wonder if you may share this information with your menfolk. The answer to the second, by the way, is that you should. Definitely! This is not information we want to keep from the males, but information we hope you share in your own way. We needed to keep numbers down so that you could ask questions easily, and we are confident in our menfolk's understanding of our ability to communicate

Thirty-one: The Passage

with them. You know only too well how we are much better at communicating than they are!" A buzz of laughter and agreement went through the assembly.

"So, let's start way back. There's a stranger in our midst. You will probably have noticed. I want to ask Jīngfēi to stand, please." Her challenger from years before stood, offering Líng and her audience a genuine smile. "This is Jīngfēi. She is the wife of the leader of the Èrlǐtou council, a man who also represents the whole Xià Empire. She will be leaving the valley shortly, but she is one person I can be sure of. Jīngfēi will not share our location with anyone. She will not share the contents of my talk today with anyone but those present. For the time being, she will not even share this information with her husband, Bóyì, who some of you may remember as the leader of the Xià army, but a man who has now reluctantly taken Yú's old job." She paused to let the import of her words sink in. What was being shared was something on a scale most of them had never even considered.

"It was Jīngfēi who first alerted me to some problems we had created. She was a Sisterhood member but had abandoned the movement. In a nutshell, she felt the Sisterhood was not doing enough for women. Is that right, Jīngfēi?"

"It's right enough, Líng. Back in Táosì, the situation was awful. It seemed they, the Sisterhood, were taking too big a view of things. They were not caring for women in their everyday lives. Líng was one of the senior members of the Sisterhood back then and someone I despised.

Líng may be about to tell you about her mistakes, but I will tell you one of mine. I had forgotten what the Sisterhood did in terms of day-to-day life. I had forgotten that most wise women, healers, and midwives learned their skills through the Sisterhood." The mention of the wise women had everyone focused. In the valley, they all knew these arts, including the menfolk.

"When we moved from Táosì to Èrlǐtou, it seemed everything was falling into place. Women and men were regarded as equal; in fact, everyone was regarded as equal. I can tell you, as of two weeks ago, when I left the town we created, it no longer seemed as if this was still the case. Gradually, the principles on which we had based our lives are being eroded. I have discussed this at length with Líng, who has told me what she will reveal to you. I can tell you that there is nothing Líng will say that my husband, who is presently the leader of the Xià, would disagree with. You will only realise when she concludes quite what an admission that is. This is important!" Jīngfēi sat down and, for her contribution, received a round of applause.

"I will also admit to spending time with Hòutú, discussing her students' future." Líng resumed, "As you know, she has had a reduction in numbers recently. For reasons that will become apparent, fewer of her students will be sent to the Xià states. The ones already there will be charged with training their successors. Some may even wish to return if they have completed their work. The fact is, we need our young, talented youth with us here. They are our future - your children. Is that not right, Hòutú?"

"She is correct. Despite her relative youth…" she paused to allow a ripple of laughter, "What Líng is saying today will be the most important thing you have heard or will hear in your lives. Listen hard!"

"And so, it's time for the confession." Líng's smile disappeared, replaced by a stern look that made her look much older than her thirty-five years. "I…and the Sisterhood…have made mistakes. I will outline the reasons.

"Firstly, there were too many innocent people who died in the overthrow of the Lóngshān…for this, I will always feel shame. Many of you lost parents, some brothers, some sisters. There is no doubt that it was right to overthrow those cruel tyrants. Undoubtedly, lifting women from the abject misery of being treated little better than animals was correct. However, there is no doubt it could have been done with far less loss of life. It might have taken longer, but it should have been done more humanely. Re-routing the Yellow River was–"

"You're not telling us that that was down to the Sisterhood, are you?" the tone of the call from the back of the audience was incredulous.

"You'll have to ask those people I mentioned earlier. Please feel free to do so when we're finished. I do not expect you to believe everything I say without confirmation. However, I am trying to come clean, telling you what was done and what will be done.

The same voice came back, "It's still going on?"

Thirty-one: The Passage

"It is, but in a very different way. The Sisterhood still exists. The sisterhood is still active in Xià lands. However, it is a very different Sisterhood. Its members will still pass on the wise women's skills, although this may change over time. They provide a network of information. The key aim of the new Sisterhood is to remove key obstacles to progress. It was they who killed Fēngbō and–" An immediate collective gasp, followed by a myriad of voices all speaking at once, caused Líng to sit for a moment until they quieted. It took a little time for the order to be restored and for her to recommence.

"You heard me right! They killed Fēngbō, with the result that Cāngbái now leads the council in Ānyáng. Some of you might know what a good job she is doing."

"She might be doing a good job, but she's still not joined Ānyáng to the Xià Empire!" A second woman had found her voice.

"Nor will she–" a second collective gasp went around, although more restrained than previously. "Nor will she...that is not part of our plans. But we will come on to the future shortly. First, we must deal with the past and present.

"The situation in the Xià Empire is that currently, two of the satellite states are led by women, Jiālíng in Dōngxiàféng and Héměirén in Sānménxiá. This is the sort of result we had hoped for. However, there are already signs that this situation will not persist.

"As you are aware, Yú joined us in the autumn. The Sisterhood has ensured that everyone in Èrlǐtou and all the Xià lands believes he is dead. One reason that Jīngfēi came was to confirm that he had not died. She is one of his best friends. The myth of his death is now accepted in the Xià Empire, and Jīngfēi needed to see her friend with her own eyes; the tale has been pervasive.

"I would like to come back to Jīngfēi. We said earlier that she left the Sisterhood when she was much younger. We have spoken in the last few days, and she has told me there is now nothing the Sisterhood is doing that she disapproves of. She is fully supportive, even though, at some point soon, this will put her and her husband at great risk. Isn't that right, Jīngfēi?"

"It is," again the guest smiled around at the group, "it is something I've been concerned about...something I feel passionately about...the

Èrlǐtou, Hénán

rights of women are too important to take second place. I believe they are now integral to the Sisterhood's plans."

"Thank you, Jīngfēi. I'm going to turn to the future. At the insistence of Lùduān, who may be both the most irritating and intelligent child I have ever met," laughter erupted while the features of the target of that laughter contorted and reddened; the girl buried her face in her hands with embarrassment. "…really…I mean it! The most irritating and intelligent child I have ever met." The laughter took a while to die down, and Lùduān had to be held in her seat by the comrades she had travelled with, "…and talking about relative youth, Hòutú, I think she beats me hands down! At Lùduān's insistence, the people of this valley, with your agreement, will take on the name of Shāng. As Lùduān pointed out, this also means 'to consult', and we will, of course, consult with everyone and note only those comments that agree with Lùduān's view!"

"You're not being fair to me!" Lùduān opened up for the first time, "I'm not always irritating!"

"It's true…not always…but…think about what else I said." Líng herself was laughing so hard it took a moment to compose herself. "One day, young lady, you might lead these people. If you think about that, you might just stop saying 'it's not fair' quite so often. I was only a few years older than you when I joined the senior council of the Sisterhood. My codename was 'Girl'. Think about that, please."

With Lùduān trying to contain herself, the time was right. The mood had lightened. Líng launched into her vision for the future.

"Whilst we in this valley will live as we feel is right, this will not be the case outside. It will take many years, but our gains will gradually be eroded. I foresee a time when the Xià will begin to take on the ways of the Lóngshān. As you can see, we may have won some battles but not the war. The war must go on. The war does not mean hating men; it means changing men. The war does not mean chiding women; it means changing women.

"Since we took up farming hundreds of years ago, women's rights have…bit by bit…been removed. We have achieved some success. However, these successes will become losses without a massive change in the societies outside. I mentioned the future, and it is in this that my focus lies. You may be content with your lot in this valley. You may

Thirty-one: The Passage

believe your children's children's children will also be content. However, it will be several hundred years before we can strike out again and change the world. When that time comes, we, the Shāng, will move our society, ideas, and inherent ideals of fairness back onto the Yellow River flood plains. That is why Ānyáng will never form part of the Xià Empire. Quite simply, many years from now, we will need it as a base for expanding the principles of our collective. It will become the age of the Shāng!"

The enormity of the message was starting to sink in. Small conversations had kicked off in Líng's audience. It would have been hard to contain them much longer. Líng glanced at Hòutú and Jīngfēi and, after receiving a nod of approval, commenced her final words.

"Whatever you might think about me being a madwoman who lives in this menagerie up here at Shāng Hill, what I am telling you is that you are the great-grandmothers of the future of our nation. You are the ancestors they will revere. Some of your names will be handed down for millennia. Some of you might come to be thought of as gods. That is how important you are! Every woman in this assembly has a part to play. Every woman is integral to our ambitions. Every woman's voice counts!" Polite applause became louder, and gradually, they began to stand for her.

"There is one last thing I should point out. Always, always remember. There are also men in this community. Those men are our equals. Yes, really! We, as women, will not succeed without them. It's true. It's your job to make sure they are with us.

"Now go! Go and talk, go and discuss, go and decide. When we next meet, it will be with everyone in the valley, with all the Shāng! We want all to be part of this vision of a new Motherland! Let us make it happen!"

As the crowd began to disperse, Líng closed her eyes as tightly as she could and prayed that her audience would not only forgive her past mistakes but also her future actions.

Èrlĭtou, Hénán

Thirty-one: The Passage
Èrlĭtou, Hénán
Year 102. Year of the Rat
Sixteen days to the summer solstice
5th June 1893 BCE

Although he was once again a reluctant candidate, Bóyì was voted in for another term. He had almost gone out of his way to fail, but Háng's manipulations had seen him past the winning post. The whole pre-election trauma had led to Jīngfēi refusing to speak to him for a few days before disappearing. Not only had he been sore about winning, but Bóyì was also distraught that his one and only partner deserted him. She had stayed away for over a month, which felt like a year. It seemed some cooling off had been in order. Jīngfēi had needed a few weeks in the mountains to wash away her negativity in the cool streams. She had returned refreshed and insistent.

"This is the last time, Bó. I can tell you that for a certainty because if you stand again…If you stand again, I'll leave you; I know you will not allow that. It's true, right?"

"That will not happen. It won't. I'll promise you now. I will not stand next year. I already announced it at the meeting to swear me in. Honest. When they offered me the yellow and then the lifetime position, that's when I told them. I said this is the last year I will serve. It seems most of them were quite accepting. In fact, Jīng, I do not understand how I could have been voted in again anyway. It's not as if I'm popular; I–"

"You're popular with me, and that's all that matters. Besides. I have news."

"I hope it's good news because the council is all over the place."

"I found Yú!" The three words that Jīngfēi uttered forced Bóyì's sad face into the explosion of an ever-widening grin. He almost catapulted

Thirty-one: The Passage

himself into his wife's arms, tears streaming down his face. "He's safe!" she comforted him.

"I told you. I told you that message was—"

"I think I told you, Bó! But, and here's the thing, only a tiny group knows he's alive. They are also the only ones who know where he is. It must remain our secret here in Èrlĭtou. You know…You know I would never have been away so long if it wasn't important, don't you?"

The conversation came to a swift conclusion as they collapsed onto their bed, thrashing around like a couple of teenagers as they ripped each other's clothes off. It was several hours before any further conversation was possible. Later, they sat naked on the kitchen floor, each nursing a jug of beer.

When Jīngfēi brought Bóyì up to date on the hidden valley, she also told him there were aspects of Líng's speech that she had promised not to reveal just yet; he was accepting. Trust between the two was absolute. However, when he described some happenings in Èrlĭtou, they approximated developments that Líng had forecast. It was hard for Jīngfēi to keep herself from nodding in agreement or interjecting with 'that's just what she said.' It seemed the decline was already setting in.

In council before the elections, they had determined to reduce the council's size. It had become too unwieldy. Surprisingly, seeing as the number of councillors was halved, it had been a popular motion. It seemed the greater good was put before individuals' ideas of status. Instead of two representatives for each one hundred farms, the number was reduced to one. They executed the simplest method of maintaining representation yet halved the council numbers, bringing it down to a reasonable size. Due to town growth and a few changes to representatives' boundaries, the new body would come in at fewer than a hundred members, representing a total population of over fifty thousand if one included all the children.

Èrlĭtou had grown enormously. The land bounded by the Luòhé and Yī Rivers was now almost fully occupied. Any further expansion of farmland would have to be outside the area protected by the two waterways. Any additional expansion project would prove expensive, which was another contentious issue for the council to argue about.

The composition of the new governing body gathered to vote in Bóyì was a shock. In the reorganisation, the requirement for one female and one male had been scrapped; the consequences were appalling. Those gathered to observe Bóyì's swearing-in were almost entirely male; the few females present felt overwhelmed. If it had not been a ceremonial occasion, Bóyì would have dismissed the council and called for a re-election. It was not a body with which he felt he could work.

"You know, Jīng, this is something I do not understand. How did we end up with all these men?" Bóyì's brow was deeply furrowed. "We've always run society equally between men and women. It's–"

"I can tell you what it is, Bó. It's as simple as this. Everyone has a bias; it's built-in. It's built-in for men and women. If you like, they're equally biased."

"What's that got to do with it?"

"Well, men are biased towards voting for men as leaders…true?" Her husband nodded, "And you would think that women were biased towards voting for women as leaders…yes?" He nodded again. "Well, that's not true. Some women are biased towards voting for women, but some are biased towards voting for men. Really!"

"So, what you're saying is that–"

"I'm saying that when you had a male and female candidate for each area, you achieved a perfectly balanced split on the council. If you don't have that constraint then, due to bias, even with an electorate split half and half between men and women, you will almost automatically end up with a male-dominated council."

"It makes sense; why didn't we think about that?"

"Who sat on the re-organisation committee?"

"Well, me and - and it was three other men - it looks like…How come the council voted it through?"

"Did you check who voted which way?"

"No, it was a show of hands."

"Well, there you are then. I would willingly offer up my evening meal to you as a wager that the vote was split, almost exactly male-female, but the balance was tipped by those female counsellors who are biased towards men. I'll tell you what; I'll find out for you." She laughed, "One more year. It'll kill you, Bó! What other disasters occurred while I was away?"

Thirty-one: The Passage

Bóyì went on to explain how Hòutú's appointees, Cóng and Cāng Jié, had come up with some disturbing imbalances in the exchequer. It seemed there was too little grain in storage, and this after two good growing seasons. People were persisting in their complaints about the contributions they had to give at harvest time, pointing to the lower taxes applied in the satellite states. It seemed some were beginning to hide their actual yields. Indeed, the stocks were down, although even the most ignorant would have expected them to be up.

"Cóng suggested putting guards on the grain storage and...Well, this is a funny thing...Cāng Jié said that would be pointless, as they'd be bribed to look the other way."

"Who by?" Jīngfēi whispered in his ear. She had just started to massage his shoulders, which felt unduly knotted, requiring her to knead harder.

"Well...they wouldn't speculate, but I think...that they think...that it's Háng. You see, his money system...Yes, that's the spot. Harder, yes!...has to be backed by an equivalent of grain and whatever he says, he does not have enough grain." Jīngfēi groaned, but Bóyì continued, "If you think that's bad, then it gets worse...much worse. Some people who have collected enough want to pay their taxes with Háng's silk *qián*. You can see where that's going to go. The exchequer could be filled with little patches of worthless cloth if Háng so much as looks at a crack in a dam wall. That's one more mess...Thank you, ah...but they discovered something else while digging into the stocks."

"Something else that's missing?"

"Yes. Remember all that jade we brought from Táosì?"

"Yes, I'd almost forgotten about it. Isn't it sitting in storage somewhere? Nobody could work out what to do with it."

"That's true, but now only half of it is in storage, so somebody determined they did know what to do with the other half."

"No one is going to miss it, are they?"

"Here's a problem, Jīng. I was told it was all there just after Yú left, which means–"

"Which means that you can be held responsible. True? Well, I'd not doubt pointing a finger on that one. He may be an old friend, but the barman has much explaining to do. You know about the passage, don't you?"

"What passage?" Bóyì playfully slipped his hand under the hem of her smock, only to receive an unexpected slap on his wrist.

"That'll have to wait!" She kissed him reassuringly. "Well, there were only four entrances into the council compound, all clear as day. All are monitored, if not guarded. However, there is now one more, and it's pretty much a secret, which is why you don't know about it. Well, that and the fact you walk around with your head stuck in the sand most of the time."

"A secret passage?"

"Mmm. A passage. It leads from Qí and Tú's rooms inside the wall into the whores' quarters at the back of Háng's central bar. It was purportedly built to make it more convenient for Háng and Qí to meet regularly. It's supposed to be guarded."

"Not by the army, it isn't - I'd know about it!"

"No, not the army, Háng's henchmen. Now, what Háng doesn't know is that not all his men are as loyal to him as the rest. One little bird told me that the passage was for convenient meetings. Interestingly, this little bird also told me the meetings tended to be between Háng and Tú and, and this is going to shock you, between Qí and the whores. I've heard that Háng pays them to keep him serviced."

"But he's only twelve years old!"

"He's not. He's thirteen. He's—"

"He's still too young. You know the rule of fourteen - it still applies."

"And you should know that hundreds of youngsters flout it every year; it's—"

"Maybe, but not with the whores. We turn a blind eye to a little dalliance between youngsters, but this is not the same."

Their discussion continued for hours about the rights and wrongs of the case, deflecting somewhat from the real focus of their concern, which was Háng. Bóyì determined he would approach the barman about the passage before widening their conversation to include more significant issues.

Thirty-one: The Passage

The following morning, bright and early, the council leader and his wife approached Háng's oldest and most central bar. They had hoped to catch the barman off guard, but the man himself was already awake and working. As usual, his attire was tidy, and it looked like he had made an effort to spruce himself up, which is more than could be said for Bóyì.

"Well, Jīngfēi, you're lookin' as beautiful as usual today. Good mornin'. It's a-lookin' like you're a takin' the dog for an early walk. Isn't it time for his bath?" Háng slapped Bóyì on his shoulder, ensuring his insult was taken as intended.

"Well, Háng, you know what it's like…once a month, we wash his fleas out, but they're always back the next day. You can tell by his scratching!" Jīngfēi peeled around, placing her arm around the barman's waist. "All this time…all this time, and I could have had you. Look what I've had to put up with!"

"You two should leave it out." Bóyì sported a playful scowl. "You know my powers extend as far as imprisoning you for as long as a month…without trial. I'll do it, you know. Insults most definitely constitute a crime, one that commands at least thirty days, and those days should be without food or water."

"The dog speaks! Have you thought about a takin' him around the countryside as a curiosity Jīngfēi? With your pretty looks and a dog that's a-talkin', you'd be a-gettin' free food and beer in every town you stopped. If they let him in, that is!"

The genuine fondness the three felt for each other would remain, notwithstanding the difficulties they had already faced and those to come. It was as if Háng regarded himself as a doting, although somewhat mischievous, uncle who believed he had provided a helping hand in Bóyì's meteoric career. There was little evidence to suggest he had played any part in the council leader's earlier role leading the army, and Bóyì's appointment to the council had been at Yú's behest. However, the barman had undoubtedly swung the two elections since. The fact that the position was something Bóyì would rather have had removed from his shoulders and one that Jīngfēi desperately wished would go away meant that, as well as longevity, a delicious irony underpinned the trio's bond.

Èrlĭtou, Hénán

"I'm afraid it's a working matter, Háng. We thought we'd catch you early before any business starts to arrive. Are you prepared to allow my scruffy, flea-ridden dog of a husband to come into your bar?"

The smile slipped somewhat on the barman's face. "And I thought you were a-comin' here to start an all-day drinkin' session. I suppose, if it's business, I can forget my sensibilities about his looks, and as you well know, Jīngfēi will be improvin' the appearance of any bar she steps into." Within seconds, the grin was back on his face.

"I found something out yesterday, and it has…err…let's say it has…perturbed me. It's this passage you've got that has been worrying me, Háng, worrying me a lot." While Bóyì spoke, the barman was desperately trying to work out how his friend might have found out. The council leader continued, "You know, one of my jobs is to ensure the council compound is secure, and I've just found out it has an entrance I know nothing about. What do you say to that?"

"Well…it does, and it doesn't; it's–"

"What's that meant to mean?" Jīngfēi was not supposed to be interjecting on council business but could not stop herself. Bóyì cast her a glance that suggested she should not do so again.

"Yes, Háng, what's that meant to mean?"

"Well, you see…there is a passage…yes, there is…but it's not an entrance or exit as such…it's an internal passage."

"That explains nothing. I'll make the question quite plain. Is there a way through which someone could pass from outside the council compound to the inside?"

"No."

"There is no passage?"

"No, there is a passage, but it's a-goin' between the back of my bar and the temporary residential quarters."

"Háng, you're deliberately obtuse. I can get from the street into your bar. Correct?"

"That's true. It wouldn't be much of a bar if you couldn't be a-gettin' to it, would it?" The barman winked at Jīngfēi.

"So, tell me. Can I get from the council courtyard into the temporary residential quarters? Yes or no, let's not have a wordy answer."

"Yes."

Thirty-one: The Passage

"So...by definition, I can get from the street into the council courtyard without being seen passing through the gates. Correct?"

"No," the barman shook his head definitively. "First, you'd be a-havin' to get past the bar staff, then you'd be a-havin' to pass through the whores' working rooms and disturbin' their customers, then you'd be a-passin' my guards, then you'd be a-openin' a barred door and then...and then you'd be a-dealin' with Tú and Qí. The answer is no: you cannot get into the council courtyard from the street. Most certainly not!"

A moment of clarity came to Bóyì. "Alright, I cannot pass from the street into the council courtyard. I understand, Háng, so...I'll re-phrase. Can you..." he put his finger onto the barman's chest, "Can you...you... Háng, pass from the street into the council courtyard?"

"Well, you've got me there, Bóyì." It was clear the obfuscation would not work, "I can do that. However, that's only because of the ordinance you was a-passin' a couple of moons back. It's why–"

"I did not pass an ordinance allowing a passage to be dug through the east wall of the council courtyard. It's unbelievable!"

"It's true. You were a-passin' an ordinance allowing for the improvement of access through the eastern wall."

"That was to improve the gate; it was falling down!"

"I think you'll be a-findin' it was non-spe...speci...specific. In effect, you ordered the passage built yourself!" The barman's triumphant look did not last long as Jīngfēi's face twisted into a glare that would have scared a giant bear. "I was just a-sayin'. That's how it was."

After the barman's confession, Háng took the time to show them the passage. It was as he had described, except for the whores, who were all sleeping as no customers remained. However, the barred gate was guarded, admittedly, by a man who was only bordering on consciousness. Háng would not take them through the door, explaining they would disturb Tú or Qí, although he wasn't clear which one. He politely asked that Bóyì request access from the other side and promised his guard would not be an issue. After saying their farewells to the barman, the council leader and his wife strolled off toward home; it was unlikely either Tú or Qí would be up and about just yet.

Jīngfēi determined it was time to bring up another issue. "You know that Háng will stop the free beer completely?"

Èrlǐtou, Hénán

"He can't do that! He'd not be given any supplies from storage. He'd find it diff…" it was slowly sinking in, "he'd…that is…" Bóyì's voice trailed off, although his head was swimming.

"He doesn't need it, Bó. He's got everything he needs, although it'll be impossible to prove; you know what he's like. He can maintain his silk *qián* system if he's siphoned off the grain stores. He can buy imports using that jade if he has it. You know outsiders love that stuff. He's already in control, Bó. All he needs now is to put someone in as council leader. Someone whom he can control." Jīngfēi sighed, "I told you not to stand…you should have listened, Bó."

"I should. All I know is that I'm not in his pocket."

"True…and…we're in this together…let's see if we can minimise the damage in the next year. Cóng and Cāng Jié are doing a good job on the accounting; he won't get to them. That's crucial. Měnghǔ seems to have the bronze well under control, and she's straight as an arrow. It doesn't matter much with the army because if the new leader isn't so good, they'll still be loyal to you. You're going to have to give Hétóngzǐ a lot of support with the water control, but he's not going to be swayed by Háng. In fact, Háng's probably not bothered about him because that irrigation stuff is too long-term. I hate to say this, but that leaves you with Lài, and we know there are serious problems with the granaries. I'd say she is the one in Háng's pocket. That's it, Bó, it's Lài! The devious cow!"

Thirty-two: The Arrest
Èrlĭtou, Hénán
Year 103. Year of the Ox
Ten days after the summer solstice
1st July 1892 BCE

Of the entire town's folk, only one person had expected things to turn out as they had. Of all the possible outcomes, it had seemed that a continuation of normality was the most likely result and, with a bit of luck, a return to what people were increasingly calling the good old days. All but a few desired that Yú should once again run Èrlĭtou. It was considered a miserable misfortune he was dead. People remembered the early years and conveniently forgot many of the problems.

In the absence of the man who, year after year, they had asked to become their leader for life, the only logical step for many was to elect his son. After all, had the boy not promised to follow in his father's footsteps and lead them with a caring hand? If they could not have their hero, they could follow the product of their hero's loins.

The meeting of the new moon, held just two days before the summer solstice, had seen the commencement of a party lasting four days. Few outside the army mourned Bóyì stepping down. After all, what was there that had been a success during his period of leadership? The list of his errors grew. Gradually, the populace found that misdemeanours and even crimes were added to the accusations and attributed to Bóyì. It was not so much that everyone accepted the charges levelled against their former leader, more that they wanted to believe them.

Everything became a little clearer with the full moon shining brightly on the town and fields. First, there had been the party, with food and drink supplied in quantity and at no cost. The affair had continued from the day of Qí's accession until late into the night of the longest day.

Following the celebrations came the arrest of Bóyì and Jīngfēi; the pair were now incarcerated in the council buildings.

The more perceptive struggled to accept Qí's response to the two questions asked with pomp and formality each year. The council members cheered uproariously when he affirmed that he would wear yellow. When he accepted the offer to lead them for his entire lifetime, the applause had been a little more delayed. The proposal, made each year, had finally been accepted. Crossing the minds of almost all the one hundred councillors was the thought that it was an enormous leap of faith to appoint a fourteen-year-old in perpetuity. They had taken a giant step without considering all the consequences; it was one that the council could not retract.

It was also customary to grant the incoming council leader three requests. Yú had always got around this one by asking for a jar of beer, a piece of bread, and asking one of the more tone-deaf councillors to sing a lengthy song at Háng's bar. His wishes had always been granted, and the crowds attending the musical performance had been legendary. One of the first indications that Bóyì would never attain his predecessor's popularity is that he had opposed the tradition and had declined to ask for anything.

Qí's requests had been strange, although not apparently without thought; they appeared innocuous enough. The first generated some sympathy from the council members when he asked people not to look at his face during meetings. The youth's disfigurement at the hands of the Wolf Pack had been considerable. Few did not look twice and stare; there were fewer still for whom his features did not elicit either disgust or sympathy. Their new leader was undoubtedly not elected due to his looks. He boldly stated that his visage should not distract the state's business. It was considered a brave appeal and granted immediately.

The second request was that they extend their leader's right to have a pause on council decisions. Qí cited the example of Háng's debts from years before. There was some surprise that he had any knowledge of the incident, as virtually none of the council could recall the precedent. However, as he pointed out, the last thing he would do was delay any emergency measures; the whole thing seemed perfectly acceptable, and again, there was agreement.

The third was more of a bureaucratic convenience and not one given more than a passing thought. Qí wanted a permanent secretary to

Thirty-two: The Arrest

the council and its leader, who would keep the minutes up to date, ensure ordinances were posted and so forth. He requested that Lài be appointed and a panel seek a replacement to run the granaries.

*

Háng had unusually slept away from his bar the previous night. He seemed to recall being dragged away by three women, but his memory of any later detail was minimal. He was not robbed; however, there were curious scratches on his body, extending across his abdomen and down his arms and legs. He was still considering whether it might have been a good night when he reached the central bar. Above the door, a nailed sign proclaimed, 'Permanently closed at the orders of Háng'. His brain still somewhat addled, he paused to allow the message to sink in.

It had certainly been no order that he had made; the message ran counter to his entrepreneurial spirit. If he had closed the bar, the last thing he would have done would be to put his name to it; that would be business suicide. 'Sorry we're closed, we ran out of beer" was more like what he would have composed. It dawned on him that someone else had written and erected the sign and deliberately positioned it to make it too high for him to remove. Someone must have it in for him.

Háng believed he was standing at the dawn of a golden age for his businesses and personal wealth, with Qí at the helm and his hand on the boy's shoulder. In addition, he had their new leader's aunt at his beck and call, seemingly prepared to lavish sexual favours on him. It seemed there was nothing that could stop him, but unfortunately, it wasn't quite going to work out that way.

"We are arresting you on behalf of the council leader." The man who had crept up behind Háng was undoubtedly confident, but there again, he was accompanied by five associates. Háng did not turn.

"I'm thinkin' that's not a-goin' to be the case. You see, if I'm a-openin' this door, an' I've got twice as many men inside as you do out. We'll soon see heads a-rollin'." Háng remained with his back towards the man. "Would you like to be a-goin' away sooner…or later?" As the door opened, the barman called inside. There was no response. A cough alerted him to the fact that those behind still accompanied him. "Are you still here? You lot must be a-losin' your minds waitin' here!" With that, he turned impatiently.

It was with some surprise that Háng noted the men all wore a flash of yellow on their shoulders. It was more shocking as it sunk in that the men facing him were none other than the staff he had been employing as security at his bars. Fear began to set in when they dragged him away.

Qí watched the scene from a distance. He liked the rule about the leader wearing yellow because it was clear he could not be their leader when he chose not to. He tossed the word around for a bit - leader! No, it was not good enough. It wasn't quite as enjoyable wearing a scarf around his face, but although he had ensured it was of the finest silk, he did not draw a second glance. Plenty of men and women covered their faces from the harsh sun of midsummer.

So, Háng was out of the way. Qí had given it the better part of a month and had learned a great deal from the barman. The flow of information and skills had begun to level off; instead, there were constant demands for favours. The new leader of Èrlǐtou considered the time had come; he would not be controlled. He watched as the barman was dragged towards the council buildings.

The list of crimes committed by Háng was so long that great care had to be taken. Qí could not consider any with which he could be implicated. In the eyes of the townspeople, the cardinal crime would be that the barman had closed up shop. The rumour already circulating was that the bar closures, a decision seemingly made solely by Háng, would be permanent. A second whisper was going around that a large quantity of stolen jade lay beneath the floors of each of Háng's establishments. There was a third, on paper, the most serious of the three, which speculated the barman's wife lay interred alongside the jade in one of the bars. It had yet to sink in with anyone that imprisoning the man who underwrote their nascent currency might cause more significant problems.

Qí had thought the plan to be excellent when his mother revealed it to him six months previously. If she could turn Háng's staff, which was not particularly hard as they were not well-treated, then he could turn them again. He could, and he did. It was so brilliant he had made the plan his own.

Thirty-two: The Arrest

If Qí had learned much from Háng, he had learned much more from his mother. Háng had taught him manipulation, his mother had taught him subtle guile, and Fēngbō had taught him how to channel and disguise his inherent cruelty in ruling. His birth father had essentially deserted him. His mother had arranged for those three bitches to smash and scar his face and dispose of his adopted father, for whom he had a peculiarly close attachment. He was an exceptionally intelligent boy with a massive chip on his shoulder.

Tú repeatedly told him his destiny had been fulfilled. She had whispered the idea in his ear for as long as he could remember. It was time the whispering stopped. He was a man now, and he was a leader. Not only was he the leader of Èrlǐtou, but he was the leader of the Xià Empire. Just as he hated using the name Qí, he hated being thought of as 'leader'; it was simply not grand enough. An empire deserved an emperor.

He was in a quandary as to how to deal with his mother. She was clearly using him for her own ends, although whether others controlled her was less obvious. To have her destroyed would be ideal, but only if he could find out what was driving her. Qí knew well enough that Tú would not give up her secrets easily or quickly; it was this that saved her from immediate execution. He would make a play suggesting that death might be his course of action, but he needed to keep her secure, which was difficult; she would need to be kept under guard.

The idea formed gradually, but his mind was never far from the whores. He now felt he had integrated them into his personal protection unit; they could be her guardians. The thought settled into a fully formed plan; his mother would oversee his harem, and the harem would keep his mother captive. There was a perfection to the symmetry. Satisfied, the new leader turned his mind from what he thought of as social policy to that of finance.

The closure of the bars had two intended effects. The first was to alienate the barman and, in doing so, strengthen Qí's popularity when he re-opened the bars. He would offer all the goods at no charge, perhaps while stocks lasted, blaming Háng for any shortages. To improve the offer, he summoned the whore's leader, a woman called Biǎozi.

"What I want from your lot is some hard work." Qí watched her face as she studiously avoided looking at his own.

Èrlĭtou, Hénán

"But…sir…my lord…we do work hard. Now you've taken those girls into the compound - we'll have to work harder to make up for those missing."

"I see your point. So, tell me what I can do to improve things for you so you can cope with more customers."

"We call the customers 'boys,' my lord, it sort of sounds better."

"Alright, how do I get you all to see more boys?"

"Well… Háng kept us in dreadful conditions. You could improve those. Better food would be good. Best of all, though…well, that would be a reward when we wanted to stop."

"You mean you receive something for the number of years you've been whoring?"

"Yes…like a farm…or some land anyway."

"I'll make you a promise, Biăozi. Let's have the girls working flat out, and I'll make sure there is better food, better accommodation, and some sort of plan for when you finish whoring. That is a deal. We can do the food immediately, the quarters within a week, and the retirement plan before the winter solstice. Does that sound fine?"

"It sounds wonderful. Thank you, my lord."

"You now have permission to look at my face." The girl raised her eyes, staring directly into Qí's, avoiding looking at the terrible scars on his face. "I am making a promise…are you?"

"I am. I promise, my lord."

"You can go now. Make sure all the other whores know. Go!"

Qí had not expected to have such an excellent idea presented to him by a sex worker. The scheme she proposed could be applied to various occupations, and the first that came to mind was the army. There may not be much land left between the two rivers, but there was plenty to the north and south. Now, he also had access to the farms Háng had taken on as debt payment. He decided that his first proclamation would assign all land to the emperor unless it were already legitimately owned. It was a masterstroke.

The bar closure's second effect focussed on Háng's silk currency. Qí had stolen the idea from the barman himself. With Háng's businesses closed, the silk swathes were worthless; many townspeople would cry into their broth over this. Qí planned to offer to buy back the silk notes at

Thirty-two: The Arrest

maybe half the nominal value, knowing that the state granaries would cover the cost in the short term. People would doubtless jump at the prospect of having something rather than nothing. After a while, he would reintroduce the exchange system at its original value, thus doubling the value of the silk he held. The people's losses could all be blamed on the barman. The reintroduction would prove popular with most, and although the losers may be somewhat upset, it was something with which he could live. In the long term, he may need to repeat the stunt; that required more thought.

Time was short. Qí summoned Lài to discuss his silk-for-grain plan. He then called for Háng's number two, whom he planned to put in charge of the army. However, the man's first job would be to test run a bar re-opening the following night. When both meetings were over, he turned his mind back to his very own private group of whores.

Èrlĭtou, Hénán

Thirty-three: The Imprisonments
Èrlĭtou, Hénán
Year 103. Year of the Ox
Eleven days after the summer solstice
2nd July 1892 BCE

The prison cell that held Bóyì and Jīngfēi was nothing more than a large room at the rear of the council chamber. The doorway housed no door, and there was no guard. Anyone was free to walk in or out except for the couple now held there. It had been King Léigōng who had devised the multiple *jiā*[34] holding system.

Most walls in Èrlĭtou, and nearly all the Lóngshān cities, were built of tamped earth. Any prisoner worth his salt could escape from such a cell with ease. Generally, a tunnel could be created, and escape could be affected in a single night. To avoid the cost of bringing in stone, Léigōng had devised a system of restraint using a wooden halter stock. These were not used singly but were usually designed for two, three or four people, as a single device could provide an enterprising prisoner with an effective digging tool. Multiple prisoners could not coordinate sufficiently.

Bóyì and Jīngfēi had been placed naked in a four-person *jiā*, which was proving somewhat heavy. They were also positioned in the first and fourth slots, meaning they were distanced from each other. It had been several days since their imprisonment, two days in the *jiā*, two days with their hands raised to head level; the pain in their arms was excruciating. Sunrise had come and gone; the heat of the summer's morning began to penetrate the room.

"I need a shit, Bó. Sorry." Her eyes begged for sympathy.

---

[34] A cangue or tcha, which is a wooden board worn around the neck, in this case the cangue had space for four prisoners.

Thirty-three: The Imprisonments

"Alright, let's go. Ready?" When she nodded, they both backed up two steps and dropped into a squat. A short burst of diarrhoea issued forth, most missing the gutter that ran the room's length. With her hands firmly fixed in the halter stock at neck level, there was no option but to allow the splatter down her legs to remain.

"Jīng, when they come back with some water, I'll ask them to throw some over you, as well as down the gutter. Are you alright?"

"I'm getting weaker, Bó. I'm not sure how long I'll last. It wouldn't be as bad if it were possible to lie down, but these cross pieces are evil."

The wooden beam she referred to ran at right angles to the main planks, a simple design that meant that even if they turned through ninety degrees and formed a file, they could still not exit through the door. It was an ingenious device, one that both Yú and Bóyì had banned from use in Èrlĭtou. It was a shock to find a working model in the town.

There was the clanking of arms from the courtyard.

"They're coming. Jīng, you should ask them. These thugs Qí's using are not army; they're Háng's enforcers. You know them well; there's bound to be some sympathy. Ask them."

A group of six men appeared at the doorway carrying a seventh; Háng drooped between them. The barman was not his voluble self and had clearly been struck in the face, for blood still streamed from his swollen mouth.

The only way for their captors to install Háng in the stock was to release the fettered couple temporarily. A knife at each of their necks provided a deterrent against any attempt to run. However, Jīngfēi's request was granted. She found it enormously challenging to lower her arms to clean herself and resorted to rubbing the shit off with her feet. One of the gaolers appeared to take sympathy, splashing water on her lower legs and rubbing at the stains. As his nose came level with her pubic hair, it was clear that lust had overtaken sympathy.

"Get off her! Now!" Someone was in charge; their leader took a dim view of one of his men sniffing out for sex. "Leave her be! Now!"

The transgressor stood, maintaining an evil grin while leaning in and whispering to Jīngfēi, "Next time…and next time it'll not be my nose pressing your fanny fur," before stepping away.

Èrlĭtou, Hénán

Háng was stripped before they were lined up once more, the wooden planks clamped around their necks and wrists, while the ropes were tied, carefully positioned so that none of the prisoners could reach them. The squad left with no further comment. It would be up to the ex-council leader and his wife to train the barman to survive the *jiā*. With their friend almost unconscious, they were obligated to support a large part of his weight. As he had been positioned next to Jīngfēi, she was taking the brunt.

"Let's hope the next person they bring in is fit and strong, Jīng." Bóyì tried to smile at his partner but found seeing around Háng's head difficult. He had a genuine concern; whilst he was fit and well, it was clear that the barman was not, and Jīngfēi was weakening rapidly. The thought of one of the two dying where they stood or dying as they fell was foremost on his mind.

It was not until mid-afternoon that his wish was granted. Still, the pleasing prospect of a fourth occupant of the group cangue was overridden somewhat by their shock at the individual's identity. The same goon squad as before dragged in a somewhat disorientated, dishevelled, although near-silent female. It was Tú.

The gaffer seemed less protective of the new arrival than he had earlier been of Jīngfēi. They were delighted when they ripped off her smock and found the tattoo. Too many fingers traced the inkwork and dwelt in regions they should not touch. Their leader's mother was receiving an unwanted mauling, which could have only occurred with permission from her son.

For a second time in the day, there was the relief of a temporary release, and with the squad more focused on Tú, it was at least possible to massage their arms. Háng's state was of great concern; he could barely stand unassisted. The addition of a fourth body would at least make the likelihood of total collapse less likely. When they were all back in position, and the guards had left, it was time to rearrange themselves. The barman hampered the coordination of their movements, but gravity was on their side. As the three of them dropped first to their knees and then into a sitting position, Háng dropped with them, Tú and Jīngfēi kicking at his legs to force him into the same poses they adopted. Eventually, they

Thirty-three: The Imprisonments

were all seated, and it was possible to use the crossbars to hold themselves in that position.

With everyone slightly more comfortable, now was the time to interrogate the newcomer.

"You're the last person I expected dragged through that door, and that was after the second last person I expected had just been brought in. What's going on, Tú?" Although Bóyì was fascinated by the latest addition, he wondered whether it would make it easier or harder to escape. However, it was not as if he had a plan. "I hope you're going to be able to fill us in a little more than Háng has."

"It seems my son has determined we present a danger to him. It seems he has determined that right now, that danger is greater than any benefit any of us might bring. It seems he has probably worked out that of all the people in Èrlǐtou, only we four could identify who he is. In a way, I'm quite proud of him; there's no denying his intelligence, and that can only have come from me," she laughed hoarsely.

"I will say, though, I've never liked him. Well, not since he passed the age of two or three. He's not a nice boy, which I suspect you have gathered from the conditions in which we are now held; it stinks of shit in here. I know Háng's only been here since this morning, so how long have you two been locked up?"

"Over two days. It's hell—Jīng's in a worse state than me. It would be great if you could help her by taking some of Háng's weight; I can do little at this end. The biggest problem is that if someone needs to piss or shit, we must be very coordinated. I'm not sure what'll happen when we get to eat, as we've not been offered anything yet. They've come morning and night with water, but I suspect it's straight out of the local ditch. Jīng's got terrible diarrhoea."

"I'll try to help with Háng, but if Jīngfēi is losing strength, it's going to be difficult supporting that end. They both look terrible. Let them sniff around my body like dogs; a lot of good it's going to do them. Look, Háng might have resisted arrest, but I didn't. I suspect he thought he was untouchable; I've never taken such things for granted."

"I think they did this on purpose, putting you two on either side of the barman. It would have been much easier if I'd been on the other end."

Èrlǐtou, Hénán

"They'll have not have thought about it. This is my son's doing. He'll have instructed them; he's a stickler for planning out detail."

"Jīng, are you alright?"

"Hanging in there, Bó. What's upsetting me is that they put you next to someone who tried to seduce you once."

"Come on, Jīngfēi. That was a long time ago. I'm hardly likely to be able to nuzzle up to him now, am I." Tú laughed before continuing, "If I did, there's not much you could do about it, is there? I know he used to fancy me – once!"

"It might be better if we apply our minds to getting out of here rather than discussing who he and she might have fancied all those years ago. I–"

"Whose talking years ago? I've seen her looking at you, Bó. The trouble is that she looks at so many men the same way. Word has it, Tú, you've been spending a lot of time in Háng's bed. Is that true?"

"It's true enough, Jīngfēi, the work of the Sisterhood is never done. Well, I say that, but I think with this…well, this might just count as retirement. I've had enough input over the years. My use runs out if I don't have access to the power base. We've got the boy emperor the Sisterhood always wanted. I'm not sure he will do what's expected, but he's certainly had the training. You know, if that stupid cow Túshānshì hadn't blown away Yú, none of this would have happened. Yú would still be leader, Bóyì would never have had to be, my son would still be in training, and Túshānshì's son wouldn't be dead. If this thing goes badly wrong, only she carries the blame."

"What? Not you? Not you for bringing up such an objectional child? You've got to take some of the blame, surely? And, you know, her…" Jīngfēi almost let slip that Yú and Túshānshì's son was still alive, managing to bite her tongue just in time.

"Shh! What's that noise?" All three listened intently. However, whatever it was, possibly a rat, was scared off by the guards' approach once more.

"Bóyì," Tú was whispering now, "I'm not quite ready for retirement. I managed to get myself put in here temporarily, even if Qí thinks it's his idea. They'll be coming to take me out, and there'll be a replacement you know well." She shook her head when Bóyì tried to

Thirty-three: The Imprisonments

respond. "Listen. There will be a rescue. I have information from outside, from the Sisterhood. Could you wait for it? Don't try to escape yourselves; they'll kill…" she fell silent as the same guards entered once more, this time dragging Shénnóng, the army's top general, the man whom Bóyì had appointed as his replacement.

"Thank–" Bóyì was silenced.

"No talking! Right, let's do all this over again. It seems that one of you is to be housed with the whores. Not any whores either! Our lead…Our emperor's private whores!" Twice as many troops accompanied the sergeant.

"I'd rather die!" Jīngfēi's look was one of murder rather than suicide.

"It's not you…it's her!" The sergeant pointed at Tú. "It's beyond me why our leader…sorry, emperor, should want his aunty locked up with his playthings, but that's the order."

"I'll come peacefully, sergeant. No fuss," Tú smiled disarmingly, "better to be a working woman than a dead one!"

The whole rigmarole was repeated for a third time. Háng could support himself this time, but he was holding on by a thread. When they were left alone again, Bóyì turned to the army leader.

"Well met, Shénnóng." They were friends from way back. Shénnóng had been Bóyì's final appointment. "What did you do to upset the boy?"

"I'm not sure I should be telling you, really."

"Why's that?"

"You might not like the idea…I refused an order."

"That's not good. Not a wise career choice."

"True, clearly it was not. I think you would have done the same. They wanted me to execute some friends."

"Who?"

"You…" Shénnóng paused momentarily, "…and her and him…all of you."

The pair were silent, which made it easier to hear that the scraping sound had resumed.

Èrlǐtou, Hénán

Thirty-four: The Escape
Èrlǐtou, Hénán
Year 103. Year of the Ox
Eleven days after the summer solstice
2nd July 1892 BCE

"It's coming from behind me, directly behind me. Can we rotate this thing?" Jīngfēi had adopted a furtive tone as if she were part of whatever was going on rather than being someone who simply wished to be an observer.

There was only just enough room to turn the massive contraption, but with Háng now able to hold his body weight, the exercise became feasible. It took time, however. As they completed a half rotation, the lower part of the wall directly in front of Bóyì began to crack. It was the end of the gutter through which their waste had exited: a short bronze dagger thrust back and forth, the crack widening by the second. Within moments, an ever-growing hole formed, through which a pair of determined eyes were visible. The stabbing became scraping, then carving, before a mop of black hair appeared, then a face. Incredibly, for the hole seemed too small even for the head, an arm thrust its way through.

"They always say…" the individual panted, "they always say if you can get…your head and an arm…through…the rest is easy. Well, you can tell that to me, and it makes sense. You try telling that to Xiǎo or Kuài because they'd get their hips stuck. Not me!" As the girl pulled herself out and upright, the four prisoners had a clear view of the tunnel she had appeared from; a rabbit would have struggled; it was tiny.

Now, five naked people were in the room: four clamped into the group *jiā*. Even when the halter was opened, they still had to exit the council compound, cross the centre of Èrlǐtou and pass through one of the gates - naked.

Thirty-four: The Escape

"My name's Dàláng. You can call me Dà. Where are your clothes?"

"Where are yours, young lady?" Jīngfēi had struggled, having a naked Tú in the room. This one looked like a smaller version, albeit with a body covered in scratches, dried mud and what smelled much like faeces. She wrinkled her nose.

"They're here." The girl pulled on a length of twine, winding it around her left hand and elbow until a small package appeared from the aperture she had recently exited. She quickly pulled a smock over her lithe, muscled body. "Now, let's make a start!"

Her dagger flashed as she hacked through the sturdy bindings holding the two halves of the *jiā's* frame. "Support the weight. Come on. You've got to help out here. What's wrong with him? That's Háng, isn't it?" The barman had collapsed as soon as he was free. Jīngfēi swiftly joined him on the floor, although her fall was voluntary. She promptly kneeled over the barman, massaging his wrists and neck alternately, ignoring the shooting pains in her shoulders and arms.

"And I know you…" she sliced through the final binding, "You're Bóyì!" The ex-council leader caught the ends of the two planks, groaning as the weight stretched his muscles almost to the point of ripping. "Well, Bóyì, where are your clothes?"

"We've no idea. We haven't seen them in over two days. Shénnóng's in the best state; he was only put in here moments ago. Shénnóng, where did they put your clothes?"

"I haven't a clue, Bóyì, not a clue. Thank you, Dà, but do you have a plan?"

"We had a plan, but that plan did not involve the four of you displaying yourselves all over town. Èrlǐtou's not a place for four naked, well-known individuals to stroll around. We'll have to make a few changes." Dàláng scrambled over to the hole in the wall, putting her mouth to it and, in a half-whisper, said, "I'm in. Problem. No clothes. Need fast exit with cover. Five of us." Before turning her ear to listen for the answer.

"There's two wolves out there, and they say they'll have an alternative in a few moments. I don't know you. What's your name?" Dàláng peered into the army leader's face.

"Shénnóng." The man was unused to being unknown,

"Well, can you kneel by this hole and call me over when we have an answer." She turned to Bóyì, "You know this place, there's four gates and my tunnel. None of you will fit through the tunnel. None of you can walk out of the gates in this state. Is there another exit point?"

"There is. But, you see, it's a bit of a problem. It runs from Qí's rooms in the compound to Háng's bar, just outside the wall. I doubt that Qí would be happy about our using his rooms, and the bar will be packed."

"It's not. It's closed." They were the first words the barman had spoken since being dragged into the cell. "Completely closed."

Dàláng pushed Shénnóng aside from his listening position. "We can exit from the bar. Do you know where Qí is?"

This time, the reply was audible to all, "He's at another bar on the south bridge. It seems they're making a big fuss about re-opening it. Sounds like another party night."

"What about Tú because, surprisingly, she's on our side?" Bóyì asked.

"Any news on Tú?" Dàláng repeated the message to the hole in the wall, "She may help."

"Nothing. We've no information." The hole spoke back. "We're going to bring a four-wheeled cart round to the front of the bar. There'll be a covering over it. We'll offload some large beer jars. We'll make it look like they're full, leaving space on the wagon for you. You'll have to lie squeezed in, and it would be better if you found some clothing if you're coming through Qí's quarters."

"The guards said they would put Tú with Qí's private whores. We can only guess what that might mean." Jīngfēi had stopped massaging Háng, who now joined in the discussion.

"I'm a-thinkin' it'll be a chamber backin' onto the whores' quarters," Háng was returning to life, although he still looked a miserable wreck, "just this side of the passage door. Qí was a-plannin' to have some of the girls for himself. I'm not sure if he had them agreein' or not."

"The questions are whether they'll help or not, whether Tú will be able to assist and whether the door has a guard. It should be easy if they cooperate and there's no guard on the door." Dàláng oozed confidence.

Thirty-four: The Escape

"If the bar is closed, they'll not be a guardin' it. For sure. I'm a-thinkin' he'll be a usin' the guards wherever he is." Háng was desperate to be seen to be helping.

Dàláng lay down, speaking again to the wall, "We'll be out sometime after dark. Make sure the wagon's up close to the bar door. See you later."

They were now all physically capable of exiting the room, although Háng required some support. There was no guard outside the room, but there could still be people finishing their day's business or even a cleaning crew in the courtyard. It was reassuring that the town had been in party mode and that most of Qí's hangers-on would likely be with him on the south side. The first gamble was to cross the space from the cell door to the entrance to Qí's quarters. Dàláng had asked them to stay put while she reconnoitred the route and was back within moments, wiping blood from her dagger.

"One guard. Now dead. I've pulled him out of sight—no one else to be seen. When we get to the door, it's open. Could you two drag the sentry inside? Jīngfēi and I will look after Háng. Got it? Let's go!"

They scurried rather than ran, Háng dragged along by the two women. Shénnóng and Bóyì scooped up the dead guard, and they were all inside Qí's quarters before being noticed. The sudden action had enlivened the barman, and once the front door was closed behind them, he began to explain the layout before Dàláng urged him to lead them. There were a few twists and turns, but it was hardly a maze. They halted before a large, bolted door.

Háng looked confused. "That wasn't here before." He indicated a second door to the left; it, too, was bolted shut. "I'm a-thinkin' that'll be where he'll have stuck his mother and…that bein' the case…she'll be in with the women he's been a pickin'. Bóyì, what are you a-thinkin'?"

"I was wondering why anyone would want more than one woman and–"

"Ooh! I love you so much, Bó!" Jīngfēi squeezed his arm, "But I'm trying to work out why he would put his own mother in with the same girls he's planning to have entertain him. It doesn't make sense. My question is whether we should open the door and free them. And free Tú if she's in there."

Èrlǐtou, Hénán

"My question is, why do you keep referring to Qí's aunt as his mother?"

They all turned to look at Shénnóng, but no one was prepared to explain; the question remained hanging and unanswered.

"Why don't we ask them if they want to be freed?" Bóyì indicated a wooden hatch on the door. "Do you think this room they're in is soundproof? Can they raise the alarm from in there?"

"I'm a doubtin' it. All the whores' rooms had pretty thick walls; it makes sense, doesn't it. You don't want all the whorin' disturbin' the drinkin'. There's profit in both, you see, but some are a-likin' to keep their pleasures separate."

"Bóyì, you speak to them," Dàláng asked, "while we get this other door open."

The Wolf Pack's hitwoman went into a huddle with the barman, examining the device holding the door closed.

If there was something that Bóyì feared, it was talking to the whores; he always had been. He did not appreciate their role in society and was uncomfortable in their presence. It was akin to a human afraid of horses, where the horse would misbehave when confronted with such an individual. Bóyì felt the whores always misbehaved with him and tried to wind him up. His hesitancy provoked Jīngfēi into taking over. She cautiously lifted the small hatch, "Is anyone there?"

"Too right there is! There's ten of us in here. Ten plus one now, since an uppity older woman has compromised us."

"Do you mean Tú? Qí's mo…Qí's aunt?" Jīngfēi, like all of them, had some difficulty getting it wrong all the time.

"Are you Tú?" the whore turned into the room, which was in complete darkness. Obviously, there had been an answer, for she turned back, "Yes. It's dark in here; we can't make anything out. She says she's Tú. That means she's Qí's aunt. What's she doing in here with us?"

"I can't help you with that one," Jīngfēi was just as confused as the whore. "How many of you want to get out of there?"

"Now, you've got to understand something. We would all like to leave this room, but we all want to be in Qí's harem. It's a dilemma. If we escape from here, he might not take us on to take care of his - how do I

Thirty-four: The Escape

put this - needs. So, on balance, we've decided we might be better off staying here."

"And you're sure you're happy with the arrangement?"

"It's much better than the 'arrangement' we had with that sodding Háng!"

"Why's that?"

"Look, this way we get a few nights off, only have to work now and then…and get good food…and new clothes…and free beds…and he promised us a room each. Now, with Háng, we had up to seven or eight customers a night. We had to hand over our earnings to him to pay for crappy food. The beds were lice-ridden, and we had only one room to sleep together during the day. It was no life, no life at all. Qí's harem is a step up, and there's always the possibility of having a boy baby and making him take even more care of one of us."

Bóyì had to force himself, but he joined in, "You are saying that Háng treated you this badly…for how long?"

"For as long as we've been here, all of us. Fēng's been here longest. She's been with Háng since Táosì." She turned her head again, "Fēng, how long has Háng been treating us like shit?" She waited for the response before replying, "Since the first year here in Èrlǐtou, it started deteriorating. It got awful after Yú left, but that Túshānshì was a bad influence on Háng for years. Fēng says she had it in for us for some reason, although I think he just saw us as a source of more riches. You know he sold two whores last year, just as if we were horses?"

Bóyì was so shocked, and Jīngfēi had to take over once more, "Let's try to get this sorted. None of you wants to escape; is that right? None of you?"

"Correct."

"What about Tú?"

"You'll have to ask her. Hey, Tú, come here."

The emperor's mother's face appeared at the hatch. She whispered, "I'll be staying too, Jīng; it seems I have more work to do. I'll be in touch. Bye." With that, the hatch emptied. All its occupants had moved away to the far walls.

"Good luck!" Jīngfēi called out before dropping the hinged trap back into place. The oddity of the circumstance was extreme.

Èrlǐtou, Hénán

    The problem with the main door was that it had massive latches on both sides, which operated independently. With a guard on either side, it had never been a problem, and a password sufficed. Now, the difficulty appeared insurmountable. Dàláng had to get a message to her sisters that they had to open the door from the other side, the problem being they would not know how to find the exit. The only option would be for her to leave the escapees. It would mean risking a trip through the courtyard, out through the gates and round to the bar. It was impossible to tell from where they stood, but it should at least be getting dark.

    She explained the plan. Bóyì suggested that if caught, she should pretend she had fallen asleep after drinking too much. It was a common problem in the centre; he had spent many evenings ejecting drunks from the council compound. As it turned out, Dàláng had no such need for subterfuge. She passed unnoticed through the yard, exiting the eastern gate and looping back to the front of the bar. Waiting for her was Xiǎoláng, dressed as a male cart driver and holding the bullocks steady, together with Kuàiláng, whose widening smile was illuminated by the moon as she saw Dàláng approach.

    The street entrance to the bar was blocked entirely by the four-wheeled cart, which had a cloth thrown over its contents. The only way to make entry was to climb onto the flatbed, writhe under the fabric and drop down the other side. A large flagon stood by the side of the wagon, ready to be pushed into place to close the gap.

    "Through there, Kuài?"

    "That's right, Dà, I'm coming with you, but you go first; only you know where we're supposed to go. Xiǎo will mind the wagon. When we return, I'll slide across the wagon and guard the street-side side. You'll ensure our human cargo is loaded, then put this pitcher into the gap, blocking them in. I'll join Xiǎo on the driver's bench, and you'll have to wait until we move off to perch yourself on the back. Unless that is, you want to pretend to be Xiǎo's wife this time?"

    "No, I'll give that a miss; thank you. Anyone around acting suspiciously?"

    "Dead quiet…not a soul. Come on, let's get in there."

    The two squeezed themselves across the cart and into the bar; it was pitch black in the indoor section close to the entrance, but further in,

Thirty-four: The Escape

open hatches in the roof allowed enough moonlight to illuminate their route. Dàláng ducked under the bar and pushed at the door; it swung open easily.

"Come...follow me!" The pair gradually got a better sense of their surroundings as their night vision improved, but the patches of moonlight made the dark shadows impenetrable. "The one problem we might have is from the room on the right, so keep quiet, Kuài," she whispered to her wolf sister. "That's where the whores sleep, and after what I've heard, they might be a bit feisty right now."

"Well, you say that, but I think they all left for the party at the south side bar. I wouldn't have said they were feisty; it seemed like they were celebrating something. Let's have a look."

Pushing the door open, the immediate impression was that they might have entered a poorly managed barn; there was a horrendous smell.

"This is where these poor girls sleep?" Kuàiláng was astonished; I wouldn't keep my pigs in here!"

"It's more of a prison cell for them," Dàláng explained. "There's a bunch of them that have chosen to be the emperor's private whores rather than continue to live here. You can understand their reasoning. To think that anyone would choose the option of a life of opening their legs at the beck and call of an obnoxious fourteen-year-old makes you realise just how bad things must have been for them. They're choosing slavery over what? Slavery! Come, close that door; we'll think about that later. Someone should suffer for this, and I think I know who it should be!"

Two more turns in the corridor, and they reached the blocked door. Voices on the other side indicated the four escapees were ready for them. The large wooden latch raised relatively smoothly, and the door swung free. As Kuàiláng led three of them down the passage, through the bar and to the waiting cart, Dàláng held Bóyì back and showed him the whore's quarters. Once again, he was deeply shocked.

The slight delay meant that Háng and Shénnóng went on first, Jīngfēi third and Bóyì last. It meant the couple had to lie on the two men already installed. Bóyì found himself face to face with the army leader, whereas Jīngfēi was atop Háng; it was not a position in which she had ever wanted to find herself. Entrapped by flagons to their sides, heads and feet, the flatbed beneath them and a heavy blanket above, it was claustrophobic, to say the least. Kuàiláng ordered absolute silence, the bullocks took the strain, and the cart creaked forward.

Their most immediate concern was to escape with their lives, so it was a matter of tolerating the close physical proximity and nudity without comment. They were perhaps only three hundred paces down the track when Jīngfēi felt what seemed to be a rock-hard erection pressing into her belly. Worming her arm between herself and the barman, she slipped her hand down his penis before grabbing his balls. Her grip tightened as she whispered in Háng's ear.

"If you can't get rid of that thing, then I can," she twisted and pulled. "I can make it go away very quickly, and you…you have been told not to make a sound…" she twisted it again as the barman groaned, "…not a sound…Now. Do you want me to stop?" Háng nodded. She could feel dampness; he was crying in pain, but she continued to squeeze. "Enough then…it had better not come back…let's make sure!" With that, she dragged rough nails along what remained of his shrivelling penis.

Thirty-five: The Shāng

The Hidden Valley, Shǎnxī
Year 103. Year of the Ox
Three weeks to the autumn equinox
1st September 1892 BCE

It was a somewhat surreal gathering made more so by the headgear worn by all. Even the newcomers had been gifted fur hats, each receiving a lengthy explanation along with the head covering. It seemed the settlers had caused something of an imbalance in the local ecosystems by killing too many wolves. Now, the *háo zi*[35], with their predators' numbers minimised, had bred like rabbits. To restore the balance, it had become obligatory to wear a hat made from the skin of one of these fox-like animals, and their flesh was utilised to encourage the wolves back; it was a delicate balance.

There had been a curious side-effect. The inhabitants of the hidden valley were now avoided, even more than had been the case previously. The rumours, which no one tried to suppress, were that the fur gifted the wearer the art of shape-shifting. Quickly, the myth was elaborated and passed from tribe to tribe. The Hidden Valley became a place that only the mad or stupid would attempt to visit.

Those wearing *háo zi* hats were shunned. Indeed, most would run away from a wearer. For the wearers, removing and hiding their headgear brought renewed acceptance in the outside world. It was the best protection their growing community could have.

The four newcomers, Háng, Shénnóng, Jīngfēi, and Bóyì, were delighted to have escaped their likely fates in Èrlĭtou, even if they were

---

[35] Racoon dogs (Nyctereutes procyonoides). In Japanese mythology they are shapeshifters.

now on Qí's most-wanted list. Anything that further safeguarded them from prying eyes was a positive, and they donned their new hats with real pride and a sense of being protected.

Shénnóng had saved the lives of both Háng and Jīngfēi on their journey north, using his extensive knowledge of herbs to treat them. His appointment to the army's leadership had come when he had considered retiring to focus on medicines. Now, there was no going back. Shénnóng would farm herbs, while Bóyì and Jīngfēi would simply farm, albeit that Bóyì had a lot to learn. With Yú settled in contentedly with Líng, only Háng felt he needed to find a role in the valley.

"I'm a-tellin' you; it wasn't my fault. The grain, the jade, and the conditions those whores were kept in. None of it was down to me. You have to understand what was a-goin' on. You have to understand my up…upbrin'in'. It was never normal, you know."

Háng sat with Bóyì and Yú, the pair of them having determined to persuade him to explain his actions since the first year in Èrlǐtou and were somewhat surprised by his denials.

"If not you, Háng, then who is responsible? There's no one I can think of. Bóyì, what are your thoughts?" Yú was less attached to the barman than his successor on the Èrlǐtou council, although he still wanted to find a way to forgive him.

"I can't see how you can say all these things were not down to you," Bóyì grimaced. "You took the jade. You took the grain. You were supposedly looking after those whores. Who else can be to blame?"

"I was a-thinkin' you might be askin' that. Only now do I feel safe to tell you. Only now, I'm away from harm. You've been a-thinkin' that these were all my ideas, and it's just not true."

"Well, who then?" Yú was becoming exasperated.

"The missus."

"You're saying your wife, who, to be honest, I've never met and actually had come to believe did not exist, is responsible? How come, when we've been friends for as long as we have, that neither me nor Jīngfēi has ever met your wife? Yú, this is unbelievable!"

"She does exist…honest…but you see, I use the term 'missus', which is what I was always a callin' her, and you assume I was referrin'

Thirty-five: The Shāng

to my wife. I was not. The missus is my mother. I've never been married. The missus was not a-lettin' me."

"You're trying to tell us that you've been living all these years with your mother? You're trying to tell us that she told you to do all these things? Are you trying to tell us you're not responsible for anything? Aren't you your own man? How could she control you?" Yú's frustration was boiling over, "How?"

"She has powers. She's a witch. She has some links to the Sisterhood, although I was never a-figurin' out what?" Háng was now sobbing uncontrollably, "She was…a-holdin' a…dagger to my neck. It wasn't my fault. I was so young. She said she would tell the authorities, and I would have been killed."

Háng's two interrogators were now thoroughly confused and, with the merest nod passing between them, determined someone with a little more sympathy best extracted the story.

"Would you rather talk to Líng?" Yú asked. Háng shook his head violently.

"Or to Jīngfēi?" chimed in Bóyì. The action was repeated. "Well, who then?"

"Kàn. Kànménrén. He'll be understandin'. I'll be a-talkin' to Kàn."

When the story eventually came out, it was left to Kàn to explain the details, and it was Kàn who concluded that Háng's tale was, by and large, truthful. Amongst the seniors in the valley, there was agreement. They would let the barman stay, although he would have to abandon his trade and deviousness. Jīngfēi was appointed to monitor his behaviours.

Kàn's explanation was complex and detailed. There was amazement that the secrets had been kept for so long. It seemed Háng had left little out, and his mother had abused him almost since birth. She turned the screws further with his involvement in the rape and death of a girl in Táosì. It was this that had been held over his head for decades.

Líng confirmed that her predecessor in the Sisterhood had what she termed a wrecker installed in Táosì, but she had never been made aware of who it might be. The organisation's wreckers operated independently and were involved in a multiplicity of devious social experimentation. She let it be known that this was a practice she had halted

The Hidden Valley, Shǎnxī

but that it had been impossible to identify or stop a wrecker once they were established, especially when their controller was dead.

In quite an official manner, there was an announcement that Háng would become a member of the valley community; the seniors did not identify details of his past. Eventually, Háng found a partner and settled into a smallholding where, from time to time, he would entertain Jīngfēi and Bóyì with his home-made beers. He would tell them with pride each time that they were the best beers in the valley, if not the whole of Shǎnxī. They would re-tell tales of their past exploits, steering well clear of anything too sensitive; their friendships blossomed.

The people of the valley may have relied on ghost stories and folklore to protect their southern boundary, but to the east, west and north, it was primarily their export of *fénjiǔ* that kept them safe. Requiring clean spring water, sorghum grasses, yeast, and herbs, which Shénnóng now sourced, the hidden valley was ideal. Huge sterilised underground vats housed the fermenting mash for around a month before the drink was ready. Carts laden with flagons took the brew to the borders, where they were transferred to wagons provided by their thirsty adjacent states. Huge demand and tightly contracted deals with their neighbours ensured their secrets did not cross the borders with their liquor. Occasionally, Háng was asked for advice on fermentation, but he was kept well away from the trade in the stuff, for which he seemed grateful. Apart from the necessary tastings, he also spurned the chance to imbibe *fénjiǔ,* sticking to his home-brewed beer as a matter of choice.

There was some opposition to the isolationist policy, coming primarily from Cāngbái in Ānyáng. With the changing situation in the Motherland's capital city, Cāngbái kept her distance from Qí. She wanted to trade directly from east to west without the inconvenience of having the trade routes looping down close to Èrlǐtou.

The mountain passes to the east were fundamental to Líng's long-term planning. She had little idea how far in the future it might be, but they were her preferred route for the eventual expansion out of the hidden valley. She saw Ānyáng as a future capital, one from which they could wrest control of the Motherland. In addition, it would provide better access to the eastern sea, particularly as the Yellow River was brought further under control. It was a grandiose plan involving people who would

Thirty-five: The Shāng

not be born for possibly another hundred years or more. Not only did Líng wish to ensure she had the geography on her side, but she was also keen to ensure those future people would derive from her preferred stock. From time to time, she compared herself to a cattle farmer. She kept the wolves out while maintaining a gate in working order and ensuring the right bulls mated with the right cows. Although the thought was there, she had not quite reached the stage of culling those she felt were less suited to her plans. However, she was prepared to discourage inappropriate breeding. Líng was often unpopular.

At the request of Líng, the Fire Horse Three all worked on dissuading the Ānyáng ruler from pursuing a direct trade route across Shǎnxī, and she eventually agreed. Consequentially, the people of the valley found themselves acting as middlemen between Dōngxiàfēng and Ānyáng. The exposure to products from other provinces was largely beneficial; it kept the valley folk up to date on advancements and sometimes regression. It was a monopolistic enterprise, and no outsiders were permitted to cross between the mountain ranges to the east and west. As a result, the mystique and associated fears grew predominant. In a few years, rumours began to abound that the hidden valleys were home to wolfmen and wolfwomen, who would use their teeth to tear the flesh of humans while they were still living.

Meanwhile, with no respect for convention, Líng encouraged Yú to plant his seed in as many of the valley's available females as possible. Single women greeted this policy with open arms, as there was still a shortage of males. She was frank about her goals; she felt maximising Yú's offspring would create a more pleasant society. All the women were encouraged to keep documentation of their offspring's lineage to prevent later inbreeding.

However, the one thing Líng wanted more than anything was a child by Yú herself; this was proving problematic. She intended to pair her father's line with that of Yú. The simplest and quickest way to achieve this was for her to have Yú's baby. Irritatingly, her womb seemed infertile, contrasting painfully with the many pregnancies in the valley. She enlisted the help of Shénnóng and many of the wise women as she could. Her body remained stubborn, but she still intended to produce a lineage from which leaders would be drawn. She refused to countenance her father's line disappearing.

Notwithstanding continued pleading and regular tantrums, Yú refused point-blank to have any relationships with Lùduān. It was as if he regarded her as his daughter. She repeatedly lied about her age in an attempt to persuade him. Since her physical development had commenced in earnest, she was not shy of flaunting it in his face. For Líng, the circumstance was more than simply irritating. She had identified Lùduān as a potential leader; she encouraged her studies and had spent time teaching her all she knew. However, the situation was untenable; the young girl needed to be moved away to develop healthier obsessions. The inspiration for a solution came from an unlikely source: a visit from the Wolf Pack.

"It's like this, Líng. We need to be closer to the action in Èrlǐtou," Kuàiláng explained. "We're thinking about the mountains to the east of Mount Song. It's little more than a day's walk from the centre, and we can set up as foresters for cover."

"That sounds good, Kuài. Are you two on board?"

"We follow in her footsteps, Líng. Me and Dà would get ourselves into heaps of trouble if we didn't!" Xiǎoláng smiled down at the big sister, who was at least a head shorter than she.

"She's right! Kuài's the boss. We have talked about it. It's not just following orders. We all agree it's a move that makes sense." Dàláng added, "We do have another problem, though. We all agree it's time to start working on our replacements. That's why we're here. We're picking your brain for ideas."

"I have someone in mind," Líng looked thoughtful, "more a tiger than a wolf, mind you. Have you met our very own *hǔ zǐ*[36]? She goes by the name of Lùduān?"

"No," the three of them shook their heads as Kuàiláng answered for them. "Is she a handful?"

"Oh yes!" Líng broke into a grin, "She's a handful, alright! She's not just any little girl. This one is handpicked for trouble. Kuài, believe it

---

[36] Tiger cub.

Thirty-five: The Shāng

or not, she's brighter than you. If you take her on, I assure you she will become your next leader."

"Not the leader of the Wolf Pack; she won't! She might be the leader of the Tigers or whatever we call them, but we are the Wolf Pack, no one else!" Dàláng spoke with pride, but her voice softened as she added, "But even wolves have to retire one day, don't they, Xiǎo? Kuài?"

"I think we've agreed, Líng. Now it's a question of whether little Lùduān wants to come."

"Her name means the beast able to detect the truth. I think it's time she detected the truth in Yú's consistent rejection of her advances. I'll talk to her. Once she agrees, you three chat with her and see if she's compatible."

"So, what you're saying, Líng, is that she's as bright as Kuài and as horny as Dà. I hope she's not as tall as me!"

With the most likely future upsets to be found in Hénán, the Wolf Pack plus one *hǔ zǐ* set off southwards. At Jīngfēi's suggestion, they planned to search for two more youngsters amongst the whore houses in Èrlǐtou. It seemed there were plenty of unwanted kids to be found there. Xiǎoláng, Kuàiláng and Dàláng were going to try to perform the impossible by giving the appearance of living everyday lives whilst training their replacements and undertaking their abnormal covert operations. Lùduān was just what they needed.

Èrlĭtou, Hénán

Thirty-six: The Emperor
Èrlĭtou, Hénán
Year 103. Year of the Ox
The autumn equinox
21st September 1892 BCE

If the escape of the four prisoners had been cause for celebration in the hidden valley, in Èrlĭtou, it was not. It had taken the Wolf Pack only two weeks to reach the capital, and it was clear that things were changing rapidly. If the hidden valley had become secure, a stronghold even, Èrlĭtou proved very different. It had achieved the appearance of security, although appearances were deceptive.

The bridges across both rivers were guarded heavily, almost entirely by men, most sporting brand-new weapons. The tracks, most of which traversed farmland, were patrolled several times each day. New structures were being thrown up at critical points, some with the intent of creating garrisons, others seemingly vast storage barns. Emperor Qí's new order was fundamentally different from anything most had imagined.

Much of it was dysfunctional. The three wolves and their newly acquired *hŭ zĭ* had no difficulty accessing the city, nor did they have trouble exiting by the southern bridge out of Èrlĭtou. They all dressed as women for a change, and it seemed they were regarded as of little consequence. It made it easy to slip in the southernmost of the bars previously run by Háng. To their great surprise, the place was nearly full, and most customers were female. They blended right in.

It did not take long to find out what was going on. Conversations were raucous and often fractious. It seemed all females in the army had been removed from their positions and sent back to the farms. Only men had been recruited to replace them. The recruitment of new troops had

Thirty-six: The Emperor

focussed on attitude as much as ability, and the once trusted army was becoming a much more sinister force.

Additionally, the townsfolk had just learned that henceforward, there would be only one vote per farm for the council. That was not considered an issue, but the insistence that it must be a male who delivered the vote caused alarm. If the Wolf Pack had picked it themselves, they could not have created a more encouraging recruitment centre.

Most of the rage was not directed at the new emperor but focused on a woman named Lài. Qí had carefully distanced himself from any changes that could be seen as unfavourable, whereas he very publicly took responsibility for any positives. When the time came, Lài would take the fall, just as Bóyì, Háng and Shénnóng were being blamed for all the town's ills presently. In addition, he smeared Jīngfēi's reputation through the mud. It seemed the emperor needed a female target. Many woes were attributed to Jīngfēi; she was accused of sleeping with any in power to get her way. It was a grand lie, but it made it easier to blame anything on the female half of the population. The appearance was of a good man at the top, fighting for control with a female monster and trying to recover from a situation made intolerable by a manipulative whore. Amongst the women around them, there was no criticism of the emperor himself.

As the Wolf Pack settled down for their second drink, a short walk to the north, in the *huì tang*, Qí argued with Lài in an attempt to foist another unpopular move on her.

"I want the year I started my rule to be called year one."

"It is possible, my lord, but it will make things very difficult." Lài knew her frustrations would count for little.

"It's not difficult. We just call it year one, which means this is year three. Nothing difficult about it at all."

"No, it's not difficult to say it, but it is difficult regarding record keeping. What do we call something from four years ago? There's no name or number it could have, my lord."

"Who cares about four years ago?"

"Our records…all our grain records go back to the year Yú came to Èrlǐtou…there's also the record of decrees and rules and the outline of events that Houtu's team are building. If we are in year three now, nothing

Èrlǐtou, Hénán

before year one exists. Well, it exists, but it's hard to have records…" Lài felt a stare hardening in her direction, "…My lord."

"This might surprise you, Lài, but I sympathise with this problem. I do understand the importance of records, but I do want there to be a clean sequence. I want the start of my reign documented as triumphant; this is the best way to do it. If it is not one, I still want an important number, a number to mark the start of my being emperor. What about one hundred and one?"

Lài was perplexed, "How did you come up with that?" The stare hardened once more, "My lord."

"Well, by my reckoning, one hundred and one is better than one. Correct?"

Lài wanted to explain that no number was better than another one but held her tongue.

"That being the case, we must work out a way of making the years work for us. My father was very old and reigned a long time, although not as an emperor; we can make him one, can't we?" It was clear that Qí's question was entirely rhetorical, although Lài nodded. "And we can forget that idiot, Bóyì; I mean, he was useless. So, on that basis, if my father ruled for one hundred years, then the year I commenced as emperor would be year one hundred and one. See, it makes sense."

"But Yú did not rule for that long; it was much less, it–"

"Who cares? Your records only go back to my father's first year in Èrlǐtou, which satisfies that criterion. It would be year ninety or ninety-one or something like that."

"And…what about the two years that Bóyì was council leader? That's–"

"That doesn't exist."

"But the years exist…my lord."

"Yes, years one hundred and one and one hundred and two. I know the years exist; I'm not stupid. Bóyì was regent in those two years; I was already emperor."

"But…you would have been twelve," the stare returned, "My lord."

"And if he were regent, then we can blame him for all the bad things and give credit to me for the good things. I'm longing to see the

Thirty-six: The Emperor

revised history those scribes have created. Make it as convincing as you did with the city rules. Have you got that, Lài?"

"I have." Lài turned her attention to the new list of rules she had just drawn up, "You are relying on people not reading these, aren't you…my lord."

"I am."

"Well, you know, there's a big difference between 'six months' and 'more than six months'. Some people will spot this, my lord."

"You appreciate the difference, Lài, but most will not. To be on the safe side, make some sort of stain on the cloth. Make sure that stain obliterates the 'more than', won't you?"

"You do fully understand the implication. That if you can suspend council laws for more than six months - then you can suspend them forever."

The stare was now more than hard; it was most definitely threatening, "I know it, you know it, but who else knows it? My life is of enormous importance, Lài; remember that! At this point forward, yours is not! Dismiss! And send in Měnghǔ."

Qí's need for the woman who had once run the granaries was declining, but he would need a replacement and had no one suitable yet. Lài had committed too many crimes to go public about his misdeeds; she would continue for a while. It was Yú who appointed her, Bóyì who kept her on and Háng who had turned her. Qí had benefitted from the acts of others; she was at his mercy. More to the point, she would be at the mercy of the crowds baying for blood.

The situation was not quite the same with the woman now approaching his raised dais: Měnghǔ, keeper of the bronze. She had also been appointed by Yú and kept on by Bóyì, but try as he might, Háng had not perverted the woman. She was as straight as she was pompous. She and Qí had only two things in common: their love of ceremony and dressing up, which was not significant enough commonality for him to save her head. He wanted to be rid of her and had devised a plan. She now waited before him, head bowed.

"Měnghǔ! Good of you to come so quickly." Qí was more than aware that the woman had been kept waiting for the better part of the day, just out of earshot.

"Good afternoon, my lord."

"You know, you remind me of my mother, Měnghǔ. I'm never sure if you're being polite or not."

"My lord?"

"It doesn't matter. What date do we do the bronze handouts to the provinces?"

"Well, that depends on the harvests, my lord, but generally, we start taking the bronze back around now and re-issue before the winter solstice. It's not hard and fast, but if we change the dates too much, there'll be some hardship."

"For whom?"

"For the farmers in the provinces, my lord. They must fit their tool requirements to harvest times, ploughing, fertilising, and planting. I'm sure you know that."

"I do. We'll be changing things a bit this year. Not the timings, mind you; we keep the timings the same. I need to know if we've got enough bronze in stock to manufacture nine large *dǐngs*[37]."

"*Dǐngs?*"

"Yes, you know what I'm talking about, three legs, big pot, some fancy artwork on them."

"How big?" Qí knew better than to give Měnghǔ hard stares; they did not work as she never even glanced sideways at his face. There was no point wasting glares on her.

"I was thinking large enough to be impressive but small enough to minimise the cost."

"What would it need to impress you?"

"They're not to impress me; they're to impress the leaders of the provinces."

"There are eight provinces now, not nine, my lord."

"There you go again, just like my aunt! I know there are eight provinces. One of the *dǐngs* is for here, Èrlǐtou, to be positioned in this hall. If I were to be impressed, it would have to stand high enough for me not to be able to see what is inside."

"What will be inside?"

---

[37] A large bronze ornamental vessel in the form of a large tripod cauldron.

Thirty-six: The Emperor

"Nothing, but that's not the point!"

"So, you're looking at nine bronze *dǐngs*, as high as a man, and that means probably half a man's height in width and—"

"Wider!"

"Alright...well, nine *dǐngs* like that will use all our reserve. That's a problem."

"It's not a problem."

"It'll be a problem when you ask for more weapons, and there's no reserve. I've never said 'no' to you, and I don't want to start. I will have to say 'no' if there's no reserve. Honestly."

"There will be a reserve. All those weapons, ploughshares, daggers, and axes due to be returned before the winter solstice will become the reserve."

"Bu...but that means we won't have anything to send out to the provinces at the winter solstice."

"And that is where you are wrong. We'll be sending the *dǐngs* instead."

"But you can't plough a field, cut down trees, or arm an army with a *dǐng*; this will weaken the provinces. They'll have to use stone for knives and axes and ploughshares. It's not going to make any of them happy."

"We'll see about that. The provinces will have a magnificent *dǐng* with 'Qí is our emperor!' etched on it. And what's more, if they need an army, I'll send ours to help them!"

"Bu..." it was slowly dawning on Měnghǔ that Qí's plan was much more complex than she had first supposed. It was also beginning to cross her mind that she would be the first target of abuse from the recipients of the intended winter gift. "May I ask to be transferred?"

"Transferred to what?"

"Anything...I'm not sure I'll survive what you have planned. I beg of you, my lord, could someone else do this job?"

"In one year...in one year, I'll consider your position. Now, dismiss! And send in Hétóngzǐ."

As Měnghǔ crept out, she could feel the penetrating glare of his eyes and the malice cast from them. She would sharpen her sword and keep it safe; one day, it might be prudent to put its point to her chest and fall on it.

Èrlǐtou, Hénán

Qí was happy. After so many years of learning, he was now wielding real power and, in the process, increasing his strength. The first two of his civil servants would not last long. He would keep Lài as long as she stayed useful, but that would be a year at most. He knew that Měnghǔ would take her own life; it was just a matter of helping her choose a time. It had to be after the new year, and he thought he could keep her stable until then. Hétóngzǐ. Now, Hétóngzǐ was a different matter.

"Come forward, Hétóngzǐ."

"Yes, my lord."

"I'm told there are growing problems with your irrigation systems failing east of Èrlǐtou."

"That is true, my lord."

"Well, why haven't you fixed it?"

"Because you prioritised draining the flood plains outside the two rivers, my lord."

"So, you're blaming me!"

"No, my lord, just pointing out that I don't have the resources to cover the areas outside and inside the rivers."

"I hope you understand that the land outside the rivers is my land, land I plan to give to those who have served the state well. To the soldiers and civil servants such as you."

"Someone told me the land will also be given to the older whores, my lord."

"And who told you that? One of the whores, I suppose. Well, whoever receives it is my gift, and it must be perfect. You are still our best water engineer, then?"

"I am, my–"

"Which means you have failed! You have failed to train replacements for yourself. It is one of the worst failings of management! Even I must train a replacement for when I die!"

"I'm not going to die soon, my lord. I'll work on a replacement."

"You will. However, I'm making a change as regards your job. I need to make it easier for you. Therefore, I will appoint two people, one to run water affairs within the two rivers and one to run water affairs outside the two rivers."

Thirty-six: The Emperor

"Which one would you like me to do, my lord?" Hétóngzǐ was relieved. He knew his present job was unmanageable.

"Neither. My decision is that two new leaders will be appointed. They will be appointees from the army. You will be advised who they are very soon."

"And what is my job to be, my lord?"

"Your job, Hétóngzǐ, will be to act as number two to both the one who runs water affairs within the two rivers and the one who runs water affairs outside the two rivers. They will take the weight of complaints from your back and direct you in your priorities."

"So, what you're saying…what you're saying is I've got to keep doing the same job as I do now, but I'm going to have two bosses, both of whom have different priorities, it's—"

"Careful, Hétóngzǐ, I sense you would be critical of your emperor's decision. This is a time of enormous growth and development. It is a time for civic pride; it is not a time to get upset about a minor change to your job. You did a good job for many years, but it is starting to look shabby; we need a shake-up."

"And I need to see my wife. I'm working all the hours I can, all daylight hours and some in darkness. She forgets what I look like. Perhaps I should step down."

"I thought you might suggest something like that." Qí beckoned one of his guards across and whispered in his ear. Immediately, the soldier sprinted off. "Now, I suppose you want to know what my instruction to the guard was?"

"Not really."

"I think your impertinence is going to halt shortly. I cannot have you punished because I need you to work. However, your needs are also important. You need to see your wife more often. I sympathise. I have ordered the construction of a wagon to follow you between jobs. Your daily needs will be on the wagon, as will your wife. I have arranged that she be chained to the wagon so you don't lose sight of her."

"But—"

"There is an alternative, which is that she is chained up here in my home. I suspect I know which you would prefer, but the offer will remain on the table. Now, dismiss. And don't let me hear any more complaints about you! If there are, she will suffer! Go!"

Water, bronze, grain, the writing of ordinance sorted and the army under the control of Háng's chief bouncer, Qí could not be more satisfied. What remained was the problem of his grandmother's students.

Qí had a sneaking admiration for Hòutú; he regarded her as the most intimidating of his adversaries, although it was a long time since he had met her. His admiration spawned a growing physical desire for her. Would it lead his grandmother to Èrlǐtou if he could turn her disciples? Could he turn Hòutú herself? The question would be more easily answered if he had a single idea of where she might be. For now, the two youngsters could operate in peace, and he would focus on his mother.

Wútóng was the man he leaned on for enforcement. It was a very satisfactory relationship. There was no way that Wútóng could have any authority of his own; he was utterly dependent upon his boss. Whereas the head of the army could beat anyone to a pulp in a one-to-one contest, he was such an unpopular bully that he could never achieve and maintain a leadership role without serious backing. The man at least had the intelligence to understand his weaknesses; he would die for his commander, for without him, he was nothing. It had been the same when he worked for Háng; Wútóng fully understood his reliance and responsibilities.

Because Qí understood his underling's weaknesses, he was careful not to treat him as he treated others who worked for him. When he spoke to Wútóng, it was as if he were a friend, a confidante or an equal. His commander grew in stature every time Qí did so, and with every slight enhancement of his ego, Wútóng became increasingly loyal. He reminded Qí of a dog he had owned when he was young. The dog eventually died when its owner tired of him and threw him into a well. It had taken half a day for the dog to drown, and Qí had watched every moment of its struggle.

"Wútóng, I want to congratulate you on ridding the army of those useless women."

"Thank you, my lord."

"However, I have found a use for them; they will work for Hétóngzǐ."

Thirty-six: The Emperor

"Who?" Wútóng reddened, "Sorry, my lord. Who, sir?"

"The water man, the one that just left. I want two teams drawn up from those women just side-lined from the army. They can all dig, can't they?"

"Yes, sir!"

"Well, pick two of your toughest lieutenants and put one in charge of each group. One will work outside the two rivers, the other inside."

"I don't understand, my lord. Are they reporting to this Hétóngzǐ or my men? The problem is that my guys know little about water management; they're more—"

"Yes, I know, they're more the bullying sort. Perfect. Hétóngzǐ tells the women what to do; your guys ensure they do it! Oh! And I must tell you about Hétóngzǐ's wife. I want her chained to a wagon and moved around. Always keep her with the group away from her husband. Could you make a point of it? Now, have you got all that?" His captain nodded enthusiastically. "Then go and get it sorted. If you have any questions, come back to me. Go!"

Qí smiled as the army commander left, a smile that became a grin and then a laugh once he was out of earshot. He had surrounded himself with such unpopular individuals that their downfall, sooner or later, was a certainty. He needed replacements for when that time came; the grooming had already commenced.

Èrlĭtou, Hénán

Thirty-seven: The Tigers
Èrlĭtou, Hénán
Year 104. Year of the Tiger
The autumn equinox
21st September 1891 BCE

Tú had learned one thing from Yú's ex-wife, and she had learned it well. Túshānshì, until she found her skills slipping under the influence of too many mind-altering substances, had exerted enormous control over men. More specifically, she had come to completely control those men with whom she regularly slept. Not only had Tú watched, but she had also discussed the techniques with the woman. She may now be a rotting corpse, but she had been the mother of the future emperor. In decidedly odd circumstances, not only had Tú usurped Túshānshì's desired role, but she was also to become the mother of her son's child.

In the fifteen months since her incarceration in the *hòugōng*[38], she had not only wriggled her way into Qí's bed but had also exerted enormous influence on his policies. Whilst her son gradually consolidated power, she was sowing the seeds of a longer-term decline. Like Líng, she had no idea how long it would take for that seed to germinate, grow and flower, but it was within her. She suspected the truly damaging effects of the weeds she was spreading would not be apparent until well after her son's death, but by son, she did not mean Qí, but the unborn one inside her.

There was an intricate irony in the beliefs of mother and son; both believed they controlled the other.

It was her time. The two whores attending her were helpful, although they were jealous. It did not seem to occur to them that they were

---

[38] The imperial harem.

Thirty-seven: The Tigers

unlikely to last the night. Anyone witnessing this event would have to be put to death. Almost certainly, all the members of the *hòugōng* would have to die, including Tú herself. She was aware that Qí had already sorted out a wet nurse. She had helped him recruit replacements for the whores who would be killed. The newcomers were presently housed away from the site, awaiting the call. No one would ever miss those to be culled; they had been cut off from outside contact for so long.

Tú had gone into labour late that morning. The birth came quickly and easily. Next to her bed, one of the women whispered aloud the checklist as she examined the baby and checked the air supply. The other whispered in her ear; it was the expected boy. The count to eighty-eight seemed to last an eternity, and when they shouted the final number, Tú had already reached for the bronze blade and kissed it. She had prepared by sharpening it to perfection; the knife almost slid through the cord.

The new mother had little time for the ritual and even less for breastfeeding, but there were expectations. If she were to escape certain death, she must leave quickly. Qí would try to minimise any possibility the news might leak out. All now depended on the Wolf Pack.

Sitting on the outer bank of the *Huángjiā Hé* moat, Kuàiláng appeared to be fishing. Her pole extended at a near-perfect forty-five-degree angle, and the line looped into the water. She would have had to be an extremely optimistic fisherwoman to try to bring anything out of the moat alive; the water stank, and nothing moved. Passing townspeople commented, suggesting she would be better off elsewhere, but her blank staring eyes and twitches persuaded them she was mad and best left be.

In the gathering gloom, only those with the keenest eyesight would have spotted the thread extending across from the fishing pole to the base of the high walls of what was now officially called the *Jīn bì huī huáng*. In the circumstances, no one was looking up at all. A dust storm was approaching, and all held their clothes to their faces with their chins tucked down.

Kuàiláng had not received instructions to get the emperor's mother out of the *hòugōng,* although there had been strong hints that it might be a good idea. Back in the hidden valley, Líng had compiled a list of Tú's contributions to the Sisterhood's cause, which made quite astonishing reading. There had been some impetuousness along the way, but Tú was pretty much unmatched regarding job completion. It was time for her to have a break, not a time for her to die. Líng's information was as good as that of the new mother. She had concluded the likely consequences well before Tú. The message had been that a wolf pack should attend the birth; for Tú, the intent was obvious.

The palace guard had been completely revamped since Tú's initial incarceration. However, they were not allowed near the compound housing or the *hòugōng*. With the raising of the palace walls, their focus was very much on the four main gates. They also monitored the outer stretch of the tunnel into the bar. It was no coincidence that Kuàiláng had chosen a spot on the eastern wall away from the east gate hidden by the protuberance that had been Háng's first bar. There may be many guards, but none would observe her clandestine activities in such poor weather conditions.

A drunk rolled down the road, pushing a barrow carrying two barrels. As the man approached the spot where Kuàiláng sat, he veered towards the moat, losing control of the cart as the barrels crashed into the water. The drunk fell on top of the fisherwoman. The resulting melee would have been entertaining if there had been any observers.

Indeed, a close observer would have noticed that as the fishing pole dropped from Kuàiláng's hands, it appeared to divide into two. A close observer might have dragged their eyes from the groping and punching between the drunk and the fisherwoman. A close observer might have seen the disturbance in the water as two small figures exited the barrels and pulled the poles onto the opposite bank. However, any close observer would probably not have been able to drag their eyes from the scene that was now developing. It seemed that the mad fisherwoman was being raped by the drunk. Kuàiláng and Xiǎoláng had to suppress their giggles as their enactment became more involved. Eventually, Kuàiláng broke away and ran down the street to the south. Xiǎoláng's performance continued as she staggered after her boss; both had to compose themselves before rounding the corner of the palace. Beneath the palace wall, entirely obscured by shadows, Dàláng and Lùduān were the only potential spectators to their comrades' staged fight, yet they were far too busy digging to appreciate it.

Thirty-seven: The Tigers

By now, close to the southern gate, Kuàiláng and Xiǎoláng had changed entirely. They had become a wife and her husband walking their way home.

"It's going to be a close call, Xiǎo. Suppose she's already dropped that baby. Who knows when Qí will act? I'm told he's away from the palace right now, but he won't be for long when he hears the news."

"We've got to try and save as many of those girls as possible, Kuài. They're all dead meat."

"The problem is whether they'll think that they are. Remember, they've chosen once, and that was to stay put. Some will make the same choice again, regardless of any warning."

"But…it's a matter of common sense, isn't it? No one can know that Qí's son is a product of his mother's womb. No one. He's done all he can to make himself look cleaner than clean and those around him as dirty as hell. He cannot afford the opprobrium this will bring down on him."

"It's a balancing act, but his safest course of action is to kill them all, Tú included. He'll then have the task of disposing of the bodies."

At that moment, a four-wheeled cart rolled past, empty barrels bouncing in the back. It pulled up at the south gate briefly before receiving permission to enter.

"I think that's just answered one question, Xiǎo. Who has ever witnessed a delivery of empty barrels to the palace? It tells me two things. Qí knows about the birth, knows it's a boy and is planning that those women in there are only coming out in those. To get them in, they'll not only have to be dead, but he'll also have to cut them into pieces. More than a few pigs and dogs will eat human flesh tonight.

"The way he works, though, nothing will happen until he's back in the palace. They'll also kill and butcher those girls one by one. That'll keep down the number in the know. Then, they'll have to deal with the soldiers who do the killing. He'll have to have one person he trusts: someone powerful."

A very similar conversational exchange was presently being conducted by the two riders travelling along the main highway from the west. Qí had made Wútóng take him to the fortifications being erected where the Luohe and Yi Rivers entered their respective gorges. It took a whole day to get out there and it would be a full day to return. The emperor had received the news of an "event" at the palace but could not speed his return. For the first time, he told his captain what was to occur but not why. For practicality's sake, he had to give the number of women that Tú would be among them and that the women's executioners would also have to die. He also mentioned the barrels. Wútóng hardly blinked.

"So, sir, we have to take them one by one. There's no other way. If we did several at a time, there's more chance of noise, and we would need more men for the killing, and then that's even more to kill. The best approach would be for them to be taken one by one to your bed-chamber; that way, they'd be thinking they'll be in for a night of pleasure, so they'll come quietly."

"True. It also means that Tú has to be last."

"Why's that, my lord?"

"Some questions are best not asked, Wútóng. Not even by you. Understand?"

"Sir!"

Dàláng and Lùduān were close to breaking through the thick wall. It had proved easier than expected. They had hit on a repaired patch of tamped earth that had not been renovated well and was weaker than the rest. A tunnel big enough for the two of them would not be big enough for a woman who had just given birth, even though they knew Tú was not enormous.

For once, Kuàiláng's project was flawed. The pair had already perfectly executed the plan to get in. Then there was the way of getting out, which would mean three or more of them having to submerge themselves in *dàfèn*[39] on the back of a cart driven by Kuàiláng and Xiǎoláng. The plan was deficient because it did not have a middle section, which is why Lùduān was on her first job with the Wolves. Her size was an asset in gaining entry. Her brain might be the tool needed to ensure they could attempt an exit. The lack of information about what they might find inside the hòugōng walls had thwarted proper planning. The odd message came out, but nothing of detail.

---

[39] Nightsoil. Human effluent, often collected at night from residential areas, used as fertilizer.

Thirty-seven: The Tigers

Tú was not entirely popular amongst the women who serviced her son. Not one of them understood why she was with them. Not one approved of her incest with Qí, even though they believed she was his aunt. They did not like her arrogance and superior air. However, they had the common sense not to speak about it openly. It was the *hòugōng's* biggest cover-up. Secretly, all the other women would prefer that Tú was not there, although not one would want to be implicated in a plan to have her escape.

The women were so used to their closed existence that it was something of a shock when two mud-splattered girls appeared from the end of their garden.

The two barrels and bamboo sticks had been pulled into the tunnel entrance and could not easily be observed from outside the walls. Inside was a different matter; it was self-evident where they had come from, even if it was less obvious why they were there. As agreed in their planning meetings, Lùduān took the lead.

"Ladies, please do not be shocked. We have been sent here by someone who wishes to allow you the opportunity of freedom. We'll take as many of you as want to come out of here with us." Her introduction faced shocked silence. As their lack of response started to become an embarrassment, Lùduān elaborated. "We know that you mostly came here of your own free will. However, some of you might have changed your minds after all this time. Do you have any questions?"

"Yes! Where the hell would we go?"

Another chimed in, "We'd not be safe, not anywhere. He'd have us hunted down and killed. We're best staying put. We would also lose the retirement homes he's giving us."

"It's not a bad life. Better than before. I don't want to go back to common whoring," a third imparted. "Who would?"

They were becoming more animated, and the majority seemed somewhat angry. Only one voice contrasted the general opinion, "Well, I want out. I want a life. I'm sick of servicing that spoiled brat. The things he makes us do, you–"

"Now, now, they're strangers. No secrets go out!" The first speaker was becoming more riled, "If anyone goes, they must swear not to tittle-tattle…Swear on their life!"

Èrlǐtou, Hénán

Ultimately, it was only one girl, much younger than the rest. She was the one who had spoken out already, desperately wanting to leave. The others gathered around her, trying to dissuade her course of action. In the ensuing arguments, only Dàláng noticed the black-cloaked figure flit down the garden wall towards their escape tunnel. Tú. It was time to move. She pulled her knife.

"You must accept that we're taking her, like it or not. Where she's going, she'll not be tittle-tattling like you think she might. I do not want to use this, but I will if I must. Lùduān, do you want to add to this?"

"We don't think you're safe here. This is your last chance. Does anybody else want to come? No? Right, go to your rooms, pretend you never saw us. You can say she must have escaped all by herself. Deny all knowledge," she paused, "and you had better pray to your ancestors you've made the right choice."

With that, she turned, offering her arm to the girl, who was a little older than herself and beckoned Dàláng to follow. Instead, her more experienced partner took two threatening steps towards the gaggle of women and snarled. It was enough. They beat a hasty retreat to the perceived safety of their beds as the wolf turned and chased after her comrade and the two escapees.

Tú was quite shaky. She had only given birth that afternoon, had now abandoned her child and was a little uncertain about her company as she had difficulty recognising Dàláng. However, passwords sufficed, and introductions were made before Dàláng dived back into the tunnel to signal her comrades outside. It was essential the next steps went unobserved and were undertaken as quickly as possible.

While they waited, Lùduān engaged the escaping pair to explain the intended methodology of their escape. Both wrinkled their noses at the mention of the *dàfèn*, but it was clear they were up for it. When she ran out of steam, she babbled, "I know your name is Tú, and I know you've just had a baby. Don't worry about leaving him; I had many mothers, and it will be fine. My name is Lùduān, but the others want to change my name to Hǔzǐ because that means tiger cub. I don't know your name, but if you joined us, you might be called Hǔtáo because that means escaping tiger. You're a tiger and escaping; it makes sense!"

Thirty-seven: The Tigers

"So, I'm going to become a tiger, am I? That'll make a change from being a whore. I like it. My new name that is…Hŭtáo," she beamed at Lùduān, "but I'll only do it if you are going to be called Hŭzĭ. Is that a deal?" Their agreement was interrupted by frantic waving from the hole in the wall.

Lùduān led the way, followed by the newly named Hŭtáo, then Tú squeezed through with Dàláng pushing her from behind. By the time the wolf exited the hole, Lùduān was assisting their two escapees in burying themselves in shit and ensuring they had breathing holes. All that remained was for her and Dàláng to follow suit. No one would be prepared to dig through the cart's contents to discover them. They felt mad enough about volunteering for the hiding place; no one else could be that stupid.

No news ever left the palace as to what happened in the aftermath. The only sign that something may have changed is that twenty new whores and two new guards appeared, but no one noticed except Qí.

The two tiger cubs formed a close bond, and the Wolf Pack stepped a little closer to their retirement.

Èrlĭtou, Hénán

Thirty-eight: The Spies
Èrlĭtou, Hénán
Year 107. Year of the Horse
The autumn equinox
21st September 1888 BCE

It was three years since Tú had fled Èrlĭtou and over four since Qí's accession. The changes in the town had accelerated, gathering a momentum of their own. The changes in the empire were harder to pin down, but of the decline, there was no doubt.

Each of the provinces had objected to the removal of support from the centre, some to a greater degree than others. Qí's Èrlĭtou-based army was now considerably more powerful than the army of any other single province. Currently, the combined forces of perhaps as many as four outer states would probably not be considered enough to challenge it. As promised, Qí protected against threats from the outside, but each time he did so, his forces dug themselves deep into positions that were also to be used for suppression. Once his armies arrived, they seldom left.

Collaboration between the provinces and the centre was now a thing of the past, replaced by coercion. In allowing the greater stratification of society in the centre, Qí, seemingly inadvertently, encouraged the same in the provinces. The latent forces of greed began to pile up against the nascent socialism established by Yú. If the dog-eat-dog mentality did not extend as far as the more distant farming communities, it was undoubtedly taking root in the main urban centres.

Even those leaders who had wholeheartedly supported Yú's principles were forced to abandon their firmly held positions. The reversion to a stone-age society, dependent on lithics for their agriculture, tools, and arms, made sustaining their increased populations impossible.

Thirty-eight: The Spies

For the first time since the great floods, following the defeat of the Lóngshān a generation ago, peasants were starving to death.

Of the Lóngshān as an entity, there was no longer any sign. As regards their way of life, there appeared to be a resurgence. For the farmers, there was a double hit. Not only were they losing more of their harvest to the exchequers of their provinces, but a growing number of robber barons frequently raided them. The armed gangs roaming the countryside would settle for a few weeks, uprooting or killing locals before devouring all foodstuffs and stripping the settlement of anything of value. The thieves would then move on before the depleted provisional armies could find them, let alone defeat them.

Some of the provinces had held out. To the west, Jiālíng in Dōngxiàféng, Héměirén in Sānménxiá and a succession of leaders in Lǎoniúpō had stayed true to the concepts of equality. In this, they were protected to an extent by their geography. However, Qí was greedily eyeing the trade in tin from Sìchuān and the copper mines of Shānxī. It seemed only a matter of time. All provinces to the north, south and east of Èrlǐtou had changed their leaders. Qí had threatened all, and all had succumbed to his vision of civilisation. It had little room for women, no room for perceived weakness and no sympathy for society.

Alone to the north, Cāngbái in Ānyáng had not only resisted joining the Xià empire, but she had also defeated Xià forces in open battle. An uneasy truce now held between Èrlǐtou and Ānyáng. Some of his generals thought that Qí would not act against the northern state because he had spent this youth there, but, in truth, he saw few advantages in terms of trade. He did not perceive Cāngbái as a threat either, something that was true. While the northern leader wanted to protect what she had, she had no desire for expansion. Qí's eyes wandered westwards, time and time again.

None of the people gathered around the Xià emperor had been in place three years before; even Wútóng, the army leader, had gone. As he had cut a swathe through his administrative staff, he had offered favours before they had left their posts. Vast quantities of land, jade, bronze, slaves, everything he could think of, had been on the table as long as they came up with a list of suitable replacements. Once Qí was satisfied that he had trusted substitutes in place, the previous postholder could retire.

Èrlǐtou, Hénán

Their view of retirement and their leader's understanding of the term differed. Qí saw their deaths as a much cheaper option. His preferred method was to arrange exposure to the citizens, preferably those his lieutenants had upset so much whilst they were in their post, quietly removing their security to ensure they were exposed. Whilst some might point to the similarity of their deaths, none could realistically point their finger at their emperor.

Oddly, Qí's popularity had not declined. He was increasingly popular with those who benefitted from the changes he made, his biggest supporters. He was also popular amongst the peasants, even if they had lost significantly. People saw him as a guardian, one who looked after their interests. His longstanding policies in this regard ensured it was his henchmen and women being blamed for any excesses of the state apparatus. The emperor did nothing to dispel these beliefs but did little to encourage them. His natural inclination was to distance himself more and more from the people.

His lofty position led to the current situation in the throne room. The peasantry was no longer allowed into the palace compound; court officials delivered their messages or pleas. Those of higher standing could access the courtyard but not the palace hall; they would have to communicate from outside, again through intermediaries. Only a tight elite circle was allowed into the throne room, but even they could not see their emperor, for Qí had secreted himself behind a screen.

He had also acquired a double. His stand-in's sole role was to stand on a platform and wave. No one expected the emperor to speak directly to the people. No one expected the emperor to reveal his face. The two combined meant the double was of similar height and weight, but his features bore little resemblance to Qí 's own. It was a deliberate strategy in case one of his inner circle was ever to devise the idea of using the substitute in a coup.

The only physical contact the emperor now had was with the whores in the *hòugōng*. They ran everything for him; personal medical advice came from that group, even the cooking staff. He had incorporated much of the exchequer into his harem. Their only contact with the outside world, or so he thought, was through himself. Control was everything.

Thirty-eight: The Spies

There was one exception. Once or twice a month, Qí would dress himself up as a peasant, in complete disguise, and exit the palace through a newly constructed tunnel to gather as much information as possible and weigh public feelings. His official physical distancing in public was making his regular outings easier and easier; there would come a point when no one would recognise him.

If it was unclear what Qí's personal objectives were, then he did not care to elaborate. Power was obviously crucial to him, wealth perhaps, his pleasure centre, the *hòugōng*, another. Some commentators saw his actions as self-serving, others as ideologically driven. No one seemed to consider, for one moment, that at the heart of their government sat a confused and lonely boy, a youth who had been manipulated into his present state by training, coercion, and abuse. He had no one to whom he could talk; his bi-monthly outings at least provided alternative and refreshing input.

With the eastern provinces on their knees, the emperor had determined it was time to move on the west. He would be happy to push through an offensive before the snows came. Notably, personal irritations spurred his decision. Lǎoniúpō had stopped sending their silks and Dōngxiàfēng its sheep. Qí had not eaten lamb, his favourite meat, in some months, and he had received no new fine silks since the previous year, something that rankled. His new army commander was more concerned about the tin supply, insisting weaponry should be a priority. Sānménxiá stood in the way.

Four armies had been prepared to move, all to fight, but three to remain in the capitals he wished to subdue. Each came fully prepared with a puppet government to put in place, piles of jade to bribe key figures and a team of spies to discover the whispers in the town taverns. If he had learned one thing from his stepfather, it was that planning for peace was as important as preparing for the battle. His father would have concurred. Where Qí and Yú would have disagreed completely was regarding the nature of that peace.

Having issued his final instructions, Qí stepped back from the screen and into the *hòugōng*. Somewhere inside, his son would be lying down for his sleep, meaning his wet nurse's breasts would be available for the emperor himself to suckle on. It was one of his favourite times of

Èrlĭtou, Hénán

day, bringing back his few warm feelings for his mother. He still speculated on her whereabouts, although he was long past wanting her return. The level of leverage that Tú had employed over her son as the emperor had only lasted a year but had left more scars on his soul than he wished to remember. It was this damage that prevented him from hunting her down, even though Qí would prefer her to be a corpse. If his guard captured her, would it not be possible for her to work her tricks again? It was a risk he did not wish to take. He shook his head to clear the memory.

If Tú's methods had been less than subtle, the team now in place was better trained. The volunteers had been required to become whores before they stood any chance of being selected for the *hòugōng*. Twelve had put themselves forward, and the Sisterhood had accepted ten, although only three had passed Qí's entrance test. All had known that failing the test would result in their deaths, for no one, other than the emperor, ever left the *hòugōng* alive. Even the three now in place knew their lives would be lived and would end in the confines of the imperial whorehouse. What had driven them were the growing inequities, particularly regarding females, something that was now swelling Sisterhood membership.

Qí kept no secrets in the *hòugōng*; he felt no need. Matters of state, imperial finances and his most likely choices for assassination were often freely discussed, although his concubines were not expected to gossip behind his back. The sisterhood's plants had two roles: to get news out and, when required, to use persuasive techniques to redirect actions as information came in.

Passing messages out of the *hòugōng* proved relatively easy; it was all about timing, a good throw, and the ability to write and tie a message around a fist-sized stone. Getting them in was trickier. The best solution was to have messages delivered in the foodstuffs, specifically in the guts of the various fish, fowl, or mammals, and sent in for preparation in the integral kitchens. Not only did the Sisterhood's plants need to know their trade as whores, but they also needed to be expert butchers so that incoming messages would fall only into their hands. They also needed to have precision throwing arms to get the secrets out.

The Wolf Pack were their outside contacts. Their roles changed significantly as time passed, with only the occasional assassination to

Thirty-eight: The Spies

spice things up. That was not entirely true, for there were the Tiger Cubs, who now numbered three: Hǔtáo, Hǔzǐ and Hǔkuáng, the violent tiger.

Kuàiláng had long since surmised that Líng's retirement had been phoney. If the truth be known, the Wolf Pack had only operated without supervision and been able to make their own decisions to a very limited extent. As the years passed, it became clear that someone in charge had selectively processed the information fed to them. They had shared their thoughts and had no real objection other than wishing they had been advised of the circumstances when they commenced. The identity of the controlling hand was unmistakable.

When they determined that the time had come to pass the reigns to the Tiger Cubs, it was unsurprising that Líng should turn up. It was her first trip away from the hidden valley in years, and she was excited to be in the field, to meet her old students and pet executioners, and at the same time to meet the new team.

"Yes, you found me out," Líng admitted, "The retirement thing was all about luring Yú to the hidden valley. In reality, I've been working hard to ensure the long-term future is more secure. Meanwhile, you three have done an excellent job on the frontline. What are your plans?"

"We're staying here," Dàláng admitted. "We've become quite good at forestry and will keep going."

"You know farms are waiting for you in the hidden valley if you want them?"

"We do, but if it's all the same, we're happy here. Dà's finally settled on one man, Xiǎo has been sleeping with the same shepherd for two years, and I plan to settle down and start a family." Kuàiláng smiled, "We will retire, even if you will not!"

"I've not just come down to see you three; I also want to see these Tiger Cubs I've heard so much about. We might have their first job for them. Are they ready?"

"If we don't get let off the leash pretty soon, we'll gnaw the Wolf Pack's arms off." The voice came from behind a door that gradually opened to reveal three women with arms folded and frowns across their faces.

"Lùduān! You've grown up! Look at…"

"Yes, I grew up so much I changed my name. I am Hǔzǐ!"

Èrlǐtou, Hénán

"And I am Hǔkuáng."

"And I am, Hǔtáo. Hǔzǐ says you are a good person, and what Hǔzǐ says is good enough for me. That's right, isn't it, Hǔkuáng?"

"It's right enough."

"Well, I'm only on a short visit to see your three mentors, but I'm also here to ask them to perform one more job," Líng paused. There was an air of expectancy. "Hǔtáo, you worked in Qí's *hòugōng*, didn't you?"

"I did. It's not a period of my life I care to dwell on."

"Well, as you know, we have three of our sisters embedded in there right now. I think it's time to get them out. A little bird has told me someone might be about to reveal their identity. Either we get them out of there swiftly, or they'll die. Almost certainly, they'll be tortured as well."

"Do you want them out to save their lives or simply to stop them talking?" Kuàiláng's expression suggested she knew the answer to her question. "Eradicating them would be easier than extracting them; it's as simple as that."

"That's true, Kuài, but perhaps I'm going soft in my old age. They've done us good service and don't deserve that fate. Can the three of you devise a plan to allow them to escape, and can the three of you," she indicated the Tiger Cubs, "Implement that plan?"

"It'll be a bit more difficult. We've done it twice with tunnels. Now, they have guards on the walls, trained to listen for vibrations. It can't be a tunnel, but it is possible." Kuàiláng was becoming excited, "Leave it with us, Líng. I think we're happy to supervise," she received nods from the other two of the Wolf Pack, "and I'm sure these three are up for it. Hǔkuáng, Hǔtáo, Hǔzǐ, what do you say?"

"Yes!" the Tiger Cubs spoke with one voice. It almost made Líng cry.

Thirty-nine: The End
Èrlǐtou, Hénán
Year 107. Year of the Horse
One week after the autumn equinox
29th Sept 1888 BCE

There were few obvious alternatives to tunnelling. While accessing the compound by one of the gates was possible, it was probably doomed to failure. Only one gate, to the south, remained in use; the others were now permanently barred yet still guarded. Háng's old tunnel was filled in, the entrance having been comprehensively blocked off, yet this, too, was protected. The new guard posts built into the walls had obliterated the covert access they had dug three years before. Each had hanging ramparts to allow their occupants to scour the internal and external length of the structure.

Although the Wolf Pack knew that Qí had a tunnel, they had no idea where it exited in the town. To compound the difficulty, whilst they knew its entrance was somewhere in the emperor's bed-chamber, they had no idea of its location nor how it opened. For obvious reasons, it was one of the few secrets he had kept from the women who serviced his needs.

The Wolf Pack had looked at the option of an entrance through the moat and into the sewage system, but Gǔn's original design meant the time someone would have to spend underwater made the idea unfeasible. Likewise, smuggling in even the smallest of the tigers in a food delivery had been examined and dismissed. All deliveries were inspected thoroughly for larger objects. Small messages may get through, but anything larger than a rabbit would not.

It had left only one route, that being aerial. As none of the tigers could fly, it would mean a climb or a vault; a combination of the two had

Èrlǐtou, Hénán

been chosen. It also required a new moon, providing a cloak of invisibility, but an additional distraction was needed.

It was the Tiger Cub's first operation and the Wolf Pack's last. Whilst the former had to undertake the extraction, the latter had to conduct an entirely new activity. The Wolf Pack were going to put on their first public dance performance. Surprisingly, Kuàiláng had suggested it, although she had been desperately trying to extract herself since doing so.

Only Dàláng had been enthusiastic, and it had been she who had planned and choreographed the spectacle. They had fitted in as many rehearsals as possible, more than the Tigers had for scaling the wall. Each group observed the other as they perfected their techniques.

The Tigers had all pointed out that the dance Dàláng had created was nothing more than an elaborate striptease. Hǔtáo had suggested that it was inappropriate, something that might go on within Qí's *hòugōng* but should not be performed on a public street. Dàláng had to point out that was the intent; to get everyone ogling was more important than any moral concern. It was a lesson in the extremes that assassins would go to achieve their objectives.

The Wolf Pack had been stunned by the methodology involved in the Tiger's more athletic routine. Each had handpicked a bamboo pole. With a suitable run-up and digging the stem into the ground, all three could propel themselves to twice the height of a tall man. It would suffice for their ascent of the palace wall. They carried a length of twine with them, tied around their wrists and leading to rope ladders that could be hauled up quickly. They had practised in daylight, and Kuàiláng had asked how they knew they could execute the manoeuvre in complete darkness, only to be shown the same stunt performed blindfold.

It was quite a plan involving an astonishing degree of athleticism. It was not particularly subtle and would certainly not be soundless. For this, the Wolf Pack had been asked to increase the volume of their dance; they had added drums. Xiǎoláng had been considerably relieved that she would wield the largest drum as it would cover more of what she considered her over-large frame. Kuàiláng and Dàláng had told her she was silly, but for their youngest member, her body was an issue of concern. Of all their stunts over the years, baring herself publicly was the

Thirty-nine: The End

one she dreaded the most. Now, as the time approached to perform, she shivered.

Lined up outside the palace wall, it was not that the Wolf Pack were cold; they had more layers of clothing on them than they would have had in the depths of winter. It had been Hŭtáo's idea; she had said the art of this dance was not the nudity but the undressing. The idea was to keep an audience guessing when they would finally see some bare flesh. It had been one more piece of solace for Xiǎoláng.

Their presence alone had attracted the attention of the guards. Their performance lights used eight oiled torches as a perimeter, blinding any observers to what would occur a hundred paces to the north.

"Time to begin, Kuài," Dàláng whispered. "Off you go.

As Xiǎoláng pounded a slow and steady bass beat, Dàláng trilled her fingers over a smaller drum, and Kuàiláng commenced her dance. Long, slow, and careful strides matched the beat, her arms moving to the more complex rhythm sounded out by the smaller drum. The first of the animal skins slid from her back as a gaggle of men wandered up to watch. At the same time, the noises emanating from the turret increased as the guards leaned over their ramparts to observe more closely.

A second skin fell to the floor. There was an appreciative roar from the male spectators and unmistakable tutting from a group of passing women. Now Kuàiláng was twisting and turning, allowing the watching men to glimpse the expanses of her thighs and the tops of her breasts.

"You know, Xiǎo," she whispered as she slid around her comrade's back, "I'm beginning to enjoy myself! Now, raise the volume on that drum. I will show them a bit more, and it's time the Tigers had the signal."

As the dance heated up down the street, Hŭkuáng, Hŭtáo, and Hŭzǐ braced themselves, counting softly before beginning a sprint that would take them to the moat. In unison, they planted their bamboo poles. The poles fell with a slight clatter and minimal splash, but no one on the street had eyes or ears for anything but the climax of Kuàiláng's dance. If anyone had been able to see them, they would have been amazed by their synchronicity as the three girls arced onto the wall.

Her two partners stood aside so that all in the audience could see. Kuàiláng was now writhing on the floor, surrounded by the furs she had shed. Even the disapproving women had come closer to see what would be revealed. As she rubbed swathes of silk against her breasts, abdomen, and groin, gradually, the furs fell away from her flesh, and the staring males caught glimpses of nipples and pubic hair, but only glimpses. She covered herself once more in a single roll as Xiǎoláng stepped into the centre of the circle of fire.

Xiǎoláng defined a big woman, but she was not fat and far from unattractive. Her opinion of her body was not shared with those in the audience. There was a gasp when she lifted Kuàiláng off the floor and over her head. There was appreciative applause as her furs fell apart, revealing ample breasts. She had expected laughs, but her comrade had primed the audience perfectly; they gaped.

"You know, Kuài," she parodied her friend's earlier remark, "I'm beginning to enjoy myself as well!"

"Well, it's time for you to keep them going. I must get my clothes back on and take over from Dà on that drum. Let's see the shaking routine."

As Xiǎoláng opened her clothing and rotated back and forth, the crowd burst into appreciative calls, stamping their feet to replace the bass drum beat and roaring on the dancers. Astride the wall, the three younger women spun out the rope ladders. They were met by three willing pairs of hands inside the *hòugōng's* garden. As the numbers in the dancers' crowd again doubled, the number of women atop the palace wall went from three to six.

Sitting up there was the most awkward and likely time for discovery. Even so, the women took a little time to take in some of the performance, waiting for the next signal. Inside the dancers' ring, Dàláng began completing laps, tumbling in twists and handsprings around her two fellow entertainers. Her energy and precision engaged the crowd to a greater extent than her complete lack of clothing. In the centre of the ring, Xiǎoláng had now lost all her garments. She was holding Kuàiláng aloft, one huge hand creating a platform for her to spin and weave, shedding her layers once again. The audience's attention flickered between the floor routine, the muscular and statuesque tower of strength, and the gracefulness of the performance. Sexuality oozed above their heads. Their audience's attention may have been divided between the three dancers,

Thirty-nine: The End

but all focused inside the circle. Even the six distinct splashes from along the track could not distract the guards from their entertainment. The Tiger Cubs and the three escapees were out.

As the dance routine wound to a halt, the Wolf Pack lined up to take a bow. As her head dropped, Kuàiláng noticed that only one of the audience members was paying keen attention to something other than their show. He was dressed in the grimy clothes of a peasant, a cloth wrapped around his face. The scarf slipped as she looked more intently, revealing a scarred, battered face and a broken nose. Instantly, the covering was pulled back up, and the features she had helped rearrange disappeared—her escalating fear related to who she saw, not the scars themselves.

As the three girls huddled to help each other dress, she whispered, "Qí's here. Let's get out fast."

It was too late. Within moments, the palace guards had formed a cordon around the crowd, their arms interlocked to prevent escape. Gradually, they allowed one person to leave at a time, the audience sloping away, thanking their forefathers that they were not the target of the troops' attention. It was not long until only the Wolf Pack remained in the ring.

Just a hundred paces from where they stood, another unit of palace soldiers was pulling six bedraggled women from the moat. They were shivering in naked fear. Both groups of women were outnumbered three or four to one; there was no opportunity to escape. It was not as if they did not try. Xiǎoláng tried force, Dàláng seduction and Kuàiláng logic and persuasion. There were similar attempts from the six sodden girls—Hǔzǐ emulated Kuàiláng, Hǔkuáng pushed, shoved, and fought, whilst Hǔtáo led the three escapees in groping and stroking the troops. It was to no avail.

Quite clearly, the men sent to arrest them had been given explicit orders about behaviour and stuck rigidly to their instructions. They did not put up with backchat; in fact, they did not respond in any way. One or two may have had to operate with erections, but they coped. The gags were applied first; shutting them up was a priority. However, it was not long before the nine women were thoroughly trussed. Poles slid through the bindings of their hands and feet, allowing them to be slung between the shoulders of pairs of men. In the case of Xiǎoláng, four were necessary. Before they moved off, the captain insisted they were blindfolded. The nine were in a sorry state when the troops carried them into the palace compound. When they reached their penultimate destination, they were dropped to the ground, wholly disorientated. Mewls of rage came from behind some gags and constricted sobs from others. A door slammed shut.

The confined women were all highly trained and committed to the Sisterhood. Dàláng chewed through her gag first, taking off half of her tongue as she did so. She had difficulty speaking, "I…I've…ot my…out." There were mumbles in response. "Is ever…is all here?" She rolled over, and her face came up against someone's neck. "Be…still. Bite ou blind…blind…off." Dàláng proceeded to bite through the cloth covering the eyes of Hǔtáo and then her gag. Blood streamed from her mouth. When she had gnawed through the rags, Hǔtáo was able to both see and speak.

"One, two, three," she counted to seven. "There's two of us missing." She looked more intently at each prone form. Yes, two. One is Hǔzǐ, and the other must be one of the girls from the *hòugōng*. Iwazaru, I think. Where are they?"

They were the last words shared amongst them. The door opened.

Upon entry, the guards immediately noticed Hǔtáo's and Dàláng's missing gags and swiftly replaced them. They did not bother with the blindfolds as they were now removing them from all their prisoners. Each woman was lifted in turn and taken into a second room, where a bed-sized table was central, and six individual *jiā* hung along one wall. Still bound and gagged, the females were placed in the halters. The last to be brought into the room was Xiǎoláng; her treatment was different. The big woman was led to the table, where it took six men to lift her and immobilise her further by placing more ropes across her and around the table's wooden legs.

As the emperor walked in, the guards turned their backs to him in a display of respect. Qí wasted no time. Pulling out a bronze dagger, he carefully thrust it half a finger's length into Xiǎoláng's right eye. He turned to the horrified and unwilling audience as she screamed in agony.

Thirty-nine: The End

"If you don't watch, by which I mean keeping your eyes open and looking this way, I will have the guards cut off your eyelids. Understand?" It was a rhetorical question, but clearly, the answer was that they did not understand, for all kept their eyes firmly closed.

Qí was as good as his word. Very swiftly, one of the troops passed down the line of women, slicing off their upper eyelids; it was apparent he had used the technique before. One unintended consequence was that whilst they may be forced to watch, the blood masked some of the horror shows now enacted. Whilst Qí made a show of interrogation, he was not serious about this aspect of his task. With the room now filled with agonised shrieks, it would have been impossible to hear answers to his questions anyway. When he had finished with Xiǎoláng, she was mutilated beyond recognition, now blinded in both eyes, ears, fingers and toes sliced off, tongue cut out, and, thankfully, finally unconscious.

"What happens next is that these boys," he indicated the troops, who still had their backs turned, "are going to take this thing off the table, drop it over there and then we're going to move on to the next one. That's you!" He pointed directly at Hŭkuáng. "Understand?"

What followed was a replay of the treatment meted out to Xiǎoláng. Then went Mizaru and Kikazaru, the two escapees, and then Hŭtáo. The volume of the squealing began to diminish as more of the woman blacked out. When Dàláng was finally strapped to the table, Kuàiláng, who was the only remaining spectator, began to cry. She cried not for what would be done to her but for whatever mistakes she had made to allow this defilement to occur to her sisters. She cried for the other women, womankind, and men who had permitted things to reach this state. When they finished with Dàláng, it was her turn. When her gag was removed, which she realised was the precursor to losing her tongue, she whispered, almost sweetly, "I can still love you, Yùtù." The use of his real name caused the emperor to recoil. "Yes, we can all still love you; there does not have to be hatred; there can still be kindness. Kiss me." Qí composed himself and planted his fist into her teeth before ripping the tongue from the unconscious woman.

If the seven women thought their torture had ended, they were sadly wrong. Another *jiā* had been suspended from the palace walls, over the moat and next to the southern gate. This new device had been designed

Èrlǐtou, Hénán

to hold prisoners suspended by their feet, heads downwards. The contraption could be raised and lowered. When lowered, their heads ducked underwater; when raised, if they were conscious, they struggled to draw a breath.

Xiǎoláng was the first to die, perhaps facing an audience, for she could not see nor hear. It would have been midday. Dàláng was the last, as the sun set over Èrlǐtou. Behind them, suspended from the wall, was something of a rarity. There were now few in the town who could read, but a few could explain the message. On a banner were seven words visible behind the seven mutilated and naked bodies:

Do you want to join the Sisterhood?

Forty: The Beginning

The Hidden Valley, Shǎnxī
Year 109. Year of the Monkey
One week after the spring equinox
29th March 1886 BCE

Four male arms held each of her own firmly, immobilising her wrists and shoulders. Two females lay across her legs, pinning her from foot to thigh. She lifted her head and tried again to push; it was futile. Two other women approached her bed, the first with a recently sharpened bronze knife.

"Let's do it!" The restrained woman heard herself say. Within seconds, there was a stabbing pain in her abdomen, followed by a searing pain reaching down to her groin. The week had started so well. Now, it was ending. She passed out.

*

Líng had not known it; otherwise, she would not have taken the trip to Erlitou those eighteen months before, but she had been pregnant. She had lost that baby shortly after hearing the news of the slaughter. In all, there had been five miscarriages. It seemed her body had not been designed to carry a baby. Now, finally, she had brought Yú's child to term. She was more than forty years of age. She was excited to become a mother.

A day earlier, in the quiet of the morning, she had been considering the continuing conundrum of Iwazaru. It had taken six months to reach an agreement with Lùduān that would work to everyone's satisfaction. Since then, and for a further year, it had been necessary to operate in complete secrecy. In effect, that meant that Iwazaru continued to be an object of suspicion, whereas Lùduān was exonerated. It was unfair, and Líng knew it. Public blame for the deaths of the seven girls lay

The Hidden Valley, Shǎnxī

on Iwazaru, who had become withdrawn and mute. No one knew how she had escaped; even if she had been able to say, she would not have been believed.

On the other hand, only Líng knew that Lùduān had been allowed to flee her captors on the command of Qí. Speculation was rife, but none of it concerned Lùduān. She had become popular, especially when she told stories of her exploits in extracting herself from Qí's clutches in Èrlǐtou.

Líng's thoughts dwelled on Lùduān. On her return, she had reverted to her original name, her only concession to grief. Hǔzǐ had been the name the Wolf Pack gave her, and they had all died. She shared the name with the Tiger Cubs, of which she was the only survivor. In one fell swoop, the girl had lost everyone who had brought her to adulthood.

It was widely accepted that Lùduān would run the Sisterhood when Líng passed on or when she retired. However, Líng wondered whether there was time to ensure her full integration and to what extent she had discarded any loyalty to the emperor. Dealing with a double agent was a delicate balancing act.

Líng laughed at the prospect of retirement; only death would stop her from working. The child who brought together her father's attributes and those of Yú kicked hard inside her. She felt damp, then a trickle down her inner thigh. Her waters had broken.

Líng's call had caused all the female elders to be drawn together. Xīwángmǔ, who had become the valley's best midwife, notwithstanding her inability to speak, and Kùàimǎ, still mourning her daughter's death at the hands of Qí, was a more than able second. Jīngfēi, Hòutú, and Tú's presence were not entirely necessary, but they would not have missed the event for the world; they were already gossiping in a corner. Finally, there was Lùduān, who was not yet an elder but someone now included in all their meetings. Yú was there as the expectant father. It was something he had been more than a few times. Kànménrén attended; as her father, he was enthralled with the idea that his family's line would continue. At the bottom of the garden, Bóyì, Shénnóng, and Háng were hiding more than ten flagons of beer and were hoping for a couple more before midday.

Xīwángmǔ and Kùàimǎ attended Líng in her bedroom. The waiting had started.

Forty: The Beginning

The full moon rose over the eastern hills. The same moon disappeared over the mountains that separated the hidden valley from the Fén River at daybreak. The day wore on, and as dusk arrived, Kùàimǎ came out of the house and gathered all around her. Either Líng's baby or her body was refusing to cooperate.

"We have a problem." It was an understatement, "Neither Xīwángmǔ nor I have ever seen a baby born alive if it is delivered more than two days after the mother's waters have broken. We are concerned, and Líng is in considerable pain. A decision must be made, and Líng believes it should be a decision involving Hòutú, Tú and Lùduān, as well as Yú and Kàn. These are unusual circumstances, and it is imperative her father and husband attend, however unusual it might be for them to be present at a birthing."

There were silent nods of agreement before the five followed Kùàimǎ into the house and the bedroom as if in a processional file; the scene was a shock.

"Are you alright, my love?" Yú sat on the bed beside his wife. Líng winced and forced a weak smile.

"No, Yú, I am not. These two have been wonderful, but they are stuck, just as the baby is stuck." She took a deep breath, pain etched on her face. "There are only two possible outcomes from this situation," she announced, summoning enough strength to raise herself slightly. "The first is that both the baby and I will die," there was a mutual intake of breath around the room, "and the second is that I die and the baby lives. Is that not right, Xīwángmǔ?" The mute woman dipped her head in agreement and gestured to Kùàimǎ to speak.

"Líng asks you to consider this. It is better to have one death than two - always. Both Xīwángmǔ and I agree with her as regards this. She knows the only hope is to cut the child from her body. She knows that there will be no prospect of recovering from this procedure. She will die; the child may live. She wants a few moments with her father, a few more with Lùduān, and then Yú. She says we should proceed as soon as you mutually agree on her course of action. We will need all of you to help."

Líng propped herself up once more. "I want you with me, not just to hold me down, which will be necessary, but as a comfort as I leave this world. Please agree. Now, all of you, leave me with my father for a while."

Tears were streaming down his face when Kànménrén joined them in the living area. Hòutú comforted him as best she could, and in a rare display of solidarity with her mother, Tú held him tight from the other side.

Lùduān was considerably longer with Líng; presumably, a few of the Sisterhood's secrets needed to be passed over. When she came out, Kùàimǎ looked around at the circle of faces.

"Before Yú talks to Líng, she wants a decision. Now, should we save the child, even if it means certain death for Líng? Just nod or shake your heads; I do not expect you to speak."

Kùàimǎ turned to each in turn, receiving a curt nod from all. Finally, she reached Yú. He nodded his assent and immediately returned to the bedroom to be with his wife; his face was ashen.

Líng's final conversations with her father, successor, and husband remained entirely confidential. Subsequently, no one ever asked the three what was said; no one wanted to know. They only opened up about matters Líng had asked them to share. It was enough to share the pain; they did not need more information.

When Yú called them back into the room, his arms were wrapped gently around her head. Her father sat on the other side, both in place to hold Líng's arms when necessary. Hòutú and Tú were at her feet, ready to still her legs. With Xīwángmǔ wielding the knife and Kùàimǎ to extract the child, it left Lùduān with the job of getting the baby out of the bedroom and into the waiting arms of Jīngfēi, who had prepared the necessary swaddling and plenty of hot water.

"Let's do it!" Líng's voice was the strongest it had been in two days. "Now, Xīwángmǔ, no point delaying. The time for talking is done. I want this child!"

Xīwángmǔ plunged her knife through flesh, fat, and muscle at a point just below Líng's left lower rib. She then dragged the knife in the direction of her feet. Líng screamed and bucked, but her friends held her down. Blood welled. After a brief halt, the blade was brought crossways, slightly above her pubic bone, at right angles to the initial incision. A second cut brought the edge back up her body towards the right extreme of her ribcage. The dumb midwife signalled to Kùàimǎ, who dug her

Forty: The Beginning

fingers into the horizontal incision and quickly pulled the flap over Líng's breasts. She screamed once more before passing out.

The womb and the shape of the baby were evident to all, as was its heartbeat. Xīwángmǔ raised her blade once more and began hacking through the side of the womb, taking care to avoid the as-yet-unborn child. It took her only moments; Líng's unconscious state helped considerably. As the womb split apart, Kuàimǎ reached hands around the baby, pulling it towards her, as her colleague swiftly cut the umbilical cord. With Líng still out cold, as soon as the newborn cried, it was passed to Lùduān, who rushed the child out. It was up to Jīngfēi to clean and return the baby as swiftly as possible.

Gently, Xīwángmǔ pulled down the flap, then the blankets, to cover the gaping wounds. All knew that there was no point trying to patch anything up. Covering the unsightly mess was all that was required.

Kànménrén gestured to have the knife passed to him. He pulled back the blankets again and made a light incision between his daughter's breasts and one across, at the point the flesh had been folded. "She wanted the Motherland's symbol on her body before she died...this is the best I can do in the circumstances." He wept as he and Yú brought the covers up over Líng's torso, bringing them to rest under her chin. "Now, let us all leave. Is that baby here yet? Bring it in. Let's leave the mother and father alone with their child."

As Kàn left, he stumbled in the doorway, turned once, and exited. All followed, each looking back, if only momentarily. As they did, Kuàimǎ pushed past them, bearing a bundle of warm blankets. The opening in the wrappings revealed only a tiny nose and two eyes screwed tightly shut. She silently handed the child to Yú, turned, and left herself. The door closed behind her.

Yú put his palm on Líng's forehead; her eyes flickered open, "Is...the... baby...alright?" she whispered. "I didn't hear the count or anything." Yú pulled open the wrappings. "Are...you...going to...tell me?"

"Yes, the child seems fine. How are you feeling?"

"Forget me. You...have...not...told me...if...it's a boy...or a girl."

Yú pulled the wrappings open further. "It's a girl."

The Hidden Valley, Shǎnxī

"Good, I thought it was," Líng made an enormous effort to lift her head to speak more coherently, "hold her up so I can see her. Thank you. Now, put her on my breast. Yú, this is the only time I will do this. I want to feed my baby. I can feel the blood leaving me. I can feel my life leaving me. I can feel me leaving me. Look, she's feeding. Look, Yú. Hold her there." Líng's head fell back to her pillow. "Hold my hand and hold her to me, Yú. Hold her there until I'm gone. Thank you."

With that, Líng's eyes closed. Within a few moments, her breathing faltered. A few moments more and her chest stopped rising and falling. With tears in his eyes, Yú released her hand and lifted the baby girl into his arms. He stood and walked to the door without looking back. He had instructions, instructions that did not simply involve the child. Líng had told him to hold a meeting. She had told him to hold a meeting immediately after she died, and, as always, Yú would do as he was told.

He thanked Xīwángmǔ and Kùàimǎ, asking them to round up all the others who had remained and have them meet him under the tree where Háng had stashed the beer. They gathered within moments, and Yú held the baby girl up so they could see her.

"Líng is dead. She died as peacefully as was possible in those circumstances. She asked me to tell you several things, and she also asked her father and Lùduān to do so.

"I would like to introduce you to Guānyīn. She is the only child of Líng and me. She is the granddaughter of Kànménrén. Líng believes she will one day be the leader of the Sisterhood, although that will depend on the present leader of that organisation. I believe this baby girl may one day be the leader of the Shāng, our community here in Shǎnxī's hidden valley. I think that you know that Líng and I did not always agree. She told me I should say that; she thought it would make you laugh.

"I'm going to ask Xīwángmǔ and Kùàimǎ to take Guānyīn from here. She needs food, and I believe they already have a wet nurse for her." He carefully handed the child to the midwives. "Let us sit down. Kàn, Lùduān and I have some important information we need to share. Líng also said we should have a beer and celebrate the birth of her child. She does not want anyone to get upset over her departure. She told me to tell you that from this point on, that means right now, there will be no crying, no mourning, and no frowns. She said to start on the beer now and stop

Forty: The Beginning

only when none was left. She said she never liked beer much, so it's fine if we drank her share. Háng, Bóyì, Jīngfēi. Let's get that ale handed out."

Yú was forcing himself not to show his true feelings, although Kànménrén was having more difficulty. The calmest individual in the group was Lùduān. "Should I go next, Yú?" He nodded assent.

Her first words startled everyone. "I am a spy in the pay of Qí, the Xià emperor." No one could speak. Around the circle, mouths dropped open. "Líng wanted me to tell you that right at the start, and it is true. That she has asked me to take over the running of the Sisterhood, which Yú and Kàn will confirm, is also true. I will remain in the pay of the emperor, and I will run the Sisterhood.

"When you start to think about it, you will conclude there are advantages, although immediately you will consider it unthinkable. However, Líng would not have appointed me if she were not confident, and I can tell you that my loyalties do not lie with Qí. It means I can access information we could not otherwise, whilst I can feed information and disinformation the other way. The first piece of misinformation heading to Èrlǐtou is that Líng is alive and well and remains the leader of the Sisterhood. I must tell you this because we do not want news of Líng's death circulating."

There was a dawning realisation among the group that Lùduān was beginning to forge a new path for them.

"Now, you are all old friends. It is right that I leave you. Kàn, I know it is rude not to hear you out, but you know I know what you will say. May I leave?" Kànménrén nodded his assent, and she left with a parting shot, "Like Líng, I do not like beer. You may drink my share as well."

Lùduān's confession had left the remaining friends bemused and desperately needing the drink. Kànménrén and Hòutú, Bóyì and Jīngfēi, Tú, Yú, Kùàimǎ, and Háng had all known each other for years, Shénnóng was the only more recent addition to their group. They knew each other's weaknesses and preferences and what would make them laugh or cry. Hòutú squeezed Kàn's hand as he rose to speak. He had shed his miserableness as if taking off a cloak.

"Líng said, 'Do not mourn', so we shall not. We must celebrate the birth of my grandchild, Guānyīn. For a long time, Líng was my only remaining family member; now, she has given me a replacement. I thank her and Yú." He raised his mug and drank.

"Now, Líng asked me to pass you her vision of the future. It is a future that you all, in very different ways, have helped to build. She was unsure when these events would occur, but her estimate was two hundred years, perhaps thirteen generations. That is a long time to wait, and none of us will be around by then. There is one possible exception, which is Shénnóng." He raised his mug again, this time towards the target of his humour, "Especially if he perfects those obnoxious herbal concoctions of his."

Yú and Kàn, in fact even the ever-serious Lùduān, had all made weak jokes. They may not have been hilarious, but they were all well-received. It seemed everyone was getting the idea Líng had insisted on; this was a time for celebration, not mourning.

"The story goes like this." Kànménrén drew a large circle in the sand with this foot. "Now it is time for the ladies. Jīngfēi?"

Jīngfēi stepped up and, using her foot, drew a vertical line down through the circle, but one that did not bisect it. Next, Tú stood and dragged her toes across the vertical. Kùàimǎ followed, scoring a second line parallel to that of Tú. It was Hòutú who rose last.

"We tend to think that what started the adventure of the last forty years was the scarring of my body in the great hall of Táosì. Some of you will have remembered that it is forty years to the day. Then, it was the full moon closest to the spring equinox; today, it is that same full moon. Following that, Tú was born. Bóyì and Jīngfēi were growing up as children in that desolate place while Háng was planning to open his first bar. Fourteen years later, Kàn, Yú and Líng arrived and–"

"And me! I grew up in Táosì also. You just don't remember me!" Shénnóng grinned at his circle of friends.

"Sorry, Shénnóng, I'm getting old and forget. Where was I? So, it was only Kùàimǎ who joined us later."

"That's partly true, but about the time Háng opened his first bar, it would have been when Mǎ recruited me."

"Sorry, Kùàimǎ, I'm getting old and forget."

"If you say, 'I'm getting old and forget' again, people will start to believe you!" Kàn laughed, "Do you remember what you are doing?"

Forty: The Beginning

"I do!" Hòutú stepped across the circle, neatly drawing in the two sidebars.

中

"It's been forty years since this was etched on my belly. We're only drawing it, so I do not have to take my clothes off again! It was more of a circle when this was carved into me; it only changed as my belly shrank. You can imagine how it felt for me, reliving the experience as Líng died and Guānyīn was born. Tú and I avoided that situation, but it was a narrow escape. I could feel both Líng's pain and her joy.

"I still think of it in those terms, a never-ending circle with no beginning and no end. We should perhaps think of our mission as having no beginning, for it will surely not have an ending. Maybe our roles are ending, although others will take our places, just as Lùduān is to take on Líng's role.

"So, I ask you to stand and raise your mugs." The friends rose as one.

"To the Motherland!" All drank. "Again! This time to the Motherland and the Sisterhood, may they always work as one!"

"The Motherland and the Sisterhood!"

Lùduān looked down on the grouping from the hillside, her countenance grazed by a wry smile. Overhead, her pigeons were heading south, overflying the group of friends and heading for Èrlĭtou. Thunderclouds hung over the southern peaks, lowering skies framed the darkest shades of grey, and lightning sparked frenetically as the atmosphere clung to all of their sensibilities.

The Hidden Valley, Shǎnxī

Below her, the pigeon fancier glanced skyward. They were not her birds. She traced a projected route; it seemed to lead to only one place, but it would be a bumpy ride.

Turning, she spied Lùduān on the ridge. It looked to her as if more severe storms were brewing.

Chinese Whispers
Book III - Philosophers
(580 - 460 BCE)

Chinese Whispers - Philosophers follows from *Sisters* and *Mothers*, although the backdrop is thirteen hundred years later. The struggles of women to occupy a significant niche in early Chinese society continue and are made worse in many respects by the nascent philosophical concepts being penned by men.

The story brings together some established characters of ancient Chinese history, a feminist force determined to prevent their ideals from taking root, and sympathetic support from roving minstrels.

Chinese Whispers
The Prequel - Ancestors
(3025 - 3007 BCE)

Chinese Whispers - Ancestors commences around Lake Baikal (in present-day Russia) and follows two bands as they migrate into what is now central China. Their journey necessitates changes to their society, which are essential elements in the shift from a matriarchal to a patriarchal society. The changes begin to snowball, resulting in the sometimes gradual but often abrupt stripping of women's rights.

Both books will become available during 2025. Keep an eye on my website's books page for a launch date and links to buy.
https://www.markwhitworth.rocks/books.

Archaeological Evidence, History & Myth

Although my story is entirely fictional, the settings, events, and characters are based on hard evidence, academic hypotheses, and Chinese mythology. It is quite a mix. Below, I have outlined some of the background information. Where relevant, I have included some details that also appear in book one.

The Xia Emperors

Some would still argue that the Xia Dynasty was a mythical construct to justify later dynastic changes. Sīmǎ Qiān, the Han Dynasty historian, is the first to tell their tale, but he wrote almost two thousand years later. He includes Gǔn in his history, attempting to control flooding, but Yú receives the credit for success. Yú's reward was to become the first emperor of the Xià Dynasty. When Yu died, he did not want to nominate his son to succeed him, preferring Bóyì. However, the populace demanded that Qí should take the throne.

Erlitou Floods

I will confess that I cannot remember where I found this information. Rolling around in the back of my mind is evidence of catastrophic flooding of the Luòhé and Yī Rivers before the foundation of Èrlǐtou. If this occurred, it might explain why such potentially bountiful land was unoccupied. I speculated that the Sisterhood chose the area because it was ideal for growing farming communities. If there were flood threats, someone (in my story, Gǔn) would have needed to get to grips with controlling the flooding.

Pigeon Post

Some argue that Neanderthals first domesticated the pigeon. Indeed, it was one of the first birds to have fallen under the spell of humankind, well before the chicken. Ancient Mesopotamian and Egyptian records show it had already been domesticated before 3,000 BCE and was used as a messenger. I have written that they were used in China a thousand years later. However, the earliest hard evidence of the Chinese using pigeons to carry messages comes from the Suí Dynasty (581-618 CE).

Halley's Comet

Obviously, the name "Halley's Comet" came later, but it was likely to have circulated the Sun every 75.3 years back then. Using basic arithmetic, I calculated back from the first documented sighting in 240 BCE and came up with 1894 BCE. I used to be excellent at arithmetic, but it failed me on this occasion. If Halley's Comet had been around at the time of the Xià, I believe the actual date would have been 1896 BCE. My mistake!

The Lajia Earthquake and Mudslide

Qinglong Wu's research identified an earthquake in the Yellow River's Jīshí Gorge and a lake forming behind a mudslide. Lǎjiā was destroyed by the quake and covered in mud. Human remains date the event to somewhere around 1900 BCE. I have chosen 1894 BCE to tell the story of Yu's turnaround as it coincided with Halley's Comet. In Lǎjiā, archaeologists unearthed the world's oldest noodles, dating them to the time of this book.

Writing

There is proof of writing from the Shāng Dynasty, but this comes later than the events depicted in the book. However, there is a widespread belief amongst archaeologists and historians that a more primitive written form must have preceded the complex Shāng oracle bone writings. Evidence presented by Paola Demattè in "The Origins of Chinese Writing: the Neolithic Evidence" shows that the earliest forms may have been discovered in Táosì. I speculate that writing had been around for much longer but that the medium on which it was written, such as sand or cloth, is subject to such degradation that it is unlikely we will ever know the truth. One of archaeology's biggest problems concerns what has not been found rather than what has been found.

The Changing Course of the Lower Reaches of the Yellow River

The Yellow River (Huáng hé) has changed course many times. Evidence for this may be found in the work of Professor Vivian Forbes, "Yellow River Changing Course". Whether there were any significant changes in the period covered by the book is much harder to prove because of the lack of records. We do not know. Many of the changes from 602 BCE were caused wholly or partly by human activity. My dating a course change to 1905 BCE was solely to link it to the solar eclipse of the same year.

The Neolithic Bronze Age Horizon

The commencement of the bronze age was of extreme importance. A spin-off effect led to civilisation, writing, government, etc. Generally, the transition is considered akin to the start of the Communications Age (the times we live in today), whereas the reality was very different. Today, there are twice as many mobile phones globally as people; cell phones only became commercially available in 1983. As the Neolithic ended, this was not the case with bronze and copper objects; people continued to use stone as a tool for thousands of years, and in some parts of the world, they still do.

I have postulated that bronze was initially used for agricultural purposes but was withdrawn by warlords seeking to arm their troops. For thousands of years, peasants did not generally have access to metals for farming.

Chinese Whispers – Mothers

Named Characters in the Story

Here is a list of the characters, compiled in alphabetical order. The character's role is the one they had when they first appeared in book two; I have not added later changes as this might ruin the tale! I have also included the character's gender, as I am aware that many Chinese names do not readily identify gender for a Western reader.

In addition, many of the characters' names have some significance or a particular meaning in Chinese myths and legends. Where there is a relevant connection, I have identified the source of the name.

Āyí Zhū (f)	Túshānshì's old nanny.	This was the name of my cleaner in Suzhou. Āyí is a commonly used Chinese term for someone who helps in the home or with children.
Běidǒu (f)	A woman rescued in Lājià by Yú.	This name means the Big Dipper.
Biǎozi (f)	The spokeswoman for the Èrlǐtou whores.	This name means prostitute.
Bórén (m)	Xià leader of the Lǎoniúpō council.	His name indicates his origin amongst the ancient people of Sìchuān.
Bóyì (m)	An Èrlǐtou farmer who had earlier led one of the wagon trains from Táosì and married to Jīngfēi.	In mythology, Bó Yì was an important minister in Yú the Great's government and the planned successor.
Cāng Jié (m)	One of Hòutú's apprentices.	In mythology, he invented writing.
Cāngbái (f)	An albino captive of Fēngbō, married to Chéng.	This means pale or wan.
Chéng (m)	A displaced person looking for his wife, Cāngbái.	A common Chinese name, but it can also mean honest.

Chinese Whispers – Mothers

Chūxi (f)	One of Hòutú's apprentices.	This means to mature.
Cóng (f)	One of Hòutú's apprentices.	A common Chinese name, but it can also mean a follower.
Dàláng (f)	A street kid in Ānyáng (sister of Xiǎoláng).	This means the eldest wolf.
Dǒng (f)	A woman rescued in Lājià by Yú.	A common Chinese name, but it can also mean east.
Dòngxī (f)	One of Hòutú's apprentices.	This means to understand clearly.
Fēngbō (m)	Leader of the last unit of the Lóngshān army.	An ancient Chinese deity who was known as the Wind Master.
Guānyīn (f)	Líng and Yú's daughter.	In mythology, the goddess of mercy.
Gǔn (m)	Father of Yú and Èrlǐtou's hydrologist.	In mythology, Gǔn was Yú, the Great's father, and he failed to prevent flooding.
Háng (m)	A bar owner.	A common Chinese name, but it can also mean a professional.
Héměirén (f)	Xià leader of the Sānménxiá council.	This means the beauty of the river.
Hétóngzǐ	The Èrlǐtou water engineer who replaces Gǔn.	This means river boy.
Hòutú (f)	A teacher, mother of Tú, wife of Kànménrén.	An ancient Chinese deity, an Earth Goddess.
Hǔkuáng (f)	The third member of the Tiger Cubs.	This name means Mad Tiger.
Hǔtáo (f)	A young whore in Qí's harem.	This name means Escaped Tiger.
Iwazaru (f)	A Sisterhood spy in Qí's harem.	This Japanese name means speak no evil.
Jǐ (m)	A shepherd on Hùtóu Mountain.	A Chinese name, but it can also mean oneself.

Chinese Whispers – Mothers

Jiālíng (f)	Xià leader of the Dōngxiàféng council.	Two Chinese names combined but meaning, but it can also mean additional effectiveness.
Jiǎn (m)	Hòutú's assistant in opening the school - married to Lín.	A common Chinese name, but it can also mean simple.
Jiāng (m)	A local Lóngshān bandit leader.	A common Chinese name, but it can also mean river.
Jīngfēi (f)	A militant citizen of Èrlǐtou. Married to Bóyì.	A Chinese name, but it can also mean to go off like a rocket.
Jīnxīng (f)	Tú's pet dog.	Named after the planet Venus.
Kikazaru (f)	A Sisterhood spy in Qí's harem.	This Japanese name means hear no evil.
Kuàiláng (f)	Kùaimǎ and Shùn's daughter who joins the Wolf Pack.	This name means clever wolf.
Kùaimǎ (f)	A Sisterhood agent, one of the Fire Horse Three.	This name means clever horse.
Lài (f)	An Èrlǐtou councillor.	A common Chinese name, but it can also mean to renege.
Lín (f)	Hòutú's assistant in opening the school, married to Jiǎn.	A common Chinese name, but it can also mean neighbour.
Líng (f)	Leader of the Sisterhood and Kànménrén's daughter.	A common Chinese name, but it can also mean clever.
Lùduān (f)	A seemingly vagrant child who helps Yú in Lājià.	In mythology, a creature that speaks all world languages and can tell the truth from lies.
Mǎjié (f)	A Sisterhood agent, one of the Fire Horse Three.	This name means horse hero.
Měnghǔ (f)	The controller of Èrlǐtou's bronze.	This name means fierce tiger.
Mizaru (f)	A Sisterhood spy in Qí's harem.	This Japanese name means to see no evil.

Chinese Whispers – Mothers

Nányīng (f)	A young girl rescued in Lājià by Yú.	Nán means south, and Yīng is a common surname. However, I made a mistake here as Nányīng is more usually a boy's name.
Nüxi (f)	Gǔn's wife and Yú's mother – previously in the Sisterhood.	In mythology, Nüxi was Yú the Great's mother.
Péng (m)	A member of Captain Jiāng's band.	A common Chinese name, but it can also mean dishevelled.
Qí (m)	Túshānshì and Yú's son.	In mythology, Qí was Yú the Great's son, although not his chosen successor.
Shénnóng (m)	The Èrlǐtou army leader who replaced Bóyì.	In mythology, Shénnóng is credited with inventing all things agricultural, especially the use of herbs and tea drinking.
Shíliu (f)	An Èrlǐtou prostitute.	This name means pomegranate.
Shuǐkè (m)	A Xià trader from Lǎoniúpō.	This name means smuggler.
Shùn (m)	A member of Captain Jiāng's band.	In mythology, he is a sage and leader, but in reality, I named him after our one-metre-tall Terracotta Warrior.
Táng (m)	An Èrlǐtou councillor.	This name means of the same clan.
Tú (f)	Daughter of Hòutú. Mother of Yútú and Líng's companion.	A common Chinese name, but it can also mean to be a believer.
Túshānshì (f)	Yu's wife.	In mythology, Túshānshì was Yú the Great's wife.
Wútóng (m)	The Èrlǐtou army leader under Emperor Qí.	In mythology, one of five one-legged demons who took sexual advantage of women.
Xiǎoláng (f)	A street kid in Ānyáng (sister of Dàláng)	This name means small wolf. As Dàláng's little sister, she was small but grew to be a huge woman.

Chinese Whispers – Mothers

Xīwángmǔ (f)	A mute woman rescued in Lājià by Yú.	In mythology, she is a god, the queen mother of the west, having power over life and death.
Yěmǎ (f)	A Sisterhood agent, one of the Fire Horse Three.	This name means feral horse.
Yú (m)	Leader of the Èrlǐtou council and the Xià empire.	In mythology, Yú was the first Xià emperor.
Yútú (m)	Tú and Yú's son.	An entirely made-up name combining the names of his parents.
Zhāng (m)	A member of Captain Jiāng's band.	A common Chinese name, but it can also mean a cockroach.
Zhèng (m)	An Èrlǐtou councillor.	This name means upright.

Sources

This bibliography includes written sources used for this book and the subsequent novel. Digital sources can be accessed at the link below; I have tried to document my sources of information accurately but find that putting these into print form is tricky.

As this research took place over some thirteen years, a few sources may have slipped through the cracks. If this is the case, I apologise.

Maps - The Times Comprehensive Atlas of the World, National Geographic Atlas of China, Atlas of China Kunyu Publishing Co. Ltd., Google Earth, and Google Maps.

General History and Archaeology –
New Perspectives on China's Past: Chinese Archaeology in the Twentieth Century – Xiaoneng Yang
The Archaeology of China – Li Liu & Xingcan Chen
Illustrated History: China – Patricia Buckley Ebrey
The Cambridge History of Ancient China – Michael Loewe & Edward L. Shaughnessy
Banpo Matriarchal Society – Banpo Museum
The Institute of Archaeology Chinese Academy of Social Sciences, various papers - He Nu

A complete list of websites used can be found on my website at **https://www.markwhitworth.rocks/post/chinese-whispers-sources-for-sisters-mothers**

Printed in Great Britain
by Amazon